HIGH
HOPES

HIGH HOPES

JACLYN JHIN

For my amazing parents, Jack and Joy;
my wonderful husband, Nick, my two sons,
Greg and Grant, and my three stepchildren, Jack,
Izzy and Oscar; and of course, all my supportive
girlfriends and mentees.

CONTENTS

CHAPTER ONE

The clock on the shelf read 5:30. Last time I'd checked, the digital image read 5:29. Just sixty seconds. *One interminable minute.*

The Columbia University admission office was issuing its early-decision announcement today, and I had promised Halmuni I wouldn't sneak a peek before I got home.

"Six o'clock," she'd insisted. "I'll be waiting on dot. Hear good news."

Halmuni was so confident in me, the only possible outcome she could imagine was an email declaring, "Congratulations, Kelly!"

I pictured Halmuni, how she was at that exact moment, waiting for me in our apartment, preparing herself to celebrate her granddaughter's achievement.

I was so nervous. I felt like throwing up.

I sneaked another look at the clock. Now, it read 5:31. I wished I could will the digital numbers to run backwards.

The bookshelves in my office were stacked with documents in manila folders. All neatly labeled, there were so many, they filled nearly every inch of shelf space. The legal paperwork inside was so important, saving even a few inches for my own personal things gave me a twinge of guilt. My boss told me I should

1

feel free to decorate my cubicle however I wanted, but in the midst of so many crucial documents, it never felt quite right to display many objects of my own.

Only on the shelf, I'd reserved about 12 inches for myself. I had my clock, of course; a little Korean doll my mom had given me when I was little; and a photo of my father, my mother, and my grandmother in a restaurant. In the photo, the table was loaded with Korean barbeque, glistening so beautifully I could almost smell the thinly sliced pork and Kalbi short ribs. In the shot, the trio smiled happily, with no clue as to the tragic fate that would soon befall two of them. Dad was a little heavyset, blond, and blue-eyed. Mom, from Korea, was slender and gorgeous, and Halmuni, my mother's mother, looked at the lens impatiently as if to say, "Enough of this camera already, let's eat!"

Other than the clock, the doll, and the photo, my entire office was reserved for the work of the Brian Chu Law Offices, B.B. Chu, he liked to be called. *"Like B.B.Q!"*

It just wasn't in my nature to decorate my workspace or "toot my horn," as B.B. always counseled me to do. Putting up photos and awards would have felt like showing off to my coworkers.

I told myself, "I'm half-Korean. That's not in our culture." But then again, Halmuni never hesitated to brag about my accomplishments. So maybe it wasn't so much about being Korean as it was just being who I was—shy through and through.

For the last month, I'd barely slept. The email from Columbia kept flashing before my eyes. Each night, after tossing and turning and finally giving up on sleep, I'd flip on my light, reach for my laptop, and read articles and blogs. Mostly, I'd gravitated toward ones like "How to Deal with College Admission Anxiety," "Seven Ways to Stay Calm When Waiting for College Decisions," and "Tips for Surviving the College Admissions Waiting Process." Some of them recommended starting a hobby or an exercise routine, but I was carrying a full load of A.P. courses. Between studying and my part-time job at the law office, I really didn't have time for quilting or jogging.

Another blog suggested getting a dog. Now I wondered if I shouldn't have taken that advice. I pictured Columbia's decision arriving in my email inbox, Halmuni distraught at the result, myself ready to burst into tears … but if I'd adopted a dog, at least there would be one creature in our apartment who wasn't crushed by the news.

Now, the clock read 5:32. There was no more putting off the inevitable. I twisted my hair into a ponytail, secured it with an elastic hairband, and reached down for my BRIAN CHU LAW OFFICES bag.

Brian—or "B.B.," as my boss liked to be called— was an excellent lawyer. He was also practically family to me. When I was little, he'd been a regular fixture in our house. For the last few years, he'd been the closest thing I had to a father. So, I may have been biased in his favor.

In addition to lawyering, he was a non-stop self-promoter. His face smiled from bus-stop benches all over Koreatown, and he insisted on his staff members carrying a BRIAN CHU LAW OFFICES bag, such a bright orange it almost hurt to look at it.

"You never can tell when the next big client will see you walking by," he would say.

I started to stand up from my desk, but I was so anxious my knees shook. I sank back into my chair with my neon orange bag in my lap. Sitting there, I glanced at the stacks of paper atop my desk. People expect paralegal assistants to be organized. That's 90 percent of the job, isn't it? So my shelves were incredibly organized. I had allocated each square of my desk as a separate compartmental thought: initial applications for trademarks, pending trademark applications, completed applications, and potential IP litigation.

No more of this. No more shyness. No more modesty. Tomorrow morning, I will come back here bright and early, stand beside my desk and shout to everyone within earshot, "I don't need to do this anymore. I'm going to New York!"

That would never happen. I would never shout in the office. I could never be anything but respectful to my co-workers and our clients. Even respectful to these tidy piles of paperwork. My heart would beat frantically with joy at my acceptance to Columbia. Or I would blink back tears. Either way, I would sit at my desk, lower my head, and get back to work tomorrow.

That's the Korean way, which I'd absorbed from my mother—though I suppose I carried it to an extreme.

Suddenly, B.B. Chu appeared in my cubicle. "Hear anything yet?"

Six-feet-tall and built like a football linebacker, B.B. wasn't a typical Korean. People joked that he must have permed his naturally wavy hair in imitation of K-pop singers. This annoyed him so much he straightened it. I would never dare to tell him it made him look worse.

"Uh-huh," I said.

"I'm going to be the first to know, right?" said B.B.

Addicted to working out, B.B. put in two hours of weight training each morning. In the old days, my dad and Brian would spot for each other. I wondered if it was the strain of all that pumping iron that had created those deep frown lines between his eyebrows. They gave his face a serious, slightly angry look that served him well in the courtroom, but didn't reflect the man I knew: approachable, caring, and humorous.

I hoisted my bag on my shoulder. "I should tell you before I tell Halmuni?"

"No way." He pretended to be horrified. "If Halmuni found out you told me before you told her, I'd hate to think what she'd do to me." He laughed before noticing the anxiety on my face. "Take it easy. And remember: Success is the only option."

B.B. was into theories like the *Law of Attraction* and books, like *The Secret*. He always lectured me about how we attract what we project.

I nodded. *Sure.*

"I'm just looking forward to getting to say, '*I told you so.*' " He smiled, crinkling the lines around his eyes.

I walked past him, heading toward the lobby, shaking my head. "We'll see."

"Let me know the good news, Kelly," he called after me. "After you tell Halmuni."

As my hand pressed against the copper handle, I remembered what I had been working on: Speak up. Be less shy. Be less *me.*

"Hey, Brian. I've been meaning to say, 'Thank you.'"

"Thanks for what?"

I steadied my nerves. It wasn't easy for me to express my feelings. "For always ... For having confidence in me."

He scoffed. "Come on, Kelly, you are a superstar! You've always worked your butt off. If Columbia doesn't take you, I will personally go to the admissions department and punch them in the nose for being so stupid."

I'd rarely heard him raise his voice in anger, but he had a habit of talking tough.

"And anyway," he said. "Who's Brian?"

"I mean, "*B.B. Chu.*"

"Like B.B.Q.!" With a big grin, he waggled a finger at me as if this was the most important thing I needed to remember in life.

I blushed and smiled. "Got it, B.B."

He acted just like my dad used to, making me laugh and annoying me at the same time.

"Go home now, Kelly," said B.B. "Halmuni's waiting."

* * *

Halmuni is "grandmother" in Korean. Back in Korea, the name signified respect and tenderness. *Halmuni. Halmuni.* It fit how I felt about her.

Today I found myself repeating the word, imagining different destinies: *Halmunnniiiiii, I got in! Halmuni. I didn't get in. Hal-MUNI. I GOT IN. Halmuni, I'm never going to amount to anything. Ever.*

Our condo hugged the border of Koreatown. Literally. Our diminutive porch stuck out like a fat lip away from the nearby units. Beside it, the fire escape crawled down to Little Bangladesh of Los Angeles. Sometimes as I stepped outside to get away from Halmuni's endless commentary on *Real Housewives of Orange County ("She did not just say that!"),* I found myself straddling two worlds.

I climbed the concrete steps, scattered with dead leaves from the maintenance man's leaf blowing this morning. Crunching my way up, I hummed the song my parents always sang together. *Just what makes that little old ant/Think he'll move that rubber tree plant/Anyone knows an ant, can't/Move a rubber tree plant.* Since I was little, I sang that song whenever I needed a lift.

Inserting my key into the lock, I hummed louder, swung the door open and stomped in. I always tried to be loud so Halmuni would hear me above the TV buzz. The apartment's tangy smell, garlic and ginger with a hint of spicy peppers, immediately hit my nose.

Halmuni heard my humming, swiveled her neck to look at me, and belted out her own version of the song. *"But she's got higghh hopes! She's got high hopes!"* She creaked forward in her ancient recliner, adjusting her ankle-length dress. Tucking loose strands of curly, grey hair behind her ears, she put her wrinkled hands in the air. "You got in," she said, as if I had already told her.

"I don't know yet." I dropped my orange bag on the beige carpet, its pattern worn from decades of footsteps.

As Halmuni bounced her knees up and down, her blue slippers fell off her feet. She was wearing her usual "outfit," which was baggy cotton sweatpants with a loose, long-sleeved tee shirt. The sleeves were too long for her because Halmuni was a diminutive figure. She also liked to buy her clothes one size larger than needed because her view was that everything eventually shrinks, but they hardly did and as she got older, she seemed to get shorter. Her face was very round, which most Koreans would say was a lucky face (since Buddha had a round face), but it gave her the appearance of being chubbier than she actually was. "You better open email before I have heart attack." She tugged her right hand out of her sweatshirt sleeve to pat her chest. "Tell me good news."

"In a minute, Halmuni." I made my way into the kitchen to avoid her stare. Using chopsticks to peel a pickled cabbage from the fresh Kimchi bowl, I popped it in my mouth.

"*Kelly*. Eat later," she said impatiently.

"Okay. Fine." Walking back into the living room, I pulled out my phone, but I couldn't make myself press the home button.

Halmuni glared at me.

"But you can't look at me."

She rolled her eyes, mumbled something in Korean, and swiveled her recliner in the other direction. "I make you comfortable," she said, and she scrunched up even further into a contorted position.

"I didn't mean you have to turn around."

"No, I just wait over here. How long you going make an old lady wait?"

"That's not—never mind." I clicked on my phone. It lit up, showing two unread email messages. Going into my inbox, I saw it: *Columbia University.* My finger hovered above the screen. All those years of late night studying, notecards under pillows, friendless lunches, all came down to this one moment ...

"Kelly. Pretty soon I read from grave."

"Okay, okay." I clicked. The screen filled with letters that made no sense to me. *Ants,* I thought. *How could one ant move a rubber tree plant? Impossible. Maybe there were hundreds of little black ants pushing at that rubber tree together.* But then one word, near the top of the screen, took shape before my eyes: *Congratulations.*

I gasped. Halmuni turned around. "What? What? You make it?"

I pitched the phone to her. It got lost in the fabric of her skirt.

"Why you throw it to me, not hand it to me?"

Halmuni's hands fumbled for it. She stabbed at the screen with a long yellow fingernail.

I squatted beside her recliner, took the phone out of her hand, and held it up for her.

She stared for what felt like five minutes, and I realized, *she doesn't have her glasses.*

I grabbed her bifocals from the low table beside her recliner, handed them to her, then raised the phone for her. She read slowly, out loud, moving her lips. If possible, this was even more agonizing than the last three months of waiting.

Finally, her mouth dropped open. "*Aigo!!*"

Relief flooded through me. I fell into the recliner, wrapping my arms around her, the edges of her glasses digging into my cheek.

"I knew it all the time. You so smart, girl."

"Halmuni, I made it." I felt tears of joy filling my eyes. "I made it; I made it."

"Your parents be so proud."

Then, knowing how proud my parents would have been, wishing they were here to share this moment with me, the tears really did start to flow.

Halmuni wiped off my cheeks with a leathery fingertip.

I looked up into her eyes and knew she had read my mind.

"Don't think like that. Time to go Ivy Leagues. Law school. Become big-deal attorney."

"Then I'll take care of you, Halmuni. Like you always—"

"Shh." Halmuni tugged me into an even tighter hug. "This a time for happiness. No Kimchi and rice tonight. We celebrate. I brag to everyone my Kelly going to New York—become big city lawyer. Make everybody jealous."

CHAPTER TWO

Seoul Garden is an upscale restaurant off Wilshire in the heart of K-town. The succulent odor of barbecued Kalbi and savory Kimchee Stew filled my nostrils as we entered. Waxy green booths lined the walls, and round tables filled the space between. Golden light fixtures hung above each polished table with its grille in the center. I'd only been here two or three times. I took it all in, allowing myself to own this moment.

Halmuni stood on her tiptoes to peek over the hostess stand. "Give us best table. We're here for my granddaughter. She get into Columbia University."

The young hostess set down her phone, gave me an expressionless nod, and muttered, "Cool."

Halmuni looked like she was about to launch into one of her scoldings, so I put a hand on her arm. "Like you said," I whispered. "This is a happy occasion."

The girl carried menus toward our booth. She didn't even wait for us to follow.

Halmuni poked me in the ribs. "Young generation. So rude. Don't you act like that when you come back from New York."

"I won't."

"I know. That never be Kelly's style."

Halmuni always excluded me from the "young generation," because she knew I never really belonged to it. My best friend was a 46-year-old man whose name was associated with BBQ, and my high school "friends" were the people who gave me a slight nod when I ran into them at the Korean market. The nods always meant the same thing: You only look a *little* like me. Why are you here?

As we passed each table, Halmuni engaged with every single family. I wondered, *Does she actually know all these people?*

"*Anyonghaesayo*, my granddaughter get into Columbia. What about your child?"

With some, Halmuni spoke English. With others, families who hardly spoke any English even though they'd lived in the US for years, she spoke in Korean. Halmuni interrupted conversation after conversation to share the news. *My* news. I didn't know whether to linger behind Halmuni and mouth "sorry" after each table, or keep my eyes plastered to the floor in case it would offer mercy and swallow me whole.

Oh geez. I tugged on her arm, trying to speed her up, but she shrugged off my hand. The hostess had reached our table, and she looked back at us impatiently. It didn't make any difference. Halmuni was on a mission, and she refused to be hurried up.

By the time we sat down, I could feel everyone in the restaurant staring at me. I scooted right next to the window, trying to hide.

The hostess gave us our menus and, without another word, headed back toward her phone.

I scanned for the lowest-priced items, my usual job when dining with Halmuni. I always tried to think of her as *frugal* or *careful,* but the truth is, she didn't like to spend money. Out of all of the English words she knew, Halmuni could probably pronounce "clearance" the best. Even on a menu, I found myself looking for those red sales tags.

Halmuni placed her bony hand on mine. Her deep-set eyes grew misty. "Get whatever you want today."

"Anything?" I couldn't remember ever hearing Halmuni utter those words. "You sure?"

Halmuni honked her nose with the cloth napkin loud enough to make the hostess turn around. "Soon you be famous lawyer. You pay me back—with interest."

Our server, a Korean boy around my age, approached our table, notepad in hand. He had short, spiky hair and two cute dimples. But who was counting?

"Hi, there." He cast a bright smile at Halmuni, then at me. "My name is Mark. I'll be taking care of you." When he smiled, his dimples deepened. If possible, they got even cuter. "What would you ladies like to start?"

"A congratulations!" Halmuni lifted her menu. "Earlier girl so rude."

"Halmuni," I whispered. I looked up at Mark, trying to send a mental apology. When I saw him smiling at me, I looked down at the table and busied myself readjusting the perfectly well aligned silverware.

"She just got into Columbia."

Mark rocked back on his heels and let out a low whistle. "Wow. Congratulations indeed."

"Thank you." Bravely, I glanced up at him. "We'll just have water."

"Right away."

As he walked off, Halmuni's eyes shamelessly followed him. "Maybe he go to Columbia, too. Be boyfriend."

"Halmuni. Please."

"Studies number one. But maybe you find nice Korean boy."

"I won't need a boyfriend in New York."

"Lots of Koreans in New York."

I lifted my menu to hide my face. "Anyway, I'll come back to California for law school. Continuing to work for B.B. will help me get ahead."

Halmuni scoffed.

Remembering B.B., I pulled out my phone. "Excuse me, Halmuni. I don't mean to be rude at dinner, but I promised to let him know."

"Good girl."

I typed a quick message: *I'm in!*

"B.B. like your mother," continued Halmuni, "but with women. He only like American girls with blonde hair." One of Halmuni's favorite pastimes was impugning B.B. Chu's love life. I usually only half-listened.

Almost instantly, my phone beeped at me. It was as if B.B. had been waiting with his phone in hand. Happy emoticons danced across the screen.

"He too old be bachelor," Halmuni continued. "What if he choke one day and no one there? He die alone."

It was pointless telling Halmuni you could still choke with someone else in the room—and also, there were many other reasons to fall in love besides having someone ready to save you if you got a prawn stuck in your throat.

"You know. It not love at first sight for your mom."

I returned my attention to Halmuni, who had flipped her menu over to peruse the side dishes. Her finger traveled down pictures of fried oysters cooked with savory pancake batter, and tofu stew.

"But it was love at first sight for Dad," I reminded her. I was no expert in the area of love, but this was one thing I knew.

She nodded. "Love at first sight for your dad. But you remember how beautiful your mom. How could any man, even a man not Korean, not fall in love with her?"

I nodded. Ever since I was a kid, I had heard the story of my parents getting together. The way my dad told it, he knew he loved my mom from the first moment he set eyes on her. Some kids would roll their eyes at hearing about their parents' romance, but not me. I thought it was sweet.

My dad, Paul, spent his early 20s teaching English in Korea and backpacking through Asia. One day in Seoul, he went into a salon for a haircut and saw a beautiful, petite hairdresser—with great hair, of course. While he didn't have qualms about professing his love after only one day, he didn't realize my mom's first impression was that he was a typical, bumbling, crass, white idiot. Still sitting in the chair with her snipping at his hair, he serenaded her with *High Hopes.* The other girls in the salon giggled, and she snapped at him, "Be still, I'll cut you." When his haircut was finished, he refused to leave, consuming the salon's complimentary tea, waiting, and asking my mom, Soo Jin, to go out with him.

"Only men have love at first sight," said Halmuni, "but it not real. Men think love at first sight, but it's just ... they want sex."

"Halmuni!"

"Your mother so beautiful, he thinking not from head or heart, but with that." She pointed downward, and I cringed.

"Women more smart than that." Halmuni nodded at me as if to say, *"You listen to your Halmuni. I know what I'm talking about!"*

I started to object—*Not my dad*—but changed my mind. What did I know about love anyway? I'd never even had a boyfriend.

Halmuni patted my hand. "You know it when time right. It take time. If it don't, you not with right man."

"So, you're telling me to take lots and lots of time."

She frowned. "Not too much time. Just be smart. Lots of men will say they love you, but they think with their thing down there. Because you are like your mom, beautiful girl. When you find right guy, you'll love him, too. Like your mom loved your father."

Not a day went by I didn't think about my parents, but as I sat there at the table thinking about love and marriage, old memories resurfaced. Stuff I hadn't thought of in a while. Some of them, I couldn't be sure if they were actual memories or if I had just heard them from Halmuni and B.B. Chu.

After my parents got married and came to LA, my mother started her own salon while my dad worked as a carpenter. We owned the smallest home on the block, but we lived in Hancock Park, one of the nicer parts of LA. I suddenly longed to step back into our kitchen with the peeling yellow wallpaper. In my mind's eye, I padded down the narrow hall to the living room with the long oak table, scratches etched into the wood. I even missed the bathroom with the broken toilet lid that would slip off the bowl if you didn't drop it just right. And I wished for one more moment with my dad quizzing me on biology, my mom yelling at us to stop—to give my "brain a break."

"What you want order? Let's share main dish."

I chuckled to myself. *Frugal,* I thought. *That's my Halmuni.* So much for picking anything I liked.

Mark came back over to refill my water glass, and Halmuni asked him for Beef Bulgogi. Once he left, her gaze wandered. When I heard her make a 'tsk' sound, I turned to see what she was looking at. A couple sat on the other side of the restaurant—one Korean boy, one white girl. They held hands.

"No good. That."

"You mean like my parents?"

"Yes, like your parents." Halmuni nodded her head, causing a few strands of thinning grey hair to escape her ponytail.

"You loved my dad."

"I loved him. But I wanted Korean." Her old eyes had moistened at being reminded of my mom and dad. "Your dad different from other Americans. Good. But messy."

A moment later, Mark returned with a bowl of raw, thin slices of marinated beef, along with green onions, garlic and sesame oil. Before he set down the food, Halmuni began coughing. I looked away as if not acknowledging this would make her stop. Whenever we went to eat, she played the sick old woman.

"Oh, dear. Sorry." She coughed again, her voice becoming a whisper. "Bad chest. Get worse with age. Do you think I could get some soup for my chest?"

I was so used to Halmuni's act it usually didn't bother me very much, but I didn't want to have her embarrass me in front of Mark.

"Oh, sure, since it's a special occasion."

"And some extra side dishes, too?"

He ran off, probably praying today would not be the day one of his customers died at the table. Halmuni resumed her posture, then seared the beef over the open flame. She pointed at the mixed couple again, using her chopsticks to emphasize her words.

"White people never understand Korean culture. Those women on *Housewives of Beverly Hills,* they *michyeosseo.* Crazy. They don't know Korean stuff." Halmuni pointed to the white girl playing footsie with the boy. I'd hoped Halmuni hadn't noticed. "Korean women wouldn't act like that."

Taking a piece of beef from Halmuni, I tried to change the subject. "I worry about leaving you here by yourself."

"Kelly, you know those just fake coughs."

"No, Halmuni. I mean in general."

Halmuni sat back. She looked out the window at the cars zooming down Wilshire. "I be fine. You taught me Spy."

"Skype."

"Spy, Skype, whatever. You go East Coast and explore. Only four years."

"I'll come back for vacations, and you'll come visit me. Think what a good time we'll have in New York."

She waved away the thought. "Too expensive. We'll talk on Spy."

"And then I'll be back for law school."

"Good. Good."

I put my chopsticks down. I wanted her to know I was serious. "Halmuni. I'm going to do everything I can to be financially independent. And to become a lawyer. I don't want to have to lean on you anymore."

Halmuni looked at me. In the right light, the brown in her eyes turned into an opaque golden.

"I know. You good girl. Always been."

Our server returned with Halmuni's soup and side dishes. When he caught my eye, I looked down. I wanted to apologize for this whole charade, but I knew my grandmother would take this as the ultimate betrayal. And anyway, it's not like I could've managed to hold his look for more than a second or two.

Halmuni let out a few more coughs. "Oh, thank you, thank you."

"You're welcome. And by the way, congrats again," he told me.

"Thank you." I felt my cheeks burning. I blamed my father's ruddy complexion for never being able to hide my blushes.

"Kelly smart girl," said Halmuni. "She got scholarship, too. So we afford your restaurant!" Then she said, "Young man, you toast with us?"

Oh, no, I thought, realizing what she was up to.

Uncertainly, he looked from her to me. "Um, sure, if you like."

"You get me some free Soju, okay? And then we toast together."

As he walked off to fetch the complimentary Soju, I had to admit, she was really good at this.

"Kelly, when you successful attorney, you look back on today as day your life began. You won't grow old in third-story condo like Halmuni. You own big house with swimming pool, like *Real Housewives.*"

Mark came back, opened the bottle, and, using two hands, poured Soju into a shot glass.

Halmuni grinned and nodded, pleased that Mark knew the Korean etiquette for pouring a drink for someone older than you. "Cheers!" she said. "Congrats to my Kelly for getting into Columbia. Not only pretty girl, but also sooo smart!" Halmuni raised her glass and clicked it against Mark's. "You think she's pretty, don't you?"

Now it was Mark's turn to blush. "Very pretty," he mumbled, embarrassed. He took a tiny sip, then asked, "So, do you need anything else?"

"We're good," I said. "Thanks, Mark." Calling him by his name felt bold. But after all, I reminded myself: I was a Columbia student now. Enough of shy Kelly. But then I thought, *Who are you kidding, Kelly. Shy might as well be your middle name.*

He left, and I breathed a sigh of relief, stirring a straw in my water. "I just want to have enough money to take care of you like my mom and dad would've. They sacrificed so much for me."

"They wanted to. When you want to do it, no sacrifice."

She finished round one of her side dishes, pushing plates of food toward me. Picking up my chopsticks, I couldn't help but look over at the couple again. They looked sweet together, not destined for failure. They seemed to be playing some kind of game with their napkin while they waited. The girl must've got the answer right because she lifted her hands in the air, throwing her head back with laughter. He grinned at her.

As I continued to stare at them, my longing turned to fear. I wondered if I would ever find someone willing to go out with a half-Korean girl who has never been in love before.

CHAPTER THREE

The moment I entered the law office, B.B. Chu's shout echoed through the office suite: "Kelly, you brilliant young lady! Get in here!"

I could feel my cheeks flushing. If the receptionist hadn't been staring at me from her desk, I might have quietly backed into the corridor and sneaked away.

But B.B. had given me no choice. I stopped in his doorway.

"*I knew it.* I knew it all along."

For a moment, I let my eyes wander up to his Boston College and Hastings Law School diplomas. How many times had I fantasized that one day I, too, might occupy the corner suite of a large office? Columbia's seal would greet others as they entered. I even pictured myself mentoring a protégé, someone shy like me. *Would I still be awkward by then? Or, would I have it together as a professional?*

I dipped my head and whispered, with solemnity and politeness that I hoped would have made my mother proud, "Thank you. You've always been there for me, B.B., always believed in me, and ..."

He held up his hands, interrupting the speech I'd been rehearsing. "My turn," he said, and I knew what was coming. He'd been preparing his own speech. I cringed. I knew I might be standing there in his office doorway for the next half hour, listening to how proud he was of me, how I never believed in myself as much as I should, how I needed to reach for the stars, how I …

His phone pinged, and I thought, *Oh, thank you, whoever you are.*

He put his finger up to give him a minute, then swiped his iPad. His shoulders sagged, and I knew it must be a message from his mother. His forehead always creased at the top of his T-Zone whenever she barged into his life on social media. I waited, expecting this might take a while.

B.B. continued to stare at his screen so long his forehead contracted into a V shape, and at last my curiosity got the better of me. "Everything okay?"

"Sorry." He motioned me to close the door.

I came back to take a seat across from him.

He slid over his iPad. "My mom doesn't understand what's private about private messaging."

I scrolled down. His mom had posted multiple times on his public news feed. Each entry presented a new, eligible Korean woman she thought he should date. And to B.B.'s mother, dating was just one short step to her real goal—marriage.

"Oh, boy."

She had written in all caps: "*Nancy! Amazing! Beautiful! Amazing!*

I saw *1 Comment,* and I couldn't help laughing. "Who comments on these?"

Then I clicked on the comment and put my hand to my mouth. *Oh God.* B.B. shook his head. *Halmuni Kim.* Now it was my turn to cringe.

"Oh yeah, she always comments. Finds them all hilarious, apparently."

I looked closer. On every post, she had written 'Pretty girl. LOL.'

"She's not laughing." I scooted the iPad back to him. "She thinks LOL means 'Lots of Love.'"

"She does?"

"She doesn't understand any social media lingo. Sometimes she'll shout YOLO at the TV, and I'm like, 'Do you know what that means?' and she'll go, 'It has a meaning?'"

"It's a wonder they can login at all."

"I feel like there should be some sort of parental blocking, but for old people—"

The door opened without a knock. "That's one gorgeous woman your mom's picked out for you this time." Dan, one of the other attorneys in the office, dropped into the chair beside mine. Dan always delivered his remarks stone-cold, without the tiniest smirk or smile in his blandly, round face. He was Korean American, but unlike B.B., he could speak Korean fluently. Overweight from snacking at work, whenever he was particularly stressed, he would carbo-load.

"Potato chips are his nemesis," B.B. once told me.

Though he had a wide face, he had very small eyes so when he laughed, you couldn't tell if his eyes were opened or closed. B.B also told me Dan had spoken a few times about getting his eyes done, but couldn't actually go through with it.

"Besides," B.B. had said. "Dan thinks women are attracted to successful men, so all he has to do is make lots of money."

Dan counted the words off his fingers as he spoke. "If you ask me, she's amazing. Beautiful, too. Did I mention *amazing*?" Dan and B.B. had a brotherly, love-hate relationship. Even after so many months of listening to their daily banter, I barely understood it.

"Dan, first of all, get off Facebook. And second, go F yourself."

"Will do, B.B., will do," Dan said. "Gonna go F myself right now." Except he didn't move from his chair. "But first, when am I gonna get to see the one and only matchmaker again in person? Any minute, I'm guessing."

B.B. picked up his stapler, threatening Dan with it.

"Don't kill me," Dan protested. "I'm just a fan of your mom. I love her ... tenacity. If her son was such a go-getter, we'd have doubled our business by now."

B.B. launched a rubber band at Dan, who casually caught it in his left hand, dropping it into the wastebasket.

B.B. let out a big sigh. "It's because I'm 46. She's freaking out."

"As she should be. You're old as shit."

Neither of them seemed to notice me squirm in my chair. They just carried on their exchange as if I wasn't there. But that was all right with me. I didn't understand the purpose of their dissing each other, but I'd gotten so used to it I usually let my thoughts wander while they threw their barbs back and forth.

This time, B.B.'s mentioning his own age made me think of my dad. B.B. and my dad had been buddies since high school. They were almost exactly the same age—or they would have been. What little Korean my dad spoke before he'd left for his English-teaching gig in Korea, he had absorbed by hanging around B.B.'s house.

"I've seen the hotties your mom brings in the door." Dan threw his long legs over the side of his chair like he owned the place. He shook his wing-tipped shoes as he spoke with nervous energy. "You say you're not gay, and I believe you, I guess. But I don't understand what's stopping you from taking all those gorgeous girls out."

"First, I can pick out my own women, thank you very much—"

"So, why don't you?"

"I do. I do. But whoever I date never seems to be good enough for my mom. And more important ..." He shot me a kind of apologetic look before lowering his voice. "I like blondes."

Dan laughed hysterically. This might have been the funniest thing he ever heard. "Oh, well. Don't we all?"

I felt my phone buzz in my back pocket, reminding me I had 50 emails to return, so I started to get up.

Dan finally noticed me. "Oh, hi, Kel. What's going on?"

I opened my mouth to tell Dan my news, but before I could, he whipped out his phone and started typing. He leapt off the chair and strode to the door, his eyes glued to his screen. "I'm off. Got more Facebook stalking to do."

Once Dan was gone, B.B. turned to me. "I'm taking you to lunch today."

"Oh thanks, that's really nice—"

"Have you read Tony Robbins's books?" he asked, and I groaned inside. "He says, if we want to direct our lives, we must take control of our actions ..."

No, I hadn't read Tony Robbins's books, but I'd heard this lecture so many times before, I felt like I knew everything he'd ever written.

My phone beeped.

"Sorry, let me just check this." I looked: two missed calls from Halmuni, and she'd sent me a text: *CALL ME! 911.*

"Sorry." I quickly stood up. "Excuse me. I'll be right back."

I ran out of the office, darting through the doors to the outdoor plaza with my heart in my throat. The sun shone in my eyes, blurring my vision. Dialing Halmuni, I prayed everything was okay. In my mind, I apologized for my words about older people not understanding social media. I imagined horrible scenarios: an intruder, the kitchen caught on fire, she fell down the stairs. *Pick up, pick up, pick up.*

"*Hola*, Kelly," she chirped happily. She had learned a few Spanish words from *Housewives of Beverly Hills*.

"Halmuni. What happened? You okay?" The breath trapped in my diaphragm released. I peered across the diamond-shaped plaza to men and women in pantsuits and blazers looking for someplace to sit and drink their paper cups of coffee. They had been a blur as I imagined Halmuni succumbing to some terrible demise.

"I need you go to McDonald's."

Now the strangers came into sharp focus. A couple gawked at me in bewilderment. I could only imagine how I looked. Sweat glistened on my face, and my hair fell into my eyes. I collapsed into a park bench beside the glittering business park pond.

My voice still shook. "Halmuni ..."

"What?" she asked innocently.

I sighed. It wasn't worth it. "I told you that stuff's bad for you."

"That food cheap. They have dollar menu: McValue Fries. 2 Hot Apple Pies. McChicken Sandwich—"

As she rattled off her disturbing knowledge of the dollar menu, I noticed Mrs. Chu approaching with an attractive Korean woman beside her. I guessed this must be Nancy from her Facebook post.

Mrs. Chu always looked incredibly put together. She wore a black barrette in her short pixie-cut hair and a black billowing maxi dress with a small, white flower print with stylish shoes that weren't too high. Her only jewelry was a statement necklace that matched her dress perfectly. She looked seriously hip for her age, and Nancy could've been her well-to-do daughter--her nervous, well-to-do-daughter.

Yes, I decided, *Nancy was pretty amazing.* Ballerina thin and very pretty, she wore a form-fitting dress with black stilettos. Her long brown hair was perfectly styled, and her manicured hand was currently in danger of being amputated by Mrs. Chu's fierce grip.

I interrupted Halmuni's McDonald's order. "Halmuni, I gotta go."

"You write that all down? You get it for me?"

"No, Halmuni. I'm not getting you junk food."

"I old woman. I live day to day. Look at Trump, all the time his KFC and his McDonald's, and he is big and healthy."

Mrs. Chu halted in front of me. A nanosecond later, Nancy came to a breathless stop.

"Okay, fine," I told Halmuni, "just text me what you want."

"Text take too long. You just remember it."

"Mrs. Chu's here. Text me, okay? I gotta go, bye."

I ended the call, and Mrs. Chu swooped me up. I felt her involving me in her game of pull-and-drag. "You're coming with us," she said. I desperately wanted to escape her, but my Korean politeness took over.

The three of us hit the lobby glass doors together, looking like the Korean version of *Charlie's Angels.* Mrs. Chu pushed through. *Whoosh!* They shut behind us as she led us down the marble hallway. My coworkers watched us hurry past as if a live hand grenade was rolling down the hall.

I leaned forward to offer Nancy a sympathetic smile.

"Hi," she breathed back. "I'm Nancy."

"I know." *Aw, she seems nice. Poor thing.*

"Byung-Chul," Mrs. Chu shouted. "Come meet Nancy!"

I didn't even have to look into his office to know the look on B.B.'s face. I imagined him searching his desk drawers, wondering if he could fit in any of them. I saw Nancy swallow. We waited for a good minute before B.B. sauntered out, all the color gone from his face. He didn't even look at Nancy; he just stared at his mom.

"Byung, this is Nancy, Dr. Stephen Lee's daughter. Isn't she pretty?"

Nancy blushed, then held out her hand. I felt bad for her. If I was her age, I might've thought B.B. was cute too, but I already knew this was doomed for failure.

"Nancy just graduated from Ewha University, a top women's college in Korea," she added. "She's visiting cousins in LA. In Seoul, she works at Samsung, in the marketing department. She speaks fluent English. I told her how awesome you were and that you two had to meet. She is ten years younger than you, but she doesn't mind older men."

It was obvious to me, and probably to Nancy, too, that B.B. would have run screaming down the corridor and leaped out the window, if only he hadn't been afflicted with that same Korean courtesy. From my peripheral vision, I noticed Dan peeking outside his office. I worried he might slip on his puddle of drool.

Now it was B.B.'s turn to have his finer points described. "This is my handsome son," said Mrs. Chu. "He doesn't speak Korean, but he is a *lawyer*. You know how hard it is to be a lawyer? He graduated from Hastings Law School in San Francisco. He would have got into Harvard if he studied more, but he was too busy chasing girls. But Hastings is a very good law school, and this is his own practice. Such a successful guy to have his own practice, don't you think?"

Nancy nodded. "Very impressive," she said quietly, with only a hint of an accent.

Mrs. Chu beamed around at all the people who were listening, then waved to all of us. "Bye, Kelly. Bye, Nancy. I have an appointment now. Take her to lunch."

"Mom," B.B. called after her, "I don't think I'll have time today. I already told Kelly I'd take her out for lunch. She just got into Columbia."

Mrs. Chu paused. "That's amazing," she said to me. "Your parents would be proud."

"Thank you."

Then Mrs. Chu straightened her skirt and looked up at B.B. "How perfect. Nancy likes food, too. Take her with you."

Nancy started to interject, but Mrs. Chu put a hand on her arm. "The more the merrier, sweetie. Have a good time."

Mrs. Chu disappeared out the glass doors, her heels clacking down the steps outside. Nancy and I turned back to B.B., who nervously rubbed his hands together. "My mom can be a bit ... pushy, if you can't tell. And you can call me B.B. People remember my name better that way. B.B. Chu. like BBQ, you know? And well, we all love BBQ beef, right?"

I saw Dan shake his head, mouth "*loser*," then close his door.

B.B. looked back and forth between Nancy and me.

I realized B.B. and I had automatically assumed the same posture: hands clenched in front of us, looking for a way out.

"So." He opened his arms, flashing a grin. "Lunch then?"

* * *

B.B. took us to Fuji Grill, a Benihana-type Japanese restaurant where they cook the food right in front of you. We sat at the corner of the communal table: Nancy in the middle, and B.B. and I on the other side of Nancy. I felt like the ultimate third wheel—or deterrent, however you viewed the situation.

"We worked together one summer, fixing up houses," B.B. said. He was in the middle of telling a story I had heard many times before but loved all the same because my father was its hero.

I could tell Nancy liked it, too. She kept her pretty eyes focused on B.B., not on the paunchy shrimp-flipping cook in the black apron. "So we show up to this woman's house and tell her we're here to fix her kitchen. We tell her we talked to her husband, and this is a big surprise for her. So she's all happy, and we start tearing apart the kitchen. The husband comes in, takes a look around, and shouts, 'What the hell are you doing to my cabinets?' *Paul had taken us to the wrong frickin' house!*"

Nancy chuckled as the dim, circular lights above us reflected off her jade earrings. I decided I liked her. She seemed calm, self-assured. I hoped B.B. might put aside his bias toward blondes for the afternoon.

The chef flipped our chicken, then scraped fried rice on our plates.

"Thank you," we said in unison.

"So, that was Kelly's dad for ya." B.B. doused his bowl with a lake of soy sauce. "Luckily, Kelly's a little more, um, straight-edged, I'd say. Responsible."

Nancy looked over at me, and I could sense she wanted to ask about my father. But no Korean woman would ever be so forward as to ask, "Has your father passed away?"

Nancy skewered some chicken with her chopstick. "Did you guys get in trouble?"

"Nah." B.B. gave her a twinkly-eyed smile. "Kelly's dad said to the husband, 'Sir, today's your lucky day. You've just won free, remodeled cabinets.'"

"No!"

"Yup. Paul said, 'Normally, this would cost $2,000 and take a week, but we're going to do it by the end of this afternoon—all for free.' Of course, I started to protest. I was ready to tell the guy, 'We'll just put your cabinets back together for you, and no harm done.' But Paul gave me that wink of his, and I knew he was playing all the angles."

"What angle?" asked Nancy.

"Paul gave the guy our business card, and we ended up getting a bunch of referrals from him. That one mistake kept us busy all summer long—and made us a lot of money."

"Sounds like a man who thinks on his feet." Nancy kept her gaze on B.B. for just a moment too long. Even *I* could tell she was trying to flirt with him.

B.B. broke off her glance, turning to me. "So, Kelly just got into Columbia. Found out yesterday."

Nancy turned to me. "That's nice."

From the look in her eyes, I could tell she had forgotten I was here. *Wow, twice in one day.* A new record.

"Yes," I said.

"You must be so excited." She kept her eyes on her food.

"Kelly really needs to get away," B.B. put in. "She needs to go party."

I shook my head. "That's not really my priority."

"It should be," B.B. said. "You're 20 years old now. Get a boyfriend! Live a little!"

I didn't necessarily disagree, although I didn't know how much "living" I would be doing at Columbia.

"And don't worry about Halmuni, either. I'll keep an eye on her."

"He's close with my family," I explained to Nancy.

Over this conversation, she had started checking her phone. "Uh-huh. Uh-huh."

"Oh, here." B.B. took a business card from of his pocket. "My friend Sophia runs a restaurant right by the university. She needs a hostess."

My eyes must have lit up with joy, because B.B. happily slapped me on the shoulder as he shoveled more rice in his mouth.

I grabbed the card. "Wow, thanks so much."

He washed down his food with a swallow of water. "Wish I could've gotten you work at an office."

"No, no, this is great. I'll take anything I can get."

"That should be your mantra at parties."

I gave him a look. Nancy glanced up from her phone with a chuckle. "I worked as a hostess for a while. It's good if you can move up to a server position. You can make a lot of money off tips."

"Plus, I thought you could use some practice talking to strangers," B.B. said to me. "You're gonna need strong interpersonal skills when you get in the courtroom."

I could feel my face reddening. "I have decent interpersonal skills."

B.B. stared at me with his "oh, gimme a break" look.

Nancy stared down at her plate.

"Don't I?"

B.B. sipped his water.

"You're sweet, but you're shy," Nancy said.

"Oh," I muttered. Was it that obvious, even to someone I'd just met?

CHAPTER FOUR

As I was about to enter the security check at LAX to board my plane to NYC, Halmuni and B.B. were both there to say their goodbyes. Halmuni gave me a bag of snacks to eat on the flight - edamames and Korean Kimbap. Halmuni knew that these were my favourite snacks. I've loved Kimbap ever since I was young - they are addictive like Doritos; once you start with one, you have to finish the whole roll. *Thank goodness, she didn't include any Kimchee; otherwise, it would stink up the entire plane*, I thought.

B.B. handed me a large, heavy, and very poorly wrapped box, which he insisted that I open before I board the plane. Inside was an Apple MacBook Pro.

"I got you top of the line - a MacBook Pro 15in with 512GB storage. Now you don't need to use the crappy, old one that you've been using."

"I don't know what to say," I said, genuinely surprised at the generosity of his gift. "This is the best present ever! Thank you, thank you! You are the best." I hugged him and held the laptop across my chest tightly, never wanting to let it go.

"Byung Chul, you are good boy. You deserve good wife," said Halmuni with a look of approval.

"It's nothing. Kelly, you deserve it. Without your help in the last two years, my files and bills would be a mess. Now get going before you miss your flight." He lightly pushed me forward. I could see that the eyes were getting watery.

I knew he didn't like it when I got emotional, but I couldn't resist, I said, "Thank you Uncle B.B. I love you for everything you've done for us," as I wrapped one arm around him and the other around Halmuni, who nodded in agreement.

"Hey, your dad did so much for me. He would have done the same if I had a kid. And didn't I tell you before, don't call me Uncle - makes me feel old, even if it is to show respect." He gave me a wink.

* * *

When I landed in JFK, I queued for a yellow taxi. I couldn't believe how chaotic everything seemed. Everything seemed to happen in a mad rush - people walked faster, the cars were going in all different directions in hyper speed, and people seemed to have a supersonic style of speaking. Once I managed to get a taxi, I knew we were in NYC as soon as we exited Midtown Tunnel. I rolled down my window and watched the city dwellers and tourists alike charged at a frenetic pace, creating a walking, talking human traffic flow. Some were drinking Starbucks, others talking on their mobiles, and even a few joggers going for a run along the busy streets. Everyone seemed busy doing something.

Everywhere I looked, NYC seemed congested and overcrowded. The mobbed streets, the jungle of vast buildings side by side, all in the same greyish color. There was also a unique smell that was inescapable — the aroma of a mixture of various ethnic restaurants, numerous hot dog stands, flower shops, and fruit stands. Buses, trucks, private cars, taxis. Vehicles honked; cabbies with their windows rolled down cursed at the universe. On the sidewalks, city dwellers charged blindly, jabbering importantly into their phones. Meanwhile, tourists like me shuffled along, gawking up at the skyscrapers, watching the world through their cameras.

Back in LA, whenever I watched street sweepers or the multitude of cars chugging up congested neighborhood blocks, I'd felt alone, a mere pedestrian swallowed up in the vastness of the city. But there, pockets of greenery had provided a bit of relief. Here in New York, there was nothing but steel, concrete, and people so sealed off from each other they might as well have been made of steel and concrete, too.

But I had already fallen in love with this city. I already felt at home.

In Los Angeles, there were so many indecipherable signs, so many rules to observe, but always the expectation that it was your duty to obey them all. I'd always worried about parking Halmuni's beat-up Honda in the wrong spot and being punished with a massive traffic ticket. As any Angeleno knows, violations can easily run hundreds of dollars just for overlapping the white lines. Maybe it was because we had no money to spare—or just because I'm hyper cautious—but I had always felt like I was encroaching on other people's space whenever I stepped outside my door. Though I'd lived there all my life, LA wasn't my town. Its streets belonged to someone else, and every step I took felt like someone was about to remind me I was out of place.

Riding in my taxi through New York's packed city streets lulled my usual fear. With so much stimulation, how could anyone expect me to be aware of all the rules, much less follow them? My breath caught in my throat and my heart sped up—but not from tension.

It was as if the city's energy, its constant movement, was making its way into my veins and nerves. I felt alive, in a way I couldn't remember feeling in … well, a long time. Maybe forever. The trepidation that had lived inside me forever slipped away just a little. I wondered, hopefully: *Maybe I can be part of this mass of people.* In a city teeming with strangers, maybe I wouldn't feel so alone.

We pulled over at Amsterdam Avenue. My driver hadn't ever turned to face me. All I knew of him was that he had glossy black hair framing a shiny bald dome.

"Where are we?" I asked.

"You wanted Columbia University, right?" He gestured abruptly. "There's the Arts and Crafts Beer Parlor. And over there is Hamilton Hall."

I had tried to memorize the campus map, but couldn't remember Hamilton Hall. Was Hamilton near the dorms? I considered asking him to circle around so I could get a better sense of where I was, but he cleared his throat by way of hurrying me up.

This was New York. You get out of your car as quickly as possible.

"Here," I handed him the wad of cash I had carefully budgeted for my one and only taxi ride until graduation. "And do you happen to know where I could find—?"

"No."

"Okay." I grabbed my two duffel bags and hoisted them on my shoulder. "Well, thanks." I opened the door, then attempted to drag my suitcase out from under the seat.

"Hurry up, miss."

He was already looking in his rearview mirror, signaling to get back into traffic. I sensed he was intent on zooming off the instant he found a gap in the traffic, whether or not some part of me remained in his vehicle. I dragged the suitcase out and collapsed backwards onto the street, landing on my butt, the suitcase springing open and scattering my belongings to the sidewalk.

A middle-aged dog walker with three yapping chihuahuas stepped around my bags, glaring down at me with a special look of derision.

Scrambling onto my knees, I reached up and slammed the door shut.

The driver sped off, narrowly missing another cab as he merged into his lane.

I sucked in a breath. It tasted like diesel fumes.

So much for feeling one with everything. For a few minutes, I'd felt part of New York's vibrancy, but I realized I was going to have to find a new pace, lot faster than I was used to, if I was going to keep up.

I stood. Lifting my suitcase by the handle, I allowed myself a brief look around. Over there was a quad, a grassy oasis in the teeming city. Surrounding it were massive buildings, historical, practically oozing with intellectual promise.

Hopefully, once I got off the street and onto campus, I could find a map—or a nice passing student. Plus, asking for directions might help me with my apparently needed "interpersonal skills."

Under the weight of my luggage, I staggered onto campus. The roar of Manhattan life grew muted almost at once. Luckily, Columbia had anticipated shy students like me. Or they were just extremely organized. There was a campus map, but before I'd even reached it, I saw brightly colored cardboard signs: 'MOVE IN DAY FOR NEW STUDENTS! FOLLOW THE PURPLE ARROWS!'

Even without the signs, I probably could've deduced where to go by following the hordes of excited teens and frantic parents.

Witnessing a mom wipe a tear from her eyes with the back of her hand reminded me of my own folks for a second. Her son didn't notice her; he was too busy looking at his phone, but she happened to lock eyes with me for a second. Caught, she smiled back at me.

I forgot to grin back. By the time I remembered to be polite, she was gone.

For a moment, I felt terribly lonely. All these other freshmen came accompanied by parents, brothers, and sisters—and here I was, all alone. I wished my mom and dad could be here with me. If they were here, my mom would've grabbed a cart and raced to keep up with the other mothers. My dad would've gotten lost behind, folding and unfolding the city map, suggesting places we could go sightseeing later—until my mom told him, "No, we'll have time to sightsee tomorrow, but today's all about Kelly and Columbia."

My dad would definitely have helped me unpack, though, all while rattling off trivia about the architecture, which he'd have dutifully researched the night before. Sprinkled between these nuggets of wisdom, he would still find time to try out a few corny jokes. I chuckled to myself, imagining my mother's expression, annoyed but amused, and full of love.

I have to stop wishing, I thought to myself, because I'd been doing that kind of wishing for quite a few years now, and it had never done me any good.

Joining the crush, burdened by my luggage, I followed a girl my age who was pushing a cart full of bedding, toilet paper, and collapsible drawers. Her mom, in a black sweater and scarf, kept trying to put her hands on the cart as if to guide it. The girl's dad, in suspiciously dark sunglasses, trailed behind, studying each building they passed.

"Mom, I got it," the girl said, pulling the cart away.

"It has a dead wheel. I just want to make sure you don't run it into anyone."

"It's fine."

"Do you remember your hall name?"

"It's on the map."

The dad glanced over at me. This time I was quicker on the draw, offering the prim, close-lipped smile I save for professional encounters. When he didn't return it, I slowed my step, realizing I was probably following too closely behind. I turned to watch other sets of families bustling along with their carts full of Bed, Bath & Beyond products. They all looked so put together, as if they'd spent the summer preparing for an eerie apocalypse with color-coordinated survival supplies.

The straps of my duffel bags burrowed into my shoulders, making me wince with pain. As ridiculous as my peers looked pushing metal carts, I desperately wanted one of my own. My suitcase kept turning on its side behind me, forcing me to halt every dozen steps to the annoyance of the parents and students behind me. Sweat ran down into my eyes. More than anything, I wanted to get to my room already, drop this stuff, and finally meet my roommate.

My roommate. This mysterious person would soon be a major part of my life. Just trying to imagine her made my stomach tighten. Typically, my overactive brain had already run through multiple roommate scenarios, every one worse than the other. I pictured a snobby former cheerleader who immediately despised me for being so uncool. Another narrative featured a sociopath with eleven fingers who liked to torture normal ten-fingered girls for fun. In my less disturbed moments, I visualized a quiet, introspective genius who preferred solitude. Of course, me being me, I also pictured a female undercover agent secretly working for the CIA while posing as a Columbia University student. That one might have been my favorite.

I approached a big sign at the entrance to the dorms with bold uppercase lettering: "WELCOME FRESHMEN TO YOUR NEW HOME!"

Any lingering connection to the city vanished. Suddenly I was very, very aware of my singularity. The solo kid. *The orphan.* I felt myself surrounded by all those other kids with their stockpiles of necessities from Costco and IKEA. I imagined them thinking to themselves as they stared at me: *Where are her parents?*

I must have been standing there like a goof because some proctor guy with a name badge stopped to ask me if I was lost. Embarrassed, I shook my head and got out of the way of the others streaming by.

At last, I found myself at the steps of Hartley Hall. Putting my suitcase down, I gave my throbbing hand a rest and caught my breath. I peered up at the beautiful, stately building.

This is it, I thought. *My new home.*

For a long while, I stood there peering up through the windows. On the other side of the glass, kids and parents milled about, taped up posters, hung clothes, argued over where to eat lunch.

Maybe if I kept looking up, I could hold back my tears.

* * *

I paused outside my door, wondering which imaginary roommate would greet me on the other side. After counting to five in my head, I pushed open the door. The room was empty and much smaller than I'd imagined it would be.

Whoever would share this space with me hadn't yet arrived. Two striped, blue mattresses sat atop wooden frames. The bed farthest from me adjoined an open window, and the white walls looked freshly scrubbed, practically crying out for cheesy motivational posters and stick-on calendars.

Allowing myself a moment to dream, I imagined how nice it would be to study on that bed and periodically look out the window to watch the falling leaves on the campus below. In my mind's eye, all this space belonged to me alone. I could do whatever I liked, be as messy as I wanted—or just the opposite, construct a super-regimented system of tidiness and cleanliness so the windowsills gleamed and the floor was so immaculate you could eat off it.

Shaking off such thoughts, I sighed and dropped my stuff on the other bed. I didn't want to immediately mark my territory in some confrontational way. The last thing I wanted was to be perceived as a pushy, difficult roommate.

I allowed myself a chuckle: *Especially if my roomie turns out to be that CIA agent.*

I looked around some more. There were two identical desks, scuffed and well-worn. I couldn't help wondering how many people had used them before us. A narrow bathroom occupied the space to the left. The bathroom contained nothing but a toilet scrubber and a chalky white soap slab beneath the mirror.

I debated my options. I could unpack. I could explore. I thought about what else I had to do. My mental to-do list, usually so insistent, had oddly gone silent.

As I rested upon a mattress in the middle of Columbia University, in the middle of a totally unfamiliar city, it hit me. I didn't *have* to do anything. No one was holding me accountable for anything. If I didn't want to unpack, I didn't have to. If I wanted to live out of my suitcase, no one was going to tell me that was a sloppy way to live. I didn't have any homework yet, no work assignments, no lectures or seminars to rush off to. I didn't even have to check in with B.B.'s friend, the restaurant manager, until later in the week.

Peering around, I suddenly felt paralyzed by this unusual feeling. *Could freedom trap you?* It seemed so weird to acknowledge this: permission to do anything, or nothing at all, could be liberating or terrifying—or both at once.

Then again, I wasn't entirely free. I had a schedule, starting tomorrow, of new-student activities. I *did* have a job to go to later this week, if B.B.'s friend liked me. In order to be self-sufficient, I needed to buy a bike to get around unless I wanted to waste my meager savings on transportation.

After a few minutes, slightly embarrassed by my paralysis, I decided my first task needed to be searching for a used bicycle. I assumed there must be Wi-Fi in the dorm, but I didn't know how to access it on the new Macbook B.B. had given me. So, I decided to find a computer in the Columbia library.

I hastily unpacked, leaving plenty of space for my roommate's stuff in the closet, then made my way to the library.

The sun had disappeared behind a few clouds, and the campus felt cooler and more inviting with a soft early autumn breeze. In the intervening hour or so, much of the freshmen and their parents must have settled in, as I encountered fewer of them as I passed through the quad.

Away from the dorms, I noticed older students who could be graduate students with backpacks heading in the same direction. The men sported more facial hair, and the women acted less giggly and nervous than the ones I'd seen earlier today.

I imagined a sense of homesickness would soon return. After all, I was still me, wasn't I? But now the buoyancy I'd experienced when I first saw the city returned. I felt weirdly light—happy, even. I wished

Halmuni was here, sure, but it was exciting to say maybe, just maybe, I could do all this on my own.

Standing outside the library, I craned my neck to see how far up it went. Palatial and regal, it looked like it could've been a part of the White House. Pushing open the glass doors, I felt like I shouldn't touch anything inside.

As I walked up and down stairs, through long aisles lined with shelves holding more books than I'd imagined existed in all the world, I breathed in the smell of newly printed pages, musty research books, and table cleaner. There were rows of wooden tables, chairs, and green-shaded lamps. I was certain I'd soon be at one of those tables.

I noticed that the students I saw were leaning over their Mac laptops. Some even possessed two laptops, plus an iPhone in their laps. I hoped having three screens wasn't a prerequisite for college success. I'd have to find another job if that were the case. As an avid reader, my usual instinct was to cock my head and read all of the vertical titles, but I reminded myself of my mission: Craigslist. Transportation. Cheap.

I found an open spot next to a young man with short hair who was snoozing on his keyboard. Was this an omen for my next four years? Quietly as I could, I sat next to him, careful not to wake him, and pulled up the browser screen. First, it asked for my login credentials, automatically adding @columbia.edu on the side.

I stared at the cursor, fingers poised on my keyboard. I could actually type my username and password and get Wi-Fi access. Because I was a student at Columbia University now. *Columbia!*

Okay, okay. Enough patting myself on the back. I hadn't actually accomplished anything yet. After successfully setting up my student account, I opened up Chrome and went to Craigslist, suddenly feeling self-conscious. Worried that the guy next to me might wake up, I tilted the monitor down and scooted closer. I typed in "bikes," specified the local area, then adjusted the price to $150 maximum.

NO RESULTS.

I closed my eyes. I guess the people who warned me New York was pricier than LA were right. My education was starting earlier than expected. Luckily, I'd come prepared. Reaching in my back pocket, I grabbed the budget sheet I constructed on the plane.

Each box represented a new expenditure. Increasing one meant I had to reduce another. It was like a painful game of Sudoku.

Looking at the obsessively straight lines, I realized why B.B. advised me to lighten up and party more. Oh, well. Maybe one day my own law practice would thrive like his, and I wouldn't have to create anal-retentive budget sheets.

Modifying my bike budget to $200, I looked elsewhere to make a minus-$50 deduction: grocery shopping. I imagined an embarrassment of Cup O' Noodles wrappers in my dorm trash can. So much for making a good impression on my new roommate.

I lowered the grocery amount. *College students don't eat real food anyway.*

Online, I scrolled through various options for a $200 bike. Within seconds, I found a decent-looking one in a nice shade of magenta with black lines across the handles.

I clicked, "Reply to Sender."

Just then, the young man beside me shook his head and sat up. I felt him look at me, but my eyes remained on the screen, typing quickly to the anonymous Craigslist seller.

The smell of honey mustard wafted over. From the corner of my eye, I watched the guy drizzle the yellowish substance on his Cobb salad. Ugh. Though, this wasn't exactly the food I'd eat or the place I'd dine, seeing him prepare his meal reminded me I hadn't eaten in a while. I didn't know if I had my cafeteria card yet, though. Maybe I could get a salad around here. I glanced at the guy's plastic lid. The price sticker read $15.99. I stifled my gasp. *Never mind.*

Now officially hungry, I reached in my bag and pulled out a Ziploc bag of edamame. The beans were warm and slimy by now, but I needed the protein—and I couldn't deduct $15.99 from any more boxes today.

While I tried to clandestinely munch on the green pods, I watched more and more students pass by, all maintaining the same expression of determination and worry. None of them seemed to be talking to each other. It was like they all knew socializing for even five minutes would undermine all their study goals. I started to feel bad for them, until I realized that would be me in about five days.

I looked up. The Craigslist seller had emailed me back. *"I can do $180. Can you swing by tonight?"*

"Yes," I typed. *"I will be there in an hour."*

Time to go meet another stranger in an even stranger place.

CHAPTER FIVE

If Halmuni knew I was about to meet a strange man from a Craigslist ad, she would've killed me before I got past the front door. Ever since what happened a few years ago, Halmuni obsessively scoured our local newspaper for reports of area murders, rapes, kidnappings, home invasions, and other violent crimes. She watched the local "Eyewitness News" obsessively like it was her own personal soap opera and kept a notepad by her recliner, ready to record any changes to the FBI's "Top 10 Most-Wanted List." Her mini-notebook, ironically covered in a rainbow font spelling out *Every Day is Beautiful!* barely moved from its spot beside our couch, where she wrote in it like a deranged diarist.

Every day when I came home from school, she couldn't wait to share the latest sensational news story with me. My friendly "hello" was met with, "You know who went missing today on news?" or "Did you hear about latest school shooting?" A backpack check usually followed.

"How come you no keep two Mace?" she'd ask, going through my bag's contents.

"I think one Mace spray is enough, Halmuni."

"Tell that to dead girl I see on news."

One pepper spray wasn't enough. She insisted I keep two containers in my purse. Thankfully, no one ever asked me about them. Halmuni would typically talk to me about whatever she just read in the newspaper or heard on the TV while I rummaged in the fridge. If the crime didn't involve armed robbery, which still stung to hear about, I could usually tune her out. There is only so much bad news you can absorb before going numb.

As time went on, and my tuning-out skills improved, Halmuni probably began to think she had raised the most heartless granddaughter in the world—one who would casually say, "Yeah, great," to the occasional inmate escape. As she breathlessly told me about online date meetups gone awry or high-speed car chases ending in fiery deaths, I started to feel that perhaps she was confusing TV dramas like *Law & Order* and *CSI* with reality.

The only way I could make her comfortable about my going to Columbia was by telling her I would hardly leave campus. I assured her I certainly wouldn't go to Morningstar Park in the evenings (because Halmuni was certain most crimes happened in parks at night) or distant neighborhoods like Harlem or, God forbid, the Bronx. I once tried to explain that many of New York's older neighborhoods were now being heavily gentrified, and she said, "You never see *Real Housewives of the Bronx*!"

But now here I was, on my first day at Columbia, going up to Harlem to buy a bike from a complete stranger. I already could picture Halmuni seeing my face keyed above an anchorman's shoulder as he matter of factly recounted the grisly details about this unfortunate Columbia student's murder during a Craigslist deal-gone-bad.

Shaking off such disturbing thoughts, I buried my hands in my pockets, trying to blend in with the sky's darkening veil, and marched to the bus stop a half-block away. Two minutes later, the bus arrived with a *hiss,* and I climbed aboard, paid my fare, and found a seat. Following the directions from my phone, I got off at Frederick Douglass Boulevard, leading me to dilapidated streets with sketchy, dark buildings, the kind of rough neighborhoods you saw on *Cops.*

I tried to walk down the sidewalk in a narrow, straight line to avoid undue attention. A nearby street lamp barely illuminated the shadows from my footsteps. I kept my head down and to the side, relying on my peripheral vision to detect any approaching dangers. Behind me, a couple in black, puffy jackets stumbled out of a Mexican restaurant, clutching their takeout boxes. They hailed a taxi and quickly got in. I wished I could afford a cab. Right now, I would like nothing more than to take it back to Columbia, back to my room, so I could safely wiggle under the warm comforters.

Turning on Frederick Douglass Boulevard, I searched apartment numbers for 308 West 154th Street. The red brick buildings all looked identical except for the people sitting on the porch steps. Some of them spoke to each other, barely tossing me a glance, while others stared ahead as if on guard duty. They gave me dirty looks, suspicious of my every step.

Then he jump out of alley, knife in hand! Halmuni's voice screamed in my head.

I sped up my walk. 300. 302. 304. Almost there. Don't make eye contact with anyone. Pretend like you know what you're doing. Keep your chin up. Dogs—and people—can smell fear. From the corner of my vision, I noticed a middle-aged man wearing a grey sweatshirt and plaid pajama pants. His grey sweatshirt said, "Don't Follow Me, I'm Lost" which made me let out a chuckle because I was, too. He must have heard me because he turned and gave me a cold leer. I looked away and walked even faster.

I was practically running to the address the bike seller had given me, but I wasn't sweating. Although it was the end of summer, the temperature had dropped since morning, and I found myself shivering. I should have taken B.B.'s advice and bought a bulkier, pricier jacket. I already needed to subtract 20 degrees from the actual temperature to compensate for my native Southern California upbringing.

My teeth began chattering, and I could see my breath. I shoved my fingers deeper in my thin pockets to keep them warm. Every sound, from a window opening to a whisper, alerted me to someone nearby who I thought would most definitely assault me.

But I had to keep walking. I had come all this way so I couldn't give up now. Plus, the price of this bike seemed reasonable. What if bike prices kept going up on Craigslist? I couldn't reduce any more numbers from my other budget boxes. I was already pushing things close. If some unforeseen emergency arose, I'd be in big trouble.

At last, I arrived at 308 West 154th Street. Rusty gates outlined the exposed brick building. Black trash bags lined the nearby sidewalk, their blue strings pointing toward the street crammed with parked cars. Some of the bags looked only half-empty and fluttered as the cold wind shifted them side to side. It wasn't just the prospect of a scary encounter with this Craigslist guy that had me on edge. Loneliness had already caught up to me. I missed the familiarity and safety of home.

I pushed open the gate and walked up to the front step, noticing a broken pot with soil sprinkling a sodden WELCOME mat. I pushed the buzzer for Apartment 2B, which had "Doyle," the last name from the ad, written on tape beside it. The door unlocked with a startling vibration much louder than the buzzer.

Entering the foyer, I noticed random graffiti. Mangled letters made up a language I didn't understand, and abstract symbols marred the concrete walls. I pulled my hoodie down to hide my face as I stepped over a Big Gulp soda, its straw broken in pieces beside it. I raised my fist at the door with peeling green paint the color of rotting cucumber skin.

Before my knuckles met wood, the door opened. Behind it stood who I guessed was Tim Doyle. Balding on top, he had a crown of reddish fuzz extending from ear to ear. Beneath the fluorescent lights, his pale complexion looked waxy. He wore a leather jacket one size too small for his beer belly. The leather made a crackly squeaking sound when he stuck out his hand to greet me.

I shook his hand. "Hi, I'm Kelly. The person interested in the bike?"

He made some kind of movement with his mouth as if he were chewing an imaginary piece of gum, loosely holding onto the edge of my fingers in a shake before grabbing the door again.

"It's in the back." The gruffness of his voice matched his tall stature.

And this is how one of Halmuni's stories starts.

I glanced past him, into a room that had probably not seen a carpet cleaning since the previous tenant. This section also seemed to be a storage space for spare vehicle parts. I detected oil mixed with cigarettes. I returned my hands to my pockets, wondering how fast I could dial 911 without him noticing.

"I think I'll wait out here," I said calmly so as not to project any hint of the fear causing my heart to pound in my ears.

I heard a sound from the apartment behind me. Glancing back, I saw a Hispanic woman with a bag of groceries. She tucked them under her chin and fiddled with her keys at the door. I mentally volunteered her as someone who might help if I screamed.

Tim moved his jaw again in that funny way of his. "All right, I'll bring it to you." He headed back inside, closing the door in my face.

I let out a deep breath. If he wanted to hurt me, he would've tried to get me to come in, right?

I looked back down the now empty hallway. My first day at Columbia and here I was, standing in what could have been a drug den. Someone in the apartment above me moved a chair. The scratching sound seemed to trail across the top of my head.

Tim opened the door again. "Here she is."

He suddenly wore a big smile, exposing slightly yellowed teeth and receding gums as he rolled out a bike.

A bike, not *the* bike I saw on Craigslist.

I stared at it. Painted with dozens of bugs running up and down the body, the word *MANTIS* stretched across the side in black, block letters. As Tim released one of his hands, he revealed a large protruding plastic insect head mounted between the bars like the bike's very own hood ornament. How could I possibly ride this eyesore to class? This wasn't a bike. It was a two-wheeled freak show.

"$180. Like we said." Tim hovered over the vehicle in a protective stance, as if my thin, frame could somehow wrest it from him.

"Um, this isn't what you put on Craigslist. You advertised a shiny, almost new, magenta bike. I did not come all the way over here to buy this—joke!" I was furious and determined not to be bullied. Like B.B. said, I needed to toughen up and show some moxie.

"Oh, *that* bike. I got that in the back, too. But that one's $300. This one's the $180 deal."

"But that's not what I—"

"Listen," he cut me off, "I don't care what you think you saw on the ad." He walked closer to me and I could smell his B.O. Although I was five-foot seven, he towered over me. I knew this type of guy. He was a bully, like the ones at school, and was looking for an excuse—any excuse —to pick a fight. So, I changed my tack and used my "be as sweet as possible" approach.

"I'm a college student on a budget. And I don't really want to go biking around at Columbia on an ... insect."

"Mantis. Like a praying mantis."

"Right. You can imagine it might look a bit silly for a grown woman to be riding around on something like this?"

He smirked. "Go to Columbia, huh? You one of those stuck-up smarty pants snobs?"

"No. And that isn't my point. I'm saying it would be embarrassing to ride a bike with a mantis head on the middle."

He whistled. "Excuse me. Didn't know who I was dealing with."

"Look. I just want a bike. A 'normal' bike."

He rolled it out toward me. "And here it is."

I looked up at him. He straddled the bike, still standing inches above it, pretending to steer it like some high school kid. "This could be you," he said, adding sound effects. "*Errr! Err!* You'll be the cool one cruising to class, studying microbiology or some shit."

I didn't have the courage to tell him he looked anything but cool, so I just crossed my arms and looked coldly into his eyes.

"Okay, okay," he said. "I'll take $20 off. And. *And...* I will throw in this."

He rested the handlebars against the door, then disappeared down the hallway. I was afraid he was going to bring out some kind of bug helmet.

I sighed, leaning against the door, the top of my hoodie resting against a sticker of a smiley face with a bullet shot through it.

The floor vibrated as he came back out and tossed me a white mesh basket. It reminded me of the one attached to the pink tricycle my dad used to push me in. Near the house I grew up in was a stretch of lawn where I always grabbed sunflowers. I'd stuff them in the basket, then ride back up the hill to show my dad. When I was finally big enough for a bike without training wheels, he gave me one with a basket brimming with fake flowers as our little joke. I knew Tim's basket, scuffed with black stains and bent edges, would probably not offer so many happy memories.

Tim clasped the basket onto the handlebars, careful not to disturb the mantis head. "You must have a lotta books, right? Being so smart and all?"

"I have a backpack."

"Bad for your back. Just put 'em in here." He flashed that yellow toothed smile again. "I'm really giving you a bargain. Bike *and* basket. Who could ask for more?"

I pointed to the insect head on the handlebars. "It even comes with this," hoping he'd catch my sarcasm.

He raised his arms triumphantly. "I know!" *Good God*, he genuinely thought the mantis head was awesome.

I felt deflated. Then I looked down at the bike. Or, more accurately, The Mantis.

Well, at least it has a basket.

CHAPTER SIX

I pedaled faster and faster beside the campus sidewalk, hoping the wind might rip the "Mantis" paint off the bicycle's aluminum alloy frame. I had managed to remove the insect head the night before with a screwdriver I borrowed from the RA on my floor. My roommate still hadn't showed up, and I didn't want her first impression of me to be strongly associated with a green carnivorous insect.

My phone buzzed in my back-jean pocket. I stopped suddenly—too suddenly. It almost made my books catapult out of the white, mesh basket. I couldn't believe I was actually using this thing, but Tim was right. Carrying all those books in a backpack really did hurt my spine.

I picked up my phone. Unknown number. Area code 917. I stopped, peering over to the hall with the widest steps—easier for kids to sit and study in solitary without being tempted to talk to one another. A bunch of them sat with backpacks hunched over their shoulders, whispering to themselves or reading.

I planted one foot in the grass and the other on the concrete, slowly lowering my bike to the pavement.

"Hello?"

"Kelly? This is Sophia from Poseidon—B.B.'s friend," she said, in what sounded like a British accent.

"Hi, Sophia—"

She cut me off in mid-sentence. "I need you to come to the restaurant right now."

"I thought we were meeting on Thursday ..."

"Leo, I told you to put that over there!" she yelled to someone off-phone. "Oh, my God, he is such an idiot." *Poor Leo*, I thought. I pictured a busboy just starting off. "As I was saying, I need you here ASAP so we can get your HR stuff processed."

I could hear the clang and clatter of activity in the restaurant around Sophia. The ambient buzz of chatter mixed with pulsing, bass-heavy music made it sound as if she was moving through the heart of a packed nightclub.

"Sure, I can do that." I really wanted to go to freshman orientation and meet my roommate, but it was more important to get on Sophia's good side.

"Fabulous. See you soon."

"And should I bring—" But she had hung up. "... anything?" I whispered, putting the phone back in my pocket.

Turning my head, I noticed several female freshmen awkwardly trying to make conversation with each other, their topics shifting quickly from music to majors to the best sororities to rush. On one level, I wished I could join in, but, never having had much time to socialize as a teenager, I lacked the skills to be "one of the girls" and didn't even know how to start. That was fine. The point of being here was to do well academically, get into a top law school, and move

Halmuni into a nice house with a yard so she didn't have to age in a grimy K-Town apartment.

More girls joined in the conversation, so right before they got any louder, I plugged in my earbuds, blasting my workout playlist. The bass kicked in to Justin Timberlake's *Can't Stop the Feeling*, matching the timing of my knees circling the pedals. I tightened the jacket tied around my waist, feeling grateful for the sun's rays. The temperature was probably only in the mid-60s, but it was a whole lot better than the biting cold from last night.

Veering off campus onto a side street felt like stepping out of a quiet museum into the middle of a crowded intersection. Passing the South Lawn, I rode onto Columbus Avenue and into Morningside Park as I continued south. The dappling sunlight made the park's grass look freshly mowed, and the pond buzzed with ducks and geese. Paved paths weaved around beautiful landscaping with historical statues rising atop concrete staircases. A dog tried to chase down my wheels before becoming distracted by a flock of frightened birds. I turned down my music to hear the quiet from the park, actually enjoying the occasional bark or flapping wing. This picturesque spot was the exact opposite of Tim's Harlem neighborhood, and I loved it.

I sped faster and faster along Columbus Avenue and finally slowed to turn onto West 83rd Street, pausing to make sure the pedestrians who wanted to cross did so. Seeing my chance to finally make the turn, I was about to resume peddling when, out of nowhere, a sports car came zipping up from behind and swerved around the corner, coming so close I could feel the air whoosh as it passed.

I gasped, swinging my handlebars far to the left and immediately losing my balance. My forearm hit the pavement first, then my wrist slammed beneath the handle bar.

I stayed on the ground motionless as people buzzed past my head, the street now completely perpendicular to my sightline. Once I realized what had happened and remembered to breathe, I untangled my legs from the wheel, pushing myself off the ground. I winced with pain. My scraped knee was bleeding into my sock.

"Whoa, you okay?" asked a slender hipster with eyeliner and orange hair.

I started to respond, but he didn't wait for my answer. Like the other people from the intersection, he dashed across to make the light.

I took off my helmet and examined my body for any other injuries. I started to reach down for my twisted bike when I noticed the maniac speed racer's car was parked on the next side street, arrogantly occupying a spot with a sign reading *Loading Zone Only*. I was almost blinded by the deep, royal blue of the car. Then a young, dark-haired man flew out of the driver's side. He and his luxury vehicle both looked like they just wrapped filming a James Bond movie.

I pulled my bike closer, glaring at him as he ran to join me. His hair was thick and dark, and he had a traditionally handsome chiseled face that only male models usually enjoyed, but you could tell he didn't make much of an effort to try to look good—he didn't need to. His tall build fit perfectly in what I assumed was a very expensive suit.

"Oh my God, are you okay? I am sooooo sorry." His voice was deep but warm.

His outfit and assertive posture made him appear older until I glanced at his eyes and realized that he must be in his twenties. They seemed to still be questioning, like he was hoping for something.

I grabbed the handlebars to see if they still worked and then squeezed the tires to make sure that they weren't flat.

"I really didn't, you were in my blind spot and—oh, no. Look at you!"

He pulled a white handkerchief from his pocket, knelt down and pressed it against my scraped knee. I stared at him. What young guy carries a handkerchief? Was this a New Yorker thing? I'm sure if I told B.B. this, B.B. would have guffawed and said that this guy was either a sissy or had some germ phobia.

"Why were you going so fast?" I fumed, pulling my leg away. I glanced over at his car. Its vertically opening doors looked as if they could sprout wings and fly.

"I'm late for an appointment. But that's no excuse."

I looked at the bent handlebars. "I just got this last night." I let out a sigh.

He reached in his back pocket and pulled out his wallet. "Look—

"And you know what else?" Hot adrenaline coursed through my body, straight to my mouth. "I could have died!"

He stood up and eyed me skeptically, which only made me angrier.

"I'm serious! Last year, motorists killed almost 20 cyclists in Manhattan alone, so you are lucky that I wasn't one of them or you would be in the news as a murderer." It amazed me how quickly I had retrieved this particular statistic from memory. Thank you, Halmuni!

As he pulled up the bike, he wasn't paying attention to me. Instead, he was looking at my ridiculous basket, reading the name "Mantis" to himself. "Is this really your bike?"

For some reason, I suddenly felt fiercely protective of it. "Yes. It is a specialty item." I have no idea why I said that, but I didn't want him to know this was the only bike I could afford.

Without hesitation, he withdrew three crisp one-hundred dollar bills. "This should cover the cost of repairs. Or buy you a new bike. Either way. If not, give me a call."

Three hundred dollars for my ridiculous Mantis bike? This obviously rich, privileged jerk clearly had no clue about the real world. But who was I to complain? Halmuni would have said, *Ask him for more! Start limping and pretend you need go to hospital.*

Next, he reached back in his wallet and pulled out a business card. Made of thick material, the card had a light beige tint, the kind of high-end card you don't print off your computer. The name IAN WILLIAM ANDERSON II appeared in embossed cursive blue letters that matched his car's hue. Beneath the lettering was a single straight line and a phone number. Nothing else. Weird.

"Do you think you'll be okay? Do you need a ride?" He held my arm up to make sure I was steady. I could feel the warmth coming from his hand—it caused a kind of tingling sensation I never felt before.

"I'm fine." I yanked my arm from his grip as I pushed his money away. "Just on my way to work." I glanced at the damage to my elbow and knee. Blood smeared into my forearm and my left shin, and I felt like that little girl on a tricycle again, counting bruises and blood spots to show Mom.

"Oh, where do you work?" He slipped his wallet back in his pocket. He didn't seem in the least concerned his super-car was illegally parked and could be ticketed or towed at any minute.

"Poseidon." I tried to sound more "adult like" and matched my posture to his. "That's a restaurant. I'm just starting today." I handed back his once-white handkerchief, which now had several blood stains on it.

"I know that place. Super trendy now. You sure you don't want a ride?"

As I stood up, I looked directly at his face. His nose and cheeks were tan, as if he spent the summer at the beach. I suddenly became very self-conscious. He was so good looking. I must look like a disheveled mess. His eyes impressed me the most. Startled by the feeling of not being able to break away from them, I cleared my throat.

"No, thank you," I managed to croak. We looked at each other for a second. I had never been pulled into someone's eyes like that. His were light, light blue, like the color of one of those unbelievably clean oceans by a private island. *No. Stop that.*

"Okay, then how about I pick you up afterwards to go repair your bike? Maybe even grab a bite to eat?" This guy was relentless. He was probably used to girls drooling over him. *Don't fall for it Kelly. He must be a womanizer.*

"Sorry. Busy today."

I leaned over to get my bike upright, but he immediately reached over and pulled the bike up. As he leaned over to reach for the bike, I couldn't help but notice his nice, crisp clean scent.

"You smell like SeBreeze-Fresh Garden Scent," I whispered, not realizing that I actually said it out loud. I was mortified.

He chuckled. "No one has ever compared my scent to an aerosol can before, but thank you?"

Completely embarrassed, I just needed to turn around the corner and speed off, way past that stupid blue car and those ... blue eyes.

I began walking around him with the bike, but right as I walked past, he bent down.

"Wait." He picked up the books from the road that had fallen out of my basket. He reached them out to me, barcodes facing up. Next to the numbers spelled COLUMBIA UNIVERSITY.

"This where you go to school?"

"Yeah." I quickly readjusted the placement of my basket, plopping the books inside. I hoped he didn't comment on Columbia like Tim—I wasn't in the mood for someone else to make a smart comment.

"Cool."

I looked up at him, surprised.

"Sure I can't change your mind about tonight?" *Yup, relentless.*

"The bike and I will be fine. Just some scratches."

"Okay." He backed away. "Well, then ..."

Voice trailing, he waved, then walked back to his car, opened the side, and got in. More pedestrians floated past. I rotated my handlebars and decided to walk the bike to the corner, or at least until I stopped shaking. I looked at Ian a second longer before he drove off, slowly this time.

I didn't need a new bike. Or a "bite to eat." I was fine. He was probably just a spoiled brat, anyway.

CHAPTER SEVEN

"About time you showed up," said a very agitated Sophia.

"Sorry ..." My voice died in my throat.

Arriving at Poseidon ten minutes after my fall, I was still in a state of shock and confusion. I could only imagine how untidy I looked: the sleeves of my beige jacket not quite rid of sidewalk debris, my jeans ripped around my scraped knee, my dark brown hair in a messy ponytail with the top of my hair inadvertently over-teased as a result of my helmet rubbing against the top of my head.

I wished I had time to fix myself up better before coming in. It also didn't help that a trail of dried blood covered my elbow and knee. But I did my best to appear confident, presenting my tight-lipped professional smile as I shrugged off thoughts about nearly dying coming here.

Sophia sported bleached blonde hair in a tight, neat bun and perfectly arched eyebrows. She didn't seem fazed by the fact I was out of breath or that I had to keep wiping sweat from my brow. Squatting behind the hostess stand, she lifted heaps of place settings as if she had magnets attached to her freckled hands.

Then, she stood up, adjusting her hair so that not a strand was out of place and straightened her black top. She stared through me as if taking inventory of each movement in the room. Without warning, she turned on her heel toward the first row of tables. Assuming I was supposed to follow, I hurried after.

Poseidon's interior was an eclectic blend of Greek mythological statues and Chinese artifacts. The vaulted ceilings seemed to stretch as high as the billboards on Manhattan Avenue. Along the entrance, tall earth-colored Terracotta style Chinese warriors stood as if guarding the restaurant, and through the arched front windows, you could see a large marble statue of the eatery's namesake, the Greek god of the sea and earthquakes—brandishing his massive trident.

Striking, deep hues distinguished the stylish décor. Well-dressed men and women in smart suits and blazers fresh from their high-paying jobs leaned up against the dark oak tabletops. Chatting loudly to be heard over hip-hop beats blasting from the sound system, they threw back oyster shooters in between nibbling tapas-sized plates of dim sum. Meanwhile, servers clad in all-black uniforms similar to Sophia's blended in with the elegant, yet chic, vibe, darting around with trays of food and cocktails.

I did my best to shadow Sophia, but she zoomed through the crush of diners like a cheetah cat, her heels barely kissing the floor. Once or twice, I got stuck between her and a four-top, a casualty of the speedy servers racing to drop off Laksa noodles and various ceviche small plates. As Sophia slowed for a moment at the lip of the bar to inspect a half-dozen specialty drinks, I rushed over to explain my tardiness. "It wasn't my fault. This guy came out of nowhere—"

"Make this one again." Sophia told a female bartender with a nose stud. Then she turned to look me full in the face for the first time. "Get here late next time, don't come back."

My mouth parted, but I quickly shut it.

She looked me up and down. "You living on the streets?"

"No, I was actually hit by a car today. That's what I was trying to explain."

"That's a good one." The faintest glimmer of amusement flashed across her narrow face. Then her green eyes hardened. "But I don't accept excuses."

"Oh, I'm not trying to give one. It's the truth."

"Leave the truth to jurors." Sophia reached over me to plop a cherry into a beverage a nano-second before the server took it. Then she rocketed off to the next part of the restaurant with me in her wake, talking over her shoulder. "I owe B.B., so I guess I really don't have a choice. I have to take you. For now."

I didn't like that last part. I vowed to make her think employing me was not a mistake.

"How do you owe B.B.?" I couldn't picture her striking up a friendship with anyone, especially him.

"We're a fusion restaurant focusing on various styles of seafood. Asian, Greek and ... Peruvian."

"Peruvian?" I didn't see how this connected to B.B.

She turned the whole way around to address me, walking backward through the crowd. Incredibly, she didn't bump into anything or anyone. "Peruvian cuisine has a rich culinary heritage unexplored by modern restaurateurs. Anyway, some fusion bistro down 112th said we were 'appropriating' their recipes," she said, using air quotes. "It was all total B.S., of course, but they slapped us with a C&D. B.B. helped us out of the legal PITA." She finally took a breath. "Man, gotta love acronyms."

"PITA?"

"Pain In The Ass." Sophia switched back to charging through the restaurant face-first. "Before that, he and I went to Boston College together."

"You went to Boston College?" I ducked under a server's tray carrying what looked like spring rolls.

"Why the surprise?" She said with some rancor in her voice. "People who work at restaurants can have college degrees, you know."

"It's just that you have a British accent, so I wouldn't have thought you went to school here," I managed to stammer out. *I hope I didn't offend her. I really need this job.*

She ignored my response and swiveled around a passing waiter to place a new napkin set up at a table beside the window. A middle-aged couple peered up at us expectantly. Sophia immediately turned on the charm, offering them an angelic smile. "Here you are. Anything else I can get for you?"

The man shook his head. "How did you know I needed silverware?"

"You must have eagle eyes," said his wife.

Sophia shrugged off the compliment. Walking away, she caught a young waitress by the shoulder. Grabbing her arm, she pulled her closer to whisper. "I shouldn't still be helping your customers."

Blushing, the girl nodded, then scurried off. I watched her go, fearing that might soon be me. I continued after Sophia, trying to keep up. At each empty table she passed, she picked up glasses, wiped off crumbs with a towel, and tucked in chairs. I was getting tired just watching her.

"On the plus side," she said, returning to the narrow bar area to pour a beer from one of the many taps. She handed it to a waiter, then clicked on a nearby computer screen. "I guess you're pretty enough to be a hostess."

I clumsily hovered beside her, not sure where I should go. "Oh, um thank—"

"But you should know," she said, handing off a glass of wine to the bartender who nodded thanks. "This restaurant business is *warfare*. You always need to stay one step ahead of your enemy."

"My enemy?"

"Yes. Time."

Before I could process this statement, Sophia raced off to the hostess stand. As I rejoined her, she brushed me out of her way to allow in a tall woman, who was so beautiful people couldn't help but notice her. There were a couple of men with those fancy, professional cameras that only real photographers use taking photos of her as she entered. She must be someone famous, I thought.

"Hi there, darling, how may I help you?" Sophia purred in her sweetest voice.

"Two please," said the woman, as an equally dapper man wearing a suit with no tie joined her.

"Great. This way." Sophia whipped out menus and place settings without taking an extra breath. "Wait here," she told me.

I stood behind the counter, looking out of place in my scuffed jacket and untidy hair. Another couple came in and smiled at me. *Oh no.* They looked at me expectedly. I glanced in either direction as if some other hostess would magically appear to save me.

"Two, please," the man said.

"Oh, um, sorry I don't actually—"

"This way." Sophia emerged from nowhere, pushing past me to grab more menus and silverware. *How did she keep appearing everywhere?*

I stood awkwardly at the stand until Sophia returned. "Remember. This is what happens when you call in sick. Other people have to rise to the occasion for you." She waved over a waitress.

A woman in her mid-20s came over. Her jet-black hair was pulled back, but hers was in a low bun, instead of a high bun like Sophia's, and the tips of a blue cactus tattoo peeked out from beneath the sleeve of her tight t-shirt. Bright lip-gloss reflected off her full lips.

Sophia grabbed a black apron from the back of the lowest row on the hostess stand. "Your apron looks filthy," Sophia said as she handed it to the woman. I couldn't help thinking it looked perfectly fine to me.

The waitress untied hers, putting on the new one. "But I spot-cleaned."

Sophia frowned. "If I can still see the shadow of brushing sauce, so can the customers."

The server glanced at me, then squinted her wing-tipped, jet black, eye-lined eyes, and said, "Next time, I'll use newbie here as a shield."

"Eva, Kelly. Kelly, Eva."

I offered my hand. "Nice to meet you."

Eva tied her apron in the back with a harsh yank at the end. Strutting back toward the bar area, she pretended to high-five a waiter carrying four plates on his hands and forearms.

"Very funny, Eva," he said.

"Gotta keep you on your toes, tough guy," she said before disappearing into the kitchen.

"She'll be training you next week." Sophia pointed to the iPad perched on the stand. "What time does that say?"

"6:46?" I felt like this was a trick question.

Sophia craned her neck, taking in the restaurant. I followed her gaze. Nearly every table was filled with patrons. Server after server rushed to keep up with the orders: in and out of the kitchen's double doors, back out to the main floor. Aspiring actors made up the staff of most LA restaurants, and I had never seen any of them work this hard.

"It's not 6:46," Sophia said, keeping her eye on the clock as the minute changed. "Nor is it 6:47. It's Dinner Rush Time."

"Right."

"Why am I telling you this, Kelly? If you know the enemy and know yourself, you need not fear the result of a hundred battles."

"Sun Tzu?"

"Good girl. You're well-read."

I would have taken that statement as a compliment if I didn't also feel like Sophia's new pet. The phone on the hostess stand rang. Its high-pitched screech bounced off the high ceilings before she snatched it. "Poseidon. This is Sophia, may I please place you on a brief hold?"

She put the phone down. A red light started blinking at its base. She sighed, the first sign of normal human life she had shown in the last 20 minutes. "In the midst of chaos, there is opportunity."

"Sophia!" someone yelled. I turned to see a woman in her 40s, clad in expensive fitness clothes. She tossed off a Lululemon headband, dropping it in a $1,000 Gucci duffle bag she used as a sports bag.

"Janet." Sophia beamed. "Lettuce wraps with scallop ceviche?"

"Honey, you always know my post-workout."

Sophia typed in the order on the iPad. "Want a glass of champagne while you wait?"

"You read my mind." Janet plopped into a seat by the door. "Bless you, woman." She seemed to genuinely love Sophia. Sophia seemed to love the love.

I watched both of them as Sophia finished inputting the order. Janet used a makeup remover towelette from her bag to rub her face. Sophia reached under the stand again, handing me a black shirt with a trident in the right-hand corner. The word POSEIDON appeared in bright orange lettering above it. "This looks like your size. And here's the application I need you to fill out for HR." She handed me a thick packet of forms.

"Should I fill this out now?"

"No. Take all that home to complete it. Bring it back Thursday. 4 pm. Be punctual. We need to defeat our inexorable enemy."

"What?"

"*Time.*"

"Oh. Right."

"You can go now." Her hand shooed me to leave.

I started to say goodbye, but Sophia left before I could form the words. As I watched her zip to the bar, I couldn't help admire how incredibly agile she was—her body gracefully glided by all the tables like a well-trained, prima ballerina.

Suddenly, I felt a tap on my arm. I turned to see Janet holding another one of her Neutrogena wipes. She circled her face with her hands and scrunched her nose. "Looks like you needed a little refresher."

Embarrassed, I grabbed the soggy cloth and forced a smile. "Thanks."

CHAPTER EIGHT

After fitting my scuffed Mantis bike between some brand-new Schwinns, I trudged up the white, concrete steps to Hartley Hall. Lifting my body step by painful step, I suddenly became very aware of my exhaustion. My intuition told me I didn't want to work for Sophia. I didn't want to ride on stupid Amsterdam Avenue, facing impending death each day, just to get to a degrading job requiring super-human energy levels only maniacs like Sophia possessed. I also didn't want to attempt that while studying the many textbooks weighing down my basket. Classes hadn't even started, and all I wanted to do was sleep.

After scanning my ID card in the electronic slot by the automatic glass doors, I stepped into the dorm's warm embrace. I padded along the faded purple carpet and then pushed the elevator button with my knuckle, this time hoping my mystery roommate wouldn't be home. No more talking. No more new people. I had enough social interaction for one day. Just let me tuck myself beneath my sheets and drift away. I could face everything tomorrow if I could just be alone for a little while.

The elevator dropped me off at the second-floor hallway. In the time I was gone, our RA found time to decorate the beige walls with inspirational posters, including quotes like:

"What we think, we become." ~Buddha.

"Believe you can and you're halfway there." ~Theodore Roosevelt.

"All our dreams can come true, if we have the courage to pursue them." ~Walt Disney.

Reading them actually made me feel better. As I continued to look on, I noticed two comfy-looking leather couches flanking a pool table in the lounge opposite the posters. Two unshaven guys in t-shirts sat in front of a big screen TV watching *Game of Thrones* while munching tacos out of delivery bags.

"But what'd you send her?" the guy on the left asked, talking over the show.

"One of those eggplant emojis followed by a thumbs up. Picture is worth a thousand words," the other one said, looking down at his phone hopefully.

"And you're wondering why she hasn't replied?"

"I'm just being straightforward!"

"You're just being an idiot."

I put my head down as they both stopped talking to stare at me. Suddenly feeling exposed, I rushed down the hall to room 203, right next to the exit for the stairs. I slipped in my card and pulled the handle.

I walked into an explosion of color. I had to blink a few times to take it all in. I had left the bare-walled room with just my monochrome-colored white sheets and white comforter on my bed, but now returned to what looked like a tropical beach house. A couple of posters of an ocean sunset hung on each side of the beds, and some smaller photos of beautiful white sandy beaches with clear blue water covered the wall between the two windows. White, beaded lights hung from the ceiling, creating a trapeze of sparkles; and there were two wind chimes made of seashells hanging above each window sill. Both beds now sported matching teal sheets, grey comforters, and striped, turquoise pillows. On each nightstand stood gigantic mugs as big as bowls, with the words HELLO, GORGEOUS printed on the outside.

I was still taking in the full spectacle with my mouth slightly ajar when a petite brunette came out of the bathroom. "Yay! You must be Kelly!"

She appeared to be about five-foot-two with muscular, toned arms and legs. Freckles dotted her nose and cheeks. She got on her tippy toes and threw her arms around me for a big hug, then stepped back to look at me.

Self-consciously, I put my hands in my pockets. "Yes, hi. Kelly Hopkins."

She brushed her perfectly styled bangs from her forehead, then tucked the sides of her shoulder length hair behind her small ears as she grabbed another string of lights from the bed. I wasn't sure where she would find room to fit them amongst the zoo lights she had already created.

"I'm Melissa. Melissa Schulman. I'm so glad you're here. I was afraid I'd have to sleep alone." She had a perky, high-pitched voice I associated with over-caffeinated cheerleaders.

"Yeah, it can be a little eerie in here alone."

"Oh, my God, you've been here forever, haven't you?"

"Just two nights."

"That totally sucks. My parents wouldn't let me go till the last minute."

I wasn't sure what to say, so I looked around the room again at the decorations. She noticed, curling the lights into her chest. "I know I went a little overboard. I just wasn't sure. Well, I mean it was pretty empty so ..."

She let her voice trail off. I didn't want to make her feel bad, especially since this was our first-time meeting. "No, no, it's great. I hadn't really put up anything yet, anyway."

"Where are you from?" She turned around, taping plastic lights to another corner of the ceiling. "I love the sunset and the beach, don't you?" she said as she readjusted one of the sunset posters, pounding the side of her fist into the wall to make it stick.

I tried to yell above the pounding. "L.A.! And YES, I love the beach, too!"

She stopped and turned around, her mouth dropping open. "L.A.? I *love* L.A. Never been, but it looks *ah-mazing.* There are so many great beaches there, like Malibu, right?"

"Yeah, Malibu, Santa Monica, Venice, Manhattan ... It can be pretty cool. Really bad traffic, though."

"So I hope you don't mind." She hopped off the bed, landing with a *thump*. She wiggled her small hips and hands to readjust her green jeans, then pointed to our matching bedspreads. "My mom can't shop online, apparently. She always orders two of everything."

I looked around more closely, realizing there really *was* two of everything: two blue rugs, two blue lamps, and two turquoise office supply sets with two gigantic paper clips and two miniature staplers. "No, that's fine. It's really nice."

"Final sale. Can't return 'em. But, hey, who doesn't like free stuff, right?"

"Always good," I said, inwardly relieved.

"And I also—" she pulled open the closet doors by my bed. Another explosion of colors hung from the horizontal metal pole. Every type of clothing selection from evening gowns to workout tank tops lined the closet, all squished together like a triple club sandwich. "Tried to only take up half the space. I saw you hung up some stuff, but I'm assuming you have more?"

I could count less than a dozen hangers on my side, draped with long sleeve shirts and hoodies. "No, not really. I'm not much of a clothes person."

"Um, okay. Well, you can count this as all yours, too. I mean if you ever need something."

"Wow, thanks." Although I doubted I'd ever feel okay borrowing her stuff.

"Of course, girl! And these bags here are the holiday decorations." She pointed to two huge trash bags on the floor by her array of shoes. "I thought we could start October 12th for Halloween. November 25th for Christmas. That okay?"

"Sure." I sat on my bed, not sure where else to go.

Melissa flipped through the hangers in the closet. "You are going to *love* it here. My family used to spend summers in the Hamptons, so I know all the good spots. Do you like going out? Because I know all the cool bars. And running! We can go running in Central Park on the weekends. Total hangover cure." She laughed, taking a baggy grey shirt off a hanger.

"I don't really run too often, but I did just get a bike."

She pulled off her blue tank top to throw on the grey shirt. I looked at the floor, not sure where to place my eyes.

"That's so cool." She unfastened her bra underneath her shirt and tossed it in a laundry basket by the door. I tried to look away again. "That'll help you get around campus, too." She went back toward her bed. "It's pretty big. Damn, you're going to look so cute on your shiny new bike all over town. I should've gotten one."

"I wouldn't exactly call it shiny. Or new."

She smoothed out her sheets before flipping onto the mattress and shoving a pillow under her head. "No?"

"Yeah. Some idiot almost took me out when I was riding to work so now it has a bunch of scratch marks."

"Are you serious? Are you okay?"

Going over to our shared desk, I impulsively started organizing the bright blue office collection. For some reason, it always made me feel better to do something with my hands. "Oh, yeah. I'm fine. Just kinda annoyed." I laughed.

"What a jerk. Did he offer to do anything?"

"Gave me some cash to fix it."

"He gave you cash? Did he throw it at you—like a gangster?"

I had to laugh again. "No, he didn't throw it at me, but he's clearly a spoiled brat because I can tell he thinks money can solve everything. He must be a trust fund baby ... he seemed like he was only a little bit older than me."

"Was he at least cute?"

I remembered his blue eyes and couldn't help blushing.

"Oh, my God. You totally like him!"

"No, I don't."

"Did he ask you out after he hit you? That would be so romantic."

"Um, actually, he did. Then he gave me his business card, which was kinda weird."

"Business card? Let me see."

I reached in my wallet and handed it to her. She looked at it, then immediately dropped it on the ground as her hand flew to cover her open mouth. "Ian Anderson? *The* Ian Anderson?"

I was flummoxed by her reaction. *Who is Ian Anderson? Am I supposed to know?* "What? Is he a movie star or something?"

"What? You've never heard of the Andersons? His dad is on like, the list of 100 Wealthiest Men in the World."

I shrugged, picking the card off the floor. "Like I said, he seemed like a brat."

"Oh, my God, this is ah-mazing! You are so lucky. You almost got run over by Ian Anderson. That is soooo cool."

I still didn't understand why she was so excited about this. What was the big deal?

She leaned forward, putting her elbows on her knees. "So tell me, exactly what did he say?"

"He wanted to know if he could pick me up after work."

I thought Melissa might fall off her bed. "He wanted to take you out?"

"Yeah."

"That's ah-mazing!"

I shook my head, opening the bathroom door. I wondered what kind of *elf*-like magic she brought in here.

"You said yes, yes?"

I lingered outside. "No. He knows he's cute. And he probably thinks he can get any girl he wants."

"Well. *Yeah.*"

I looked at her.

"Ahhh, I see. Playing hard to get. All right, I get it."

"I don't play anything." Entering the bathroom, I couldn't help counting the number of lavender aromatherapy candles currently lit on our small counter (seven). I called out to her as I began washing my face. "And he wasn't even asking me on a date. He was probably worried about his liability or something."

"Girl, my parents would die if I dated someone like Ian. Well, a Jewish version."

The phone rang. I peeked my head out the door. We both looked at each other in confusion. I had forgotten the room came with a landline like a hotel. We searched for the ringing sound, picking up plastic bags and pillowcases until we found a cord leading to the device at the corner of the floor.

Melissa tentatively picked up the handset. "Hello?" She listened for a second, then her mouth dropped open. She covered the phone. "You. Lucky. Girl."

I shifted my weight to the other foot, unsure I wanted to know who was on the line. Melissa handed me the phone with the faded eggshell-colored cord spiraling. I twisted it in my hand. "Hello?"

Melissa sat on the nightstand, bouncing her knees and biting her lip.

"Kelly?" a man's voice said on the other end. "It's Ian. From before, with the um—I was the jerk. The jerk from before."

"How did you get this number?" I tightened my grip on the cord.

"All the freshman names are in this booklet. We get it the first day of class."

"Wait. You go to Columbia?" I tried to remember his nonchalant reaction from before.

"Yes. I'm a first year at the law school."

I frowned. Melissa put her knees to her chest.

"Why didn't you say so?"

"I don't know. Look, I swear I'm not a stalker. I just feel really bad about what happened, and I'd like to make up for it by taking you out to dinner."

I covered the mouthpiece and looked at Melissa, who had her hands clasped, raised to her chin. She mouthed, "SAY YES!"

I sighed, then pulled the handset closer to my mouth. I tapped my foot a couple times against the floor until Melissa suddenly grabbed my arm and pulled me close. "If you don't say yes right this second, I will use my impeccable acting skills to mimic your adorable, naive voice and do it for you."

She let me go, and I stood back, shifting my weight to the other foot. I shook my head, then tried to muster an indifferent tone. "Fine."

Melissa threw her arms up in victory.

"How about Thursday?" Ian continued. "I'll pick you up at seven."

"Wait. So you already know my dorm room, too?"

"Is that a problem? It's in the book."

"It's a little creepy."

Ian laughed. "Columbia always wants you to know where to find study help, I guess."

"I guess."

Melissa threw me a tentative thumbs-up. I shook my head again.

"So, seven on Thursday?"

I hugged the phone closer to my chest, something I realized I hadn't done in years. My parents used to have a landline when I was a kid. Suddenly, I remembered picking it up when my mom forgot something at the store. I always played with the cord, and she always made comments about how I tangled it.

"Fine."

"All right. See you then."

"Okay, bye." I put the handset in its cradle before catching his goodbye.

Before I knew it, Melissa's arms flung around me. She was so tiny, it felt like a little kid hugging me. "This is so cool!"

I slowly circled my arms around her, patting her back before she released me. A wild look came into her eyes as she dropped onto the nightstand, swinging her legs over. "We have to celebrate."

"Oh, no, it's okay. School's starting soon, and I should organize."

But she wasn't listening. She slipped beneath her bed, opening a box bursting with even more decorations. Amongst a forest of rainbow streamers and glitter, she located two portable black Bose speakers she plugged into the wall. "And we have *two* speakers."

I sat down on my bed, trying to ignore the warm feeling growing in my stomach. *No. This was not*

a happy thing. This was just another activity on my
already packed to-do list. Think of it like a business
meeting. Or a tutoring session.

"Okay, I'm not trying to be racist," Melissa plugged
her iPhone into the dock of the speaker. "But you must
know EXO, right? The Korean pop band?"

I picked up my planner, flipping to Thursday's
page. "...Yes."

"Who's your favorite?"

"Probably D.O. or Kai," I said, their latest music
video flashing through my head. I always felt a little
crush bubble up when I watched them and realized
this warm feeling in my stomach matched that. But
that was stupid. D.O. and Kai could dance and sing
while looking beautiful, while Ian's abilities stopped
and ended at being rich and driving at reckless
speeds. So why was I experiencing the same feeling
for him?

Growl started playing. *"Yo, okay ... Sexy."*

Melissa started dancing, and I couldn't help but
smile. It was so refreshing to see someone so carefree.
Then she started bouncing around the room, arms
up in the air, jumping between our beds. I burst out
laughing. She laughed, too, motioning me to join her.
I shook my head and stood still. I wondered what it
would be like to be that carefree. I knew her type: the
kind of girl who could start jumping up and down and
head-banging in the middle of a crowd. They were
rarely judged because people could tell *they* didn't care
what anyone else thought. I managed to quietly sing

some lyrics when she looked at me expectantly, but mostly I pretended to busy myself with my planner on my bed while she continued to enjoy her white-people dancing skills.

I opened up to Thursday. *7:00pm - Ian Anderson.*

* * *

I felt immense relief seeing Halmuni's familiar face, even if the only thing I could see was the tip of her nose. She hadn't quite yet figured out how to use the front-facing camera on her iPhone. A day had passed and Melissa had gone out for the night, probably to join the five new friends she'd already made in our hall. I sat up in my bed, trying to explain to Halmuni she could tilt the camera up and still be able to see me.

"Halmuni, I'll stay in the same spot. But I can't see you very well."

"I just need see you."

I rolled my eyes, hoping she could see that. "Okay, fine."

"So what you have tell me? Be safe in Columbia?"

"Oh, yeah." I decided to leave out my risky trip to Harlem to buy my bike as well as its near-fatal aftermath. "And my roommate is really nice."

"She Korean?"

"No, she's white. Her name's Melissa."

"Make sure she no introduce you to white boys. Have you found Korean club?"

"Halmuni, it's only my fourth day here." I sunk into my pillow.

"There must be one. There you meet nice Korean boy."

"Sure."

"You meet any yet?"

That stupid warm feeling surfaced in my stomach again. I wanted to tell Halmuni about Ian, only because it was more exciting than hearing her complain about the female news anchor's overly-tight blouse again. But I also knew my excitement would ebb once she began her ranting about how mixed-race couples were doomed for failure.

"No," I said. It was the truth; I hadn't met any *Korean* boys.

"Maybe in classes."

"Yeah." But I already knew how class would go. In your daydreams, you expect to meet the cutest, sweetest, smartest boy who just happens to sit next to you and asks you to be part of his study group. In reality, a bunch of silent Korean boys would barely notice me. And if they did, it would only be to ask me to scoot over for one of their friends.

"Anything else tell Halmuni?"

"I miss you." I did. Even her ridiculous rants about TV made me feel at home. I would never admit it because it would make me sound like a baby, but I missed her short but tight hugs. They reminded me I was where I was supposed to be.

"Aw, *bogoshipuh,* Kelly."

I smiled. "I should let you go. I have a big day tomorrow." I glanced at my planner and saw the word

"Ian" circled in red. Somehow, Melissa had sneakily drawn a heart around his name.

"Ah, yes, school soon."

"Yeah, I gotta go. I have to start studying already," I lied. I had a feeling tomorrow's "date'" would be enough of an educational experience.

"Okay, love you. Bye bye." She finally faced the camera so I could see her brown eyes.

"Bye, Halmuni." I waved, trying to smile.

Maybe if I smiled big enough I could convince my brain I didn't want to return home.

CHAPTER NINE

I craned my neck to take in all of the massive building. Judging by the logo, a couple of crossed spoons, and its title *Merci, Amour,* I realized this was not, in fact, a billion-dollar hotel; this was where we were eating dinner. I watched as Ian shook hands with the valet, and then his action-movie car zoomed away. Why did Ian have to look like he just stepped out of a Tommy Hilfiger ad? He wore a plain black jacket, a blue polo, and dark denim jeans. His dark hair looked naturally ruffled. The shirt perfectly drew out his blue eyes—or maybe it was the other way around?

He smiled as he joined me, and I instinctively tugged at my skirt. Melissa had spent more than an hour helping me pick out what to wear. When she finally had me try on her A-line purple dress paired with my one and only black cardigan, I told her what I had on was fine and if she kept making me try on other dresses, I would be late.

She reluctantly let me go and said, "Have fun and I want to hear every little detail when you get back!"

I held tightly to the clutch I also had borrowed from Melissa, hoping it would steady my nerve, as we ventured toward the entrance with its huge, double glass doors. Ian opened them, and I hurried inside, reminding myself he must have done this exact same thing many times before with other girls. I wasn't special.

"You'll really love this place—it has two Michelin stars. And they have the best *foie gras.*"

I didn't know what either of those things meant but decided to keep that info to myself. Entering, I felt like I had stepped inside a crystal ball. I have never been to a restaurant so beautifully decorated. One-way mirrors made up the walls, and sky-high cellars of wine seemed to float on the ceiling. Hundreds of bottles from the bar reflected off the tinted glass counters, making everything appear bathed in gold. The tables curved in different shapes, each one with a burning white candle. Menus consisted of a single page without any listed prices. Waiters in suits with pristine aprons danced past the tables, jazz music playing in the background.

Where was I? For a moment, I thought of Sophia. What would she make of this very posh eatery? Where we worked was nice, but this place blew Poseidon out of the water. No comparison.

We sat down at a plush crescent-shaped leather booth. Before I had time to say anything, a heavy-set man dressed in a tuxedo approached Ian. "Monsieur Anderson! *Comment allez vous?* We haven't seen you here in a while." He turned to me with outstretched arms. "I'm so glad to see you have brought a beautiful young lady with you." He kissed me on both sides of my cheeks. I tried to pretend this was a normal occurrence.

"*Je vais bien, merci.*" Ian smiled. "This is Kelly. She's new to New York, so I thought it'd be great to bring her to the best French restaurant on the island."

The maître d' bowed so deeply his bald head nearly touched the table. "*Bien entendu.* We will ensure your meal is absolutely *magnifique!* If you don't mind, why don't I pick the best chef's recommendation for you and your Kelly?"

"That would be great, thank you. And is the rooftop still available?"

"We knew you were coming, didn't we?" He smiled. "This way."

He led us through various tables all the way past the kitchen before stopping beside an elevator. *An elevator* in *a restaurant*?

"Please." He motioned to me as the doors opened.

I stepped in, and Ian stood against the wall. I caught him sneak a glance at me. No way had I mastered hiding my awestruck expression. A little smirk passed across his face.

"And how is Miss Beverly?" the maître d' asked.

I cringed, conjuring a Beverly in my head. Beautiful. Thin. Blonde. *White.*

Ian took the question in stride. "She's doing well, thank you."

"Giving you enough space?"

Embarrassed, I dropped my eyes. It was one thing to assume Ian took his models here. It was another to have it thrown in my face.

"Well ... you know how mothers can be." Ian and the man shared a chuckle. The doors opened, and I breathed relief. *Of course. He meant his mom.*

We stepped out onto a cozy cobblestone rooftop. A ring of heating lamps exhaled warm air into the autumn cold. Blue candles glowed atop the glass tables. Couples held hands, talking over glasses of wine and plates of food I couldn't even pronounce. As I glanced over the edge at the city, I felt suspended in the night sky itself and had to pinch myself this was real. I had only been in New York for less than a week and somehow landed here.

We only passed two tables before someone recognized Ian. Middle-aged with long bangs that fell past his brow, the man looked like he was deciding between embracing silver-fox status and giving up his youthful, surfer days.

"Ian, how are you?" he asked through porcelain veneer teeth. "I saw your mother at the Met. You should've been there. You would've loved *La Traviata*."

"Mark, hi. Yes, I'm sorry. Had to study. I've seen *La Traviata* many times with my mother. It's one of her favorites." He turned to me and said, "May I introduce you to Kelly?"

I shook hands with Mark as Ian continued talking. "Did Myles' fencing team make the semi-finals?"

Mark's face lit up. "We're heading to Boston next week for the tournament."

"Oh, that's great. And Angela's rock climbing now, right?"

"Taking classes over on 4th. You should join sometime. She even got me to try it."

Ian shot me a small smile, almost like he was trying to telepathically tell me something. I smiled back, hoping it also relayed my dislike toward small talk.

"I'll see you at the N.Y. Nonprofits Gala, right?"

"Wouldn't miss it for the world."

Ian applied the lightest of touch to my arm for a second before swiftly guiding us through the crowd. I actually wished it lasted longer.

At each table we passed, Ian seemed to know someone. Whenever they stood to greet him, he would politely ask them to sit down as he introduced me. By the time we reached our corner spot offering a breathtaking view of the skyline, I felt dizzy.

The maître d' bowed to us again as he pulled back my seat.

"Thank you," I said.

He replied something pleasant in French before disappearing into the inky darkness. When he was gone, Ian turned to me. "Sorry."

I sipped my water. "For what?"

He tilted his head toward Mark and all the people he'd spoken to. "Hope it didn't sound like I was putting on an act back there."

I shook my head.

"Just something I've learned. Memorize a couple names and facts, people think you know their whole life."

"So it's all fake?"

"Not at all. My dad insisted I learn the art of conversation. He used to tell me networking is one of the keys to success."

He looked so serious I felt like I had to lighten the mood. "Should I be worried if you start asking me about people I know?"

"Well, you don't have any kids, do you?"

I almost snorted out my water. "Definitely not."

"Then, you're good," Ian said with a smile. He unfolded his napkin in his lap before lining up his silverware. "I really don't know that many people. These are all my parents' friends. They have a place on Central Park East, so we come here on weekends. My mom would drag me to the Met at least once a month. Have you seen *La Traviata*?"

"I've never seen an opera. I've always wanted to, but the tickets were always so expensive."

"*La Traviata* is a beautiful love story."

"What's it about?"

"Basically, it's about a young aristocrat, Alfredo, who falls in love with Violetta, who is a beautiful courtesan in Paris. Alfredo's dad threatens Violetta, demanding that she leave Alfredo. So Violetta returns to her life as a courtesan without telling Alfredo why. Eventually, Alfredo finds out the truth. He goes to be with her, but it is too late, because she dies from T.B."

"That sounds so sad. Why did Alfredo's dad tell her to leave his son?"

"Because her previous life as a courtesan was an embarrassment to their family. But I don't want to tell you more or it will spoil it for you when I take you to see it." He leaned over the table to get closer to me and said, "I want to know more about you. You said you're from LA. You miss it?"

I was still processing what he just said about taking me to see *La Traviata* that I couldn't think straight.

"Kelly?"

"...Huh?"

"Do you miss L.A?"

I suddenly pictured Halmuni's disapproving face. "Sometimes."

"I've been a couple times. My mom loves Beverly Hills and West Hollywood. Great restaurants. But my father never liked LA. He hates driving, especially the freeways. Can't understand why everyone always says, 'the' before them, like *the* 405."

"Or *the* 5."

"Right."

"So, besides the freeways, did you like what you saw?"

"Yeah. Once I ditched my folks and went surfing in Malibu."

We both laughed. I noticed his eyes never seemed to leave mine.

"What part of L.A. are you from?"

"Koreatown."

"That's so cool."

Really?

"Do you miss it?"

"What?"

"Koreatown. Do you miss it?"

"Yeah. So, where—?"

"So that's where your family lives?"

"My grandma."

"Oh, nice. Are you close?"

"Really close." I fiddled with my cardigan.

"Sorry. Don't mean to interrogate you," he laughed.

I smoothed out my dress under the table. "Not at all."

A server brought several small, beautifully presented bite size starters the waiter called *amuse-bouche* and then a scallop salad, which he described as "pan-seared scallop with black truffle and crispy pumpkin seeds on a bed of arugula and kale." I'd never tasted anything like this before, so I ate slowly, letting the flavors linger on my tongue.

The food gave me a reason to focus on something other than Ian. I had been staring at him too long and needed an excuse to not talk. In between bites, I looked out beyond the edge of the rooftop. The buildings looked like a twinkly circuit board. *Halmuni would love this place. If she got over the fact Ian is white.*

Ian must have sensed my embarrassment because he said, "It's so nice to see a woman enjoying her food. Usually the girls I know have a few bites and stop because they don't want to gain any weight."

"Yeah, my grandma would make fun of girls like that, saying 'what is life if you can't enjoy your food?'"

"I like the way your grandmother thinks. It would be nice to meet her someday." Would he ever meet her? Would Halmuni even *want* to meet him?

After we finished our salads, the next plates instantly replaced them, this time with what appeared to be a greyish mound atop a brioche.

"Have you ever had *foie gras* before?"

I shook my head.

"It's delicious. Seriously. Try it."

I picked it up cautiously, taking a small bite and expecting the worst. Instead, I couldn't believe how the dish melted in my mouth. Silky and tender, it was so good I immediately went back for more. As I chewed, it occurred to me I had barely asked Ian any questions. I didn't want him to think I was uninterested—or rude. "My roommate told me your dad is on *Forbes Wealthiest 100 list.*"

Ian's face changed. Crap, why did I ask that? He must've thought that's the only reason I agreed to go out with him.

"Was." Ian wiped his mouth with his napkin.

"Oh, I didn't mean to—"

"That's okay. I've gotten better about talking about it."

"Talking about it?"

"The crash." Ian's jaw tightened. It looked like he was having trouble speaking. "He, uh, died in a helicopter accident last year."

Floored, I looked back at him until he averted his gaze. I remembered how many people told me *sorry* when my parents died. I never knew how to reply when they said that. What do you say? *'Oh. That's okay.'*

"You must have had to grow up fast," I said.

He sat back in his seat, dropping his perfect posture. For the first time tonight, I felt less distanced from him. Like I could tell him more about my life back home. But something inside told me not to mention my parents. It felt like if I did I'd be playing a who-has-it-worse-game. I stayed quiet for a long moment. So did he.

"That's kind of a second-date-after-drinks-story, though." He broke into his handsome grin again. I couldn't help but hope for that second date. "Anyway, if you're going to be hanging around here, I should probably teach you a few French words."

I used my water glass to cover my smile. "I'm going to be hanging around here again?"

"*Oui.* Now how about some more vocabulary lessons. "*S'il vous plait*—that's 'please.'"

I was still thinking about what he just said, so my 'please' didn't come out very polished.

"And '*merci*' is thank you."

"*Merci.*" I tried to roll my R, but it sounded like I had a wad of food in my mouth.

Ian laughed. "We'll keep practicing." He grabbed a bottle of red wine from the other end of the table. "*Un verre de vin?*"

"Oh, I'm only 20."

"It's okay, no one's going to card you."

I raised my glass slowly. "Then ... *s'il vous plait.*"

"So, if you're 20, did you take a break before coming here?" he asked as he poured me wine.

"I took two years off to make some money for college." The dark liquid touched my lips, stinging my nostrils and leaving a bitter taste on my tongue. I tried not to make a face.

"I worked before going to law school, too—just wanted to make sure it was actually something I wanted to do. Worked for my dad. Decided I definitely wanted to be a lawyer, instead of a hedge fund manager."

I nodded, thinking how he would have checked off all of Halmuni's boxes. Maybe it was the splash of wine going straight to my head, but I suddenly wanted to tell her all about Ian: how he knew everybody and never made me feel left out of conversations, how he introduced me to new foods, how he teased me in a fun, sweet way. But I knew what her first question would be.

"You finished that fast." He nodded to my wine.

I looked at the empty glass with a ribbon of red at the bottom. "I've never really drank before."

"Just let me know when you start to feel it."

I didn't have to tell him. After polishing off our pepper steaks and deliciously salty caviar, it became clear I found him very, very funny.

"... And that's when I realized I should stop playing pranks on study groups. They just don't appreciate it."

I tilted my head, and the rooftop became slightly diagonal. I didn't even care about the size of my smile. "That's a good story."

Ian paid the check with his credit card, and we stood up. I shivered, not from nerves, but from a gust of wind. He took off his jacket and put it around my cardigan.

"You're very nice." I giggled.

"And you're tipsy." He put his hand on my upper back, guiding me through the restaurant. I realized I was smiling and nodding at everyone who made eye contact with us, not like before when I kept my eyes glued to the ground. He waved to people at tables and said thank you again to the maître d' before walking out to grab his car from the valet.

"Thank you for dinner," I said.

"Of course."

I tensed up as I thought about the fact our date was ending and the end of a date usually meant a kiss, or more. But I wasn't sure if I actually wanted him to kiss me. The shivers returned, even in his warm jacket.

When we got back in his car, he instantly veered in and out of lanes like he was playing the expert-level of a video game. The car was so low to the ground I felt like I could reach my arm out and touch the gravel of the speeding pavement. As we weaved in and out of traffic, we passed blocks of construction workers and metal poles rising up to be future buildings. I felt like I was in a submarine in some undiscovered part of an ocean, a witness inside a claustrophobic hull.

I smiled as we drove past the crosswalk of our first meeting. He must've noticed, too, since he slowed down.

"Not going to take anyone out today?" I giggled again.

"I don't see any pretty girls on bikes."

"Ha."

Suddenly, a speeding taxi veered in front of us. Ian slammed on the brakes, barely missing the guy's bumper. I lurched forward in my seatbelt, gasping. He honked, making a couple people on the sidewalk look over.

"Really, asshole?" Ian yelled, pounding both hands on the steering wheel. He sped around the vehicle and flipped the driver off, raising his finger next to my face so the driver could see through my window. I flinched. He slowly decelerated, moving over to avoid a parked car, then returned to his lane.

"Sorry. That really pisses me off."

His knuckles were still white, gripping the wheel. I glanced in the rearview mirror, making sure no other taxis were about to speed around us.

"Maybe he was late to a meeting," I said half-jokingly, hoping to defuse the situation.

He didn't respond. He just kept driving.

A moment later, he looked over at me, as if realizing I was still in the car. "Sorry. Sometimes I can't help losing my temper."

"You just need to remember to breathe."

He stared at me for a moment too long, and I felt stupid for saying anything. Why did I pick now to work on my interpersonal skills?

He took three deep breaths then said, "You're right. I do feel better." He turned to me again. "Really. Sorry."

"It's okay." For some reason, maybe because of the wine, I reached over and put my hand on his forearm and gently stroked it.

His shoulders relaxed as he exhaled, and I dropped my hand back in my lap. I liked how comfortable it felt to touch him. He slowed, obeying the speed signs, maneuvering through traffic, returning to his expert level driving status.

Back at my dorms, I hoped to delay the inevitable. I knew he was probably going to try to kiss me. I pursed my lips, still tasting the red wine in back of my mouth. We walked up to my door, and I pretended to have a hard time finding my ID card in the clutch.

"Well, I'm glad I convinced you to come out."

"Yeah." I took off his jacket. "Oh, and thanks."

"You can keep it if you want. Give it back to me on our second date."

He smirked and realized I had taken a second too long returning to my clutch. He leaned in, putting one finger on the bottom of my chin, tilting my face toward his. I was always afraid I wouldn't know what to do when I got my first kiss, but he made it easy. It was short, but soft, and I realized I instinctively knew what to do. He smiled as he stepped away, and I felt like I could still feel his lips on mine.

"Get some sleep, Kelly." He put his hand on me. "And remember, don't slack off in your first year."

He was almost around the corner when I thought I should probably reply. "Okay. Thanks."

But he was already gone.

CHAPTER TEN

I slipped into my room, prepared to see Melissa right where I left her: on my bed, arms crossed, anxiously waiting. Instead, I walked into blackness. A sliver of moonlight pierced our window blinds, allowing me a glimpse of a blanketed lump atop her bed. Melissa was sound asleep. I closed the heavy door as quietly as I could, flinching when it thudded shut. I realized with a tinge of disappointment just how excited I had been to tell her everything about my date.

Opening up her clutch, I found my phone, using the light to guide me so I wouldn't crash into my bed post. I tugged off my cardigan and grabbed a hairband from my nightstand. I changed into a sweatshirt and sweatpants, wishing I could take the smile off my face, too. My cheeks were starting to hurt, and I still felt flushed from the wine. Maybe it was a good thing Melissa was asleep—she would've totally made fun of my blushing cheeks.

As I lowered myself into bed, the dinner and the kiss replayed in my head like a scratched DVD stuck on the same scene. I felt a wave of energy surge through me. I needed to do something. I thought about taking my bike out or going on one of Melissa's suggested runs through Central Park. Usually being around other people drained me, but Ian made me want to join a flash mob.

The way I felt right now, there was absolutely no way I could fall asleep. I needed to tell someone about my date, even if they wouldn't be as receptive as my roommate. I pulled open my phone and clicked on the Skype button. As L.A. was three hours behind New York, I knew Halmuni would still be up, probably watching TV and eating her nightly bowl of edamame. But she was bound to ask me if Ian was Korean. No way to avoid that question. I tapped my fingers on the glass screen as I tried to figure out what to do. Maybe I could just tell her some general details about the date. She didn't need to know everything. I could skim over the part about Ian being very, very white.

Rummaging through my nightstand drawer, I pulled out my headphones. Careful not to wake Melissa, I grabbed my ID card and stepped into the hallway.

As usual, the fluorescent ceiling lights washed out the corridor so brightly it felt like morning. My eyes had grown used to the dark, so I had to squint. Down the hallway, I could hear faint voices and what sounded like a car chase on TV. I didn't want to risk other people hearing me go on and on about my first date, so I walked into the enclosed stairwell.

I sat on the first step, looking up at the white walls and painted metal railings. The old building's heater didn't work too great in the more remote parts of the building, so I inched my sweatshirt sleeves up around my fingers and pulled my hoodie around my head. Leaning back against the cold grey steps, I stretched my legs out, grateful for the chance to have some space to my own. My voice echoed loudly in here, but I didn't think anyone with a life would bother eavesdropping in the emergency exit just to hear about my date.

I pressed the button to connect with Halmuni. Even if her name wasn't listed in all caps with a string of meaningless numbers, it would be hard not to find her. She was my only contact who accidentally took a screenshot of her chest instead of her face for the profile pic.

Lowering my elbows to my knees, I held the phone up so she could see me better. It rang for a while. I imagined her hurrying to turn off the TV, adjusting her recliner, and stabbing at her phone screen, all while exclaiming Korean curse words.

Finally, I saw the bottom of her chin. "HI, KELLY!"

I immediately yanked out an earbud, wincing. "Ow. You don't need to yell."

"WHAT?"

I slipped out the other earbud for a moment as I turned my phone volume way down. "I said I can hear you just fine. No need to yell."

"Okay then," she still yelled, just a little softer.

In addition to not understanding how well her voice carried, Halmuni didn't use her tablet like other people. For some reason, even though I had corrected her repeatedly, she still thought she needed to place her device so the camera shot straight up. This allowed me to see only the bottom part of her chin and up her nostrils as she walked around her kitchen.

"I make some ramen while we talk." She put the tablet on the counter, affording me a super view of the kitchen ceiling. Maybe this wasn't the ideal way to recount the most romantic night of my life, but at this point it would have to do.

"I see B.B. at church," said Halumni before I could say anything. I could hear her chopping onions. She liked to add them and eggs to her ramen because it made the dish seem a bit healthier. "He miss you. Say be good girl and call him."

"Okay, I will."

"How Columbia? You tell me everything."

"It's great. My roommate, Melissa, is a lot of fun and very chatty. I got all the classes that I wanted," I hesitated a moment, then, "Halmuni, I have something exciting to tell you."

I heard her turn on the stovetop, the flame crackling. "Okay, tell Halmuni."

"I went on a date tonight."

"A date?"

"Yes." I readjusted my body on the cold hard step. "With a sweet guy."

"See, I tell you! What you do for date?"

"Well, he took me to an elegant French restaurant. And he was so kind—I mean he pretty much knew everybody. But he never made me feel left out. And he reminded me of dad with his jokes."

Halmuni puttered around the kitchen, banging open drawers and sorting through the fridge.

"I don't like French food. Why they make dish so complicated? Korean food easy and fast."

"French food is delicious. I tried this thing called *foie gras,* and it melted in my mouth." I licked my lips just thinking about it.

"What? Fo Ga? So tell me more about boy. You say he make you laugh?"

"Yeah." I chuckled as I remembered one of his pranking stories about switching out his old room-mate's furniture while he was sleeping to make him think he grew giant-sized overnight.

Halmuni peered over her tablet and smiled, holding up a wooden spoon. "That good."

"And he's very handsome."

"Well, of course. Only handsome men for Kelly."

"I don't know if I like this feeling, though, Halmuni," I said, laughing. "It's really distracting. I feel like I can't think of anything else."

"Ah." Halmuni stirred something loudly in a metal pot. She said something else, but I couldn't make it out over the racket.

"Halmuni? Halmuni? I can't hear you."

She dropped the utensils with a sigh and wiped her messy fingers on the top of her blouse, leaving big, oily streaks.

"I said, that go away. You see."

A warm, happy feeling rippled through my stomach. "I don't know if I want it to go away."

"Just wait when he starts to annoy you. You wish you never meet. Just ask me. I know."

I shook my head. "I don't know."

She chuckled like she knew something I didn't, then propped up the phone so I could see her arm stirring the spoon in her pot. "So what his name?"

"His name is Ian. Ian William Anderson." I smiled again just thinking about it. I liked the way it sounded. Regal. Like a senator or a judge. Then my smile evaporated, and my eyes widened. I thought I would be sick. I lowered the phone so she couldn't see my face. *Crap.*

For the first time, Halmuni used the camera correctly. Her face appeared large on the screen, her glasses tapping against the lens. Her drawn-on eyebrows looked like thin diagonal streaks.

I hurried to change the topic. "Did I tell you he's super sweet and nice? And fun? He is so fun. In fact, while I was sitting there at dinner, I kept thinking about you and how much you two would get along. And did I tell you he's in law school, too, and he makes me feel really special—"

"White."

"Yes, but we had such a great time—"

Behind Halmuni, I could see smoke rising from the pot. For a moment, it looked like steam was literally rising from her head, like in an old cartoon.

"Halmuni, behind you."

She didn't hear me. Her lips pursed, and her eyes narrowed to slits. "What'd I say about meeting Korean boy? First chance you get you go after white boy."

The smoke was really rising now. Whatever she was cooking was burning. "Halmuni!" Now I was the one screaming. "The stove!"

She turned around. She picked up the pot handle and yelled, *"Ah ttu gu!"* followed by some more curses, half in Korean, half in English. I heard her still muttering as she poured the pot's contents into the sink.

When she returned to the screen, her face was red. I wasn't sure if it was from the pot's steam or her own. "You no respect me."

"I do respect you."

"Then why come you disobey first chance you get?"

"It wasn't like that. I didn't even plan on dating him. It was just something that happened."

Little beads of sweat trickled down Halmuni's face. She seemed angrier than I could ever remember seeing her. "I go."

"Where?"

"KFC." She grabbed her keys from the counter.

"Can't we talk about this?"

"We did talk. You make me burn my food. I'm hungry."

"No." I gripped the phone. Behind me, I heard voices in the hallway. I hoped they weren't coming to investigate all the yelling. "Please don't."

"Kelly. You not go all way to New York for meet stupid American boy. You went there study."

"But—"

"I told you, white boys trouble. Look what happened to your mom. If she never married, she still be alive. Goodbye, Kelly."

The screen went black. I sighed, dropping the phone between my knees. I took my earphones out and put them in the pocket of my sweatshirt. I hugged my knees to chest. My arms covered the letters of my sweatpants that spelled out BRIAN CHU LAW OFFICES.

Though I used to think B.B.'s self-promotion was a bit over the top, at this moment, I was glad to see the familiar words. It reminded me of home--even if home included a person who was very angry at me right now.

CHAPTER ELEVEN

In high school, no one took the first day of school seriously. The teacher usually tried to fill 50 minutes by doing a popcorn reading of the syllabus and reviewing the school's policy on plagiarism for the fifth time that day. The nicer students pretended to focus while those who were boy and girl crazy secretly scouted out potential hookups—someone they hadn't seen before or someone who suddenly looked good enough to text and flirt with—not to mention invite to the Winter Formal or Spring Swing.

At Columbia, however, no professor had time to set expectations. By the first day, you were supposed to already know them. And no one seemed to care about the attractiveness of the person sitting beside them. Instead, we all had eyes for our teacher, the person who would make or break our average with the touch of fingers to keyboard. As if the subjects of a mass hallucination experiment, we stared haplessly back and forth between PowerPoint slides and our laptop screens. I realized within five minutes that every person's laptop offered a way to transcribe the entire class. The professors not only understood this, they expected it from us. We were supposed to type *everything*. I sent up a silent prayer of gratitude to B.B. for my laptop—after all, I would have succumbed to carpal tunnel from handwriting notes within days if he hadn't bought it for me.

Professor Baker taught this class, *Readings in Law & Justice*. It was part of Columbia's core curriculum, and I had jumped at the chance to take something related to the study of law. Now, however, I was not leaping at the opportunity to read a 120-page assignment due in two days.

"A discussion will follow, and of course you will be graded on participation," Professor Baker said, returning to her podium.

Professor Baker was the one-woman show we paid thousands of dollars to see. Her lecture hall was designed like a small theater with all the chairs positioned on an incline facing a massive flat screen. I was used to doing Socratic circles in high school— essentially formal discussions in which the teacher asked open-ended questions, scribbling check marks every time someone participated. Always the shy student, I skated by with the bare minimum amount of talking. Unfortunately, I couldn't expect such a non-participatory approach to save me in college. Even if I tried to dominate the conversation, though, I'd barely pass. Professor Baker and the other professors weren't satisfied unless you spilled your guts.

Nervousness made my shoulders ache with tension. If only I could just read and write without having to talking to anyone—

"... And 10 percent of your grade will come from the group project at the end of the term," she said, deflating me further.

Rubbing my neck to ease the strain, I stared up at Professor Baker. Lanky with long arms and legs, strands of curly brown hair fell past her navy blue fitted blazer. Her lips were thin and her chin was hard and pointy, complementing her coldly intelligent green eyes. I read her bio before attending her class.

It was no joke. Page after page listed cases she won, degrees earned, firms she was a partner in. Though she intimidated me with the curtness of her questions, cutting right to the core of a topic, she also intrigued me. I wondered if I could ever follow in her footsteps someday, not just instructing others, but performing in the courtroom, litigating. For a few seconds, the luxury of dreaming about my future allowed me to forget about transferring to another class that didn't require group discussions.

Suddenly, a notification flew past the right side of my screen. IAN ANDERSON. Another text. I hated my reaction to seeing his name, the excitement. Now, whenever an e-notification popped up with a course email or a reminder about my low bank balance, my heart leapt with hopes it was him.

"Hey, how's your day so far? :)"

Right after I finished Skyping with a less-than-enthusiastic Halmuni, I was glad Ian had texted me, thanking me for giving him a chance. I had texted right back, matching his number of smiley faces even as Halmuni's words ate at me. Her disapproval had always been the toughest to bear. I *was* here to study—everything I had worked for brought me to this class, even if that meant participating in dreaded class discussions. I X'd out of the notification, returning to type every word from Professor Baker's mouth.

"Don't expect grade curves. Unless they happen to fall against you," she smirked. A couple of students shifted uneasily in their seats. All of us here were former AP students, high achievers. We were used to gaming the academic system. We were just beginning to understand how easy we had had it. Now, things were about to change.

As my fingers pushed on, pounding out word after word, page after page of notes, I kept waiting for a bell to ring or the morning announcements to segment the day. This wasn't really a conscious thought, but rather something in the back of my mind. After a while, I realized how stupid I was behaving. High school was over. The old rules no longer applied. If I wanted to, I could walk out without a bathroom pass or the teacher's permission. Nothing was keeping me here, except for the cold inertia of wanting to do right by my new teacher. All those years of schooling must have burned that desire into me.

Near the end of the hour, Professor Baker flipped to a slide listing our homework assignment, then motioned to the door. "See you all Thursday."

Everyone started packing up their stuff, shoving MacBooks into bags and slipping on jackets. A few of the bolder ones dared to mumble about the "insane reading" assignment.

Next to me an Indian girl with heavy eyeliner chuckled mirthlessly. "Well, shit. I was warned freshman year sucked."

"Uh huh." I carefully placed the books I needed to read first in my backpack.

"Some of us are going to that coffee shop around the corner. Maybe plan for the group project. You wanna come?"

"Oh." I swung my backpack over my shoulders. "Thanks, but I usually kind of like to study alone."

She flashed me a smile. This one projected warmth. "Well, we're kinda getting to know each other today."

"That's okay. I'd better start reading."

Even as I said the words I knew they were the wrong thing to say.

"Okay, no worries." She shrugged. "See you Thursday."

Then she caught up with a couple guys in the row farthest from me. Somehow already the best of friends, they hugged her, exiting together. With a sense of inevitability, I knew the social part of college would be a lot like high school. Once again, I planned to keep my head down. Like Halmuni said, I came here to succeed.

* * *

"Okay, roomie. Update time."

I hadn't even closed our door before Melissa sprang out of her bed like a contortionist, pulling me down beside her. As we landed, we spilled the pile of Gummy Bears she had been nibbling on.

"He asked me how my day was."

Ignoring the mess on the floor, Melissa threw back a rainbow palm full of Gummies as if she were watching a movie and the gossip of my life was the main attraction. "Aw, that's so sweet."

Scooping up the candy, I threw them into the wastebasket before falling into bed. The soft pressure of the mattress felt good against my sore shoulders.

Melissa continued to stare at me as she chewed noisily. "You know what you should do? You should text him back with a slightly funny anecdote that will non-threateningly reveal your personality."

I didn't even try to answer. I knew when Melissa was on a roll.

"Maybe you shouted something clever in class that made everyone giggle." Before I could respond, she was onto her next suggestion. "No, I know. They were having a campus fair and you signed up to participate in a charity that's close to your heart. What are you passionate about? Philanthropy-wise."

I rolled over to my backpack to retrieve my laptop. "I don't think there was a fair today."

"Damn, you're right. Okay, well you still have to say something."

I looked at my planner, trying to figure how I would spend the next few hours. "I was actually thinking I should probably just not reply."

Melissa sat straight up. "You're seriously going to *ghost* Ian Anderson?"

"He knows I'm busy."

Bing! We both looked at my screen.

"*Also—there's a concert on campus this Friday. Some guitar player I've never heard of—Guess he's really good though. You down?*"

Melissa reached over, putting her greasy gummy hands on my keyboard. I swatted them away, leaning back on my bed and pulling my laptop closer. "No. I have to study the rest of the weekend. I have to read over 100 pages."

"100 pages? That's nothing. I bet you're one of those speed readers."

I took a deep breath, then typed the message I'd been mentally composing. It was lame and mean and made me feel like shit, but what choice did I have? *"I'm sorry, I can't. And I'm sorry to 180 on you, but I need to focus on school. I'm here on scholarship, and I don't think we should see each other anymore."*

I squeezed my eyes shut and clicked "Send," guilt replacing my nerves. I snapped my laptop closed as if that would make the texts disappear and laid down.

Melissa must have seen what I wrote, because she began pacing. "I can't believe this. I can't believe this."

"Don't feel bad. I'm not rejecting you."

"Sure feels like it," she said curtly. I turned to see she had plopped back into her bed with a fresh handful of gummies.

* * *

"Melissa," I said, gently shaking her shoulder. I didn't feel bad about waking her. After all, it was 2 pm on a Wednesday and an American Literature textbook laid open across her lap. *"Melissa."*

She awoke with a start, almost smacking my hand before I moved it. She crumpled up the teal comforter between her fingers and sat up. "What? What?"

"You fell asleep again."

She looked at her phone to check the time. "Damn."

"He texted me again."

She covered her face with her hands. "Do I even want to know?"

I read off my phone. "He just said, 'I totally understand feeling overwhelmed in your first year or if you're just not interested in me. I just wanted to say that I wish you the best of luck at school and let me know if you ever need anything.' Ugh, why does he have to be so freaking nice!?"

"Girl, listen to me. Ian Anderson is probably the most eligible bachelor in New York … No, take that back, in all of America! And you're telling him to pound sand. Face it, you're an idiot."

"I really do have to study, and he's a distraction." I was trying my best to convince myself of this, so I kept repeating it to myself.

Melissa threw her covers off, returning to her textbook. "Hey, on the subject of studying … you don't have Adderall, do you?"

"No."

"Man. I knew I should have bugged my brother for some before I left." Grabbing a credit card-sized remote control, she suddenly doubled the volume of the music that had been playing in the background. The music blasted through our walls, making me feel bad for our neighbors. I put my phone down on my nightstand. "I'm going to leave this here. No distractions. I'll be in the library."

"What?" Melissa shouted over the music, pulling out two huge garbage bags from our closet.

"I'll be in the library!" I screamed back.

"I'm getting hungry, too. Bring me something. Tacos, please."

I shook my head as she dove through her bag of décor items, looking for things to hang up. This wasn't new. Whenever she felt stressed out, she told me she like to redecorate. As I took the stairs two at a time down to the ground floor, I made a silent vow. As of now, Ian did not exist for me. Text messaging did not exist, either. I didn't want to talk to anyone. I just needed to do what I did best in a quiet place with books: study.

* * *

It occurred to me I needed to start setting timers for myself, tracking the amount of hours I could study in one sitting without giving up and going back to my dorm. Right now, I was at two. From other students, I'd heard people reached up to 10 by the end of their first year. New goal. I swung my heavy backpack around, rubbing my left shoulder before grabbing my ID card out of a side pocket to get back into my dorm. It was around 9 pm, so I inserted it in the slot, pulling the door open slowly just in case Melissa had fallen back asleep.

When I pushed the door open, even brighter chains of lights exploded luminosity across the room. It looked like Melissa had bottled Thanksgiving into our tiny dorm room with small red and green lights, pictures of autumn leaves, a faux pumpkin vase and candles surrounded by pine cones. All that was missing was a Thanksgiving turkey. It took me a second to recognize the male figure occupying the chair at my desk.

Ian.

Ian was in my room. Sitting at my desk. In my room. In front of me. I froze, looking between him and Melissa who was on her bed, frantically waving a book in the air. She mouthed the words: "I'M SORRY."

Ian rolled back in the chair, gave a small wave, and then smiled in his cute boyish way that made me require the door for support.

"Heeere she is. The beautiful Kelleee," he said slowly. I could smell the alcohol on him. He was drunk.

"Kelly! I'm *so* glad you didn't take your phone to the library so I could tell you about our guest." Melissa pretended to smile in an overblown way, matching the insincere tone of her voice.

I glared at Ian. I had to remember his being here was not a good thing. How could he be so audacious to just show up in my room unannounced, uninvited? And on top of that, drunk? Even though I was angry, I felt my heart beating quickly and felt uncomfortable knots forming in my stomach. "Are you drunk?" I said angrily.

"Maybe a little," he said sheepishly. "I'm not much of a drinker. Two shots and I'm gone. Somehow ended up in your room." He pointed to Melissa. "Your roommate was gracious enough to let me stay for a bit."

My eyes burrowed into Melissa's. She made an "oops" face and shrugged.

I dropped my textbooks on the desk with a loud thud as if the act could somehow reclaim my space. "What are you doing here?"

Ian could see I was annoyed so he tried his best to seem sober by sitting straighter and articulating his words with precision. "Kelly. I know you can't be *that* busy. You have to let me take you out again. We had fun."

"What happened to your text about totally understanding?"

"Then I was sober and polite. Now I'm drunk and honest." He offered another one of his adorable grins. "Please. Just give me one more shot. If you say no after that, I promise I will leave you alone forever."

Why does he have to wear those dark-wash jeans? And plaid shirt? Ugh, my kryptonite.

Suddenly he dropped out of the chair and onto his knees, putting his hands in prayer position. "Please."

I widened my eyes in horror. This was not happening.

Melissa appealed to me with her arms outstretched. "Kelly. How can you say no to a man on his knees? I mean, it's like he's proposing to you."

I shot Melissa a look and she turned away, suddenly fascinated by something on the ceiling. Then I crossed my arms, thinking about what I should do. Ian's sexy eyes seemed somehow even more clear and bright today than ever. For some reason, it popped into my head that if someone were to ask me for a word to best sum up Ian's personality, it would be hopeful. The guy was a determined optimist. I wanted to run over and kiss him for that, but I had to maintain my angry expression. After all, I began this way, I couldn't just give in. I took one more deep breath. "*Fine.* But only if you *promise* that you will not show up to my dorm unannounced again."

"Of course, your royal highness." He kissed my hand as he stood up. "So, Friday night—the concert?"

"Yes!' Melissa blurted out. "I mean … Kelly?"

"Fine."

He smiled at me, and I think he would've kissed me again if Melissa hadn't been sitting right there. I wished he had. Instead, he leaned over, grazed the top of my head with his lips and whispered, "Fine." Then he turned and waved to Melissa. "Thanks again for the hospitality."

"Anytime," she blushed.

Ian closed the door, and I put my hands on my head, trying to slow the adrenaline coursing through my veins. Melissa threw her book across the room and flopped backward on her bed. "Well, I don't need that anymore."

I looked down where the paperback had fallen. A shirtless guy appeared on the cover beneath the title, *When The Night Takes Over.*

I shook my head and sat down on my bed, trying not to scream.

"I am so happy for you." Melissa joined me. "I mean he's not just super hot. He's *super* rich. Like super MEGA rich."

"I don't care about that."

Melissa scoffed. "You obviously haven't lived in Manhattan long enough."

"I don't know. My family and I never had a lot of money, but we were happy. Especially my parents. Everyone always said stuff about my dad not being Korean, but my mom didn't care. He made her feel special." I played with the strap of my backpack, smiling to myself. "I just want someone who makes me feel that way, too."

"Ian!" Melissa said, as if she just found the answer to the million-dollar question.

"Maybe." I tried to keep my expression neutral.

"You know why?"

"Why?"

"Cause he's rich." She picked up her book, nestled back beneath her covers, settling in for more of her steamy romance. I looked back at my planner, realizing I needed to readjust my study schedule. My dad's advice rang in my head: *Live life without regrets.*

I picked up my phone. No regrets. Halmuni had to understand that, too. I decided to send her a text.

Halmuni -

I know you are not happy that I am dating Ian. But I'm going to see him again. He is a really nice guy. Mom and Dad would've loved him, and I know you will, too. Don't be angry. Xoxo Kelly

At midnight, I finally fell asleep. No new text messages.

CHAPTER TWELVE

So much for only being at Columbia to study. The concert with Ian turned into a third date, then a fourth. Whenever I could step away from schoolwork, Ian always had somewhere exciting to take me, like indie films at the arthouse or exhibits at MoMA. But those were perks; I really just liked the chance to spend time with him doing the little things: walks in the park, holding hands on the train, kissing on the stairwells when no one was looking. It was so much fun—even if I could feel my clothes (or, more accurately, Melissa's outfits) tightening a bit from all the sushi dinners and weekend brunches.

I had become less selective about my wardrobe lately, anyway. Though it gave Melissa incredible joy to choose my apparel, I started grabbing things from my own limited array of discount fashions. The more I got to know Ian, the more I realized he didn't care about my financial standing. I felt like he liked me for me.

As the semester wore on, the homework grew ever more challenging. Pop quizzes came hurling at us like a barrage of cannon balls. Gone was the easy camaraderie between instructor and student. The professors became the enemy, pushing us to achieve—or drop out. I noticed less students watching TV in the lounge with each passing week.

Meanwhile, some inspired would-be anarchist kept tearing down our RA's inspirational posters as a silent protest against all of the clichés about hard work and success.

Melissa became nocturnal, finding it easier to cram at 2 am and then sleep between classes during the day than keep any kind of normal sleep routine. She also began letting off steam by partying at campus bars, armed with her fake ID. In the mornings, I would find empty K-Cups overflowing our wastebasket, and she began to dress like everybody else, wearing pajamas to class, looking overworked and overwhelmed. But so far, I hadn't cracked. Probably because this is what I had always thrived on: the challenge, the pressure, the knowledge that only a few thousand kids in the whole country even had the opportunity to compete in this marathon of physical and intellectual endurance. And I was one of this chosen few. I might have actually enjoyed the constant adrenaline rush if I hadn't had a spectacular reason *not* to study.

When I did get a few moments to myself, I tried contacting Halmuni, but she still gave me the silent treatment. One night, I scrolled through my call log to see how many times I'd called her, and a red arrow appeared by each attempt, mocking me. My mom told me that, while Koreans tend to get fiery when angry, the rage would dissipate quickly. She blamed our red-hot tempers on all the spicy Kimchee we ate. Well, if that was the case, I didn't understand why Halmuni was still upset. Why did she even care that I wasn't dating a Korean? My dad was white. He and my mom loved each other so much that others would tease them about it. So why had Halmuni cut me off?

These dark thoughts swirled through my head even as I worked at the restaurant, which was proving more and more to be a significant hindrance, despite the money I was bringing in. Sophia always prepared her hostesses to step into server roles, meaning I had to memorize every offered item and their ingredients. At the end of my online-study Quizlet for all of my Columbia classes, I listed "Poseidon Appetizers," "Poseidon Entrees," and "Poseidon Beverages." I needed to study them just as much as my academic courses. It was exhausting, but I had no choice. I couldn't afford to lose my job or my scholarship.

One Friday, Sophia took a breather at the end of the dinner rush to inform me in painful detail everything I was doing wrong.

"You need to organize these in-between customers." She ducked behind the podium and flipped over the silverware. "The logo must face outwards. People walking from Tables Five or Eight can see all of these mangled looking sets."

There was no way customers could actually see the hidden silverware, but I nodded my head, anyway.

"Hello, sir, how many in your party?" I said to a man in a leather jacket coming through the door. My fingers gripped a pile of menus, at the ready.

"Just a seat at the bar."

"Of course, right this way." Smiling, I motioned for him to follow.

"You're getting better at that," Sophia said when I returned to my post at the door. She was already busying herself, using a rag cloth to wipe down the menus.

"I already did those." I pointed to the clean, laminated surfaces.

She raised her eyebrows. "I know."

I sighed quietly, leaning against a pillar. It was going to be one of those nights. Looking at the clock on the POS machine, I saw the time was 8:05. Ian would arrive any minute. At least that would make the night better. If Sophia would let me go. Maybe she forgot? I should remind her—

"So, let's go over Happy Hour again," she suddenly asked. "What are the weekday specials?"

I imagined the virtual flashcards on my laptop, trying to recall all the different food categories. Then a flash of blue crossed my peripheral vision. I looked out the window to see Ian's car pull up along the curb. My heartbeat sped up as he put it in park.

"Um ... they begin at five?" I said, still watching him.

Sophia stopped mid-swipe of a menu, squinting at me. "And you go to Columbia?"

Ian walked up alongside the restaurant. "Sorry. It's just that I thought my shift was done at eight, and I have—"

"No, *I'm* sorry."

I breathed a sigh of relief, removing my apron. Could it be she had decided to be nice to me? "No problem. I just have to change real quick and—"

"I'm sorry you think you're the one who decides when you get to leave," she said sarcastically as she picked up another menu and went on cleaning.

I froze. I knew it was too good to be true.

"I'm the one who tells you when your shift is over. Not the schedule. Understand? I have a lot of applications stacked up in my office. Don't take this job for granted."

I gulped, nodding.

"Also, Happy Hour begins at four, not five, and ends at six. On the weekdays. No Happy Hours on Saturday. Sunday, it runs from three to six."

"Okay—"

"Half off bottles, half off appetizers. With just a few exceptions. Not that hard."

Except it's not just a few exceptions. Which is why I have an entire Quizlet dedicated to learning it.

Sophia stopped cleaning, stood up straight, and faced the entrance. I turned. My heart thundered in my chest even more as Ian looked at me.

"Hello, Mr. Anderson," Sophia said with a deferential smile.

I blinked. *She knows him?*

"Hi Sophia, good to see you." He nodded to her, then smiled at me. "Ready?"

Sophia's mouth gaped open. She looked at Ian. Then looked at me. Then back at Ian. She was putting two and two together and couldn't believe they were making four. Composing herself, she grabbed a take-out menu from the display and handed it to me. "Memorize this. I'll see you tomorrow."

I detected something different in her face. What was it? Jealousy? Respect? I didn't want to do anything stupid that might upset her, especially after she just said she had no problem firing me. "I'll try to be more on my game tomorrow, Sophia."

She nodded, then Ian took my hand and led us out of the restaurant. I couldn't help but smirk inwardly when I saw Sophia's incredulous expression through the restaurant window.

"You saved me." I wrapped my jacket closer around my waist and then got in the car's passenger side.

"Oh, good." He warmed up the car, putting his hands in front of the heater. "You okay?"

"Yeah." I could see my breath, but already the vents were blasting hot air.

He shifted into drive, and we pulled into traffic. "I have a surprise."

"Uh-oh."

"We're going ice skating."

This was not the kind of surprise I had been hoping for. Although I loved to watch figure skating competitions on TV, growing up in L.A., I had never seen a real ice rink in my entire life. Sure, I had loved watching pair skating in the Winter Olympics—the couples were like ballet dancers on ice—but the physical skill necessary to execute those amazing jumps, spins, and leaps seemed, to me, virtually super-human. I figured I had as much chance of being an ice skater as I did playing professional basketball.

I started to shiver as soon as we entered the ice rink. I wasn't sure if this was because it was cold or because I was terrified I was going to embarrass myself.

"Don't worry. You'll get the hang of it," Ian promised. As I sat on a hard wooden bench, he slipped the skates he had brought for me onto my feet like Prince Charming fitting Cinderella with her glass slippers, then looped their laces around my ankles for extra support. Then we both put on black gloves, and I squeezed his hand in a death grip as we approached the rink.

Ian opened the door as I waddled to the edge, feeling uncertain on my feet. It felt weird walking in skates—like stumbling around in the most precarious high heels you ever wore. And if you made one wrong false move, you'd land flat on your butt.

Once on the rink, the biting air cut right through me, making my fingers stiffen in Ian's grip. Passing through the swing gate, I hesitantly put my skates on the ice, fearful my legs might give out on me at any second. I clung to the metal railing. *Be positive. Concentrate. Remember what B.B. would say, "Believe in yourself."*

Ian tried to suppress a smile. "You're doing fantastic."

I glared up at him in mock anger. "I don't appreciate your sarcasm."

"Sarcasm? Me?" He laughed, gliding past with ease. The adorable show off had the gall to skate backwards toward me.

I looked around. Everyone our age made it look easy, circling around with their friends or dates. The only people on the railing were seven or eight year olds and their parents, and they already looked more confident than me.

After trudging a couple laps looking like I had a hernia problem, I finally ventured a few feet from the rail. When I began wobbling, Ian put his arm around my waist.

"Thanks."

He scooted us out a little further, leaned down, and drew me in for a kiss. We could've been in the middle of Madison Square Garden or in the middle of a cornfield in Iowa, I didn't care. I pulled at his jacket, hungry for another kiss, for the first time not caring if I slipped and fell. It would've been worth the bruised knees.

After I lost the feeling in my feet and Ian reminded me it had only been 30 minutes, we sat outside the rink. I yanked my skates off, almost taking Ian out with a blade to the face.

He ducked, taking them from me. "How about I return these?"

I covered my mouth, laughing. "Okay."

I looked around as I sat back on the bench. Ice shavings sprinkled the blue carpet beneath my socks. A few feet away, middle schoolers crowded around an air hockey machine, shouting at each other as Mariah Carey sang in the background. Past the ice rink, passing headlight beams from nearby cars lit up the cloudy night.

Ian approached the rental stand with our skates. It was interesting to watch him, unobserved. He walked with such relaxed confidence. Not exactly a swagger, but you could tell he felt comfortable with himself. After dropping off his skates to a teenage girl with spiky orange hair, he walked over to the café. When I saw him get in line, I shook my head, but he didn't notice. He was always getting us something—spoiling me.

He returned with two hot chocolates steaming from Styrofoam cups. He let me stretch out my sore feet on his lap and put his hand on mine.

"They're already preparing." Ian pointed to a half-decorated Christmas tree. String lights were wrapped around fake leaves, but they hadn't been turned on. "We haven't even had Thanksgiving yet. Can't they let us celebrate one holiday at a time?"

"Yeah. Always a good time for hot chocolate, though. Thank you, by the way." Sometimes he gave me so much stuff I forgot to say thank you.

"After I dragged you here, I thought I could at least defrost you."

"You never *drag* me anywhere."

He put his fingers around his cup. "So … speaking of dragging you places and Thanksgiving, do you have any plans for Turkey Day?"

Ugh. This answer would inevitably involve money. I didn't want him to think he had to help me pay for anything more than he already had. I took a long sip. "I need to talk to Sophia about picking up some shifts so I can fly home and see my grandma." *If she still even wants to see me.*

"Oh. Are your parents out of the country or something?"

I took my feet back from Ian, glancing at two pre-teen boys disputing an air hockey goal. One of them threw the puck at the other and missed.

"Actually, my mom and dad passed away when I was 15."

I could feel Ian staring, but I didn't dare look in his eyes. For some reason, *I* felt bad, like sharing this information would be too much for the moment.

"Kelly, I'm sorry. I wouldn't have ... you didn't say anything."

"I know."

We both sat in silence for a moment. I stared at my black socks, thankful he didn't say anything—that he wasn't trying to fill the silence, because the silence wasn't awkward. For the first time, I actually wanted to tell someone about what had happened.

Faint 90s music played in the background. I guessed it was the Backstreet Boys. In the rink, they turned on the strobe lights. Kids raced each other, and a couple who skated well enough to be professionals did intricate figure eights under the glowing neon green and yellow.

I tightened my grip on the bench. "I remember the day they died," I said, unsure how the words would feel on my tongue. Ian put his cup down beside him and leaned his elbows on the knees, listening. I was grateful he wasn't looking at me. "I was in biology class. I got called into the principal's office and remember being worried and confused because I'd never been in trouble before. When I got there, I realized something was really, really wrong. I thought maybe something had happened to Halmuni. But then the principal said, 'I don't know how to tell you this. Someone burglarized your mother's store. Your father was visiting. They were both shot. Paramedics came, but there was nothing they could do. I'm sorry.'"

I stayed quiet for a few moments. When I looked up, I saw Ian slowly shaking his hand, staring at the floor.

"I can't imagine," he finally said.

"I feel like you can, though."

"I don't know. And you were so young."

"But Halmuni and I are … close." I didn't know whether to make the "are" a "were."

"That's good." Ian came closer, putting his arm around me. I quickly melted into his chest. Whenever I laid there, I forgot about everything else. "I wish I could thank them," Ian said with gentleness in his voice.

"Who? My parents?"

"Yeah. For you." He pulled me even closer.

Some of the kids from inside the rink poured out, almost falling as they adjusted to walking on carpet. They went over to the café and begged their parents for hot chocolate. An exhausted-looking dad pulled a crumpled five-dollar bill from his wallet and gave it to his badgering son.

"My father was never really around because of work," Ian said slowly. "When he was, he was always super stressed and yelled at me all the time. I was closer to my grandfather, Jack. He was kinder. Calmer."

"Jack. I like that name."

"You, too? I always thought if I had a son, I'd want to call him Jack. After him."

We both turned our heads so we were facing each other. "So, my mom is actually inviting some guests to our house for Thanksgiving. Would you want to come? Then you could fly back to L.A. for Christmas."

I leaned back on the bench. "I don't know."

"Trust me, you'll be fine. It's just canapés, cocktails, and dinner."

"Canapes?"

"Like *hors d'œuvres*. And everyone will be nice to you because you'll be with me." He smiled, but it didn't make me feel much better.

"What about your mom? I don't want to intrude."

"She'll be fine. I've brought friends over before. Although … this will be the first time I'm bringing my girlfriend."

I almost spit up the hot chocolate in my mouth. "Your girlfriend?"

"Well, aren't you?"

"No, no. I mean, yes. Sorry. I was just surprised." I laced my fingers back in his. "I like that."

He relaxed. "So ... does that mean you'll come?"

"Only if you promise to stay with me the whole time."

He held out his pinky finger. "Promise."

CHAPTER THIRTEEN

Maybe if I stood in front of my closet long enough, new clothes would magically appear. Or maybe I could find a secret portal in the doorway, one that would transport me to an alternate reality where I could actually afford designer brand clothing. Unfortunately, neither occurred, so I paced my dorm room, fiddling with a hanger as I tried to decide what I could possibly wear to meet Ian's mother.

I thought I felt okay about my limited wardrobe until Ian invited me to Thanksgiving in Connecticut. Today, we were scheduled to drive out to meet his family, and I desperately wanted to look like one of those women on the rooftop of Merci, Amour. Like I belonged. But browsing through my collection of worn jeans, hoodies, and a couple of dresses from Topshop, I realized this would be a challenge worthy of Hercules.

Buzz. Buzz. My phone almost fell off the nightstand from the vibrations. I reached over my "no" pile of denim and plaid shirts and picked it up. Melissa's contact photo popped up, the one she secretly took when I wasn't paying attention. All I could see was her purposely widened eyes and the corners of a facetiously large smile. I slid the bar over and put the phone to my ear.

"I forgot about Waldo."

I looked over to her nightstand, recently adorned with a small, round fishbowl. An orange-and-white clownfish looking just like Pixar's Nemo swam to the gravel bottom beside a little castle. This fish was a gift from a boy in her study group, intended to make a romantic impression but now just represented unwanted responsibility. Poor guy, I thought. There was no way she would ever date that boy now.

"I'm looking right at him."

"No, not forgot him, forgot *about* him."

I circled my finger on the glass edge, waving hello. "Don't worry, I won't let him die."

"But I forgot to feed him before I left yesterday. Can you do it? His food's in the drawer of my nightstand."

"Sure." I shook out the container, watching as Waldo eagerly swam to the surface to nibble up the sparkly granules. "Okay, done. He looks happier already."

"Phew. Thank you. So how's the dorm? Is it a ghost town? You miss me already?"

"Yeah, but I, um, actually better go."

There was a pause, then she squealed into the phone. "Oh yeah! You're going to Connecticut today. The big family reunion. You nervous? Don't worry. I mean, his mom's gonna love you."

"I'm not nervous," I lied.

"Let me guess. You're stressing about what to wear?"

I put down the hanger, sinking into bed.

"Maybe a little ..."

"Well, don't be. You have two closets to choose from."

I looked over at Melissa's side, brimming with possibilities. "That's okay, I already wore some of your stuff already. I don't want you to think—"

"Girl, I don't care. Try some of my stuff on and take selfies. Send 'em to me. I'll tell you what's best."

"Really?"

"Seriously. Do it. I'm about ready to lose my mind watching my little brother play video games. It would give me something to do. *Anything* to do."

"Uh. Okay." I did as told, changing into Melissa's dresses, blazers, and skirts, sending her pictures of each option. I hated taking photos of myself in the mirror. I felt like one of those middle school girls who got an Instagram account way too early. I tried picturing this holiday get-together as a job interview instead. I had to be prepared—and look the part. Melissa, of course, played a role too: the highly opinionated style coach. After I sent her a photo, she would immediately text back her feedback.

"No!"

"Yes X1."

"Yes X2."

"8.5."

I became more and more confused by her complex rating system.

"No. I don't even know why I have that."

"72 percent."

"4X10."

"OMG! YESS! THAT ONE!"

I smiled, put down my phone, and looked back in the mirror. I wore a black skirt with a white blouse and one of her grey jackets. My phone buzzed again. Melissa's slightly terrifying face covered the screen.

"That's it. With the Alice + Olivia jacket, you'll fit right in."

I breathed relief. "Thanks. You solved, well, one of my problems."

"You're freaked about his mom. I've read up on her. Seems like a bitch if you ask me."

Then how did she end up with such a nice son?

"Look. Even if she turns out to be a heinous bitch, you gotta be super positive. People like positive people, you know? Play up your whole Columbia thing if she gets all snooty. How you got a major scholarship to the same elite place her son goes. Or how much you love it here, with your AWESOME roommate, that kind of stuff."

"Well, I mean, I'm nervous to meet her, but there's a bigger problem."

She paused. "What? You allergic to turkey?"

I put my hand to my forehead and resumed pacing. "I'm spending the night there." I didn't know why I was whispering. I turned away from Waldo as if he could hear me.

"Oh. My. God. K. I get it now. It's going to be fine. Remember where you just got the fish food? In the back, I have this travel-sized bottle of lube, a few condoms. Just don't use the Crown brand. Those suck. They were free from the health center but—"

"Melissa! Please. Stop."

"Sorry, I just want you to be prepared. I mean, you *are* spending the night."

"But that could mean anything." I left my hand frozen on the drawer handle. "Right?"

"Sure." She elongated the word to two syllables.

I wasn't convinced. Taking the mismatched clothes from my bed, I scooped them up, placing them on hangers. "And this *is* his family's house. That'd be weird, right? If anything did happen?"

"Only if the walls are thin."

"Okay, I'm going. Bye." I started to hang up.

"Wait! It's going to be fine. Just ... maybe don't pack the pajamas you usually wear. You know, the ones with the penguins on them?"

Good*bye*, Melissa." I tossed the phone on my bed, then looked at my duffel bag on the floor, so far packed with a Ziploc bag containing my toothbrush, toothpaste, and my blue, penguin-*themed* pajama pants. I looked back at Waldo, then at Melissa's nightstand drawer, then back at the bag. I took out the pajamas and threw them back in the closet.

* * *

"Kelly, you look amazing."

Ian and I had met outside the entrance of the dorm halls. I held my duffel bag in my right hand

and brushed out Melissa's skirt, sending her a silent prayer of gratitude.

As usual, my handsome boyfriend (it still felt weird to call him that) looked like he stepped out a page from an Abercrombie catalog, though slightly more dressed up in his tan slacks and dress shoes. "Ready?"

I exhaled. *Was I?* "Uh-huh."

He tossed my bag in his trunk, while I cozied up in the front seat. I was more comfortable in his car now and immediately plugged in his iPod to the aux cord so we could start my Road Trip playlist I had created especially for our ride. We sang along to Bruno Mars' *Versace On The Floor* while flying down half-empty streets, heading out of the city. A few minutes in, he lowered the volume and turned to me. "Sorry, gotta go to the bathroom, and we're right by my apartment anyway. You mind?"

"Sure." I hadn't actually been in Ian's apartment yet. We always went out places or came back to my dorm, and I would never be so forward as to invite myself over.

Ian's apartment building was not what I expected. It looked—well, normal. Nothing outrageously opulent or over-the-top like you might expect from a guy whose family could officially be counted in the 0.1 percent. We pulled into an underground garage beside the three-story brownstone he pointed out as his. Street level, the block teamed with other similar early 20th century buildings, all painted a honey graham cracker hue with wrought-iron staircases leading up to double doors.

He killed the engine. "You should come up, meet Kevin and Roy."

These were his roommates and buddies he talked about all the time, and it would be good to finally put faces to their names. Before we even entered, I could hear men's voices shouting from inside the apartment.

I stepped in, careful to stay on the linoleum foyer in my heels. Exposed brick lined the walls. Tasteful framed shots of beaches at sunrise added a nice touch, reminding me of an earlier conversation where Ian told me Roy dabbled in photography. A long narrow iron-crafted coffee table ran the room's length. I was surprised to see it wasn't topped with beer bottles, but instead with coasters and mugs, one of which featured Garfield and the quote, "I hate Mondays." Just past the living room, I glimpsed a steel refrigerator and high-backed bar stools along a marble countertop.

Two guys around Ian's age, also good-looking and clean-cut, sat on the couch in front of their 65-inch wall-mounted HDTV. It looked like we had just interrupted some heated conversation.

"And you must be the one and only Kelly!" said the skinnier one with a surprisingly good tan for this time of year.

"Yes, hi." I gave a little wave to both of them.

"Kelly, this is Kevin and Roy. Guys, Kelly."

"Skip the Anderson shindig and hang with us," said Roy. "Kevin's cooking a Turducken."

"That's turkey, chicken, *and* duck. Much better than just a boring old turkey," explained Kevin.

"Sorry, guys. Save me some, though."

Kevin sipped from what looked like a tiny espresso cup, leading me to believe these guys may actually have their very own espresso machine in the next room. The word "hipster" formed in my head. "Sure you don't want to join us? There's cranberry apricot compote in the fridge. Made it last night," he turned and said to me. "Secret recipe."

I just smiled back.

"Tempting," Ian said. "Usually, I just go for the stuff out of the can." He squeezed my arm. "Give me a sec, okay?"

Then he was gone. I shifted my weight from foot to foot, not knowing where to look or what to say. Some people are good at small talk. I suck at it and hoped this wasn't a foreshadowing for the rest of the weekend.

"You can join us." Roy motioned me with a welcoming arm.

Their friendliness reminded me a bit of Ian. I sat on the designer ottoman and crossed my legs. I plucked a blonde hair from Melissa's jacket just to give myself something to do.

"I heard Ian almost killed you." Roy sipped what looked like chai with two hands from a huge clay mug. *Hipsters. Definitely hipsters.*

I smiled. "He did say he was sorry afterwards."

"Ah. And who says chivalry is dead?"

Kevin laughed. "We kid, but Ian's a good dude. Top of every class and does all this work outside of school.

If we weren't best friends, we'd probably kill him out of jealousy."

"*Envy*," Roy corrected him.

"Yeah, whatever you say 'Mr. Right'," Kevin muttered.

"I'm not *envious* of anyone," Roy emphasized the word. "Except maybe John Oliver. Dude's whip-smart. Although I miss Jon Stewart. That guy was genius."

Kevin rolled his eyes. "Kelly doesn't want to hear about your man crush. We were talking about Ian." He turned to me. "Seriously, Kel—can I call you Kel?"

I nodded my head. I found myself liking both of them already.

"Kel, everyone, even Roy over here, totally hates Ian for being annoyingly perfect."

"Which means we love him," Roy chimed in.

"You meet his mom yet?" asked Kevin.

"No, first time."

Kevin shot Roy an apprehensive glance. Roy looked away. It seemed like they wanted to say something more, maybe to warn me, but Ian came out of the bathroom before they could go any further.

"Shit-talking about me?" Ian grabbed his jacket off the couch.

"Always."

"Ready to go, Kelly?"

"Of course not," said Kevin. "She told us while you were gone that Turducken intrigues her."

"Sure she did."

I stood up, smoothing out my skirt and still worrying what Kevin and Roy's shared look might have meant.

Kevin hopped off the couch and opened his arms wide. "I'm a hugger."

"Me, too," said Roy.

After both of them embraced me, Ian led us out the door. "Okay. That's enough scaring her for one day."

"We'll miss you," said Roy.

"Good luck," Kevin added.

I tried not to think about the warning tone in his voice as Ian and I drove out of the garage.

* * *

The drive to Ian's family home in Connecticut took only two hours. The sun came out just as we left the city limits, spreading so much warmth we shut off the heater, cracking open the window to let the cool, autumn breeze filter in. I wasn't used to seeing the changing seasons and loved the panorama of blazing orange, reds, and yellow leaves as we headed into the open countryside.

"Illinois!" I shouted, pointing at the out-of-state license plate zooming next to us on the freeway. "Isla Laminated Ladders ... In N' Out Of ... Irene's Shoes. Boom!"

Ian looked down at his watch. "Ohhh, just shy of 15 seconds!"

I punched the roof.

Ian laughed. "I think that's part of the other game. Although I don't know if I can count 'n' as a word."

"One of the most successful burger chains counts it."

"I told you, we don't have those here. I barely know what you're talking about."

"Just because you're ignorant doesn't mean it doesn't count." I smiled, shrugging my shoulders.

Ian shook his head. "Am I seeing the competitive side of Kelly, now?"

"Maybe."

A slower song came on the satellite radio, and I relaxed back in my seat, enjoying the window view of cottage-like houses and expansive green fields. Ever since leaving Ian's apartment, I had tried focusing on anything else but meeting his mom. Whenever my thoughts wandered, they returned to Halmuni and the fact she hadn't texted me back in weeks. I couldn't believe she was being so judgmental. At the same time, I missed her. This would be our first Thanksgiving apart, and she hadn't even bothered to call? Okay, I really needed to think of something else. Remember what Melissa said. *Stay positive.* Then I found myself thinking about the sleeping arrangements again. What if we really did stay in the same room? No. I couldn't think about that, either. I was going to start sweating through Melissa's jacket.

I turned to look at Ian. I had never felt more at ease with someone, even Halmuni. It's no wonder his roommates adored him. It was weird, but I already trusted him like he was part of my family. I just had this great gut feeling he would always be there.

"I'm okay sharing a room with you," I blurted out.

Ian looked over, wide-eyed, like *where the hell did that come from?* I was so surprised by my own words it felt like I saw them flying toward the windshield. *Splat.*

"Are you sure?" he asked.

I tried to smile, then nodded my head, scooting closer. I put my head on his shoulder. Then he reached down and put his hand on mine.

CHAPTER FOURTEEN

I was dozing off to an instrumental song on Ian's satellite radio when he gently nudged me. "This is our street."

I sat up, looking out the window. This could not be real. The otherwise empty private road was wide enough to easily fit four cars side-by-side. We passed tall, perfectly manicured pine trees, well-groomed bushes, and majestic gates. Each entrance looked like it guarded a separate neighborhood, but we were the only car in sight and all of the well-swept curbs were empty. The more tucked-away mansions we passed, the more I felt like I was on a movie set for a film about some European royal family.

As we curved left, I noticed the edges of a colossal house—if that's what you could call it—peeking out behind a forest of greenery.

"Here we are. Home sweet home."

Ian drove up a long and winding driveway that went on forever. A maze of bushes surrounded us on either side, expertly pruned down to the very leaf. I had to remind myself to keep breathing as we drew nearer.

"This is where you live?" I tried to keep my voice even. "It looks like a castle."

"My mom likes things BIG. Jewelry, homes, that kind of stuff."

I wondered if the people who lived in this area even knew their neighbors or if they all behaved as if they lived on their own private island—which they also probably owned. Ian stopped in front of a seven-foot-high gate with spiky metallic arches. An intercom stood atop a metal post a few feet away. Ian rolled down his window to press the button, then retracted his arm abruptly. He stared at the button as if deciding whether or not he should press it.

"You okay?"

He took a deep breath. "Sure."

I studied him. *Is he just as nervous as me?*

He took another deep breath and pressed the button. There was a crackling noise, then we heard a man's voice. "Anderson residence."

"Franco, it's me. Can you open the gate?"

The gate buzzed open, revealing a narrower driveway bordered by the healthiest, brightest green grass I had ever seen. The compound stretched in all directions with no clear end in sight. Readjusting my seat belt, I stared ahead. My nerves were settling in. The length of the drive made me feel like there was the possibility we might never arrive, but now everything I feared—his family, friends, our impending night— loomed right in front of me.

At last, we approached the Anderson mansion. More palace than house, it reminded me of an old Manhattan department store building, only with sheer white drapes in every window and multiple porticos jutting out to the extensive lawn. In the distance, I thought I could see the stable Ian mentioned. He had said his mom liked to spend her time there with her horses ever since his father died.

I tried to stuff down my growing anxiety and nausea as we pulled up alongside the fountain. Two statues representing baby angels playing flutes stood amidst columns of water jets five feet high. I was still staring at the gorgeous display when a man in a red uniform jacket opened my door.

I looked up. He was in his 50s or 60s and took my hand with a friendly smile. After bowing, he addressed Ian. "Welcome home, sir. Do you have any luggage?"

"Hey, Franco," Ian threw his arms around him. "Yeah, we have two small bags in the back. And this is my girlfriend, Kelly."

Franco bowed again. "Hello, Ms. Kelly. Pleasure to meet you."

Franco took our things and escorted us inside. When he opened the giant, gold-trimmed doors, I felt like I needed to hang on to Ian for balance. A two-sided spiral staircase the color of ivory led to a magnificent second-floor landing. Tasteful sculptures and paintings adorned the vast foyer. A checkered marble-floored hallway broke off in different directions, leading to various wings of the house like the world's biggest, most intricate honeycomb. I felt like I had just stepped into an issue of *Architectural Digest*.

Ian led us to the kitchen, which looked large enough to prepare meals for a small army. Everything sparkled and gleamed, from the polished countertops to the stainless steel appliances. (There were *two* refrigerators, each larger than my dorm room closet.) Ian immediately went to the bar overflowing with liquor bottles and poured himself a glass of Scotch.

"You want anything?"

Before I could answer, a pair of well-toned arms rushed toward him, outstretched. "Ian? Is that you, sweetheart?"

Extremely attractive, Mrs. Anderson did not look old enough to have a son Ian's age. She had perfect porcelain skin, manicured nails, and long, blonde, perfectly styled wavy hair. She also had Ian's piercing blue eyes.

When she released Ian from her hug, she saw me, then stepped back. "And who is this?"

"Mom. I emailed you—this is Kelly, my girlfriend."

Emailed?

"Ian, I get emails all the time. I ignore most of them. You should have called. I didn't even know you had a girlfriend." She gave me a quizzical look, as if I was supposed to explain this phenomenon. At last, she came forward with an outstretched palm. "Hello, Kelly. Where are you from?" She said this in an overtly saccharine tone.

Before I could reply, she added, "And how did you manage to snare my son? He's never brought a girl home before."

She said this last part with a little chuckle, but I couldn't help thinking she was deadly serious. *Snare him? He went after* me!

"It's nice to meet you, Mrs. Anderson," I said trying to remain calm. *Think of this as an interview*, I thought. "I'm from L.A. I didn't mean to intrude. I didn't know you didn't know. If I'm intruding, I can always ..."

I began wondering how much it would cost to take a train back to Manhattan.

Before I could finish my sentence, Ian said, "Don't be silly." He put down his glass with a thud. "You're staying." He took my hand.

I looked to his mom, trying to smile, but she did not seem pleased.

"Yes. Of course, you are staying." She waved her hand dismissively, like it was all some big mistake. Her eyes said something different. "And you can call me Beverly. *Stay.* If my son has fallen for you, then I should get to know you."

Fallen for me? She made it sound like I duped him.

She leaned a bit closer and scanned me slowly from head to toe. I felt like she was inspecting a horse to decide whether or not she should buy it. "I do hope you brought something appropriate to wear for today's party."

This isn't appropriate? Why didn't Ian say something? "I ... I'm sorry. Ian said it wasn't formal. I hope this is still okay?"

Beverly pursed her lips. "Dear, if you didn't know what to wear, you should have asked. Do you at least have some decent shoes?" I was wearing my favorite black pumps, the ones I wore when I worked at B.B.'s law office. They seemed okay to me. But now, looking down at them and comparing them to what Mrs. Anderson was wearing, which were patent leather, pinkish beige, four-inch-high stilettos with small grey spikes along the side, my shoes looked drab and cheap.

"I ... I only brought this pair."

"Well, nothing we can do about it now," she said in an exasperated tone.

She patted me on the shoulder, kissed Ian on the cheek, then walked out. "Miranda!" she called over her shoulder.

A second later, a Hispanic woman in her mid-40s emerged with Windex and paper towels, hurrying after her.

I turned to Ian. "I should go."

"No way. It's fine. No one is gonna care what you're wearing. And, besides, you look gorgeous."

"But she doesn't even want me—"

We heard the front door open, and a slew of guests entered. Couples offered their coats and hats to Franco. All of the women wore lavish designer outfits. My heart sank as I saw a blur of various colors of impeccably fitted dresses, black cashmere or fur wraps, and four-inch high heels (similar to Mrs. Anderson's) whisk by. Stunning in all of their jewelry, the ladies looked like aristocrats you might expect to see in a royal ballroom. Beside them, the men wore tailored, dark suits with button shirts and French cuffs, nodding at Franco while adjusting their silk ties. I felt like I had stepped into a different time period, one in which every person had been required to go to etiquette school as a teenager.

Staring at them in their tailored finery made me blush with humiliation. I looked down at my own plain skirt, jacket (not even mine, actually,) and stupid shoes, wishing I was anywhere but here. I wanted to run as far as possible.

Ian must have seen the expression on my face, because he took off his blazer so he was just in his white-collared shirt. "Now we'll both be underdressed."

I know he was being sweet, but I wished I could take his jacket, wrap it around my whole body, and disappear. After all, no matter what he did, Ian was Ian. The host's son. He could've shown up in a hairy gorilla suit and people would've simply applauded his sense of humor. I was the one who would receive the unfriendly stares. I was the one they'd shake their heads at, wondering why I looked so out of place.

"Let's join them." Ian took me by the hand, leading me toward the crush of people surrounding the entrance to what could only be described as a dining hall, emphasis on the word "hall."

Ian and I ventured into what could have been our school cafeteria, if that cafeteria was set to entertain some of the richest, most powerful men and women in America. Waiters dressed identically to Franco in red uniform jackets darted between groups of guests, offering champagne flutes and appetizers ranging from caviar toast to jumbo shrimp cocktail.

A massive oak dining table with engraved place settings occupied the length of the room. A small army of buffed and shined utensils accompanied each fine china plate. With a sinking feeling, I knew there would be no setting for me, making today even more awkward.

More and more guests streamed in the room, each looking more elegant than the next. There must have been 40 in attendance. If I didn't feel so terrible, I would have taken out my phone to send Halmuni a photo with this text: "Here's what the *Real Housewives of New York* look like."

To my horror, Ian took me by the arm, leading me to the head of the table. The last thing I wanted was to be on display. I started to tell him so, but a woman cut us off.

"Ian, sweetheart, how are you?" Though the 60-something female had silver-grey hair and wrinkles around her eyes, her slender body looked like that of a 30 year old. She wriggled out of her coat, handing it to me. "Oh, thank you, dear."

I dumbly accepted the cashmere coat, feeling its softness in my hands. Then she handed me a purple colored, crocodile-patterned bag.

"Mrs. Williams, this is Kelly, my girlfriend. We both go to Columbia."

Mrs. Williams looked back at me with a slightly confused look. Just like Beverly, Mrs. Williams stepped back to examine me as if I was a lab specimen. "You are very exotic-looking. Are you Asian?"

I could see Ian tensing up. No wonder he was drinking his second scotch. "I'm half Korean. My mother was Korean."

She put her hand on my arm. "Oh, I adore Korean food. Especially their barbecue. I can't remember the name of it, but you know what I'm talking about. Although, it really makes you smell afterwards."

I opened my mouth to speak, but wasn't sure what to say. I shifted her coat and purse to my other arm, wondering what I should do with them. Ian stopped a passing server to grab two glasses of champagne. He offered one to me, but before I could find a way to take a much-needed sip, Beverly materialized.

"Korea?" she said. I wondered how much she had heard. *Is she eavesdropping?* "I've been to Japan, but never Korea. I hope you didn't come from North Korea, with that ghastly fat little dictator? Were you born there? When did you immigrate to the U.S.?" Beverly didn't care to hear my answers because she turned to Mrs. Williams and added, "We already have far too many immigrants in the country, don't you agree?"

Mrs. Williams nodded in firm assent.

"I'm not an immigrant," I said too loudly, making me come across defensive and pouty. "I was born in LA. My dad was American."

"Was?" Mrs. Anderson and Mrs. William said in unison.

"Both my parents died several years ago," I said, struggling to keep my gaze upright on their faces.

Mrs. Williams shook her head. "Terrible."

Then she recognized someone and scampered off. I sipped my champagne, still fumbling with her coat and purse. "I should put these away for her."

Ian reached for them. "No, Kelly, give them to me—"

"Really, it's okay." I gave him my glass and walked away.

Entering the main lobby, I searched for Franco. Noticing him near the doors, I headed in his direction. Suddenly, a splash of pink entered my line of sight, followed by a *smack*. Cold liquid spilled all over me. I looked up to see a model-thin blonde in a light pink dress, holding a glass of red wine, sharing a similarly shocked expression.

"Jesus!" she said.

To my horror, the red wine seeped onto Mrs. William's coat and bag, dripping onto the floor. Then, I heard a high-pitched scream.

I turned to see Mrs. Williams speed walking over to us, spilling champagne out of her own glass as she hurried over.

"My bag!" She yanked it away from me. "How could you be so careless?"

"I'm so sorry, I was looking for—"

"You came out of nowhere," the blonde said. "What, were you texting or something?"

"No, I just—" I could feel the lump in my throat forming. *No. Do not cry.* "It was an accident."

"Kelly, don't worry about it." Ian came over, his mother's steps behind. A waiter with a dishtowel appeared at my side, and I took the black linen, trying to wipe off the bag. Mrs. Williams swung it farther away from me.

"No, don't wipe it. You'll make it worse."

I wanted to die. Right here. Right then.

"Mrs. Williams, we'll replace it," Ian said.

"Who will?" Beverly pointed at me. "Her?"

Hot tears pooled at the corners of my eyes. I dared not blink.

"Kelly, why don't you go to the bathroom and freshen up? I'll stay here and help," Ian gave me a look. He was trying to get me out of this.

Thankful for the exit, I followed the waiter to one of the many restrooms. I closed the door behind me, trying not to break down. *It's not your fault. She spilled wine on you.*

I collapsed onto the closed toilet lid, breathing in chamomile incense. Tiny hand towels sat stacked beside a wicker basket holding fresh soap the shape of white roses. I stared at their simple elegance as tears continued to well. *Don't cry. Don't cry.*

I took a deep breath, then looked in the mirror. I fixed some smeared black eyeliner, steeling myself. The right sleeve of the cardigan was stained burgundy. I would Google how to get it out later. If that didn't work, I would work extra shifts to pay it off. I would even work to pay off Mrs. Williams' bag—for the rest of my life, if it took that long. I halted at the door, willing myself to leave. Then, I heard Ian's voice and stopped.

"Mother, give Kelly a break. It was an accident. Why did you have to embarrass her like that?"

"Don't blame me," she whisper-yelled. "That Birkin costs over $30,000. She should be apologizing to *me*. Embarrassing poor Mrs. Williams in front of everybody."

"It's not Kelly's fault someone decided to spend thirty freaking-thousand-dollars on a purse that looks like the skin of some swamp creature. If anything, Mrs. Williams should be *thanking* her for getting rid of that ugly thing."

"What have I told you about being judgmental? You have no idea it's sentimental to my friend."

"Sentimental? What? Is she chairwoman for the Florida Alligators Board?"

"Why did you even bring her into our home? Are you really so bored you have to go chasing—"

"Mom." Ian cut her off. "Kelly is a wonderful person. If you gave her a chance, you'd see that."

I felt nauseated. I knew exactly what Beverly meant even without her saying it. I wasn't part of their class. I was *common*. I didn't want to hear any more. I wanted to leave, to get as far from this place as possible. I opened the door loudly on purpose to alert them of my presence. Ian was on his knees, wiping up the spilled wine with paper towels. Two uncomfortable waiters kept trying to intervene. Ian passed a towel to one of them, stood, and took my hand.

Then he turned to his red-faced mother. "I never gave Kelly a tour."

He guided me past her, taking the grand staircase two steps at a time. My feet ached in my heels, but I said nothing, happy to get away. Entering a long corridor on the second floor, we passed a few closed doors and abstract art pieces until he opened one on the right hand side. We slipped inside a massive master bedroom with a king-sized bed in the middle that was overflowing with golden comforters and throws. It looked like it had never been touched, much less slept in. I saw Ian's bags in the corner.

Ian dropped on the bed with a loud sigh. "Just had to get away for a second. Unless you really want a tour."

"That's okay."

"I do need to tell Franco to get your stuff."

Before he reached the door, it opened from the other side. Beverly glowered in the doorway with her champagne in hand.

"I thought you might stop here." Then her face changed in an instant. She smiled at Ian as if the last exchange had never occurred. "Did Franco get your bags, sweetie?"

Ian backed up. "Yes. Right here."

"Did you show your friend the rest of the house? Seemed like an awfully quick tour to get here." She eyed me. "But maybe you're the kind of girl who's been in a lot of houses like this."

Did she think I slept around to get invited to swanky Thanksgiving parties like this? "Oh, no." I didn't know what else to say.

"Mother, where are Kelly's bags?"

"In the east wing."

"*What*? Are you gonna buy her a bus ticket there, too?"

"Ian. Tone."

"That's on the complete other side of the house. Where the maids..."

I dropped my eyes, silently wishing I could leave again.

"We have a full house. Your second cousins are here. And I didn't know she was coming." She stepped closer to me. "You understand, don't you?"

I nodded. "No problem."

"No. It *is* a problem." Ian picked up his bag, swinging it like a javelin. It crashed against the dresser, knocking down a framed photo. It landed on the floor with a loud thump. I had never seen him so angry.

Neither Beverly nor I moved as he seethed between clenched teeth. I honestly thought he might hurt someone.

I put my hand on his arm and spoke softly. "It's fine. Really."

Ian glared at Beverly. "She can sleep wherever the hell she wants."

I squeezed his hand and leaned into him, turning my head so I could whisper. "Breathe."

He closed his eyes and took a few deep breaths. No one said a word. A moment later, he turned and gave his mother a small smile. She looked suspicious. She didn't like what just happened.

I tried to defuse the situation. "I'll sleep in the east wing. It's fine."

"See?" Beverly raised her hands. "Problem solved."

She eyed both of us again, cleared her throat, then exited, pushing the door so it stayed wide open.

CHAPTER FIFTEEN

Ian could only stay away from the party for a few minutes before it became obvious something was amiss, so we had to return. Entering the dining hall, I placed my hand over my right sleeve to cover my wine stain. He adjusted his white shirt. Despite his "underdressing," I still felt like I looked like an eight-year-old at a teenager's birthday party.

By now, the hall buzzed with chatter. Even more people must have arrived since we left. At the end of the cavernous room, right in front of stained-glass windows composed of blues and greens forming abstract shapes, a long line snaked around the buffet. Serving tables abounded with mind-boggling varieties of dishes all attended by red-coated waiters.

Ian and I passed polished silver tray after silver tray on our way to the back of the line. I couldn't believe the selection. Turkey was just one protein option, along with prime rib, roasted honey ham, barbecue short ribs, chicken tenders, pork chops, lamb chops, sausages, and venison. There were boats of gravies and sauces and something called *gravy bordelaise.* The only reason I even knew the last one—or the venison—was because of the little cards denoting each in cursive font. Forget cans of cranberries, the Andersons went all out with pickled cranberries, dried cranberries, and spiced cranberry sauce. The salad bowl put Olive Garden's to shame. You could choose between six different dressings in various porcelain bowls, each labeled in different calligraphy. Beyond the usual holiday fare, more exotic selections awaited us, including a sushi station and a place to design your own pasta.

I was still trying to grasp all the amazing choices when we encountered an older, petite woman wearing a monochrome beige dress. Her jewelry was expensive but tasteful, and her dark brown hair shone as if it had been brushed with a good 50 strokes. She had a sweet face with wrinkles that creased when she smiled.

"Mrs. Granoff, how are you?" Ian said.

"Oh, honey. It's so good to see you!" she patted his cheek.

"Mrs. Granoff, this is Kelly, my girlfriend."

Hearing him again call me his *girlfriend* lifted my spirits as I shook her hand.

"We've got some choices to make." He pointed to the buffet. More servers crewed each station, picking up crumbs just as soon as they appeared. I couldn't help but think how they were missing out on celebrating Thanksgiving with their own families.

"Too many. Your mom loves to overdo it," she chuckled.

"Why don't we try the kids' table." Ian pointed to a smaller area with a black tablecloth. A female server lifted the silver handle from a tray, revealing creamy, baked mac 'n' cheese to a crowd of eager children with smaller-sized plates. She also scooped up baked vegetables and a fruit salad, which they seemed less excited about. "That mac is amazing."

Mrs. Granoff put her hand to the sash on her dress. "No thanks. I have to watch my girlish figure."

"You always look fantastic," Ian said, giving her a sly wink.

As Ian handed Mrs. Granoff and me our plates, I wondered if his interpersonal skills would ever rub off on me.

Following them as they made their selections, I considered whether I could get away with just taking a little bit of food for appearance's sake. It all looked so delicious, but my stomach was still tied in knots.

Two huge, silver tongs rose above my plate with mixed greens and croutons. "Salad, miss?" the waiter asked.

Ian touched me, and I turned. Holding a phone to his ear, he covered the bottom, whispering, "Be right back."

"Oh, okay." I tried not to let my voice waver, hoping he would return soon; otherwise, Beverly might stick me at the kids' table. Or worse, beside her.

As I made my way down the line, I scanned each perfectly bended card in front of the tray, only asking to be served the things I could pronounce. Reaching the end, I realized, out of all the fancy options, I chose the ones most closely resembling Halmuni's attempt at a Thanksgiving feast: turkey, cranberries, and mashed potatoes. Without the addition of rice and Kimchi, of course.

I slowed down, hoping to buy myself more time. Ian still hadn't returned, and I dreaded what was in store for me at the table: uncomfortable questions, remarks about my outfit, thinly veiled racist comments. With growing apprehension, I desperately searched the room, but he was nowhere in sight.

Slowly, I grabbed the gravy boat at the very end of the line, allowing the seconds to draw out, praying he'd return. I wanted to feel his hands on my shoulder, his smile reassuring me everything would be okay. I held the boat over my plate as long as I possibly could, pretending to decide where to pour until the man behind me let out an audible sigh. I looked out of the corner of my eye for Ian. No sign. I poured gravy over my turkey and potatoes, almost spilling it due to my shaking hands.

Though I tried extra hard not to be clumsy, gravy still dribbled onto the table cloth. I apologized to the man behind me before a waiter rushed over to wipe it up. Then I also apologized to the waiter.

There was no escaping the fact I needed to sit down. Anymore time dawdling and people would start to wonder about me. I searched for a place to sit. This was worse than high school. I looked for Mrs. Granoff since she was one of the few people who seemed friendly, but she was already surrounded by others.

Everyone looked so relaxed, laughing with their neighbors or shaking hands with someone across the table. They sipped from their wine glasses as if they had been born with an anti-spill gene. It was like they were all listening to the same song and everyone knew exactly when to clap and step to the right. Just as I was seriously contemplating the kids' table as the most suitable option, I felt a warm hand on my arm.

"Sit by me, won't you?" Beverly motioned to the head of the table.

I nearly dropped my plate. It felt like every eye in the room followed me as I followed Beverly to our seats. I could swear people stopped their conversations mid-sentence just to stare. My number one desire was to flee from more attention, and now I was becoming the center.

I sat to Beverly's left, being extra careful setting my plate down. With my trembling hands, I worried the contents would end up on the floor, or worse, I would spill on someone else.

To my relief, Beverly spoke to Mrs. Granoff a few seats away, taking some pressure off. I used the distraction to deduce the silverware setup. Two different-sized forks occupied the left side of the plate, no doubt perfectly arranged to make sure they were equidistant. Two knives and a spoon sat on my right. Meanwhile, a miniature plate was arranged across from my wine and water glasses, with an even tinier spoon and fork at the top of the plate. I didn't know how anyone could focus on their meal with so many cutlery options.

I began with the forks. One had to be for the salad, but I had forgotten which. I thought of Sophia. If she were here right now, she'd shake her head at me for not paying enough attention to her lectures. I checked to see what other people were doing, but it was difficult to tell since they all faced me. And of course, I couldn't ask Ian.

At last, I settled on the outermost fork, weighing it in my hand. Then, I put it back down. No, I should pick the larger one closest to the plate. That would make sense—after all, you eat the salad first. Though my stomach still felt queasy and I had no desire to eat, I dug in.

The dressing was perfect, like a burst of lemony ranch exploding in my mouth. I was so focused on taking miniscule bites with my trembling fork I didn't notice Beverly staring at me.

She put a hand on my arm, smiling that fake smile again. "Kelly?"

Picking up the linen swan in front of my plate, she unfolded it. "This goes on your lap."

Though I could feel my cheeks heating with a blush that must have gone all the way to my ears, I tried to laugh it off. "I was so excited about the food I forgot."

"And this fork is for your salad." She picked up the smaller one farthest from my plate, the one I had picked up first. "Always start at the outside and work your way in each course."

"Oh. Thanks."

The chair next to me scooted out, and I looked up to see Ian. *Phew.*

"My apologies."

Beverly trained him well. He pulled his chair in, then immediately unfolded his swan napkin, placed it in his lap, and picked the right fork.

"Where were you?" Beverly asked.

"Someone interested in the company."

Beverly groaned. "Don't they realize it's a holiday?"

"That's what I said." He whispered in my ear. "You okay?"

I nodded. It was better just to play along in front of Beverly. Plus, I didn't want to ruin Thanksgiving any more.

As the meal continued, conversations and red uniform coats swirled around us. A rainbow of ladies in pretty dresses swept past Beverly, patting her on the shoulder, thanking her for hosting. Diffused light from the stained-glass window waned as the afternoon stretched to dusk. Soon, the chandeliers glowed, bathing the festivities with a dim but elegant illumination. Looking up to the source, I saw hundreds of vertical crystals dangling from chandeliers across the vaulted ceiling. I tilted my head down; I didn't want to be caught staring in awe.

No matter how much water I drank, someone was there to refill my glass. Every few minutes, another server offered a different selection of wine or a bowl of creamier mashed potatoes. I politely declined each time. Despite my sincerest efforts, my plate appeared to be growing.

Mid-meal, a few loose peas scattered across my dish. I tilted my fork to catch them, but couldn't scoop them up, so I used my fingers to put them on my fork.

Beverly cleared her throat. "You should always use another utensil to do that."

Which one? "Oh sorry, I—"

"Makes you look like you're not well-groomed."

"*Mother*," said Ian annoyed.

"What?" Beverly speared a slice of turkey. "These are important things one should know."

I set down my fork and put my hands on my lap, trying to chew and smile at the same time. It felt like Beverly was watching everything my every move, just waiting for me to make another mistake.

She confirmed this a moment later when she looked at my hands. "You're a nail biter." I could tell she meant to make her tone upbeat, but it wasn't convincing.

"Oh ... yeah." I placed my hands in my lap, removing them from sight. "Just when I'm nervous." Tonight, I had all but gnawed my nails to the quick.

"You have to let them grow out." She said softly so Ian couldn't hear. "Otherwise, they'll always be an eyesore."

"Mmmm, I guess you're right," I replied, not knowing what else to say.

"So, Kelly. Are you working your way through school?"

I noticed some of the people sitting beside us lean in to hear us better. Once again, I felt like I was some sort of specimen.

"I work as a hostess at a restaurant called Poseidon. I'm training to be a server."

"Must be difficult to keep a job while studying," Beverly said more to her audience than me.

I sipped at my water glass. "Yeah, it's tough, but I really like it."

She pointed her fork at me. "*Yes.*"

I automatically put my hands back in my lap, wondering what I did wrong this time. Beverly was quick to tell me.

"Don't say 'yeah.' Say 'yes.'"

"Mother, *please.*" Ian scooted closer, squeezing my knee under the table.

"What? I would have appreciated it if someone took the time to tell me these things growing up."

I tried my best to look appreciative for Beverly's wisdom. When I turned to Ian, he tilted his eyes toward the door.

"Are you sure?" I whispered. I noticed he hadn't eaten much, either.

Instead of answering, he took his napkin off his lap and set it on the table. "Well, thank you very much, Mother. I'll show Kelly to her room now."

Her eyes widened. "So soon?"

"It was a long drive."

"I'll come with you, dear. You don't know where the fresh slippers and robes are for that room."

"We'll manage."

Ian took my hand, and we exited the dining hall, followed by stares. We passed the front entrance where the wine glass incident occurred, then broke into a near run down the hallway. My heels clacked against the marble flooring. On the walls, I noticed portraits of a young Ian with his dad. He looked a lot like Ian with his strong jawline, only his hair was more salt, less pepper. Beverly's happy smiles in the pictures surprised me. Not only did she seem younger, her face once held a now absent softness. I noticed these were the only decorations that didn't fit in with the otherwise formal decor. They seemed, well, normal. One blurry photo of Ian as a baby caught my eye. I took a mental snapshot for later—he was a pretty adorable kid.

It didn't take long for me to understand why Ian had said I would need a bus to get to the other side of the mansion. The hallway must have been a recent addition. The further we walked, the colder it became. Similar to how one's toes and feet can miss out on receiving the body's core warmth, the further extremities of the mansion didn't receive the same heat from the central furnace. In fact, the more we traveled, the more it felt like we were going underground—if the underground in question were somehow constructed of expensive granite and marble.

At last, we reached a white door with a silver knob. After jiggling it several times, Ian pushed it open. We stepped onto wood flooring. A main hallway extended another hundred feet with four or five doors to each side. One was open: a bathroom with the fan humming. According to Ian, this wing was where the maids lived, which helped explain why things looked less sophisticated.

Ian led me to the edge of another room at the end of the corridor, where I saw my bags sitting on the bed.

"Sorry again," he said.

I shrugged. "It's fine. But I'll miss you." I reached up to kiss him. He started to kiss me back when we were interrupted by a harsh voice.

"I see you found it."

Immediately, I withdrew from Ian and looked down at the floor. I felt like a scolded child, but he held onto my hand, unfazed. Beverly approached, staring at my hand in Ian's.

She passed between us, forcing us to let go. "I would be remiss as your hostess if I didn't show you around."

We stepped into the simple room, furnished with a double bed, desk, and medium-sized closet. The carpet was brown and reminded me of a hotel. Clean, white blinds covered the windows. A lonely-looking painting of a mountain landscape took up one wall. It felt like everything here, especially the person in the bed, would be a temporary fixture.

Beverly opened the closet, revealing two shelves above the hangers and a white, fluffy robe. Clean, white towels hung from the steel bar above a pair of beige slippers.

"There's a shared bathroom down the hall, but the maids will be very busy today, so I doubt you'll see them. And I'm sure you can find everything else you need. You're a big girl. Don't need your hand held, do you?" She smiled tightly. "Ian, let's leave Kelly to get unpacked and all that. She looks tired."

Ian sighed, looking at me. I nodded. He had endured enough battles for one day. He leaned down to give me a peck on the forehead.

"Come, come." Beverly waved him away.

Watching Ian go with his mom, I could swear they both tried to appear straighter than the other, each struggling for situational control. It took everything I had not to yell out for Ian, to grab his hand, but I said nothing, did nothing. At least I felt relieved to escape Beverly.

I shed my stupid clothes and changed into my non-penguin pajamas. I pictured telling Melissa that absolutely nothing happened between Ian and me. The more I thought about it, the stupider I felt for thinking something could have. Collapsing under the full weight of my exhaustion, I snuck under the heavy, brown, quilt-like comforters and stacked two white pillows beneath my head. I stared up at the beige, bumpy ceiling and felt the ends of the fuzzy blanket at my feet.

Within moments, a heater crackled to life, then I felt a brush of warm air seep into the room. I thought about where I might be if my parents were still alive. Probably at our table at home in LA. I pictured my dad droning on about Thanksgiving as if it was the best thing ever. My mom would roll her eyes, begrudgingly helping him prepare the turkey. At some point, she would bring the conversation back to something Korean to remind me this "silly holiday" was only half my identity. Meanwhile, Halmuni would hassle my dad for his cooking, while laughing at his jokes and taking seconds of his stuffing.

I pressed my palms against my eyes to try to stop the memories. It did no good. Tears trickled down my cheeks. I shook my head as they fell, trying to shake them off. "I miss you, Mom and Dad," I whispered.

I couldn't sleep so I reached across the floor, still halfway in bed. Grabbing my bag, I removed my phone. I pulled up Halmuni's name and sent her a text. *"I love you."*

I laid back against my pillows as I wiped my eyes. She probably wouldn't reply, but I wanted to feel it vibrate if she did. I turned my head so the soft fabric could catch more of my tears and curled up with my knees to my chest, grateful to be alone.

My phone vibrated. I sat up.

"LOL," I read.

I stared at the screen, then fell back on my pillows, laughing in spite of myself—in spite of everything. It was the thought that counted. The phone buzzed again.

"Be happy with Ian. Happiness good."

I wiped away more tears, making my vision blurry as I read the words over and over again.

CHAPTER SIXTEEN

Someone touched me on the shoulder, and I opened my eyes slowly, feeling the crick in my neck from the stiff pillow. I had pushed the comforter and sheets down to the foot of the bed sometime during the night.

I blinked up to see Ian.

"Hey," he whispered.

I groaned like I did whenever my mom tried to wake me for school, then flipped over to the other side. Strands of my hair fell in my face. I left them there. I wasn't ready to face the day, especially not another one at the Anderson compound.

Ian laughed. "Okay, sleepyhead."

I turned back around and mumbled a good morning, wondering when his mother would burst in.

"I'm sick of it here. Thought you might want to go home," he whispered into my ear.

That was the best news I had heard in a long time. I immediately sat up, feeling lighter already. "Seriously?"

"Seriously. I mean, we can stay if that's what you want," he chuckled.

Although I didn't want to sound like an ungrateful guest, I'm sure my earlier reaction had clearly exposed my true wishes.

"No, really. Trust me. I'm ready to get out of here, too." He kissed me on the forehead. "I'll be back." He walked to the door, then turned back before closing it. "Hey. I like your pajamas."

I looked down at my light blue cotton pants and matching cropped top, saying a silent prayer of thanks to Melissa for talking me out of the penguin PJs. As I tossed my sheets aside and dove into my backpack, I realized Ian was the first boy to see me dressed this way. I really was a newbie in the romance department. Not wanting to dwell on that, I threw all my energy into getting ready. If anyone saw my smile, they probably would have thought I'd won the lottery. *I'm going home!*

I pulled on my jeans, a light-yellow T shirt, and grey Columbia hoodie, almost getting the latter stuck on my head in my haste. After slipping into my shoes, I hoisted the backpack over my shoulder, then looked back to make sure I didn't forget anything. *Crap.* Should probably make the bed. Actually, I should probably make the bed perfectly.

I fluffed out each pillow and blanket, fitting them around the edges of the bed frame, trying to straighten everything at the top as I arranged the sheets and blankets. When I was done, it all looked a bit lumpy, so I started all over again, trying my hardest to smooth it out as I went. It looked a little better the second time, but still wasn't flawless, so I tried again. When I was done, I stood back to examine my work. *Ugh. Why can't I get this to look just right?* At last I gave up with a sigh of defeat, imagining Beverly *tsk-tsking* my work in her judgmental tone.

I opened the door. To my surprise, Ian was leaning against the wall. He handed me a mug of coffee. "It might be a little cold by now."

After thanking him with a proper kiss on the lips (after first checking for his mom), I motioned to the bed. "Does it look okay?"

He wrinkled up his nose like he just smelled something rancid, making my blood pressure skyrocket.

"Oh, no. I'll do it again."

He broke into a grin. "I mean, if it was me? I'd probably pour some black paint on the whole thing and remove all of the feathers from the pillows. Might even rip the sheets a little."

I rolled my eyes, pushing him out the door. "Okay, let's go before you get any more bright ideas."

* * *

Eerily quiet, the house was a far cry from the noisy party the night before. Ian told me his mother took an Ambien with a glass of wine every night, so I felt confident we wouldn't encounter her prowling the breakfast nook or anywhere else as we trekked along the mansion.

Even the maids and servers hadn't yet risen, so it must be early. I couldn't help but feel like a trespasser or a burglar as we tiptoed through darkened hallways. Ian held my hand, guiding us to the bathroom where I cried last night. Careful not to make a peep, he didn't even turn on the light for fear of hitting the fan switch. He opened the window, gesturing me to sneak out.

"It's not much of a drop," he whispered.

This was my first time making a window-exit, and I felt a rush, like I was one of those bad kids from high school who slipped out of the house to go clubbing. It dawned on me as I stepped onto the toilet seat to reach the sill that Ian must have done this before because he knew right where I should place my feet and hands. I didn't even get a scratch as I landed beside a rose bush. Then we circled the long mansion's gargantuan perimeter, my Converses squishing in the wet grass.

Ian used his key to unlock the exterior garage, packed with luxury European cars and Teslas. He made a big jokey show of opening my door for me like a valet, then ran around to the driver's side and jumped in. We giggled as we sped off like crooks who had just gotten away with a daring bank heist. I couldn't help thinking we made perfect partners in crime.

As we approached the gate, I peered out my window. It was a crisp autumn morning, and the sun had just risen, offering soft orange light through the dense clouds. No one was in sight—no early risers out for a walk with their dog, no fitness junkies jogging the premises. I inhaled a big gulp of cool air, letting it calm me. The grass was freshly watered from rain the night before, and gravel crunched beneath our slick tires. The enchanting storybook splendor of the grounds became more beautiful as the mansion receded in the rearview mirror.

We turned onto the main road back toward familiar streets: ones with chalky lines down the middle, debris on either side. A few scattered cars surrounded us, heading somewhere after the holiday. This part of the world more resembled the remote sections of Northern California I remembered visiting as a child. I liked the wind in my face with the window down as we cruised past thick patches of colorful trees.

Before long, we reached signs for freeway entrances, and the knot in my stomach relaxed. Soon, we would be transported back to the frantic busyness of New York City. I longed for its anonymity—its camouflage.

Ian interrupted my thoughts. "I had no idea that would suck so much."

I rolled my window back up. "It's okay."

"No, it's not. You didn't deserve to be treated like a second-class citizen. It was really disgusting."

I didn't know what to say, so I kept my eyes on the road, watching Ian weave in and out of lanes.

"And I shouldn't have blown up at my mom," he continued. "My dad used to do crap like that, and I hated it."

I put a hand on his arm, feeling him relax. "It's okay. *I* feel bad. The purse, the—"

"No, no." He took one hand off the wheel. "Seriously. I already have a plan to pay back Mrs. Williams. Lord knows she needs some more fresh alligator flesh. How would you like to break into the zoo with me tonight? You did pretty well sneaking out the window."

"Ian—"

"Seriously, though. Mrs. Williams can go screw herself."

I put my hand over my mouth, trying not to laugh.

"Anyways, I want to make it up to you." He pulled his phone from the console and handed it to me. "Can you Yelp some bed and breakfasts? We can pick whatever one looks the best."

I felt my face flush. Part of me was thrilled by the idea of being alone together, yet another part—the one that still slept in girly pajamas—recoiled in fear.

I took his phone but stopped short of unlocking it, even though I knew his code.

Ian noticed my hesitation. "Do you just want to be alone today?"

I didn't want to be alone. But something held me back. I watched the cars on the highway as I allowed myself to imagine what this step would mean. I could feel tension mounting as the awkward silence dragged on. *Is there anything worse than a painfully quiet moment between two people?*

"Kelly?" Ian said at last with a pleading look in his eyes. "I wanted our first Thanksgiving together to be memorable. In a *good* way. Let's do it again, but this time a thousand times better."

I took a breath, then smiled at Ian, opening the app. He was right. We still had a chance to save Thanksgiving. After reviewing listings and user reviews, I chose a quaint-looking place called *Cozy Home Inn,* its photo featuring mid-century furniture and an adorable tabby cat. It had five stars and was very close to our current location.

Several exits later, we pulled onto another gravelly dirt road surrounded by a few trees and a sign reading, "BED AND BREAKFAST" with a blocky, black arrow. We passed an old truck with blinking hazard lights sitting in the corner, and the buzz of the distant freeway gradually muted.

Another sign out front declared this location to be an historical monument, and I detected candles glowing in the windows. We swung around a small cul-de-sac to the front of a white clapboard house. Two stories high, it had a corrugated roof and large shuttered windows on the second floor. Two slight chimneys exhaled tufts of smoke into the early morning air. A tidy white picket fence encircled the property, reminding me of *Tom Sawyer.* More signs for parking directed us to the back.

I imagined returning here with Ian at Christmas time, daring to think this could be our little spot. I secretly pictured the lawn covered in white powder, the glow from within even brighter against a sheet of ice as we cuddled up against the warmth of the hearth with cups of hot chocolate.

We exited the car and approached the wrap-around porch. The chipped wood creaked as we stepped on the front steps. A plush red couch greeted us with grey pillows knitted with *"Home Sweet Home"* in embroidered cursive lettering. On the other side of the porch, an inviting hammock swung a little in the breeze. I suddenly imagined a hammock on the future house I had already built in my head. I pictured the two of us pressed together on it, reading books together, kissing.

"Kelly?"

Snapping out of my fantasy, I realized Ian was carrying all our luggage.

"Oh, my gosh. Totally spaced." I took my backpack from him.

His face looked earnest like he was trying to read mine. "You okay with this?"

"Yes," I said softly, touching one of the white pillars near the door. I felt like I was in a dream.

He took my hand and, with the other, pushed open the door. A blast of heat enveloped my goosebump-covered arms. An older woman dressed in a thick, red sweater and black slacks sat in a tall rocking chair at the desk. I peered around the living room, or more accurately the lobby, catching the flames of a fireplace out of the corner of my eye. Pop magazines covered a long wooden table. Comfy-looking couches surrounded it on either side, draped with cozy quilts. The goosebumps started up again as I spied a narrow staircase leading up to the rooms. *Where we'd finally be alone.*

When Ian asked if she had any rooms available, part of me held back. If she said no, then that would be it. I would be off the hook. But that was stupid. I wanted to be here. More than anything. *Why do I have to be so nervous?*

"You're in luck." She opened a ledger, and I realized there wasn't a computer in sight. A bowl of pens sat on the counter next to a stapler, some rubber bands, and stacks of papers. Everything must have been handled here old school, the pen and paper way. I liked it. "I have one room with a queen upstairs."

Ian turned to me for approval, a small gesture, but it made me feel more comfortable. I nodded.

"Frank's already in the kitchen. You can grab some breakfast."

Ian thanked her and deposited a hefty amount of cash in the glass vase labeled "*Tips.*" Entering the dining room, we saw Frank, an older, bearded man wearing a checkered apron, flipping pancakes on a grill. Sunlight streamed through the kitchen window, draped with green and white plaid bows. A painting of a rooster hung above his head, and steam from the grill wafted above the seashells lining the windowsill. I wondered if Frank and the woman at the front desk were married.

Frank must've sensed we were there, because he didn't even turn around before talking. "You want any shapes?'

"What?" I whispered to Ian.

"Mickey Mouse," Ian said.

"You got it," the guy said, his back still turned.

"Of the pancakes," Ian said to me.

"Oh. Um, a square."

Ian looked at me. "Out of all the options in the world, you choose a *square pancake?*"

I shrugged. "It's non-conformist."

He smiled at that. A few minutes later, Frank served us perfectly flipped pancakes on two bright, yellow plates, along with scrambled eggs and bacon. Ian's Mickey Mouse ears came out perfectly, but my pancake looked like a sad hexagon.

"I don't have as much practice with those." He pointed to mine.

"No problem."

We carried our bags up the stairs, balancing plates in our hands. I could tell this was not exactly welcomed by the lady at the front desk.

"No messes," she yelled to us. "This is a one-time exception of eating in the bedroom."

"Appreciate it. No messes," Ian said.

* * *

Ian unlocked our door with an old-fashioned metal passkey. The bed was in a beautiful dark oak frame with miniature spires arising from each corner. A polished antique dresser hugged the corner at the end of a rug decorated in beige and gold patterns. A little handwritten welcome note and what appeared to be homemade chocolates greeted us on the pillow. The only modern touches were a small DVD player hooked up to flat-screen HDTV. Otherwise, the room could have passed for a time when radio was America's primary entertainment source.

I put my plate on the wooden nightstand and lowered myself onto the bed. Ian was still busy checking out our surroundings, peering into the closet and checking out the bathroom.

"This place is nice," he said. "You like it?"

"Yes!" Though I was starving from not eating much the day before, I couldn't start until he sat down.

Ian looked around for the remote. "TV?"

"Yeah, let's do it."

He opened up the cabinet beneath the screen. DVDs lined the shelves. "Oh, my gosh. They have every Will Ferrell movie ever made. Didn't expect that. *Blades of Glory?*"

"Sure. Never seen it."

"Then we are definitely watching it." He slid the disc into the player, then hopped on the bed with me, grabbing his plate.

We snuggled our legs under the comforter, and I put my foot on his.

He took a bite of bacon and pushed *Play*. "Now this is my kind of Thanksgiving."

After eating and brushing our teeth, we lost track of the movie. The story about two grown men competing in pairs ice skating was kind of funny, but I lost interest as soon as we started making out. We sunk down in the sheets, pulling the comforters over our head. He put his hand on my side as I ran my fingers through his hair.

I broke away, keeping my hand on his shirt. "I want to," I whispered.

He smiled and nodded. He came out of the covers for a second to turn off the movie, then met my eyes as he scooted back underneath. It was warm in our little cocoon, and I started kissing him again. I wasn't nervous. I didn't even care what I was wearing or where we were. I was just glad I could be with him like this, in a place only we knew.

* * *

I laid my head on the pillow and let one arm rest on the comforter. We held hands beneath the covers, my foot on his. I turned to face him and smiled. He had been so gentle, so careful to make sure I was okay. I felt so lucky.

"I have a confession."

My smile vanished. Not exactly what I wanted to hear right now.

"I totally planned for you to meet Kevin and Roy."

I thought of how he suggested we visit his apartment before setting out on this trip. "You didn't have to go the bathroom?"

He covered his face with his hand. "Nope."

"But why?"

He snuggled even closer, pulling me nearer to him. "Before we went to my mom's, I just wanted you to see that I was normal, too. I also wanted you to, like, get verification that I'm okay from my friends. It sounds dumb when I say it out loud."

I propped myself on my elbow. "So they were your references? Should I call anyone else? Any former employers?"

He playfully touched my lip with his finger. "Stop."

"I'm just kidding. That's cute." I laid back, stroking his chest. I liked how he had just the faintest patch of dark hair below his neckline.

We kept looking at each other.

"What?" he asked.

"Nothing. You're just cute."

He turned on his side to face me better. "And you're beautiful." He ran his hand along my side and kissed the top of my head.

I had never heard that from a guy before, and it took me a second to register it, almost as if he had said it to someone else. *Beautiful...*

Even so, I couldn't help but feel insecure after all the things his mother said to me. "Ian, do you think I'm good enough for you? I mean, you can have your choice of women, and I'm not exactly ... your type."

Ian stretched out his legs. "Are you kidding? If anything, I'm not good enough for *you*. I know you heard lots of crap from my mom yesterday. Just ignore her. She can be self-centered. It matters to her what others think of her. I can't stand it when she's like that."

"She loves you. You can tell."

"She was a complete jerk to you. You don't always have to be nice about her. We're miles away now."

I shrugged. "I'm sure she means well behind all that. Somewhere."

"Yeah, maybe deep, deep, deep down. Like on a molecular, or sub-atomic level deep-down."

I couldn't help laughing.

Ian gently stroked my arm. "I've known plenty of girls my mother would just love. And they're all spoiled brats. I love that you're not spoiled, because I want to be the one to spoil you. I don't want you to have to worry about anything anymore."

I forced a smile. "I just felt so out of place when I was there last night..."

"Those people may know which fork to use, but a lot of them—well, they're empty inside. They know the price of everything but the value of nothing. You put them all to shame." He kissed me deeply. And then he said it. "I love you, Kelly."

I've never heard anyone say that to me other than my parents and Halmuni. I couldn't believe that someone as wonderful as Ian could actually love someone like me. I didn't know how to respond. Did he even expect a response? Should I just stay silent? My heart told me to be honest with him. To trust him completely.

"I love you, too." As I said it, I felt a warmth in my body I never felt before. It just felt right. "But I'm scared, too. I'm scared you'll get bored with me. I'm scared you really want a life like your mom, you just don't know it yet. What if you change your mind later?" I looked into his eyes. Was I being too honest?

"Kelly, I don't say 'I love you' easily. When I say it, I mean it. You don't have to be scared. And as long as you'll have me, I'll always be there for you. And God, no, I don't want to end up like my mom. You have to believe me."

"Pinky swear on that?" I said as I held out my left pinky.

He crossed his pinky with mine. "No. Honestly, I actually want to be an attorney with the ACLU. I want to help others, not just make a boatload of money to host fancy holiday parties with waiters who don't get to see their families."

So he noticed our servers and thought the same thing, too.

"This is going to sound naïve," he continued. "But I'd like to just give away that stupid house. Do you realize how many families could live there? We could turn it into an academy for needy students. You saw how many people fit inside."

I felt myself drawn closer to him. "I love that you think that way."

"What about you? What do you want?"

As he looked deeply into my eyes, I could actually picture us in bed together in a real home, not a bed and breakfast, with both of our diplomas on the walls downstairs, both with busy schedules, maybe a child in one of the other rooms. But that was crazy. There was no way I could say that.

"I want to help others, too. But I also want to be like B.B., my old boss. I want my own private practice someday."

"I have no doubt you will," he said.

I smiled, squeezing his hand, imagining he'd be there to see it. With me.

CHAPTER SEVENTEEN

Christmas break was my chance to return to L.A. and recharge. During my three weeks at home, Halmuni and I binge watched *Real Housewives of Beverly Hills* and whatever we could find on the HGTV network. In my absence, Halmuni had grown obsessed with home renovation and remodeling. She loved seeing the amazing transformations the *Property Brothers* or the *Flip or Flop* couple managed on even tight budgets. Each time a host would reveal a renovated home, her eyes would widen with excitement and she would scream something encouraging in Korean.

She made a special point to take me to our favorite restaurants and indulge in all the dishes I had missed while at Columbia. While the places Ian had taken me to were world class, I sorely missed my dose of simple, authentic Korean cuisine. B.B. would occasionally stop by with his latest girlfriend, a blonde with toned legs and arms (turned out that they worked out at the same swanky gym), with pearly white teeth almost blindingly white against her Californian tan. The two actually looked good together. It was possible she was "the one" for him as long as he ignored the fact she was half his age.

When I returned to Columbia the second week of January, Ian and I fell into a comfortable routine, making school manageable again. I could actually study for more than an hour without being distracted (in a good way) by his texts. By the end of the second semester, I had pulled off straight A's, much to Halmuni's delight. I had also redeemed myself with Sophia, memorizing each item and its substitution on the menu, finally working my way up to a server position.

So much for lacking interpersonal skills. After a few months on the job, I could go up to any stranger and ask for their order without hesitation. It was almost like performing on stage, and I was getting used to putting on the same costume every night. To top it all, Beverly offered to be my friend online.

This last development I wasn't so sure about, mostly because I didn't believe Beverly really wanted to be friends. I felt she must have some ulterior motive in mind. As soon as her request arrived, I spun my laptop around to show Ian my page. We were sitting together in the dead-silent library, communicating through hand motions and text messages. The strict staff made their zero-tolerance policy on noise very clear. Even a sneeze threatened to undermine their well-ordered sanctuary.

I pointed out Beverly's picture to Ian in my Friend Request bubble, my cursor hovering over the Confirm or Delete buttons. I raised my eyebrows at him questioningly.

Ian looked wary at first, mouthing a silent "No."

But I felt bad declining the offer. Maybe Beverly really did want to get to know me? I clicked on "Accept" and returned to my notebook, re-organizing my notes from Professor Baker's class.

My computer dinged. In the stillness, the unexpected sound split the air like a shrill fire alarm. All around the room, heads turned in my direction. Embarrassed, I stabbed at my mouse, desperate to hit my mute button.

Beverly had already messaged me! I turned my computer to Ian again so he could read along with me: *Hi Kelly. If Ian hasn't already told you, I just wanted to apologize we got off on the wrong foot. Ian said you weren't feeling well and that's why you rushed off — Hope you're feeling better!*

Ian rolled his eyes. Another bubble popped up. Beverly was still typing.

I thought it would be nice if we got together again, just the two of us. How does a Girl's Day sound? We could do lunch, shopping, maybe get mani/pedis. Let me know and I'll have my assistant schedule it.

I cringed. That sounded like a *terrible* way to spend a day. True, I did enjoy getting pedicures with Halmuni, but that was only because I got a kick out of watching her freak out over her ticklish feet. But manicures for me were pointless because, as Beverly herself had so noted, I was a nail biter, and there was scant little left on my fingertips to cut or polish. I also only shopped occasionally, and then only by myself, so people wouldn't feel the need to give me their opinions. But worst of all? Lunch with Beverly. One-on-one. *What if I messed up the forks again?*

I tried to convey all of these negative thoughts to Ian via facial expressions, but he didn't get the message because he gave me two big thumbs up. I shook my head, then sighed audibly.

"Shh!" said a passing librarian. *Jeez.* If I wasn't more careful, they might throw me out of here.

Ian leaned in close to my computer and began typing. He nudged me in the arm, then showed me the message: *You don't have to. Make up a terminal illness.*

I tilted the computer and wrote my response.

No. I care about you so that means I care about getting to know your family.

Ian smiled, then squeezed my arm.

* * *

Ian's butler, Franco, held the limousine door open for me with a smile. I returned it with a tight-lipped grin, self-conscious of the fact I looked like a spoiled brat entering such a luxurious vehicle. It wasn't Franco's fault I felt so out of place. Honestly, I would rather have spent the day hanging with him than his employer.

"Miss Kelly," he said warmly, helping me inside.

"Thank you, Franco."

I adjusted the long black cardigan Melissa lent me and scooted the skin-tight dress down to my knees. I hoped the baggy cardigan would cover up my navy-blue dress. It was the only thing in my closet that looked suitable for this outing, but I had grown out of it a bit.

As I slid into the cavernous rear passenger compartment, Beverly leaned over, giving me a quick, perfunctory hug.

"Hi," I said, doing my best to be cheerful.

"Hello, dear."

Beverly's big gold diamond hoop earrings reflected off the tinted window. She wore a black fedora hat, a black-beige tweed jacket, and faded jeans that cuffed right around her suede ankle boots. She dressed like she had just walked off a Paris runway. Chic and stylish.

Instantly, I became aware of how lame and unfashionable I looked in comparison. I was also hyper-aware of my posture and how I arranged myself. The leather seats felt sticky on my hands, and I didn't know how to cross my legs without stretching my dress. Beverly wasted no time zeroing in on my discomfort.

"That dress looks a little tight." Beverly inclined her head toward my legs. "Wouldn't want you to look slutty." She leaned in and whispered the last part, as if it made it sound any better.

Would I ever dress right for Beverly? I draped my cardigan more fully over my legs. "Sorry. My mom's friend used to work at a fashion magazine in L.A. She'd given me a couple of the sample clothes once they were done with them." No response at all from Beverly. I wanted to thrust a nail in my mouth and bite it. "She worked in the petite section, but all those models are like way thinner than me so the dresses can be tight sometimes."

"Then it's a good thing we're going shopping."

The car started and Beverly addressed Franco on the other side of the partition. "Barneys," she said in a commanding tone.

As we pulled away from the curb, I took a good look at my surroundings. This was my first time in a limousine, and its opulence amazed me. I remembered back to something Ian once said about how his mom liked the biggest and best of everything. This just confirmed it. Our royal carriage had a mini bar built into the door on Beverly's left, and I saw it was stocked with bottles of water, champagne, and two Baccarat glasses. Fold-out trays, like the ones you would see in an airliner, graced each seat along with a miniature flat screen monitor tucked above the tray. I had just begun to notice the heating button for my seat when Beverly returned her attention to me.

"Ian hasn't returned my calls or messages since Thanksgiving. I don't know what I did to upset him, but this is not the Ian I know." She sounded agitated. I sensed she thought I was to blame for her problems.

"I didn't know that," I told her. Ian never mentioned he hadn't spoken to Beverly since the party.

"He was always such a good boy. Always did what was asked of him and never argued about anything. I'm not sure what you're doing to him, but if it means I have to make an effort with you, then so be it." Well, she was certainly getting right to the point. It was clear she casted me as the villain in her maternal psychodrama.

"I'll make sure he calls you."

"I hope you do that, otherwise it'll just make things difficult between us. You wouldn't want that, would you?" I didn't like the tone in her voice. It sounded almost like a threat you'd hear on *The Sopranos*.

"Of course not. I promise to talk to him as soon as I see him."

"That's a good girl. Now, let's focus on having some fun together. Tell me, what are your favorite brands?"

I had no idea how to respond. Does Topshop or Zara count? I was aware of famous brands like Chanel, Gucci, and Prada because of all the reality shows Halmuni watched, but I had never actually stepped foot in one of their stores. Halmuni would scoff at how much money the "housewives" she saw on TV dropped on shoes, saying, "Why they waste money on stupid things? What so good about 'Lu Be Ton?'" I think she meant "Louboutin," but I never dared correct her. I chuckled to myself just thinking about Halmuni.

"Was something I said funny?" Beverly asked, obviously annoyed.

"I was just thinking about what my grandmother used to say about women who spend too much money on shoes."

"Shoes can be works of art," she snapped. "And like all fine art, the best ones are worth paying more for."

Oh, no. I did it again. I'd managed to upset her.

"I didn't mean it that way. Umm ... I don't really have any favorite brands. I just buy comfortable things that I like, but I rarely go shopping anyway. My mom used to take me on my birthday and stuff. We would plan ahead to make sure we would go on sale days, and then we would get an Auntie Anne's pretzel and Cinnabons with extra frosting —"

"Ugh. Those things are horrible for you."

"Yeah ... I mean, yes. But we only had them once in a while. Like a treat, you know?"

"Try not to say, 'You know.' It's a bad habit. Almost as bad as saying 'like' in every other sentence." Beverly eyed my dress again. "Shopping is important. Your clothes are a reflection of your character. When you buy cheap outfits or borrow from a friend, they are more likely to lose their shape. Or shrink. Which will make others think less of you."

"I'll keep that in mind." My words came out stilted, as if I was reading from a script. But I couldn't help it. I felt like she would attack me at any second for saying the wrong thing.

If Beverly's criticism was bad, her silence was worse. After my last comment, Beverly clammed up, and so did I. The next 20 minutes passed with painful slowness, both of us looking out the window or at our phones to avoid eye contact. At long last, Franco dropped us at the corner of 60th Street and Madison Avenue. Perhaps someone else would be excited to venture into an exclusive department store with Beverly Anderson, widow of a billionaire mogul, but I would've rather been anywhere but here. Looking up at the display window mannequins clad in their high-end couture, I got the sickening sense even they were judging me, reminding me I didn't belong.

As usual, Beverly took charge, pushing open the glass doors for us. Sophisticated purse and shoe selections lined the walls. Racks of stylish and tasteful outfits beckoned to us. Unlike the discount stores I shopped in L.A. where every square foot was designed to yield their owners the maximum possible profit, here everything was spread out, allowing each item to breathe. Meanwhile, soft recessed lighting shone down, making the colors pop. Every inch of the displays and counters were immaculately kept with not a speck of dust in sight.

A young, well-dressed saleswoman in a tight skirt and fitted blazer approached us with a chipper smile. "Mrs. Anderson, such a pleasure."

Beverly didn't halt her stride. "I'd like to see the latest collection, especially in Chloe, Valentino, Dior, and YSL."

The woman presented us with different selections. All the clothes looked way too trendy, too sophisticated, too tailored. Certainly not the loose, comfy clothes I preferred.

I was so focused on thinking of a joke text to send Ian, I didn't realize women were both staring at me.

The saleswoman gently touched my shoulder, then ran a finger down my arm. "Maybe a size 36."

"Yes, yes. Let's try that," said Beverly. "We'll try them all. Start a room."

"Yes, of course." The woman eagerly sifted through the hangers.

The way in which the saleswoman and Beverly kept poking and prodding me made me feel like I was in a doctor's office, instead of a dressing room. They spent more time talking to each other than to me as they readjusted blouses or slacks, reviewing potential sizes and styles. I wanted to call Ian and beg him to save me. I was tired of dressing, undressing, dressing, undressing, only to model for two people whose only response seemed to be: "Definitely not." I just wanted to rip off this stupid, expensive clothing and go get my pretzel.

Wriggling a constricting bold printed silk chiffon blouse over my head, the price tag scratched my arm, and I took it out. $595. For a *blouse*? They had to be joking. I put on the rest of the outfit they had chosen to go with the blouse—black flare pants with a cream wool belted blazer—and looked at myself in the mirror. It fit me well, accentuating my legs and hips, but it looked like a business outfit a middle-aged professional would wear.

I stepped outside anyway.

"Lovely," Beverly cooed. "Definitely a yes."

The saleswoman nodded her approval. "Do you want the black Sergio Rossi pumps, as well?"

"Yes, she will take those, too. Add a pair for me— size 8."

I returned to the dressing room and froze. *Wait, she doesn't expect me to pay for this, right? No. That can't be possible. But what if she does? Doesn't she know that there's no way I can afford this? What if this was her plan all along? To publicly humiliate me...*

"That outfit looks so much better than what you were wearing. Very sophisticated," Beverly said through the door.

I tugged it off, barely getting the blouse over my head. "I don't think I really need this."

"Don't you want to earn the respect of your peers? Future employers? When I was your age, I would save for months to buy one item of designer brand clothing."

I left the dressing room with the new items draped over my arm. Beverly met me at the counter with her credit card. *Thank God she's paying and not me, but at the same time, I don't want these things. It doesn't feel right having her buy them for me.*

She took the items from me and handed them to the saleswoman. "We will take these and don't forget the shoes."

"Beverly, thank you so much. But I feel so bad. They're so expensive," I said, thinking of all the more useful things I could have used the money for.

"If we're going to spend time together, I need you to look presentable. So think of it as *you* doing me a favor. Now, we'll have lunch, then get our nails done."

"Really, that's okay. You've been so nice already," I replied, hoping that I could get out of the lunch and mani.

Beverly took my hand in hers, examining my fingers. "You're still nail biting, aren't you? You'd better nip that in the bud."

I was too tired to argue. After profusely thanking her, we went upstairs to the building's ninth floor to a restaurant called Fred's.

"This place is fantastic. You will love it," she said as she marched towards the hostess.

There was a line, but the hostess recognized Beverly immediately. "Mrs. Anderson! I'm so happy to see you again. Please follow me to your table." She grabbed two menus and sat us by the window.

Our waiter, a younger man with a tan and slicked back hair, ran through the daily specials. The restaurant was packed and noisy with chatter. The afternoon sun shone a little too brightly through the glass, and I scooted my chair to the side, trying not to let it hit me in the eyes.

"I already know what I want," Beverly told the waiter. "The chopped chicken salad, please. No onions, and I would like the dressing on the side. And a glass of that Chardonnay you know I like."

"Very good." The waiter turned to me. "And for you, miss?"

"Can I have the club sandwich? With fries, please. Thanks."

When he was gone, Beverly put her hands together with a deep breath, preparing herself like she was trying to explain something incredibly simple for the hundredth time. "Dear, you shouldn't pick meals on the menu that may prove difficult to eat, especially those you have to pick up with your hands."

"Okay," I replied quietly.

"And also ..." she looked me up and down, "... consider fresh fruit or a small salad for your side."

I picked up my water glass and drank from it deeply, using the time to get my rage under control. *Why does she have to pick on me so much?* I already felt inadequate. *Will she ever stop?* I had to remind myself she is Ian's mom. I had to do my best to get along with her for his sake.

Beverly continued to lecture me about the importance of taking care of one's appearance. She went on a rant about proper skin care: *I need to use SPF every day, I should make sure I am using the right facial cleanser and use Vitamin C serums.* Then she continued on about how to keep my weight in check: *I must stay away from gluten, try 16-hour fasting, and abstain from junk food.* I knew she meant well, but I wasn't interested in what she had to say. I pretended to listen, nodding so often I felt like one of those bobble-head dolls. She didn't seem to care I hadn't said a word since ordering.

Finally, our food arrived. Removing the toothpick from the sandwich, I tried to lift it as carefully as I could with my fingers. Even as I did, a piece of bacon fell out of my sandwich onto the table top. *Perfect timing.*

"This is why you shouldn't order things you must eat with your hands. I would suggest a soup or salad next time."

I chewed slowly, counting silently to 10 to keep from screaming.

"In general, as I said, sandwiches should be avoided, not only because you have to use your hands, but bread is pure starch," Beverly continued. "As you get older, your metabolism slows and carbohydrates pack on pounds."

I put down the french fry I was biting into. I looked down at my plate: the sandwich with two bites in it, the steaming french fries—they all looked so beautiful in their greasy, high caloric glory. What I wouldn't give to be in Ian's car, munching on chicken wings from KFC, laughing and carefree. Not here. *Anywhere but here.*

Beverly ordered another glass of wine, and soon it became clear her salad wasn't buffering the increasing alcohol in her bloodstream. Her face flushed, and her gestures became exaggerated. I noticed her elbow on the table and restrained myself from the urge to remind her of "manners."

"Kelly. In some ways, you and I are not dissimilar."

I wanted to snort. We were as different as the *New York Times* and *The National Enquirer.*

She took another sip of wine. "Like you, I came from the *lower* class. Well, lower-middle class. Married up."

I sat back in my seat, pushing my plate away. *Oh, boy.*

"I wasn't that in love with Ian's father, you know." Except the "father" came out as "fodder." "He drank; he was angryyy. But he had a lot of ..." She rubbed the fingers of one hand together in the universal sign for "money."

Baffled as to what to say, I wore a neutral expression.

Suddenly, Beverly put her glass down. "So I know a gold digger when I see one." She squinted at me.

Huh?

"Look, let's be honest with each other," she said in a measured tone. Suddenly, she didn't seem intoxicated anymore. "Ian can have anyone he wants. As my son, naturally, I want him to have the best. I want him to be with someone who can add value to his life. Do you understand?"

I felt my face flush with rage. "No, I *don't* understand. Just because I don't have money doesn't mean that I don't 'add value.' Life is about more than money. In fact … there are times that I wish he didn't have any." I was furious. Did she really think I was so shallow?

"Yes, yes, I've heard it all before," she said wearily. "All the girls say 'I don't want his money.' And we all know they're lying through their teeth. Ian is probably just dating you because he finds you 'exotic' and maybe he even feels sorry for you. He was always the kind of boy to bring home stray puppies. But, to be honest, him dating you is a bit … embarrassing. I'm trying my best to teach you how to be a lady, but you don't even know the basics. Nor do you seem to care."

The gloves were now off. She had no problem punching where it hurt most.

"I'm sorry you find me *embarrassing*. I love Ian, so I'm trying my best," I blurted out. I couldn't believe I told her that I loved him. But it was true. I loved Ian.

Even if he didn't have a penny to his name, I would still love him. And I knew he loved me, too.

"Pleaasse," she said with a dismissive eye-roll. "You two don't even know what love *means*. You are both young and naive. As for your attempt at 'trying', I don't see it." She put her napkin back on the table. "I would suggest you consider etiquette school. That made a real difference for me. If you are serious about 'trying' as you put it, you should *seriously* consider it. For Ian." The way she said "seriously," it didn't seem like I had an option.

I put my napkin back on the table, too. Then I leaned away, frantically searching for the waiter.

He saw both of us staring at him and rushed over.

"Check, please," we said in unison.

* * *

I flopped onto Ian's bed. He sat at his desk, facing me. I could hear Kevin and Roy playing *League of Legends* in the other room and wanted to join them, or even escape into the game. Anywhere, really.

"How was it?" he asked.

I sat up. Could I go into everything? The expensive and itchy clothes, the dressing rooms, the condescension, the lunch, the incessant rambling about cultivating the correct appearance, the gold-digger accusation. But then I noticed the concern on his face, the way he leaned toward me, arms crossed, waiting. What good would my venting do, anyway? Beverly wouldn't change. And what if he confronted her? It would only make her hate me more.

"Fine." I put on my waitress-performance face. "It went fine today. I'm just really exhausted from all that shopping."

"Cool." He leaned back, relieved. "So it went okay?"

I smiled. "It went great. Oh, and Ian, can you please call your mother? She misses you."

CHAPTER EIGHTEEN

"I'm glad you decided to stay." Ian leaned back on his hands. His eyes were shut, and he wore a look of contentment. We were both sitting on a stone bench in the middle of campus, tilting our heads back, letting the sun play warmly across our faces.

This campus square and lawn had become my favorite part of Columbia University. There were multiple, miniature grass quads, each partially blocked off by little, black poles with connecting chains curving to the ground. Like outdoor classrooms, each quad possessed a tight circle of students pouring over textbooks or creating mnemonics for their next exam. The sun, a pleasant breeze, and the scent of freshly mowed grass lightened everyone's mood. People here were definitely more relaxed than the hyper-focused coeds in the school library. I loved sitting here, people watching, listening as they chattered about molecular biology as if it was the most exciting thing in the world.

The main walkway ran past the bench where Ian and I sat. Made up of red and gray brick squares looping inside each other like an artistic maze, at the center of the walkway stood a concrete fountain with a circular base and a wide, water-filled basin. Here, I watched as a girl paused, put a penny to her lips, gave it a kiss, and flipped it into the water.

"Do you think they had that in mind when they designed the fountain?" I asked.

"Could be," Ian said. "Columbia students are wound so tight. Maybe someone thought they could stand to have a little bit of fun."

"Let's give it a try," I said with a giggle. Taking a penny from my wallet, I stood up from the bench, walked over to the fountain, paused for a moment, then tossed it in. "Let's hope it works."

"What did you wish for?"

"If I tell you, it won't come true!"

"Come on," he teased. "I hope you didn't waste it wishing for good grades."

"No. I wished that all the days this summer will be like today. Beautiful weather. Relaxing and carefree." I returned to where we were sitting and stretched out my arms, hoping the sun might turn my flesh golden tan. Maybe I didn't need a magic fountain, because already I could tell this summer in New York City was going to be glorious. I looked up at the sky. It seemed like some cosmic-scale artist had mixed dozens of different shades of blue, from robin's egg to royal, and splashed them across the heavens. Wispy clouds hung there like spun sugar, and a jetliner's contrail made a straight white slash.

"Ian, I'm glad I decided to stay, too." I put my hand on Ian's. "But how you managed to convince Halmuni ..."

Ian laughed. "Now, *that* was a team effort."

I nodded. "Quite a team we make."

Ian turned and gave my hand a squeeze.

A week earlier, Ian had sent Halmuni a basket of gourmet goodies and a pricy bottle of Soju along with a note saying, "I look forward to meeting Kelly's Halmuni. Sincerely, Ian." She had loved it. Then we had both Skyped Halmuni to convince her my working here for the summer at Poseidon made more financial sense than coming home. Airfares were outrageously high during the summer, and besides, I had just gotten a raise.

(While these financial arguments were all true, they weren't exactly the *real* reasons I wanted to stay. That reason was sitting right beside me on the stone bench.)

Ian had ended our Skype conversation by assuring Halmuni he would take care of me and thanked her for raising such a wonderful granddaughter. I knew that, like my dad, Halmuni couldn't help herself—she liked Ian. I think she also realized it didn't matter that he wasn't Korean. She told me that she recently watched a Korean documentary and was shocked to learn the divorce rate there was sky high because Korean men were hardly ever home—they called them "MIA husbands." The report also said many Korean wives no longer saw any value in marriage after years of being with uncaring or unfaithful men. After that program, she said, "Forget Korean men. Doesn't matter. Just need honest, smart and good man – like Ian."

I looked over at Ian. He wore a blue shirt that matched the shade of the sky, bringing out the brilliance of his eyes. A recent haircut uncovered his small, almost delicate ears. He preferred to keep them hidden, but I thought they were adorable.

He caught me staring. "What?"

I gave him a smile. "Nothing." I looked back out toward the walkway, feeling reenergized. No more homework meant lots more time together. More spontaneous adventures. But there was one small catch. "It's such a pain they close the dorms for the summer. But at least Melissa found us a small apartment in time."

"Look. I don't want you to think I'm moving too fast or anything." He looked into my eyes, and I had the sense that he'd been thinking about saying this for some time. Maybe he had even been rehearsing.

"Yes?"

He looked away, as if he'd suddenly gone shy. "You can use my family's condo in the city. We have a place near Central Park. And then, well ... I could visit you a lot."

I felt a tiny flutter in my chest at the thought of Ian visiting—a lot. "But wouldn't your mom be over all the time? I'm not sure she would like me staying there."

"She won't mind. She's hardly around this time of year. She spends every summer in Europe, either St. Tropez or Lake Cuomo."

"Can I think about it?"

I looked back across the lawn. The thought of the condo was appealing because it could become our own special place. No more dancing around roommates or trying to be super-quiet tiptoeing in at 2 a.m. And no Beverly checking up on us.

Beverly. Her words from our lunch kept ringing through my head. I needed to prove to her I wasn't a gold-digging social climber, that I could fit into her son's world. But how? She mentioned going to etiquette school could make a real difference. Maybe that might show her that I was trying. That way at least she wouldn't be so embarrassed in public with me. It bothered me to even think that way, but I knew I needed to stop feeling bad about myself for not knowing her way of life; I just needed to learn it. I could become just like one of her Thanksgiving guests, with their perfect manners, fancy clothes, and elegant jewelry. Maybe I should take at least one piece of Beverly's advice—for Ian, and for myself.

I looked at our hands intertwined on the bench. I leaned toward Ian, lying my head on his shoulder. The summer sun seemed to envelop me, comforting and encouraging. Yes, I could try. For Ian's sake. He made it worth it.

I took his hand as I imagined letting Melissa down softly about the sublease. "Yes," I told him. "Okay, let's do that."

* * *

Ian and I stood in the parking lot of a recently repainted Victorian mansion. Above the front door, a skilled artist had painted a fancy plate setting and a triangle napkin. In calligraphy, the sign read, *Manners, Please!*

"Are you sure?" Ian asked. "You really want to do this?"

"I've thought about it a lot. I want to show your mom I'm good enough for you."

He crossed his arms and gave me a stubborn glance. "You're *too* good for me. And I told you before, I don't care what she thinks."

I felt bad, but I felt even worse he couldn't see what I did. Or maybe he just pretended not to see the gap in our "life experiences."

"I'm doing it for me, too," I said, trying to sound cheerful.

Ian looked skeptical. "Only if *you* really want to do this."

I wanted to put on a brave face for Ian, but the truth was I was nervous. Unconsciously, I began to quietly sing my dad's song of encouragement: *'Just what makes that little old ant/Think he'll move that rubber tree plant/Anyone knows an ant, can't/Move a rubber tree plant/He's got high hopes/He's got high hopes...'*

Ian heard me and started laughing. "There you go again with that song about the ant!"

Embarrassed, I playfully shoved him away. "Go before I show up late for my first class!"

He shook his head, then kissed me. I snuggled against him for a second, then stepped away. "Really, I can't be late."

"Okay, I'm going."

As I walked up the porch steps, I reminded myself this would be like any other class. Unfamiliar at first, perhaps a little scary, and then comfortable as I settled in.

I opened the door and approached the front desk. An older, heavy-set woman sat there, with wrinkles only slightly covered by caked-on makeup. I already felt like she was evaluating me.

"Hi," I said softly, stepping forward to the counter. "I'm Kelly Hopkins. I'm here for etiquette school. Beverly Anderson said she took care of my registration?"

"Yes, Ms. Hopkins, we've been waiting for you."

It occurred to me this might be some kind of test so I gave her my sweetest smile. She stared at me for another couple seconds, then her face softened. I seemed to have passed. Or, I just wasn't worth worrying about.

"Here is your schedule." She handed me a piece of paper with instructions in a loopy font. Classes ran from 9 a.m. to 3 p.m., with only a small break for lunch. I sighed. I could survive. It was only for a few days this summer.

"Thank you." I readjusted the shoulder strap of my small purse.

"They're right in there." The woman waved toward a doorway down the hall.

Stepping inside was like entering a wholly different building. A huge, dark, highly polished dining table filled a good part of the room. Mounted on the wall was a giant flat-screen TV monitor. Across a light pink screen blazed the words: *"Welcome to Etiquette School!"* The hardwood table was surrounded by a dozen chairs, each upholstered with some kind of sparkly fabric. The place settings looked like they did at Beverly's, although the forks were larger and the wine goblets taller.

Ten or so men and women were already seated, quietly chatting. They were all dressed in what I understood as "business casual," whereas I wore a T-shirt with jeans. Was there a dress code that I wasn't aware of? I looked around, trying to figure out the safest spot to sit.

"Ms. Hopkins?"

Mrs. Williams stared right at me. She wore glasses and an elegant business suit, and her hair was in a lacquered upsweep, reminding me of a wave cresting on the shore. She stood next to a lectern with an agenda in hand.

I feigned excitement, though I felt my heart sinking lower. No wonder Beverly had suggested this school. Mrs. Williams, the lady whose bag I ruined during Thanksgiving dinner, was teaching the class. "Hello, Mrs. Williams. What a surprise."

"You're here for etiquette instruction? Seems appropriate."

Ouch.

"Sit right here, please." She pointed to a seat at the front beside a brunette in a black pantsuit with a single strand of pearls around her throat.

As I walked toward my place, I realized everyone had gone silent. I tried to avoid their eyes, especially Mrs. Williams'. Not knowing where to put my small, grey, zip-up purse, I hastily stowed it under my seat. I scooted in my chair. Feeling self-conscious of my hands, I decided to place them in my lap.

Mrs. Williams gave me a curt nod, then addressed the room. "Hello, everyone. We are happy to have you and look forward to contributing to your success as a professional and as a member of society. We will be covering various topics over our seven days together, including first impressions, how to dress, formal dining, afternoon tea etiquette, and posture. Today, I will give you a brief overview of each topic. Let's begin with first impressions."

She walked around my side of the table, stopping beside me. *Uh-oh.* "Ms. Hopkins, in your opinion, what should everyone keep in mind when attempting to make a good first impression? And, as you do so, make your *own* first impression to the class."

I felt like I couldn't breathe. I did not want to do this. *Maybe Ian was still in the parking lot. Maybe if I hurried outside I could...*

"Ms. Hopkins?" Mrs. Williams cleared her throat. "We're waiting."

I swallowed and tried to sit up straighter. "Hi, everyone, I'm Kelly. For a first impression, I think you should, um, be yourself. And, you know, ask the other person a lot of questions so you don't just sit there and talk about yourself."

Mrs. Williams tilted her head, smiling. "And how important are first impressions, Kelly? If you make a mistake, what might that lead to?"

I turned in my seat and looked up at her. I couldn't believe her.

"It might give you a bad reputation," I said quietly.

"Their perception of you may last for a long, *long* time." Mrs. Williams returned to her lectern with a cheery smile. "That is why we will begin our course by learning how to give the very best first impression."

I looked around the room. I was definitely the youngest person here. Everyone else probably had successful jobs and were only here for personal development. Yet here I was, the 20 year-old who couldn't even say a sentence without an "um" or a "yeah."

"Ms. Hopkins, would you please be so kind as to be my demonstrator?"

No no no no.

I carefully tilted in my seat so my knees were out from the table and my feet were firmly planted on the carpet. I stood, tucking in my T-shirt, then went to stand beside Mrs. Williams.

"When it comes to first impressions, body language is important. Let's look at how Ms. Hopkins is standing right now. Now, don't move."

Out of all the things there were to do in the world, at that exact moment, all I wanted to do was move.

But Mrs. Williams gripped my upper arm a little tighter than comfortable and repeated, "Don't move."

I clenched my jaw. I was painfully aware of everyone analyzing me.

"Ms. Hopkins is holding her hands clasped in front of her. Her shoulders are raised high, and her feet are close together. What does this communicate?"

An older man with glasses the shape of checker pieces raised his hand. "She seems closed off. Nervous."

You think?

"Very good," Mrs. Williams said.

My jaw clenched even tighter, and I could hardly keep from saying out loud, *Well, why don't you come up here, then?*

"When you're making a first impression, you want to seem open, not closed off. So, Kelly, relax your arms, relax your shoulders, lean forward slightly, open up your feet, raise your chin up, and smile."

She gave her instructions so rapidly I couldn't keep up. I tried to do as instructed, but felt like a marionette whose strings had gotten tangled. I stood there awkwardly with my feet apart and my hands by my sides.

"Better. Now you're not undermining your credibility. One more thing," Mrs. Williams looked around, inviting the others to chime in. "Let's take a look at her wardrobe. We have a T-shirt, black jeans, and blue flats. What do we think about that?"

I wished I could tell her what I thought about her bleach-blonde hair and heavy strokes of MAC blush, but I just stood there with all those eyes on me.

The woman I had been sitting next to raised her hand. "Depending on where she's going, she'll want to change her outfit. Black is good, but if we see pockets, that means they're jeans material. The T-shirt is too casual. She should only wear T-shirts when she is at home. Maybe she could wear a nice blouse and some earrings and liven up her hair. That would show she cared a bit more."

"Excellent!" Mrs. Williams said. "But how about what you don't see? Women should wear a full bodysuit in place of individual undergarments to keep everything nicely packed in. Even though Ms. Hopkins may not think she needs it, all women can use a little help." She took out her agenda. "Good start, class, let's move along. Ms. Hopkins, you can sit down."

I returned to my seat, scooting in my chair. It creaked against the floor. If only I'd known Mrs. Williams taught this class, I would never have agreed to come. *Full bodysuit?* This was so degrading.

For the next hour, Mrs. Williams went through every utensil at our mock dining table, passing out diagrams for us to take home and study. We practiced eating toast with our hands in the cleanest way possible, as well as soup, salad, and a small piece of steak. It was like assembling a bomb; if you moved any piece incorrectly, it was likely to explode. At least, it seemed to make Mrs. Williams explode.

I was just finding success with the angle of the knife against the medium-rare piece of meat when she snuck up behind me and tapped me with her knuckles, hard on the shoulder. I frowned up at her.

"Excuse me?" I asked, though my first impulse was to say something less polite.

"Posture!" she barked. "Sit up when you are eating or talking. And do not cross your legs at the knee. It should always be at the ankles."

She went around the room to deliver the same message, but everyone else took that thump on my shoulder as their warning and sat up firmly in their chairs before she could get to them. I straightened my back, trying to position my arms in the right way to cut the slab of non-seasoned meat.

At a signal from Mrs. Williams, several female staff members cleared their table. They kept their faces expressionless, but I couldn't help but think they were also judging me.

Once the food was cleared, Mrs. Williams taught us how to fold our napkins and place them gently on the table.

"Like this." She showed us. "Ms. Hopkins, this should be easy for you. I assume you did a lot of origami back home?"

Astonished, I just stared at her. The woman next to me broke her strictly straight posture to lean toward me. "Oh, I *love* origami. It's so beautiful!"

I refrained my correcting either of them that origami originated in Japan, not Korea.

Once again, Mrs. Williams stood by me to deliver her next announcement. "Everyone, once you're finished, please turn to your neighbor. We are going to practice eye contact and active listening during our small-talk exercises. This is an imperative part of making your first impression."

I turned to the woman next to me. I hoped she wouldn't use this exercise to comment on my clothes again. Up close, her eyes creased when she smiled, and I could see her perfectly drawn-on eyeliner. She was pretty and classy, someone Beverly would probably like.

"The person nearest to the television, you are the listener. The other person, begin a conversation about your last job."

The room buzzed with chatter. My neighbor smiled eagerly. "Hi, I'm Selina Carter, and I—"

"Ms. Hopkins." Mrs. Williams leaned between our chairs. "I know, especially with etiquette, there are usually some cultural differences. Usually, I let people converse and I walk around the room, then we talk about what to improve based on what I'm hearing. But, Ms. Carter," she smiled sweetly toward Selina, "if you notice any oddities, please stop the conversation and let Ms. Hopkins know. I just want everyone to be on the same page."

Selina reached out and touched Mrs. William's arm. "Of course."

"Thank you so much, dear."

Selina turned back in me. "So, in America—"

I slapped the palm of my hand down on the table. Selina's face went slack with surprise.

"Will you excuse me?" I reached down for my bag. "I'm going to use the restroom."

"'I need to use the restroom, *please*,'" Mrs. Williams corrected.

"Whatever." I stumbled away from the table. If I stayed in that room a second longer, I knew I would pass out from lack of oxygen. I burst into the lobby, not even glancing at the cold-eyed receptionist.

The bathroom here was not as fancy as the one at Beverly's mansion, but I found myself doing the same exact thing: sitting on the closed toilet lid, desperately trying to keep the tears from streaming out of my eyes. At last, I stepped out of the stall and went to the sink. I pressed my hands against the granite countertop. No way would I return to that classroom, I decided. This certainty gave my body the freedom to cry itself out, and I stood there shaking.

I looked into the mirror. Streaks of eyeliner racooned my eyes. My mascara was smeared. Mrs. Williams would be wondering what happened to me. I didn't care anymore. I was going to leave this bathroom, walk past the receptionist, and phone Ian. Usually, I hated quitting, but I could not live with regrets, and I knew I would regret it if I walked back in that classroom.

CHAPTER NINETEEN

Apron. Keys. Notepad. Extra ponytail holder. I patted my black jeans and black Poseidon shirt again, thinking I had everything. I unzipped my purse: wallet, cell phone, Tylenol, Mace spray. Backup can of Mace spray. Okay, I was good to go. I looked up at the clock above the TV in the living room. 11:15 am. Perfect. That would give me 10 extra minutes to review tonight's Happy Hour specials. I slipped on my black tennis shoes, hopping on one foot across the condo's slippery wood flooring, and then opened the front door.

"Ah!" I took a step back, hand on my chest, catching my breath. Beverly stood right in front of me. She had been looking for her keys in her bag when I opened the door.

"You beat me to it," Beverly said.

I stared at her. With her sunglasses on top of her head, an off-the-shoulder top with linen pants, she looked like she had just gotten back from a beach resort.

"Beverly. I thought ... you were going to Europe?" I hadn't come down from my shock enough to hide my disappointment.

"Decided not to. I didn't feel like spending nine hours cooped up in a plane, and St. Tropez is getting so passé."

She pushed past me, dragging her beach bag along like she owned the place. Which, she did. She removed her espadrille platform sandals, setting them in the three-tiered silver shoe cabinet by the door. She stood in the entrance gazing around the condo. I followed her eyes.

The condo was a designer's dream. It had spectacular panoramic views of Central Park through floor-to-ceiling windows. The ceilings themselves were 11 feet high, which made the condo seem even more massive. The beautiful open kitchen had only European-brand commercial-grade stainless steel appliances, and it opened up to an enormous living and dining area. The L-shaped plush couch was a light taupe, and the two modern black leather arm chairs across from it contrasted with the large, colorful impressionist paintings hanging on the walls. It boasted three guest bedrooms, plus a master suite to the right of the living room. The master bedroom had two large French doors, and it featured a walk-in closet the size of our kitchen back in L.A. Halmuni would have probably said this condo was better than all the "after" pictures of renovated homes she had seen on HGTV.

Beverly took out a cotton handkerchief and blew her nose. She then moved to the shelves opposite the couch. Reaching up on her tiptoes, she wiped off the shelf with her hand. "I'm sensitive to dust, and my nose is telling me you have not dusted. I'm guessing that you couldn't find the duster?"

I swallowed, eyeing the opened front door. I had only 10 minutes to be at Poseidon on time. To Sophia, *officially late.*

Beverly approached the powder room, and I followed, hoping Ian did not make a mess when he rushed out earlier this morning. She found the hand towels in disarray around the sink counter and tissues on the floor. She picked up one with a look of disgust.

"Kelly. *You* need to make sure you clean properly. This is really unacceptable." She dropped it into the waste bin with a frown before inspecting the next room.

Oh, no. *The bedroom.* Ian and I had been tossing dirty clothes on the floor instead of using the hamper because we'd both been so exhausted from work. My suitcase was still open on the floor, rows of folded shirts splayed out for easy grabbing.

"Look at this mess. How can you live like this? There are clothes all over the place," said Beverly, clearly annoyed. "You are a guest in this house, and as a guest, there are certain protocols you must follow, such as making an effort to keep the place clean."

"Oh, yes, I was going to pick up. I'm usually a neat person; it's just been hard to find time to unpack with work—"

"And etiquette school?"

My breath caught in my throat. Beverly smiled slyly, waiting for me to fess up. Refusing to take the bait, I silently followed her to the kitchen.

Six leather and chrome bar stools framed the marble island in the gourmet kitchen's center. The fridge was massive with two large steel doors, and the commercial-grade appliances were all state of the art.

Beverly grabbed a bottle of mineral water from the fridge and then a Ridel water glass from one of the cabinets, checking the inside for stains before filling it. She turned her attention to me as if she expected an explanation. I just looked at her.

"Mrs. Williams told me you haven't been going to class." She dumped the water in the sink. "Ugh, I can taste the soap." She rinsed out the glass. "I expect you'll be back tomorrow. After all, how will it look if you don't follow through on your promises?" She set the glass down, and then riffled through the fridge, re-sorting my eggs and milk. *Why?*

"Also, 'neat' is different than 'clean.' This house is neither."

I looked at the clock again. Officially late. I jingled the keys in my hand.

"Am I keeping you from something?" She closed the fridge, keeping one hand on the handle.

"I'm going to be late for work."

"Ah. That's why you're dressed like that." She took a seat on one of the bar stools, her olive tan enhanced by the lamp. She waved her hand at me. "Well, I won't keep you."

I squeezed the strap of my purse to prevent her from seeing me shaking. If she noticed, she didn't say anything. Removing her iPad, she began scrolling with her perfectly manicured thumbnail.

"I'm really sorry about the mess. I promise to clean it up when I get back from work."

"Kelly, do you know how many times you have told me you're sorry? I don't need your apologies. I just need you to do things right."

I almost said "sorry" again but caught myself.

I walked quickly in the other direction, closing my bedroom door on my way out. Praying she wouldn't go through my private things. Secretly knowing she would.

* * *

As I ran into the restaurant, breathless, Sophia looked up from her shift schedule. "You're late."

"I bumped into Beverly Anderson." I hoped this might warrant the tiniest bit of sympathy.

She remained impassive. "You're tables six through 10. You already got someone at seven. Ask if they want a drink."

I started off.

"You going to clock in, scatterbrain?"

"Right," I breathed, stabbing the POS system beside her. *Have a great day!* popped up after I clocked in. I hated that thing.

I still felt shaken from Beverly. It was amazing how just ten minutes with someone could revert you into an eight year old on the playground, flailing to control your emotions. And now it was affecting my work. My customer at table seven wanted a Diet Coke. I got him a Sprite. I confused sweet and sour sauce with French dressing. Forgot to ring someone out for Happy Hour. One mistake per shift and you were human. Any more and Sophia stalked you.

When one of the chefs handed me my customer's salads, I cringed. *Damn.* I forgot to request no wonton strips. I hated that feeling: the moment you realize you messed up but have no one to blame but yourself.

Sophia must have sensed me choking because she stopped me in the kitchen. "What is going on with you today? Do you need to go home?"

"I'll do better. I'm just off."

Sophia's nostrils flared. Not a good sign. My stomach hurt. I needed this job. She pushed the salad back to the expo line. "No wantons." She turned to me. "I'll get this. Take your 10. Then come back with your head on straight."

My mouth was dry. "Okay," I squeaked.

I holed up in the lounge at the little table where we would sneak off to wolf down employee-discounted food in between customers. I flung myself into a black plastic chair and typed out my S.O.S. text to Ian.

"So your mom is back. She came in when I was heading to work and told me how messy everything was. She was really upset."

I pressed send. I didn't care anymore. He responded immediately.

"What?!? I'm so sorry. I didn't think she'd stick around. Let me talk to her."

I sighed as I pressed my thumbs into my temples. I didn't know what to do. Ian's talking to her might just make it worse—on both of us. Plus, I hated bothering him with this, knowing he was busy interning at the human rights advocacy firm. I counted to five, breathing in and out, trying to calm myself.

Something was eating at me. And it wasn't Beverly. It was myself.

* * *

I wore the outfit Beverly had bought me for my return to etiquette school. I let the shoulders of the narrow blazer constrict my movements, hoping this might ground me. I pretended I was walking into a professional office, keeping my chin up as I nodded coolly to the receptionist. Then, I padded along that stupid purple carpet again in my stylish, yet very uncomfortable, new shoes. That's who I would be today—Ms. Professional. I wouldn't let Mrs. Williams criticize me for my outfit again. Tamping down my anxiety, I opened the door with my best attempt—at feigning confidence.

Mrs. Williams looked at me in surprise. The same people from the first class lined the chairs. A vacant spot near the front was still open, taunting me.

"Ms. Hopkins returns," Mrs. Williams said from behind her lectern.

"Hello. Good day, everyone." I sat down, crossing my legs at my ankles underneath the table. The class quieted and looked at me.

Today, the discussion was about afternoon tea etiquette. Mrs. Williams was showing everyone the proper way to stir their cups. Everyone in the class watched her intently as she said, "Never ever stir in a circular motion. You must stir in an up and down motion—12 o'clock position in the cup and then down to 6 o'clock—and only two to three times. And do not, repeat, *do not* dunk your biscuits in the tea! Now, everyone practice."

Mrs. Williams approached me. "I have to say, this is quite unprecedented. Someone misses etiquette training for days, then shows up without any communication."

"I had a lot going on—"

"Not to mention the fact the last time you graced us with your presence, you disappeared to the restroom without another word. Is that the sign of a person with proper etiquette skills?"

The room felt like it was closing in on me. "I'm here now."

Mrs. Williams' expression didn't change in the slightest. "And it looks like you're already forgetting your manners." She harshly tapped me on the shoulder again. "Posture! Chin up, shoulders down."

As I straightened, I happened to notice that twenty-something female with long, brown hair. She gave me a small, sympathetic smile. Before I could return it, Mrs. Williams was onto something else. "Now, Ms. Hopkins, since you've missed so much of our program, I'm sure you wouldn't mind being a demonstrator again?"

Seriously?

She motioned for me to join her at the podium. "You'll absorb more information this way."

I rose to my feet. "That would be fine."

Here we go again.

* * *

I welcomed Saturday with open arms. Embraced it. It was my 21st birthday. Sophia gave me the day off, and I didn't have etiquette school. This allowed me to savor my freedom. Well, and to study. At Columbia, if you didn't start preparing for your fall classes in July, you were setting yourself up for failure.

Enjoying a few minutes of birthday liberty, I went through my Facebook wall, "liking" each birthday post from the high school acquaintances who barely spoke to me. Even Halmuni figured out how to write something. *Is she getting better at social media?* I thanked her for sending a pic of Christopher Hemsworth as Thor mouthing "Happy Birthday," then went back to my *Philosophy of Ethics* textbook.

Despite the occasional Facebook distraction, studying with the sun streaming through the beautiful glass windows gave me motivation. I sat at the kitchen table with my back to the fridge, gazing at the tips of skyscrapers as Ian's shared playlist pumped through my Bluetooth speakers. Acoustic guitar and a man's folksy, relaxing voice filtered in.

I was just clicking onto a new tab to research a professor's background when I heard the door click open. The only other people who had a key were

Ian—and Beverly. I heard a woman's voice and sank in my chair.

"Do you see what I mean?" I heard Beverly's laugh trickle in.

Holding onto my mug of lemon tea, I walked across the living room, hyper aware of my pajamas and fluffy slippers. *Is dropping in going to be a daily thing?* I began to wish I had sublet that closet of a loft with Melissa. Though ludicrously small, it still offered privacy.

Beverly and a middle-aged sturdy looking woman in black jeans and a grey T-shirt stood in the doorway, buckets of cleaning supplies at their feet.

"Hi," I said, holding my mug close for protection.

"This is Lynette. She's been with me since before Ian was even born. Lynette, this is Kelly, Ian's friend."

I held onto the mug with one hand, while thrusting out the other assertively, like Mrs. Williams taught us. "*Girlfriend.* Nice to meet you."

"You, as well, Miss Kelly," Lynette nodded. She had kind eyes.

"Kelly, I brought Lynette here to teach you how to clean. Lynette, call me when you're done, and I'll have Franco pick you up." Beverly put on a pair of Chanel sunglasses and then walked out.

Once the door was shut, Lynette set the cleaning supplies against the wall. "Miss Kelly, I just want you to know I usually don't do this. Usually, my clients go about their day while I clean. But Miss Anderson was, well, insistent."

"It's not your fault. Do you want some water or tea or anything?"

"No, thank you. Should we start with the living room?"

"Sure." I set my mug down on the nearest surface and rubbed my hands together. "This will be my birthday present."

She started to hand me a duster, then stopped. "Oh, dear. Today is your birthday?"

"Yeah, but it's okay." I glided the fuzzy duster on one of the shelves, lifting up my mug.

Lynette came over. "Do it like this." She took the duster from me and flicked her wrist back and forth, revealing a shinier surface underneath. She grabbed a spray can from her bag. "Then use this finisher."

I used a white cloth to wipe down the finisher. "So you've worked for Beverly for a while?"

She paused. "She didn't always used to be this way. She changed after her husband passed."

I gave her back the cloth, now covered in grime.

"Let's do the bathroom and bedroom next. Here, put this on." She gave me a respirator mask before pulling out a spray can. She spoke through her shield. "This liquid is an Anderson family secret. I have a hunch it's a secret because it can kill you. But, man, does it get toilets clean."

I smiled through my mask. I never thought I'd spend my 21st birthday on the floor of the bathroom, wiping bathtubs and cleaning toilets. But at least Lynette made it endurable. After cleaning the toilet bowl, I leaned back against the bathtub to take a break. Cleaning was exhausting. I had no idea how Lynette did it every single day. *How would I ever manage it even once a week to measure up to Beverly's standards?*

"Hey, birthday girl. You're half my age." Lynette sponged the bottom of the toilet. "If I can keep going, so can you."

I pushed myself up to polish the handles of the tub. Removing the rug from the linoleum floor, I laid it outside the hallway. Then I pushed the mop back and forth, catching strands of hair and pencil shavings from my eyeliner.

"You said Beverly wasn't always 'this way.' What'd you mean by that?"

Lynette flushed the toilet. "I mean, she's always been uptight. But after Mr. Anderson died, everything got worse. Not with me. But I've seen a big shift in how she treats other people."

"So I shouldn't take it personally that she hates me?"

Lynette lowered the toilet lid and peeled off her rubber gloves. "Ian is the world to her, especially now that her husband is no longer around. She just wants to protect him."

"I wish I could find a way to relate to her," I said wishfully.

"Hon, you probably will never be able to relate to her. You and her are made from different cloth. You just have to give her what she wants. Always remember she is used to getting her way. This includes the way she decorates her homes, the way she dresses, the way her housekeepers clean, and also who her son dates. Just keep trying to give her what she wants. I'm telling you, she really doesn't like it when people talk back to her. So if you really love Ian, then tell Ian what is going on, be honest with him, but keep your mouth shut when you are with her.' Just look pretty and say, 'Yes, Beverly.'"

"Okay, got it."

I stopped mopping. Looking at Lynette, I wished I had her courage and resolve. "You kind of remind me of my mom."

"That a good thing?"

"Yes," I said, laughing a little. "A very good thing. I miss her a lot."

"Well, I have an eight year old at home. I think once you're a mom to one, you become a mom to a lot. Now pick up that mop and get to it."

I chuckled. "Yes, ma'am."

* * *

"It's perfect!" I reassured Ian. I sat down at the kitchen table across from Ian and the bags of takeout he brought. He had gotten all of my favorite Korean dishes, a bottle of red wine, and two cupcakes with chocolate frosting and rainbow sprinkles.

"Work ran late again. Otherwise, I could have taken you to a really nice restaurant. But I figured this was the next best thing."

"You do know what I like. Soon Du Bu, Kimbap and Kalbi on rice!" Actually, I preferred Korean take-out over any fancy restaurant hands down.

"For the wine, I know I should've let you have the enjoyment of *buying* your first bottle of wine yourself now that you're officially 21, but I still wanted to surprise you."

"No, no, I love it. Besides, I wouldn't even know what to buy." I eagerly poured the food into separate bowls, realizing just how ravenous I was from all the cleaning.

Ian turned on some soft music from his phone as he dimmed the kitchen lamps. "It looks so clean in here. Did Lynette come by?"

"Um." I grabbed us both chopsticks and spoons and dug into the Kalbi. "Lynette came by. But she actually taught me how to clean."

"You mean you asked her?"

"No." I tentatively put a spoonful of soft rice in my mouth. "Your uh, mom, came by again. And told Lynette to teach me how to clean properly."

Ian put his piece of Kimbap down. "Wait. What?"

Lynette was right. I needed to be honest with Ian. I had to tell him how I was struggling with Beverly. "Look. I didn't want to say anything, but your mom is driving me insane. I want her to like me, but I don't know what to do. Whatever I do, it never seems good enough for her."

I felt tears forming. Worse, I felt so stupid for saying this, like a spoiled brat. He put his arms around my shoulders, and I buried my head in his shoulder. "Babe, I'm so sorry. You should just tell me this stuff. Actually, I should have suspected it was too good to be true. My mom has never been an easy person to deal with. Look. I'll make it up to you."

"It's okay—"

"No, come on." He gently took my arm and led me out of the kitchen, punching up the volume of the music on the way out.

"What are you doing?"

He pulled me closer to him, walking toward the bedroom. "I said I'd make it up to you."

He turned off the bedroom light. Then he walked over, kissed me, and pulled my shirt up over my head. "Didn't you say you wished you got more massages?"

He led me onto the bed and told me to close my eyes. I heard him open a lotion bottle and rub it on his hands. The room filled with the smell of lavender. I loved the bed's comfy softness and breathed in the clean, fresh sheets as I relaxed. The next thing I knew, I felt his warm hands on my back. I melted into the mattress, forgetting about everything—etiquette school, cleaning, Beverly.

I just let myself drift away under his loving touch.

CHAPTER TWENTY

I scrolled through Netflix for the umpteenth time. I could barely move. TV was my only realistic option. Using what little strength I had, I sat up on the couch, reaching for the Kleenex box. Another episode of *MasterChef Junior* sailed across the screen. Why I was torturing myself watching food shows when I couldn't keep anything solid down, I couldn't say. Maybe it was because the kids were so adorable.

I blew my nose, emitting an almost cartoonish *honk!*, then let myself sink back into the couch's recesses, the ache in my neck and back flaring up. Yesterday, it was my stomach; today, my whole body hurt. Turning over on my side, I wrapped the blanket tightly around me. Maybe tomorrow it wouldn't feel like I had shards of glass in my throat each time I swallowed. Maybe tomorrow the throbbing pressure in my ears would ebb. Maybe.

The key turned in the lock, and my breath quickened. I craned my neck to see who it was. *Please be Ian, be Ian, be Ian.* I saw a large, non-manicured hand open the door. Phew. He walked in, sporting one of his flannels and a take-out bag, one of my most favorite sights in the world.

"Hey, how you feeling?"

Too tired to pause the show, I laid my head back on the couch. "Still dying."

Proving beyond any doubt he was a good boyfriend, Ian sat down beside me, rubbing my feet over the blanket. "I brought some soup. Chicken noodle."

"Thank you." I blew into another tissue, then curled up even further, hiding half of my face with the cream knit sofa throw. Why was it that the worse I felt, the better he looked? He wore a fitted charcoal suit accentuating his lean frame. A simple black tie hung over his starched white shirt. I had no problem at all picturing him as a high-powered attorney making partner, landing his own corner office overlooking the island.

"Are you gonna stay with me?" I said in my raspy, nasally voice.

"Wish I could, but I gotta get back. Things are heating up with that mosque case I told you about. Not even supposed to be taking a lunch break we're so swamped."

Did I mention he was a good boyfriend?

"Right, right. Back to saving the world."

Ian shook his head. "More like filling out paperwork. But it's good experience."

I put my feet on his lap. "Save some trees. Stay and keep me company. Please?"

He gently removed my feet and got up off the couch. "I'll be back afterwards, sickie. Just fall asleep to the soothing voice of Gordon Ramsey, and I'll be back before you know it."

I sat up. Too fast. It felt like all the blood went directly to my forehead. I felt dizzy and debated bolting to the toilet before anything serious happened.

"Woah, careful. I got this." He took off the lid of the soup and gave me a spoon. "Here."

The smell only increased my nausea, so I had to wave him away.

He put it down and kissed me on top of my head. "I'll be back, okay?"

"Okay."

I didn't dare turn my head to watch him go. I kept staring at the floor until I heard the door shut. Then I fell backward waiting for the room to stop spinning. I took some cold syrup—the one that knocks you out. Sometime later, I was half-awake, half dreaming I was a kid again. My mother stood over me as she gently nudged me into the tub of steaming water. I tried to tell her I didn't want shampoo—it seeped into my eyes—when a creaking sound tore me away.

"Ian?"

I slowly looked over. *No no no no no.*

"Hello, Kelly." Beverly strode in, this time wearing black skinny jeans with a white blouse and hot pink pumps.

"Hi, Mrs. Anderson," I croaked. I wish she didn't just come and go as she pleased. It was nerve-racking. I did a quick mental survey of my surroundings. If she thought the place was messy before, she must be revolted now. I was too weak to pick the pile of clothes off the floor, dirty pans overflowed the sink, and the leftover take-out containers were still scattered atop the kitchen's island. "How many times do I have to tell you to call me Beverly? And you look absolutely dreadful." She gazed down at me with a look of insolence.

"Yeah, I *feel* terrible." I tucked a sweaty strand of hair behind my ear. I hadn't looked in the mirror once today; I probably did look terrible.

"Mrs. Williams told me you quit class again."

Jesus. Did that woman have anything better to do than gossip about me?

"I'm not quitting. I just couldn't get out of bed today."

"I can see that." Beverly flopped onto the leather armchair, flipping through one of the many architectural magazines that stacked up here every week. "What's the problem, exactly?"

My problem is you won't leave me alone. No matter how many times your son asks you.

"Fever."

"How high?"

"101."

Beverly dropped the magazine with a very audible scoff. "Oh, please, that's practically a normal temperature. Ian used to get 104 fevers as a child, and he still wanted to go play outside."

I closed my eyes, trying to hold down the nausea creeping up my throat. "Well, I also didn't want to get other people sick. That didn't seem like good etiquette to me."

"Nice try." She laughed. "We gotta toughen you up, hon'!"

I glanced over at her, unconcerned my eyes were probably leaking contempt. I could barely lift my arm to grab more medicine, let alone humor her.

"Oh, don't look at me like that. Women need to be prepared for everything. You never know what this world will throw at you. You need to be strong. I'm sure you are making Ian worried. He has to work, so you shouldn't bother him with your small cold."

"It's the flu!" I shot back, using what little energy reserves I still had.

God, why is she even here? Why won't she just leave?

"Perhaps you're not getting the nutrients you need. Korean food is just rice and beef, right? Oh, and that horrible smelling, red cabbage thing. Not a very balanced diet, is it?"

I couldn't take it anymore. Whatever inhibitions I'd had before had been broken down, along with the rest of my influenza-wracked body.

"You are a horrible person," I heard myself say. "I've let you get away with saying nasty things to me because you are Ian's mom, but I've had enough. You are mean and selfish and petty and rude and ignorant. I can't believe Ian is your son." My face was flushed with anger and once I finished, I realized what I had done. OMG, I wish I could take back what I said—at least the last bit.

Beverly sat still and put her magazine down. Not saying one word. The silence was painful. With a rising sense of panic, I didn't know what to do, so I just stared at the TV. We said nothing as three eager kids stirred batter and fried meat on screen, racing against the clock, while Gordon Ramsay looked on critically from the distance.

At last, Beverly broke the silence. "See that girl over there?" She pointed to the TV. "She's so careless with that breadcrumb mix. It's because she doesn't know what she is dealing with. She may think she can stir the breadcrumbs that way, but she doesn't realize that this one mistake will cost her everything." She said it slowly in a steady way that scared me.

"I ... I'm sorry. I wasn't thinking. I didn't mean it that way. I want to get along with you, but it's just been so hard," I said, my voice wracked with regret.

She got up. "There you go again, with your 'sorries.'" She glared at me. "You say I'm ignorant? Look at the way you dress, the way you talk. *That* is ignorant. And I don't like any of it. You don't belong with Ian. He deserves better. Someone civilized and accomplished. Let's see who ends up winning, shall we?"

Winning? Was this a competition? Suddenly it dawned on me that perhaps she was highly competitive. I mean, super-competitive. She must have felt she was competing with me for Ian's love. For a second, I wondered if that was the reason Ian's dad had such anger issues. *Was he duking it out daily with his wife?*

"I meant ... you don't know how the rest of the world lives. Most of us barely have enough to live on ...," I whispered, gently wishing that I could just go back in time and take back everything I said.

"ENOUGH!" she said and with that, Beverly grabbed her purse from the chair and stormed out.

I started sobbing. She hates me. I shouldn't have said what I said. *But, what do I do now? Should I just give up? Should I end my relationship with Ian?* I reached down under the table and grabbed his iPad, pushing on the Skype button. I put my knees up and propped it on my legs, feeling better just from the sound of the Skype dial tone. Pretty soon, I saw the edges of our bird-themed wallpaper in the living room, along with Halmuni's face—mostly.

"Hola, Kelly!" Halmuni yelled. I could tell she was reclining in her chair from the weird tilted angle.

"How are you, Halmuni?"

"Better than you! You look terrible. You crying?"

I sniffled. "No, no. I just have the flu."

"If I there, I take care you. Where Ian?"

"He's at work. But he's been super sweet."

"He get you soup?"

"Yes. And he even went on his lunch break to get here from downtown."

"What kind soup? Korean chicken ginseng soup?"

"No, Halmuni. Chicken noodle." I propped up another pillow behind my head so it wouldn't hurt my neck so much. "Although I do miss your ginseng tea."

"Yes. Always perfect amount honey."

In my mind's eye, I saw Halmuni sitting up with me, running the shower so the steam would thin out my coughs. How I wished she were here with me right now.

"I miss you so much."

Halmuni smiled her Halmuni smile, showing the gap between her front teeth. I could almost feel her rough sandpapery hand on my head, her hot breath against my ear. Even though it always smelled like cabbage, it had a calming effect on me. She was the one who squeezed me in her tight hug and made me feel safe.

"How crazy lady?"

I had told Halmuni about Ian's mom on multiple occasions. After describing her in a way that matched the cast of *Real Housewives of Beverly Hills*, she had a clear image in her mind and loved discussing her antics.

"Please don't call her that. I'm already having enough problems with her. Beverly came today. Said I should 'toughen up.' And I got so angry at her I said some mean things I probably shouldn't have."

Halmuni grunted. "First of all, if anyone gonna tell you toughen up, who do you think it be?"

I smiled. "You."

"Yes. You running fever, your body telling you something. Now tell me, what you say to her?"

"Well, I told her that she is mean and selfish and ignorant."

"Ha! Sounds like just what that crazy woman needed to hear. I'm happy you say that."

"No, Halmuni, this isn't good. Now she'll never approve of me, and it puts Ian in an uncomfortable position. Should I just give up and end it with him because his mom hates me so much?"

Just then, my phone buzzed on the counter. It was Ian. He had sent a GIF of an orangutan falling off a swing set. *"I know you feel like this right now but it will get better."*

I smiled at the GIF, but tears swelled. My life seemed so much more complicated now, but life without Ian seemed so dark and empty.

"You thinking stupid. If you love him, who care what his crazy mom says? Hey, why you not looking at me?" said Halmuni.

"Ian just sent me something."

"Kelly, you need to stand up for yourself. Be like *Housewives*. They tear each other's hair, rip clothing. Very strong. Be more like that."

"Yeah, cause that's totally me."

"You are in New York now. Say it changed you."

"Look, I want Beverly to actually *like* me. But maybe you're right, why should I care what she thinks of me?" I put my phone down and looked back at Halmuni, who had now reclined all the way back in her chair, playing with her tablet. "Halmuni. Please—stop tilting it. You're making it worse."

She tried to sit up and must have dropped the tablet because now I had a perfect view of our ceiling. Still, Halmuni kept talking like nothing had happened. "Who care about crazy lady? Why you even want her to like you? She dumb for not like you already. Watch *Real Housewives*. Then you learn about Beverly. And Mrs. — what's her name? The other crazy lady with stupid bag?"

"Mrs. Williams. Lovely Mrs. Williams."

"I don't know why you need to learn more manners. Me and your mom taught you enough."

"This is the One Percent kind of manners."

"Why you need to learn when only one percent?"

I chuckled. "Goodbye Halumni."

"LOL."

I chuckled. "Love you, too."

I ended the call and put the iPad back on the table, picking up the remote. I went back to the master list of all the streaming devices the Andersons paid for and clicked on the search icon. I already felt ashamed but I started typing anyway. R-e-a-l...

CHAPTER TWENTY-ONE

I thought I felt happy after my high school graduation, but graduating from etiquette school made me positively ecstatic. I no longer had to see Mrs. Williams or endure her "teaching tactics" for three hours a day. More important, I proved her wrong. I showed her I could present myself just as well as everyone else in class.

The final day lasted only an hour and included a mini awards ceremony, during which we each received a Certificate of Completion. Demonstrating our new poise in action, we had to properly stand up and carry ourselves toward Mrs. Williams' waiting hand.

We posed as we shook it, looking her directly in the eye just as we were taught. Maybe it was the hired photographer snapping photos of us dressed in our smartest outfits, or Mrs. Williams' solemnity about the whole thing, but it all made me feel like I was back in grammar school performing for adult approval.

As might be expected, Mrs. Williams called my name last. I smoothed out my knee-length, black skirt under the table before approaching her with the cardstock paper in front of my chest. With fancy scrolled font and my name plugged into the middle, it looked like any generic certificate. I imagined shoving it into the bottom of one of my drawers as soon as this was over.

"Beverly is an old friend of mine," said Mrs. Williams out of the side of her mouth as the camera's flash bulb popped. "She told me to go hard on you. But you didn't crack."

I smiled in spite of my anger, teeth showing, my cheeks uncomfortably stretched. I was about to return to my seat when she caught me by the shoulder.

"I used to think Asians lacked manners. I mean, look at how quickly they eat. But you proved me wrong. I'm happy you made it through."

Made it through. That was an accurate description. Part of me wanted to tell her the real definition of etiquette was being sensitive to others. That preening and sitting with your shoulders back didn't qualify you for acceptance into society. What really mattered was how you treated people, especially those who had every reason to feel uncomfortable for any number of reasons: their class, their race, their innocent mistakes.

Instead, I said nothing. I returned to my seat, the edges of the certificate dampening from the sweat on my fingers. I put my hands in my lap, wiping my palms on my skirt beneath the table.

"Congratulations, graduates." Mrs. Williams gushed. "Feel free to enjoy the refreshments."

Excused at last from the formal ceremony, my fellow professionally-dressed cohorts made their way to the buffet line. I watched as they carefully selected their tiny plates of mixed fruit and chocolate chip cookies, daintily sipping from china tea cups. They all looked depressingly uniform, like a bunch of robots.

Walking over, I stood behind the ponytailed woman who always gave me sympathetic smiles in response to Mrs. Williams' criticisms. I knew I was supposed to use my new skills to effortlessly mingle, but I just wanted to leave. Why couldn't Mrs. Williams have taught us polite exit strategies out of uncomfortable social situations? Excusing oneself to the bathroom then sneaking off wasn't approved, so what else was there?

When it was my turn at the refreshments table, I carefully used the tongs to place a few raspberries and slice of pineapple onto my white fine bone china plate. Putting my napkin beneath my plate like I had been taught, I approached Mrs. Williams. Mustering all of my courage, I prepared my remarks. I was going to tell her she was a bigot, a hypocrite, a phony.

"Yes?" The deep ridges between her eyes creased.

I shakily extended my hand. "Thank you for everything."

Walking away from the group of perfectly composed graduates, I placed my plate on top of the table and headed for the door.

* * *

It was mid-summer, and I still hadn't gotten used to being away from home. Still, Skyping with Halmuni every week helped ground me, especially whenever I felt overwhelmed by school or work. For someone else, it might've felt like a dream to live in a multi-million-dollar condo in the Upper East Side rent-free, but I could never get comfortable here. It wasn't just the random drops-ins or the cleaning tutorials or *re-tutorials;* it was the overwhelming sense I didn't belong and never would. I wasn't a resident or tenant. I was a guest and could expect to be barged in on at any time or kicked out for any reason.

Homesickness haunted me. As I lay perched on the windowsill overlooking Central Park and the crush of honking motorists, joggers, dog-walkers, and power-walking executives from day to day, nagging questions ran through my head. Once you left your hometown, I wondered, did every place feel temporary? Maybe transitioning to adulthood meant finally finding your identity apart from a location, achieving permanence when everything appeared so temporary.

Tonight, it was quiet. August had blanketed the city in a sweltering cloud of humidity and sweat. Most of the usual crowd below had retreated to their air-conditioned apartments and condos and co-ops, and even the cars pushing their way up to the blinking traffic lights seemed sluggish.

Ian had been invited to a meet-and-greet networking thing to help entice donors to the ACLU's defense fund, and Sophia had given me the night off. Even though I had recovered from my flu, I retreated to chill mode, curling on the couch with my laptop perched above the cozy grey blanket.

I instinctively clicked on Facebook, not because I enjoyed glimpsing my distant relatives' fantastic meals, but because it was mindless. I could skim over pictures and videos at my own pace as I vegged out.

My finger stopped suddenly when I saw Beverly's post.

It always saddens me there are people in this world who still feel the need to take advantage of others' hard-earned work instead of working themselves. Instead of pretending to be something they're not, wouldn't it be best if they just showed their true colors?

I read the post three times, feeling an extra lump in my throat. Unless she just had a fling with some new gigolo, the only person she could be talking about was me. I clicked on her wall. Reading the posts, my jaw dropped.

So hard as a mother to fully protect your son from others who try to use him— *feeling emotional.

Another:

You'd think, after all these years, people would stop trying to dig for gold!!!

And this:

So proud of my Ian who is interning at a human rights advocacy firm. I only wished he could have someone at his side just as admirable. One day! A single mom can still dream of a 'daughter,' right?

I stabbed at the keyboard, pulling up my messages and finding Melissa's name. Then I screenshotted the posts and sent them.

"WHAT DO I DO??????"

I sat there, reading the posts over and over, waiting for Melissa's reply. I needed advice. I couldn't believe it. I knew Beverly wasn't my biggest fan, and it didn't help that I said some unpleasant things to her recently, but her messages were vindictive jabs at me. She was clearly convinced *I was with Ian for the status and money.*

At last, Melissa's text messages arrived, one after the other, like little bubbles of relief and validation.

"OMG! WTF is her problem?"

"Can she just be a normal person? Ever?"

"Dude. I think you need to tell Ian."

My fingers paused on the keyboard. Ian barely checked Facebook, so I assumed he hadn't seen any of this. That didn't help much. In fact, it made it worse. If I told him, he would probably side with me. Hopefully. But then he would confront his mom, leaving me more vulnerable to Beverly's ire.

On the other hand, he might just defend his mom, especially after I tell him what I said to her. If that happened, I would come across like the complaining, ungrateful girlfriend.

Something, or someone, had to break eventually. I clicked out of Melissa's message box and typed in Ian's name. *"Let's have a picnic lunch tomorrow. I need to tell you something."*

* * *

Ian and I sat under the shade of two oak trees, our legs intertwined. We picked out food from a small blue cooler between us, unwrapping the aluminum foil to get to my hastily thrown together turkey and cheese sandwiches. I had thought about eating something with our hands, especially given Beverly's warnings, but in my rush to prepare our last-minute date, I had just grabbed some meat and cheese I found in the fridge and smacked them between two slightly stale pieces of white bread.

I slowly unwrapped mine, looking over at him. I was restless and fidgety. He was totally calm and didn't seem to mind my picnic was not exactly Zagat-rated. Happily chomping away, he peered out at Central Park's wide pond. Situated below street level, its remoteness muted the urban rumble only a hundred feet away.

Cooler today, a refreshing breeze would swoop in every so often to break up the heat's oppressiveness. I had planned it so we weren't alone. Several other couples and families milled about, some of them feeding crumbs to the waddling ducks. We were only a little ways from the Bethesda Fountain, with its angel overlooking the water. I loved riding my bike here alone. Sometimes, I would stop and study the angel's face, trying to pin a description to her baffling expression.

"So," I began. "You know how your mom and I are Facebook friends now?"

Ian lifted his sunglasses from his eyes and slid them on top of his head. "Is she commenting on every single one of your posts? She'll do that."

"No ... she just posts a lot. About gold-diggers."

Ian turned to me at the mention of that last word.

It was hard to say this. "I get the sense that she's talking about ... me." There. I said it.

Ian didn't respond. Removing his legs from mine, he crumpled up the aluminum foil and tossed it back in the cooler, wiping his hands of crumbs. Oh, gosh. This was terrible. I lamely held onto my own untouched sandwich, wondering if this would be the last time we ever sat together this way. I desperately fought the tears pooling in my eyes. But then he put his arm around me.

"Babe, I had no idea. I think she's going a little crazy because I've never been so ... serious about someone."

I started sobbing uncontrollably. He does love me, I thought.

He squeezed me tighter.

"I ... I also, need to tell you something else." I continued, "She came over when I was sick. She made a bunch of nasty comments about Koreans, so I couldn't help myself. I told her she was a mean and ignorant person and that I couldn't believe that you were her son." I couldn't look at Ian. I felt vulnerable, but I also felt I could breathe again. "Ian, I'm so sorry. I really am. I should never had said those things." I wiped away my tears with the picnic napkins. "But then she went completely nuts and told me she just does not like me and you deserve better than me. Maybe she's right. Maybe I am not good for you." My tears kept coming.

He leaned back on his hands, planting them in the soft grass and looked up toward the sky. He didn't say anything for a while.

"Ian? Can you please say something?" I asked him pathetically.

"Kel, I understand. My mother has always been difficult. I'm really annoyed with her because all I wanted was for the two most important women in my life to get along. But she is used to getting her way. She has an idea of what the perfect woman is for me, and I know the 'type' she likes, but I don't like that 'type.' I've dated someone my mom liked, and she wanted me to marry her, but I felt suffocated." He took my hand and kissed it. "I think the best thing to do is to avoid her for a while. I will try to talk to her, but I'm not sure she will listen to me. I love you, Kelly. And that's all that matters."

Looking out at the still green water, I noticed two ducks fighting over a scrap from someone's burrito. The fatter one used its bill to scare away the other, snatching the prize for itself.

"So... who's the girl you dated that your mom wanted you to marry?" I put the sandwich back in the wrapper. I tried to sound nonchalant, but my stomach was churning. I knew Ian had dated other people before me. But that reality always seemed to float out there in a fog. It was something I avoided thinking about. Now, as I tried to picture those other girls, a pang of jealousy hit me.

He brushed a bug off his shorts. "No one worth mentioning. No one who I wanted to be serious with. Let's not talk about that, okay?"

I wanted to tell him we *should* talk about it, but didn't want to seem jealous or stupid.

"What does it matter? I'm with you now," he said reassuringly.

He made a good point, but it didn't make me feel any better. That knot of jealousy twisted harder in my stomach. When he tried to put his arm back around me, I moved back, outside his reach.

"Fine," he said. "You really want to know? Just a girl without a lot of depth. She was one of those girls who would take 10 minutes to decide which Snapchat filter to use."

His blue eyes flashed sincerity, but I couldn't help thinking about Beverly's post: gold-digger. *Is he just saying this to make me feel better?*

"She was like my mother. She only cared about herself."

The knot eased, and I laid back down on the grass. He fell down next to me, taking my hand. I looked up at the sky, wondering if being "deep" was code for something else. He playfully tangled his foot on my leg.

"You okay?" he asked.

I said yes, but didn't mean it.

* * *

I didn't know why I was doing this to myself again. After my lunch date with Ian, I returned to Facebook. It was like having one of those painful hangnails you just couldn't stop picking at. You knew it was going to hurt when you did it, but you went for it anyway.

I pulled up Beverly's profile, readying myself to read some new tirade. Instead, a photo popped up of a young beautiful woman my age.

I looked closer. Beverly must have posted it today, around the time Ian and I were together. I hovered my mouse over the photo, right above her thin, modelesque face. My heart stopped. I had seen her before. This was the girl I ran into at Thanksgiving who spilled the wine on my blouse! *Was she one of Ian's exes!?*

In the photo, she wore a skin-tight dress, even tighter than the one I wore on my shopping excursion with Beverly. She had black pumps, and her perfectly straightened light brown hair was highlighted with streaks of blonde. I couldn't imagine how long it took her to get ready in the morning. Beverly had an arm around her, and they both leaned into the camera, smiling.

I read the caption. *Ran into this gorgeous lady at Lucky Fashion Show. Still struttin' her stuff! — with Camy Miller.*

Camy's name was in blue, so I clicked on it, going to her own Facebook page. Every photo was professionally shot, featuring her laying on some beach or sitting seductively in a chair, as if she just happened to find one with a photographer nearby. I kept scrolling, hating myself with each click, reading more and more comments. Then my heart stopped on Ian Anderson: "*Beautiful,*" he had written with one of those smiley face emojis with hearts as the eyes. No no no no. *Okay, breathe.* It was time-stamped two years ago.

"A girl without a lot of depth ..." His words rang in my ears. I couldn't help wanting to hide my entire body underneath the blanket. Objectively, I was not nearly as attractive as this person. Maybe he liked my conversation, but there's no way he could get someone who looked like this out of his mind.

I opened up a new tab and Googled her name. Camy even had a Wikipedia page. No wonder Beverly hated me. I read her "Background" and learned she was an international fashion model. Her mother was a renowned dermatologist. Her father was a real estate developer who came from a prominent family. Both of them had their own pages. This was torture. Facebook was bad enough. You should not be able to see a full history of your boyfriend's exes on Wikipedia.

I opened my messaging app again and typed in Melissa's name.

"Can you come over?"

She got back right away.

"I'LL BRING THE ICE CREAM!"

* * *

"Stop looking at Camy's pictures. Click on that." Melissa put the spoon back into her pint of Haagen-Dazs so she could click on the screen for me. The page loaded an article titled: *5 Signs of a Narcissist.*

Melissa sat on the couch, feet up on the table, the laptop shared between our knees, stabbing at our ice cream. She took a scoop of her Vanilla Swiss Almond as I put my Cookie Dough back on the table and scrolled.

Melissa pointed at the screen with her spoon. "That's totally Beverly," she said with a full mouth.

"Perfectionism. Exaggerated need for attention. That's like what she is doing on Facebook. Why else would she post that crap? Okay, keep going … need for control. *Totally* Beverly."

"Yeah …" In my head, I was replaying the scene from Thanksgiving from Ian's perspective. *I literally ran into his ex-girlfriend.*

Melissa pointed at the next article, interrupting my thoughts. "No boundaries! Didn't you say she just like, appears?"

"Uh-huh."

"And look, no empathy! Remember how frickin' vindictive she was to you when you were sick?"

In my head, I was composing my own Wikipedia page: Columbia Undergrad, Etiquette School graduate. *What had I achieved so far? Not much.* "She told me 101 degrees wasn't really a fever."

Melissa jumped up, nearly flinging her spoon across the room. "I told you. Narcissist. Classic case." She clicked on another article.

"I don't know. I mean, it can be dangerous to diagnose like that."

"Dude. She literally matches everything. Look: Can't be vulnerable. Deflection. This is all her."

The timer went off on my phone. I gave her the laptop and picked it up to silence it. "Crap. I have to get ready for work." I had totally forgotten. "You can stay here if you want."

"Call in sick." Putting her ice cream down, Melissa lounged back as if this had already been decided.

"That's lying."

Melissa snorted. "Uh ... so? People do it all the time. Come on, pleeasse? This is so much fun. Ice cream. More WebMD." She waved to the massive flat-screen TV. "Netflix."

I looked down at Melissa: Her hair in a messy ponytail, no makeup, in a T-shirt and sweats she borrowed from me. I looked similar and had no desire to change. It *would* be nice just to take a break from Sophia and lounge. Plus, I had barely gotten to spend time with Melissa all summer.

She picked up my pint of ice cream and moved it in a circle beneath my face. "You ... want to ... stay ... home ... all day ... and do nothing..."

I grabbed it from her and shook my head, smiling. "Okay. Fine."

She clapped her hands together, proud of her accomplishment, then handed me my phone. "Call in sick and make it convincing!"

* * *

"I hate working at the restaurant. I just feel like I shouldn't be here. I mean, I go to Columbia and used to work for B.B. Chu. I should be interning at a law firm, not working at some bar!" I said in a defensive tone.

Onscreen, Halmuni nodded in her recliner. I had spent the last few days goofing off with Melissa and felt bad about it. Now, I needed to talk to my grandmother to get back my rhythm. I also needed to vent. A lot.

"And did I tell you that Ian's exes are freaking fashion models? *Models*, Halmuni. I don't look right, I don't act right, I don't speak right. I just can't do anything right here." I rubbed my temples. "Sometimes I wish I hadn't come here." I looked away from the screen, not wanting to see the disappointment on her face.

"You stupid girl. So what, model, who cares? They can't eat, and they so skinny. After 30, no more job. I could have been model in Korea, but I say NO. No way. I don't give up eating."

I doubted someone ever asked Halmuni to be a model when she was young, but who knows.

"Kelly. You make me so proud. Don't give up on dreams," Halmuni continued. "Don't let fake people get you. You real. You sweet. No other girl so nice, pretty, and smart. You deserve be happy. Don't care about skinny model ex girl. You don't need to compare with anyone else. Enjoy your own life and don't have any regrets. Halmuni loves you. Your parents looking down from Heaven and saying they love you, too."

She was right. But I was starting to wonder if my happiness could possibly include Ian.

CHAPTER TWENTY-TWO

I had decidedly mixed feelings about staying in Beverly's condo. Although it constantly reminded me of her, it did offer me the chance to spend more time with Ian. He came over and spent the night as much as he could. When he worked late, he stayed at his own apartment, which was closer to his office. During the day, when I wasn't working, Melissa and I would hang out and binge-watch Netflix. I think Melissa liked being here even more than at her family's vacation house in the Hamptons. Together, we would munch on yummy junk food while watching old episodes of *Friends* and *Suits*. She also gave me much-needed advice about what to do about Beverly, which basically boiled down to: *Ignore her.*

Since my picnic lunch with Ian, I had managed to avoid Beverly. It had been at least three weeks since, and there was still no sign of her. Ian must have told her to stop coming to the condo unannounced and stop posting offensive comments on Facebook. I was glad I didn't have to deal with the woman, but I felt bad for Ian because I was the one who had caused this rift in his family. I wish I was more like Camy. Beverly would have liked me more if I was sophisticated, famous ... and rich.

I was still trying to get over what Melissa insisted on calling Facebook-Gate. I kept trying to erase the image of beautiful, perfect Camy from my thoughts, but she was never far. Even as I stood over my bed, tucking in the corners of my comforter, the woman haunted me. *Why couldn't I just let her go?* I never thought of myself as the jealous type, yet my relationship with Ian had started to expose all of my flaws. Maybe Beverly was right that I'm not right for Ian. Camy and Ian looked like the perfect couple and would certainly have perfect-looking children.

Finished tucking, I scanned the room. Remnants of Melissa's snacks littered the floor just like when we had dormed together. I was reaching down to pick up one of her empty Red Bull cans when my phone buzzed. The caller ID: Poseidon. Ugh. I hated when they called.

But then I thought about the world's karmic balance and how people had covered for me whenever I had gotten "sick" this summer. I answered in my friendliest voice. "Hi, Sophia."

No greeting. She just launched right into it. "I need you to pick up a dinner shift. 4:30."

But Ian. We were supposed to get together tonight. So much for karma. Let someone else take the shift. "I'm really sorry, but since it's my day off, I already made plans. I don't think I can get there that soon, anyway."

"Make it 5:00 then. I'll take care of your prep duties."

"Yeah, but—"

"Don't even push back on this. I need you here."

Didn't she understand things were tenuous with Ian and me right now? This was not a good time. "The thing is, my boyfriend and I—"

"Don't care. You've missed a lot of work. If you don't come in tonight, don't bother coming back."

Wow. I was glad she wasn't stooping to an ultimatum or anything. I squeezed my eyes shut, letting disappointment wash over me. "I'll be there."

I dove into the laundry basket to find the dirty work clothes I was supposed to wash. I'd just have to douse them in body spray like Melissa did. And Ian would just have to wait.

* * *

I could barely think straight. My mind was awhirl with constant requests for refills of Diet Coke and San Pellegrino. Still, every now and then, Camy would break through my consciousness like a bad penny that kept showing up. Why couldn't I let her go? Maybe I could if Beverly stopped parading her around on Facebook. Every other update featured the two new BFFs.

It took every ounce of personal strength to quash my jealous thoughts from swirling into a nightmarish loop: *Will Beverly ever like me? Why do I care if she likes me or not? Is she right that someone like Camy would be better for Ian than I am? Does Ian even know his mom is palling around with his ex? Should I care? Of course, I should care! What do I do?*

Shaking off my worries, I surveyed the room, watching the flow of well-dressed middle-aged couples and parties of thirty-somethings occupy every available seat. Classic soft rock music filtered in above the groundswell of chit-chat humming throughout the restaurant.

I watched as the newest hostess, a blonde so young looking she could have passed for a high school sophomore, seated me a four-top. The whole family was clad head to toe in MLB gear, including caps and jerseys, leading me to guess they had left early from Yankee Stadium.

I speed walked to the kitchen, avoiding a waiter with too much gel in his hair. Grabbing a quartet of glasses, I filled them with ice and water.

I was halfway back to the table when the barely 18-year-old hostess stopped me. "Hey, that table is complaining they haven't been waited on yet."

I looked back to see a group of middle-aged women peering over their menus, seeking me out. "They must have just got here."

The hostess shrugged. "They're upset."

"Okay. I'll take care of them."

After dropping off the waters, I made a beeline for the problem table. As soon as I saw her, my breath died in my throat, and I dropped my notepad.

Beverly.

Reaching down for the black leather case, I could feel the blood go straight to my cheeks. This couldn't be happening. A bevy of immaculately dressed women gawked at me. All dressed in dark colors, they looked like they were uniformed in accordance with some sorority dress code. In addition, they all had microbladed, perfectly contoured eyebrows, filler-injected plump lips, and botoxed foreheads.

In the middle sat Beverly, the Queen Bee of Manhattan snobbery. Her perfectly quaffed hair fell past her shoulders to form a diagonal "V." A Chanel necklace rested on her black sheer silk blouse. As her lipsticked mouth formed into the beginnings of a cruel smile, I realized this would be one of those moments I would have to endure—*to get through.*

No way this was an accident. Beverly had shown up here on purpose. To torture me.

"Kelly! So you're the reason we've been waiting." Beverly gazed back at her friends with a flourish of her arms to indicate me. "Everyone, this is Ian's little friend."

How many times must she get this wrong? "Hello, actually, I'm Ian's *girlfriend,*" I corrected her.

"Yes, well." Beverly's smile stayed plastered on her beautiful face. She turned to her friends, "They're sleeping together, but honestly girls, if they were serious, why would Ian ask me to stay away from her?" Her friends looked appalled at such a thought and stared intently at me with disapproving looks. I felt like I was a puppy in a shelter and they were trying to ascertain whether they thought I was a well-behaved, cute puppy or one of the ugly, untrainable mutts no one takes home. I could tell from their looks that they thought I was the latter.

I ignored her snide comment and tried to remain calm and professional. "May I take your drink orders, please?"

Beverly tapped at the laminated menu with a long, French-manicured nail. "Get your pen ready, dear. We already know what we want."

Small chuckles chorused around the table. I imagined them all coming out of a cloning machine, each with the same tastes and thoughts. *East Coast Stepford Wives.*

"We would like a bottle of this Sauvignon Blanc." She pointed to one of the more expensive bottles in the menu. "For appetizers, two orders of chicken satay. We don't like the peanut sauce, so no need for that. And two orders of Peking Duck rolls. Make sure they don't overdo it with the sauce."

The women nodded their heads in unison. At least they were consistent.

"For mains, bring us eight quinoa kale salads with the miso salmon. Do not overcook the salmon. No quinoa for her and her," she pointed. "They just want the kale and salmon. A bowl of edamame for the table now. Oh, and gluten-free bread for the table. With dipping oil and balsamic. Also, a Diet Coke for Pamela."

I was scurrying to write everything down when I saw the ink fade. *No way. My pen was not dying right now.* I made it to "Quinoa" before I started practically impaling the paper. "I'm sorry ... that was how many kale salads?"

Beverly rolled her eyes and chuckled at the table, like *isn't this hilarious?* Then, she spoke in her trademark slow voice perfected for simpletons like me. "There's eight of us. Therefore, eight salads."

Of course.

"She looks flustered," said a lady who looked like she could be Barbie's mom.

"I'm fine. And that was a Coke?" I said, trying desperately to keep my composure.

"No. A *Diet* Coke."

"Gotcha."

"Kelly, you mean, 'got it', not 'gotcha'. Please use proper language around my friends and not street slang."

I collected all of their menus, trying not to make eye contact with Beverly. "Yes, of course. I'll be right back with—"

"And you will take our menus, right, Kelly?"

"Yes, I was just about to ask you for them," I said through gritted teeth.

I hurried back to the computer, eager to input these orders.

"Ouch!" I felt a sharp pain in my arm.

I turned to see the hostess from before carrying a tray of dirty plates. One of the knives had stuck me. Realizing what had happened, she apologized.

A small bead of blood the size of a ladybug began to form. I dabbed it away. "Just. Be more careful."

She looked genuinely remorseful. Suddenly, I could see myself in her position months ago, trying to get the hang of this job. I wished people had been nicer to me back then. "No, it's okay. I'm just stressed."

"Can I help?"

"That'd be great. Can you grab eight waters and a Diet Coke?"

"Yeah, got it. Also, you have another table on three."

Crap. I hadn't been back to the baseball family yet, and I still needed to swing by the bar for wine. Sophia squinted at me from the hostess stand across the room. No doubt she could tell I was flailing with her hawk eyes.

"You okay?" she mouthed.

I nodded before rushing off. Twenty minutes later, all my tables had been handled in some capacity. With the help of Emily, the hostess, I had delivered their food and drinks. I was standing beside a column formed in the shape of conjoined mermaids, taking a split second break, when I noticed Beverly waving.

Quickly, I darted over, determined not to let her faze me. When I reached the table, she lifted the plate of chicken satays I could barely hold, it was so hot.

"Kelly, honestly, I can't believe you didn't check this before it came out." She pointed to a pink piece of meat. "Do these look cooked to you?"

I silently cursed the kitchen staff. Of all the tables to mess up an order. "Of course not. I'll fix this."

I ran to the kitchen. Just as I slid the plate back over the metal expo line, Emily called out to me. "Hey, just sat you another table."

What? I was already slammed with the big party.

"Okay. Fine. But can you please, please, get them waters?"

It was never a good idea to tell the cooks they made a mistake, but it couldn't be avoided today. I showed

Raul, the nicest one, the undercooked meat. "Can you make it again?"

Raul did nothing. He just stared at the plate like he had never seen one before.

"And please ... HURRY!"

I was just rushing back to refill Pam's Diet Coke when I ran into Sophia. I had never seen her so angry. Her eyes had narrowed into tiny slits of rage.

"Table Three just asked to talk to a manger. *Me.* Because they said they haven't had anyone even take their drink orders in *fifteen minutes*?"

Shit. I completely forgot about them. "I just—"

She put up her hand like she was swinging back for a karate chop. "What did I tell you about mastering time? I had to comp their desserts."

I looked over at Beverly. She was laughing with her friends, enjoying herself. I wanted to stomp over there and slap her across her smug face.

"I'm really trying. Seriously."

"Try harder." Sophia walked around me.

Returning to the kitchen, I waited by the partition between the serving area, pressing my hands on the warm metal. Behind me, I could hear Raul grumbling to the other chefs. *Great.* I just made another enemy.

Sophia appeared out of nowhere. "Two servers already helped you pass out food to Beverly Anderson's table, so I don't know why you're standing there."

She was right. I was feeling sorry for myself. I hadn't thought about Derrick or Emily who had lent me a hand earlier. I hurried to the counter to deliver plates to their tables. There were so many entrees it took me a few minutes. By the time I returned to the kitchen, the re-cooked chicken satays were ready. I thanked Raul, then rushed off.

When I arrived at Beverly's table, I was in for a shock. It was empty. Dirty plates lined each side, crossed knives and spoons placed in the center. Napkins were re-folded beside them, empty wine glasses arranged together in the center. Someone else must've cashed them out. *Why hadn't they told me?*

I grabbed the receipt. Their total was $425. I couldn't believe my eyes — the tip was for $5. At the bottom was a handwritten note from Beverly. "My girlfriends were VERY unhappy with the service. It took us forever to get our salads. You are lucky that we…"

I crumpled the receipt, stuffing it my pocket. When I looked up, I realized some of the people at my other tables were staring. One man I vaguely remembered walking in raised his hand to snap his fingers.

He was bald, a corporate executive type. "Yo!" he said, snapping away.

He continued snapping, even though I was on my way over.

Someone yelled at the bar. A waitress laughed at something a customer said. The baseball family was chatting away. The sounds all whizzed past my ears, blending together in one big swell of noise as my heart thumped in my chest.

The man kept snapping at me. I saw another guy at a table. He was laughing and pointing at me, muttering something to the person beside him. They both looked like yuppies in their dark tailored sports jackets.

"Yo!" More snaps.

I threw my notepad at the bald asshole's face. "STOP SNAPPING AT ME!"

The pad hit him in the mouth.

"Do you know hard I've been working tonight? You can wait two more minutes to get your fucking beer!"

The whole restaurant quieted. I felt two strong hands grip my arms.

"Get out of my restaurant," I heard Sophia whisper. "You're done."

I didn't move on my own volition. Someone else led me out. As I passed the hostess stand, I noticed Emily. As soon as she saw me, she dropped her eyes.

I heard voices behind me. The snapping man.

"*What the hell was that?* Don't you interview your people?"

"Sir, that has never—"

The sounds died off as I passed through Poseidon's doors for the last time.

* * *

I dropped my purse on the floor and wilted into my bed, not even bothering to take my shoes off. I stayed on my stomach, feeling my breath go in and out, hoping the exhaustion would lull me to sleep.

When the phone rang, I made myself sit up. It was B.B.

"Hey," I said, trying to hide the tiredness in my voice.

"Kelly." He sounded strange. Not his usual jocular self.

My hand gripped the phone. "Is everything okay?"

"It's Halmuni. She had a stroke."

CHAPTER TWENTY-THREE

When I was a kid, I used to see how long I could hold my breath under water. I would sink down, squeezing my eyes, holding my nose shut with my finger and thumb, waiting to touch the public swimming pool's cool, white concrete floor. I would feel my long, brown hair float away from my face, suddenly weightless, basking in the depth of silence.

Then, the pressure would start to build. The moment between serenity and panic. The moment your heart really made its presence known through vehement thumping. Sometimes I would try to defy that feeling, staying under until the thumping hit my brain. Then, finally, I had no choice but to let go and push for the surface—the desperate need to gulp in air and fill my lungs. But the wonderful thing about that swimming pool was no matter how desperate my situation appeared for a few seconds, I always knew fresh air was just a kick or two away.

After hearing about Halmuni's death, I felt like that kid again, underwater, but I couldn't kick up to the surface anymore because there was no surface to break. I was drowning. I was left reeling in the moment of panic, the one where my lungs seized, legs flailed, my hands reaching for any solid perch. And I had absolutely no idea how to find fresh air.

"What can I do to help?" Ian asked.

My lips remained shut, my hands busy tossing things into my suitcase.

We were standing in the guest bedroom of his family's condo that I've been using over the summer. The sheets and comforter lay half on my bed, half on the floor. A couple pillows had been tossed around. Half my closet was now in this suitcase, shirts and pants thrown together in one mass of wrinkly fabric.

I turned, Ian blurry in my misty vision. For once, his confidence melted. I could tell he felt completely powerless. I glanced down at his feet, one set awkwardly in front of the other as if still deciding whether or not to stay in the room to watch me pack. From the moment he arrived, he had tried to swoop me up in his arms, but I had pushed him away. I didn't want to be touched. I just wanted to see Halmuni.

"I should have spent the summer with her." I zipped up the suitcase.

"There's no way you could have known this would happen."

"Doesn't matter." *I shouldn't have spent my entire summer trying to impress your mom. She'll never be happy with me. Ever.* I stood up and walked past him.

He grabbed my arm. "At least let me take you to the airport."

"I already called an Uber." I had never spoken to him like this: the minced words, the indifference. I kept thinking about how he was the reason I didn't say goodbye to Halmuni. It was because of Beverly and that dumb etiquette school, but really I wouldn't have cared about Beverly if I hadn't cared about *him*. I knew I was the one who had ultimately decided to stay in New York, but if I had never met Ian, then maybe my life would be different right now. Simpler. Easier. Happier?

He looked at me, stung, as I made my way to the silver shoe stand and grabbed my black work shoes.

His hand made its way to my arm again. "Please, don't leave like this. I'll go with you."

I stopped my erratic movements for a second, finally really looking at him. He had rushed over from work, his button-up shirt and slacks clinging to his muscular frame, tie slightly undone. Fear etched across his face.

Every good moment between us had been displaced. All I could feel were my lungs pulsing, screaming for air. *Why did I even come? Or stay?* Everything with Poseidon, etiquette school, and Beverly now seemed like a giant and tragic waste of time. And I needed to get away from Ian so I could think clearly again.

He put both hands on my elbows, locking eyes with me. "Please."

Just tell him. You can't do this kind of thing over text. "I need time away from you," I said, shaking. "I need to see what I want."

I went to turn, but he kept his hand firmly on my arm. "No."

"I'm sorry." Breaking away, I picked up the handle of my suitcase.

"Kelly." His eyes softened but his hand gripped harder around my arm. "I don't think ... I don't think you can make this decision right now," he pleaded.

The exhaustion of crying seeped through my whole body. I relaxed my arm in his, wrapping my hands around his waist. This was my sip of air. I inhaled the smell of the fabric softener he used on his clothes, trying to remember what life was like just 24 hours ago.

I looked up at him, seeing his own tears match mine. I pulled him closer and kissed him, feeling his lips press harder. It would have been easy to stand there, collapsing into him, letting him move my body for me. But this was not where I belonged. Family was the most important thing, and with Beverly in the way, I would never be able to find it here.

I broke away, ending the kiss abruptly. "I can't." I grabbed my suitcase and walked out. I heard him yell out the first syllable of my name before I slammed the door behind me.

* * *

Halmuni's funeral would last three days, keeping in line with Korean tradition. B.B. and a handful of extended family members, faces I vaguely recognized from childhood, stood beside me, clumped together on the shiny wooden floor in the mourning room of the Jang Ryae Shik Jang. This Korean funeral home was beautiful, the altar sprawling with calligraphy, bouquets of white flowers surrounding an old framed picture of Halmuni. All of us wore black clothes and socks, but no shoes. I wondered if I should have asked B.B. to request everyone wear white; Halmuni had grown up before Korea adopted the western tradition of black funeral attire.

I squeezed my eyes shut, wishing I had recorded our Skype sessions so I could hear her voice again. I hadn't stopped crying since I left New York. I only felt worse when I thought about Ian. I kept telling myself it was for the best that we had this time apart. We needed to think about what was right for each of us. My heart was broken. I had lost Halmuni, and now I might lose Ian, as well.

I felt B.B.'s strong hands on my shoulders. "Kelly."

I realized we were the last ones left in the room. I kept my eyes locked on Halmuni's picture as he guided me into the dining hall. *Halmuni, Halmuni ... I'm so sorry I wasn't here for you.*

Tables set with white cloths displayed an arrangement of rice, vegetable soup, and, of course, Kimchi. I was thinking I should have brought Halmuni's all-time favorite food: KFC. She would have loved that, I thought. People milled about, picking up black plastic plates and silverware, sitting down at tables adorned in bundles of white flowers. I looked around, wondering if I would ever speak to these people again. Maybe Halmuni was my last real tie to my Korean heritage. Maybe Halmuni had been my only true family.

"Can I help you?" B.B. asked.

I looked up, frowning, but realized his eyes were above my head. I turned around and gasped.

Ian, wearing a black suit, black dress shoes, and hair recently cut into a close buzz, stood in the doorway. He had his hands in his pockets and gave me a small smile like *Yeah ... it's me.*

Everyone stared. For once, he was the one who looked wildly out of place. I would have laughed if we had been anywhere else.

I had no idea what to say. The way he looked at me made me think he couldn't see anyone else in the room. But I could sense the wheels in B.B.'s head turning behind me: *Who is this guy?*

"I couldn't stay in New York," Ian said. I could tell his eyes were swollen from crying, his usually creamy skin reddened. "And I realized..."

He trailed off, slowly walking toward me. My breath quickened. I immediately put my hands in his. Instinct. The shock of Halmuni's death made it easier to block out my feelings, but now, with him here, I couldn't control my emotions. I had told Ian I didn't know what I wanted, but now everything in my body was screaming: *You just want him.*

"I'm sorry, who are you?" B.B. asked, breaking the spell.

"Sorry." Ian stuck out his hand. "I'm Ian Anderson, Kelly's boyfriend."

B.B. barely shook it before turning to me. "Is that right?"

I could feel my face blushing. Any other time and place, I would've loved to introduce B.B. to Ian, reveling in the inevitable banter that would include B.B.'s corny jokes and Ian's charming deflections.

But now Ian was just the weird white guy who had interrupted a funeral reception.

"I just, um, I really had to do something today." He squeezed my hands. All I wanted to do was reach for the back of his neck and kiss him, but he didn't give me a chance to rise to my tiptoes—because he was currently getting down on one knee. *Oh, my God.*

"Kelly. For a while, I've been imagining spending the rest of my life with you. But yesterday, after you left, I realized I couldn't spend the rest of my life *without* you. I just want to be with you. Through everything. Good days. Bad days. Funerals. For as long as you'll have me."

I thought about the last time I had been in LA: pining over a love story like my parents, wishing anyone would notice me. Now, I had one of the most beautiful people—inside and out—wanting an entire life with me. I took my eyes off his for a moment to look toward the mourning room. I wondered if Halmuni was watching. I had a feeling she would be smiling. My heart felt twisted again, aching for her to witness this, overwhelmed by the fact I would have to go through many more of life's milestones without her.

"Kelly, will you marry me?"

I looked away from Ian's eyes, willing myself to peer around the room. I saw the dropped forks, the Kimchi poised in mid-air, no distant cousin sneaking a bite amongst the dead silence of surprise. More than anything, they were staring at Ian, playing the game I had been playing all my life: *Which item does not belong?*

"Ian." Shaking, I grabbed his hand, trying to pull him off his knee. His face fell. "Look, I—"

He put both hands on my shoulders. "I know. It's impulsive. Crazy. But I think we both know this is *it*. And if we get married, my mom will have no choice but to be nice. She can be crappy to my girlfriend, but she can't be crappy to my wife."

I slumped in his arms. *This isn't about me.* Everything went back to the one person I was desperately trying to get away from: Beverly.

"Ian, I love you. And I do want a life with you. I want to be your wife ... someday. But not like this. And I don't want a mother-in-law who hates me."

"My mom will love you. She just needs some time. And she'll try even harder if we're engaged."

My stomach flipped. I did not want my grandmother's funeral to turn into a marriage proposal, and I did not want my marriage proposal to turn into a fight.

I heard B.B. behind me. "Okay, kids." He slapped Ian on the back, like he had just fumbled a touchdown pass. "Let's take a breather."

Everyone started whispering in Korean as we took our seats. I met Ian's eyes. I could tell he was starting to sink with me, not quite at the same depth, but just enough to feel a little scared.

* * *

Even though had I rejected Ian's proposal, I realized he was right: I was in no state to break up with someone. I was reverting to instinct, the one I exercised during etiquette school: to flee. But I didn't want to run from Ian; I wanted to run from Beverly, Sophia, the busyness of New York. I wanted to seek comfort in the arms of Halmuni--which reminded me not to take what I had for granted.

Ian and I were standing on the porch of Halmuni's apartment. I kept my hand in his, glancing over at his chiseled profile as he watched the gradual sunset. I smiled. Fresh out of his funeral suit, he wore a T-shirt with HASTINGS LAW printed on the front and a pair of basketball shorts with CHU LAW OFFICES on the side.

We had gone out here to sip some iced tea Halmuni had left in the fridge after spending the day sorting through her belongings. Before, I couldn't imagine him coming with me, but now I couldn't imagine what this experience would have been like without him.

"So, I know you don't want to get married now, and I don't blame you." He set his drink on a glass table beside the stack of Korean newspapers Halmuni had piled up. "But I want you to know I'm crazy about you. So ... this is a promise to you that someday soon we'll be together." He wiggled his hand in the pocket of the shorts, revealing a small, black box. Oh, no. Was he going to propose *again*?

"I got it express shipped," he said, reacting to my surprised expression. "It's a family heirloom."

He opened the box, revealing an elegant ring with silver bands intertwined around a gorgeous pear-shaped diamond.

"You don't have to put it on now. I just wanted you to know I want you to have it." He smiled at me, the sunlight highlighting the sparkle in his eyes, almost comparable to the ring. Looking at him in his B.B. Chu regalia, I couldn't help but chuckle. It didn't matter where we were: his home, my home. He always found a way to belong. And I belonged with him.

I cupped his face in my hands, my heart beating faster. "Yes."

He raised his eyebrows, almost uncertain, and then his face exploded into a smile, reaching down to kiss me.

"I love you," I breathed, realizing the gravity of the phrase. But it was true, and I suddenly wanted to repeat it over and over again.

"I love you, too."

We both marveled at the words, how easy they felt to say. How obvious it had already been to each of us. A warm feeling gushed through my chest, relieved to hear him say it back to me.

I hugged him again, crying, the happiness soon replaced with a nagging, sinking feeling. I was in Halmuni's apartment, deciding a future with Ian. *Why couldn't she be here?*

"Hey, let's get out of here," he said into my hair. "Celebrate with some champagne?"

"Okay," I said quietly. I guessed it would be better than staying at Halmuni's, although I still wasn't entirely sure. Was it better to live in the grief or try to forget it?

Ian suddenly grabbed me in a hug, and I squinted out at the lowering sun, wondering if I would ever feel completely normal again. I knew I wanted Ian. I knew I wanted to share my life with him. But I still didn't know if I could live the way I should without Halmuni beside me.

CHAPTER TWENTY-FOUR

New York welcomed me back with slippery arms. After being warmed by the always dependable California sun, I found the battery of frigid downpours sweeping through the city unsettling. Halmuni would have understood. She always thought rain was an ominous sign: the universe's way of warning you about some impending doom. While the joke was that, in L.A., traffic ground to a halt the moment someone spit on a windshield, no amount of precipitation seemed to halt this city's frantic buzz.

I stood at the arched window of the condo, opposite the kitchen I had just cleaned. The whole place practically glowed with a spic and span shine. I did exactly as Lynette taught me, dusting the crevices behind the flat screen TV and wiping behind the sink faucet with Beverly's potentially toxic cleaning solution. After all, now that I didn't have a job, I might as well do something valuable with my time.

I felt warm in Ian's blue Columbia sweatshirt. I pressed my fingertips against the living room glass panel overlooking the street below. Hoods of heavy rain jackets flapped in the wind as people darted between parking meters, keeping their chins down to avoid the steady downpour. Brake lights blinked in gushes of water, punctuated by a cacophony of annoyed honks, creating a swell of only slightly controlled chaos.

I still had a couple of weeks until my sophomore year at Columbia began, and I had been spending all my time on the couch or at this window, vacillating between scouting on-campus jobs and people watching. Whenever I took a moment's breath, I thought of Halmuni. Whatever memory popped up in my head either made me laugh or burst out crying. More than a few times, I pulled up Skype just to look at her profile picture—the shot out-of-focus, only capturing half of her face. It reminded me of the person I missed so much. Lessons from my parents' death came back to me in glorious Technicolor. Once again, I confronted the hard truth. When it came to real grief, there was no quick way out. I would have to endure the suffering until the passage of time made each day slightly easier.

I traced the squiggle of a raindrop on the glass with my finger, then noticed a limo out of the corner of my eye. I followed its snaking path, the enormous vehicle looking out of place amid the bumper-to-bumper traffic. It stopped outside my complex, and a man with a navy-blue rain jacket rushed out. Ian? *Shouldn't he be at his internship?* Then again, he had been full of surprises lately.

I turned, smiling, then tightened my ponytail and readjusted my sweatshirt. I reached for the doorknob. Maybe we could have a romantic, rainy day in, cooking, making out and—

The door opened before I could reach it, making me jump back. I must have left it unlocked. Ian stood there, hoodie still over his head, water trickling down his nose. He pushed through the door, tearing off his jacket, leaving a puddle on the wooden floor. Despite the cold, he was steaming.

"Are you—?"

"Well, that certainly backfired!" He pumped the air with his arms. His grey T-shirt was splattered with water, and he wore black jeans with red Converse sneakers. He must've skipped work today. *Where had he been?*

I started toward him, reaching out a hand. "What backfired?"

He pulled away, as if my touch would only make things worse. He paced the living room and the kitchen. I had never seen him wound up like this. His movements suddenly seemed childish, like an impatient teen I had to counsel, instead of comfort. I wasn't sure if I wanted to do either.

"Can you believe it? She *disowned* me!" He threw his hands up again, then let them fall. I noticed his cropped hair had already begun to grow back, framing his angry face.

"Who?" I asked, stupidly.

He wasn't even looking at me, just staring out the huge, rain-spattered window. "Who do you think?"

"Because of our engagement?"

"Well, *duh!*"

Okay. No need to be a jerk about it.

"And she wants you out of here immediately. Like, okay, Mom, just make Kelly homeless, that's cool!"

I dropped onto the couch with a sigh, hoping he might follow my lead. Instead, he increased the pace of his agitated pacing. *I couldn't live here anymore?* Sure, it was only a couple weeks until school started, but this was so sudden.

"Wait, so when do I have to—?"

"I thought about it. It's fine, you can just stay with me until you move into campus housing with Melissa when school starts. Kevin and Roy won't mind. But I'm pissed off at my mom. Fuck her! Fuck *this*!" He circled the kitchen table in a frenzy, knocking napkins and cutlery off the counter. So much for cleanliness. In a matter of seconds, it looked like a tornado had torn through the place.

"She's always been like this. I'm so sick of it." He pounded his fist into his palm with loud, meaty smacks that frightened me. "I wish Grandpa Jack was here. He would've talked some sense into her."

"Calm down, Ian ..." I tried to speak calmly. "I'm not sure even Grandpa Jack would have been able to talk sense to your mom."

"Grandpa Jack would have at least told her to stop being an idiot."

"Okay, but didn't you say that once we got engaged your mom would be better about our relationship?" I asked, still trying to be as calm as possible.

"Yeah, yeah. I did, but, boy was I wrong. Does that mean that you will leave me again?" He sat down on one of the stools, rolling his fingers into fists, making the muscles and veins in his forearm pop.

I slowly moved toward him. "We were only apart for a day," I said, trying to add a laugh, even though it felt misplaced.

"You *broke up* with me." He finally looked over, the sparkle of his eyes replaced by smoldering disdain. "Remember?"

I let out a small scoff. "It was after Halmuni just—"

"I mean, if I hadn't flown all the way to L.A., we would probably be done. You probably would've just been like 'screw it.'"

"That's not true."

Was it? This was an arena I had never stepped foot into, and I had no idea how fair the match would be. I couldn't believe he was bringing this up. Was he trying to start a fight to ruin our relationship?

Ian shrugged. "It *is* true. I mean, if I hadn't put in the effort, who knows what could have happened?"

"Wait. You don't think *I* put in effort?"

I crossed into the kitchen, almost slipping on the debris from Ian's tantrum. I switched on the industrial lamps above the table, illuminating Ian's glowering face. As I sat down across from him, I motioned for him to do the same, but he wouldn't stop crisscrossing the room in wide figure-eight arcs.

"I'm not ... I just ... I just think that, yeah, sometimes I put in a little bit more."

I wanted to laugh. Like a crazy, maniacal laugh. *He thought he put in more effort? What, did he re-enroll in cotillion?*

"That's not fair." I rose to my feet. "I have done so much—trying to please your mom. To make her like me." Frustration over the unfairness of it all ballooned inside me. I counted off each item with my fingers. "I went to etiquette school, remember that? I survived racist Mrs. Williams, a dusty old relic from last century insulting me in every possible way. I went shopping with your neurotic mom, endured her condescending comments and dressing me up like a Barbie doll all day. I had to look at all of her Facebook posts about gold diggers, knowing all along she meant me in each one of her rants. What about all of that?" My frustration boiled over into furious anger. Now, I was the one charging around the kitchen, yelling. "What about the time she visited me at Poseidon with her mean girl friends? And last, but not least, how about Thanksgiving? That was one of the most humiliating experiences of my life. But you know what? I did it—I put up with all of the bullshit because I love you."

"But ...," he tried to interject.

I was on a roll, with no intention of slowing down. "And now you're mad because I left you after my grandma died? You left *me* at Thanksgiving! At a table with those horrible people!"

"I didn't say I was mad." His tone neutralized, his eyes meeting mine.

I sighed. Why did he have to comment on only the last thing I said? *Was he listening to all the other things?* "Okay," I said dismissively.

"I've already apologized a million times about Thanksgiving. And I just got disowned over you. What else do you want me to do?"

"Nothing! And I'm not asking you to do anything. I just ..." I trailed off, looking away. I watched the appropriately gloomy weather outside, praying this would all end. It scared me how quickly this had escalated. This wasn't like a fight with a friend where you worked out your issues quickly because you were hungry and wanted to get sushi. We were at each other's throats. I didn't see any way it would end without one of us screaming at the other to get the hell out.

"I never wanted you to be cut off by your mom," I said quietly. "That's horrible. But you always told me that money and status don't matter to you. If you are now worried about losing everything, then let's end it and you can go back to what you're used to."

"Here you go again. Your solution to everything is to just run away. I'm upset because now I won't have a relationship with my mother. It has nothing to do with the money, inheritance, or lifestyle."

Tears pooled at the corners of his eyes. His anger had devolved into sadness, and he stood slumped in the corner. He started to say something, but his voice broke.

I could see he was hurting, but I had to tell him this. "My reaction is to run away because I don't know what else to do. I've tried so hard to get along with your mom, but I will never be good enough for her. I also just wished you would've taken my side more."

"Taken your side—" He put both hands on his head, staring down at the table. God, this was terrible. He wouldn't even look at me. I had never felt more uncomfortable, so distanced from someone I cared about. *How could you make it all normal again?*

He finally looked up. "Look, sometimes, Kelly ... I just feel like you kind of play the role of the victim. When you don't need to. Like I didn't ask you to do those things with my mom. I didn't ask you to go to etiquette school."

"*Victim?*"

"Not like that. Never mind."

"Then like what?"

"I said never mind."

I hated those words: "never mind." As if anything could be dismissed with just two little words. He looked up at me, his eyes pulling me in. How could I want to keep fighting with someone and simultaneously pull them onto a bed at the same time? It was all very confusing. "Well maybe you just ... don't know what it's like. I've lost both my parents and now my grandmother. I have no family. I've had to support myself and my grandma for the last six years. Not to mention having to study my ass off so that I could get into Columbia on a scholarship. While most teenage girls were out doing girly things, I had no time for such luxuries. I had to budget for everything, including how much we would spend on food. So, yeah, maybe that does make me a victim. But, while I feel sorry for you that your mom disowned you, I never asked you to marry me.

I've never asked anything from you. I only wanted you to love me. You don't realize how lucky you are to have all that you have. Things have been given to you on a silver platter. You never had to work for any of it."

"Woowww. Have you forgotten that I lost *my* dad, too? Did you know that, when he *was* alive, he was verbally abusive? We all have issues, Kelly. No one has the perfect life." He shook his head, keeping his eyes trained toward the living room.

I looked away, too, trying not to complete my eye roll. I suddenly could imagine so clearly his fights with his exes. Immature arguments about petty things. It would've made me feel better if I didn't feel like we were fighting the same way.

"You don't think I do everything in my power to *not* be associated with my family? To do things on my own?"

I looked down. I didn't mean that he didn't work hard for what he had. But he also didn't know what it was like to grow up without wealth and privilege. He always had a safety net with piles of cash to fall back on. That was a lot different than living paycheck to paycheck and hoping one day you could grab a steady job. And here he was, accusing me of feeling sorry for myself? Of course, I didn't say any of this out loud. I was too tired to continue this argument.

"I just want to feel like we're a team," I decided to say. "And I haven't told you about a lot of this stuff because I never wanted to pit you against your mom. But sometimes I just feel, like, totally alone in trying to be someone who fits in with your family."

That seemed to crack him. His eyes softened. "But that's what you don't get. I don't want someone who will fit with my lousy family. I want *you*."

I came closer. I couldn't help it. Maybe this was the other side of love: the mood could drop instantly, but it could also resolve quickly. I met his hands halfway and wrapped my fingers around his. "I want to be with you, too." With the backdrop of the city behind us, I suddenly imagined pulling him out in the rain, not caring about the shivering cold. "I love you."

"I love you, too." He squeezed me close. "And I'm sorry for saying you feel sorry for yourself. I know you've been through a lot, and I should be more sympathetic about what you've been through. I think I'm just frustrated about this whole thing."

"It's okay. I'm sorry for calling you a rich, spoiled brat."

"I didn't think you did."

I laughed. "Well. I'm sorry."

"Me, too."

I pulled him to me. "Can we please just go sit on the couch and cuddle?"

He chuckled. "Sure."

We settled in together as I wrapped the blanket around us. He wrapped his arms around me and kissed the top of my head. There was nothing more comforting than this position: hearing his heartbeat, feeling him stroke my hair, knowing I could fall asleep peacefully.

"And, I just want you to know, once I finish law school, I'll find a job," he said. "I don't need her money, anyway. We can still have the life we want."

I craned my neck, looking up at his clean-shaven, now relaxed face. "You sure you still want that?"

He kissed me on the mouth. "Yes. That's exactly what I want. To be with you. My mom is used to getting her way because of her money. It actually is liberating not to care anymore." Suddenly he sat up, jostling us both so that we nearly fell off the couch. "And you know ..." he tilted his face down to mine. "Because of that ... we could just get married right now. Go to a courthouse. Today. If you want."

I shook my head. "Ian. You're upset. I don't want to get married just so you can get back at your mother."

"But I *want* to marry you. That's why I gave you this." He pointed to the ring on my finger.

I looked down at it, hesitating for a moment. No Beverly sounded fantastic. But someone needed to keep her head on straight. "And we will. Trust me." I took his face in my hands, kissing his nose. "Just not right now."

Halmuni taught me the importance of family. I always imagined marrying someone whose loved ones took me in as their own. I hadn't realized how much I wanted or needed that until Halmuni's death. And while Ian, so much of the time, seemed like enough, I didn't want to rush into something with the fear something was missing.

He held his face close to mine, smiling sadly. "Okay. I'll have to wait a bit longer to make you Mrs. Kelly Anderson." He kissed me again, then sat back, letting me return to my favorite position—arms wrapped around his stomach, my head on his heart.

CHAPTER TWENTY-FIVE

"As I mentioned at the beginning of the semester, this exam will not be graded on a curve. That means—"

I tried to focus on typing, filtering in Professor Mendez's words, but it felt like the edges of the world were folding in, blurring. I could barely breathe. A sheen of sweat slipped down my back. *You're not going to throw up.* I pressed my eyes closed.

Halmuni used to stream *Grey's Anatomy* when I got home from school. I remember one scene where Meredith kept puking. Her friend, the one who always hooked up with the hunky redhead, told her she could stop, that it was mind over matter. That scene now replayed in my head on a loop, the repetition inciting its own brand of nausea.

I looked around to see if anyone had noticed my clenched fists, the determined expression on my face to not puke publicly. This had been happening for the last four days, and I wanted to cry from frustration. Melissa chalked it up to exam anxiety. But when I woke up, I never had a single thought beyond the need to rush to the toilet. How could it be anxiety if I had to vomit before even having a coherent thought?

Sinking further into my chair, I tried to keep my head down, my fingers on my keyboard. Everyone around me typed away with fervor, their backs straight against their antique-looking, wooden chairs. My problem wouldn't go away, though. Mind over matter could only subdue the rupturing feeling in my stomach for so long. I felt the surge of warning in my esophagus. Slamming my laptop shut, I leapt out my seat and bolted across the aisle. Ignoring Professor Mendez's look of surprise, I raced through the double doors toward the restroom.

After flushing and wiping my face off with a damp towel, I headed to the health center. This could not be anxiety. Maybe it was something I ate at the dining hall. Or some parasite. All of those clickbait stories with gross images swam around in my head. *A six-foot tapeworm found! Parasite kills man and his dog!*

I fumbled for my backpack, pulling out my phone, looking for Melissa's name. *"Still happening,"* I texted. *":/ Going to the health center"*

"OH NO!!! I'm so sorry!! Yeah definitely go, they can hook u up."

Luckily, I was close to John Jay Hall. After completing the short walk, making sure to tread beside the nearest trash cans, I stood outside the building, catching my breath. I stared at the black lanterns with their nasty spikes and black trim, imbuing the building with an ominous look, despite its sparkling clean, white interior.

As I stepped into the lobby, a dozen students greeted me in plush blue chairs arranged around a white, circular table decorated with gossip magazines and Columbia catalogs. A sign next to the receptionist read, PLEASE TELL THE RECEPTIONIST OF ANY CONFIDENTIAL CONCERNS, right next to a vat of hand sanitizers and a box of facemasks.

To the left sat a table littered with pamphlets on STDs, contraception, and a fish bowl full of those Crown condoms Melissa warned me about. I looked back at the lobby, trying to calculate how long it would take to be seen. A chorus of coughs and sneezes echoed behind me, and I hoped I wouldn't catch anything else while I was here.

"Can I help you?" The receptionist, a woman in her early 30s with straight, strawberry blonde hair, asked.

"Um, yes, hi. I'm here for—"

She cut me off by handing over a blue intake sheet. "Fill this out, please."

I filled out my name, student ID number, and the reason for the visit— *nausea/vomiting for the last 4 days*—then handed it back. Weaving around the center table, I searched for an empty seat in the corner, away from the floating germs.

Minutes later, a nurse with a blonde bob and pointy glasses opened the white door. She reminded me of a dainty bird. "Kelly?" *That was quick. I guess they must think my symptoms are pretty serious.*

"Hi." I followed her into the white hallway. The door swung shut behind us as she led me in a room on the left-hand side.

A medical examination table was set against the wall, with a thin, paper sheet on top. I hopped up and sat on it, crinkling the paper and accidentally ripping an edge.

I almost kicked a red trash can labeled BIOHAZARD below my feet before settling my hands in my lap.

The nurse opened up her folder, reading off the sheet. "So, repetitive nausea and vomiting."

"Yeah." I crossed my feet, eyeing the instruments hanging on the side of the wall—the pointer that went down your throat and ears, the new kind of temperature gauge they rolled across your forehead.

"Have you gone to the bathroom in the last hour?"

"...No."

"Do you think you can go?"

"I think so."

She stood up, opening up a cabinet below the sink and grabbing a small cup with a red, twist-on lid. "We should do a pregnancy test just to rule that out."

I slowly grabbed the cup from her. Pregnancy? I hadn't even thought of that. *Why hadn't I even thought about that?!* I wanted to kick myself. I was so meticulous in every other area of my life; why had I been irresponsible in the most potentially life-changing one? Either people told you it was scary-easy to get pregnant or it took years. I guessed I found false comfort in the latter. Ian seemed so lax about it, too, which only made it easier for me to forget about the potential consequences of our love-making. I was mad at both of us for being so blasé.

The nurse opened the door with a sympathetic smile. As if she knew exactly the kind of beat-myself-up thoughts that were swirling in my mind.

I hopped down from the table. The results had to be negative. This would all seem stupid the minute I got them back. Then I would tell Ian we needed to use two methods of birth control. Melissa told me horror stories about The Pill, but I'm sure Ian and I could figure out something.

Opening the bathroom door, I realized there was another feeling bubbling in my stomach: excitement. *What the hell am I thinking?* I was NOT excited. The potential implications were horrible—I was not ready to be a mom. I could barely take care of myself. A child would derail my whole future. Then again, I really did see myself having a child with Ian. Still, the timing would absolutely suck. I was only 21!

I locked the bathroom door. A Wicks air freshener was plugged into the wall, wafting in the faint touch of lavender. Black shelves on the opposite wall contained tampons and toilet paper. This was it. This sterile building was where I would learn if I had a child inside me.

But it had to be something else. It just *had* to be.

* * *

I sat on the examination table, swinging my feet, waiting to see that blonde bob whisk back in the room, waiting for her to say, "negative."

After 10 painful minutes, she returned. The sad smile gave it away. She seemed a little nauseated herself. "It's positive."

Sometimes you can reveal more of yourself to strangers than you can to a person you've known your whole life. Perhaps it's because you know you may never see them again. But I didn't want to react to the nurse. I didn't want to respond at all because I didn't want it to be real.

Instead, I let the edges blur again, the sounds mute. I laid back on the table and stared up at the ceiling. It was the only way I could control the wild thumping in my heart, the squeal of worry jumping in my throat, the fingers curling by my sides.

"You have some options." She turned to the wall of brochures.

I squeezed my eyes shut. I was actually pregnant. There was no rewind. Nothing to fix. This was my fate now: being a parent in college.

"I'm not sure what you'd like the next steps to be, but—"

I bolted upright. "I'm going to keep it."

I could have deliberated. I could have taken days to mull things over, to analyze every part of this decision's potential impact. But I didn't want to dwell over the life of my child. The child I was having with Ian. We were going to get married; we were going to have a child. The timing sucked, but I still felt it was meant to happen. And telling the nurse this, in this moment, meant I couldn't go back; it meant cementing the decision, the one only I could make, the one I thought I wanted. I was functioning off adrenaline: off the fear, off the strangeness of a life-altering moment, off the confusing flare of slight happiness.

The nurse nodded, slowly. She started talking again, but I was in another world, preparing how to tell the person who was about to go through the same emotional rollercoaster as me.

* * *

This wouldn't be like one of those cute viral videos of a pregnancy-reveal, pink or blue streamers flying around the room. The fact that I didn't know what to expect only made the uneasiness in my stomach worse, diminishing any previous excitement.

I sat on the edge of Ian's bed, looking out a window covered by half-open blinds. Ian worked on his computer, studying for a test. I told him it was important. He obviously didn't realize how important.

"Sorry, one sec."

I felt the soft, slightly scratchy fabric of his Columbia blanket beneath my fingers, watching him. He was wearing one of his red flannels again, with black sweatpants and mismatching blue and white socks. His room smelled like that fabric softener, the pillows perfectly propped up behind me. He kept pressing his fingers to his temples and rubbing them. Already stressed. Great.

"Okay, done." He closed the laptop, then turned around, elbows on his knees, giving me his full attention. Usually I appreciated that, but now I wasn't sure I could handle it. *What will he say!?*

"What?" He laughed. "The look on your face is freaking me out a little."

These life changing words – *I'm pregnant*. Then the reality would hang above both our heads.

He reached out his feet to kick mine and I instinctively smiled at the touch. Maybe he would be excited. Happy.

"So, I haven't been feeling well these last few days."

He frowned, waiting, his feet no longer kicking mine.

"I went to the health center." I slipped one of the strings of the blanket through my fingers, looking down. "And, well, I'm pregnant."

The pause that followed made me wish we were fighting instead. Anything but this. His whole body froze, and I felt like I could see the heart in his chest stop beating. This was not a precursor to a happy reaction.

"How is that possible?"

"Well—" I wasn't sure whether to go into contraception effectiveness or reproductive biology.

"We used condoms." His words crunched together angrily, like if he built a good enough argument, he could make the situation disappear. As if a pregnancy could be overturned with by well-considered debate.

"Well, they aren't always effective. And you know, you really should have a backup—"

"How could you not -?" He snapped at me. He put his hands on his head, not finishing his sentence. I didn't want to hear the rest of it, anyway.

"Me? I told you I wasn't on the pill."

He spun around in his chair, running his hand over his hair a few times. He looked out the window while I stayed sitting on the bed, feeling the dark hue of the walls closing in.

Maybe he wasn't really mad. Maybe he felt like me: scared to death. I put down the blanket and walked over to him, squatting down on the floor, touching his arms. "Hey." I realized he was crying. He hurriedly wiped off his face. "I'm scared, too."

He nodded, and then let out a breath. "I'm sorry. I'm upset. This was just ... unexpected."

I let myself laugh a little. At the ridiculousness. The ability of one moment to completely change our future. It didn't seem right.

He reached down to hug me, and I felt that little flutter in my stomach again, the little reminder of potential happiness.

He suddenly put both hands on my cheeks, looking me straight in the eyes, unblinking. "I will not leave. Okay?"

I nodded and he lifted me up and wrapped me in a hug. I let myself imagine the doctor's appointments and ultrasounds with him by my side. "And we can name him Jack," I said. "Or Jackie. I kind of have a hunch it's a boy, though."

He smiled through the tears, and I could see he was starting to imagine the future, too, the one we wanted together, even if it seemed too early. "I'd love that. Come here." He pulled me into his lap, pausing. "But, um ... what about health insurance? The school doesn't have maternal coverage. And my mom ... she won't help. And you don't work at Poseidon anymore."

I could tell he was trying to make these things sound non-accusatory, but it made me sink further into his lap. "Well, I can go on Medicaid," I said, hoping it would be enough to cover it. "But what about you?"

"I'm not the one pregnant. I'll be fine." He put his arms around my waist. "Plus, I'll get a part-time job. I'll move out of this place, and we can get a small apartment for the two of us and the baby. Then you won't have to pay for your dorm."

I turned and kissed him, communicating what we already knew: we would be taking on this future together. And it would be worth it.

I broke away from his lips, smiling, then pulled out my phone. "I'm just going to tell Melissa that we will be living together. I don't think I can handle her reaction about the pregnancy right now."

"Good idea."

"Hey, Ian and I will be living together after this semester is over!!"

"AHHHHHH!! LEVEL UP! But also don't leave me lol. Jk. Just don't forget about me, you little slut!"

I shook my head, laughing. Yeah. I would definitely wait until tomorrow to tell her about the pregnancy.

CHAPTER TWENTY-SIX

Ian put his head on the pillow beside mine, running his hand along my stomach. I was only 12 weeks pregnant, so you couldn't really see anything there, but Ian liked to rub my tummy, anyway. These were our evenings now: me lying in bed after class, textbook in hand; Ian curled up next to me, hand on my belly.

I had spruced up the room with some of my dorm belongings, the maroon pillows offsetting the dark blue comforter, the fuzzy, green rug resting against his black desk chair. Otherwise, it still looked like Ian's home: the dark walls, the Columbia paraphernalia, the lacrosse stick and baseball bat standing in the corner. Luckily, his bed was a comfortable queen, and I already made the nightstand my own, decorating it with my matching office supplies.

I aced all my classes last semester and was already into my second month of my sophomore year. The baby was due in early August. I would be 22 years old when the baby arrived. It seemed too young, but I kept reminding myself my mom was around that age when she had me.

Ian was in his second year of law school. He would say, "One more year to go. Then I can get a job in a law firm that pays well. Then we can finally move out of this rabbit hole." Although we lived in a small studio apartment, I was happy. I liked being creative in terms of where we could store things. It reminded me of one of Halmuni's favorite programs on HGTV, about living in small homes that totaled less than 500 square feet. She would say, "Oooh, Kelly look, look ... bench that turns to dining table and storage, too! Soooo smart."

Ian and I agreed we would get married in the summer. We were both too busy with school work to even think about a wedding. Ian was also working part-time as a paralegal at a small firm to support us. Even though we couldn't eat at those fancy restaurants and had to live on a very tight budget, we were excited about our future together. We finally felt light-hearted and free.

Even with Ian by my side, I continued to think about Halmuni. It was difficult to feel happy over milestones when she wasn't there to see them. Plus, I really needed her advice. Sure, it would have been quite a tense phone call telling her I was having a mixed-race baby out of wedlock, but she would've come around, just like she had come around about Ian. Still, I couldn't wallow in those type of thoughts too long or else or they threatened to become all-consuming, especially with the rise in hormones circulating through my body. I just had to believe she was still watching me, looking out for all three of us.

Turning my head toward Ian, I inhaled the scent of his shampoo. I loved how much he always wanted to be next to me and the baby. Sometimes I thought he would never take his hand off my stomach. He was determined not to miss the first kick, even if that probably wouldn't happen until months from now.

I kissed him on his forehead and then flipped to the next page of the textbook propped up against my thighs.

"What color do you think his eyes will be?" Ian wrapped the white blanket around us, covering up his black work pants and dress socks.

"Probably brown. Sorry."

"Why sorry? I love your eyes."

"But blue is so much prettier."

"They *are* a recessive gene."

I closed the textbook, telling myself I would learn about due process later, then scooted next to him, pulling the blanket over our shoulders. "You've already done some kind of gene chart, haven't you?"

He smiled sheepishly. "Maybe. You know what I also learned?" He leaned on his elbow, propping his head on his hand.

"What?"

"Babies can hear music even when they're in utero. But I don't know what to sing."

I smiled, thinking of the perfect song. "I can teach it to you."

"Okay." He sat up, rubbing his hands together like a dutiful student.

I started to hum, but my shyness stopped me.

"Oh, come on."

"Okay. But I don't have the best voice."

"Neither do I. Just do it."

"Once there was a little old ant/Thought he'd move a rubber-tree plant..."

A smile spread across his face. "I've heard you sing that song a lot. That's the song your dad used to sing to you when you were young, right?"

"Yeah, it's called *High Hopes*. It's an old Frank Sinatra song. When I was young, my dad used to tell me that if I sung it, then all my problems would magically vanish. Really silly of me, but I believed him!"

I proceeded to tell him the story of my dad chasing my mom. When I was done, Ian sat up, propping another pillow behind me. "I love that. I wished I could've met him."

"Me, too." I sat up a little, looking at him from the side.

I continued teaching him the words, and pretty soon we were both singing toward my stomach, trying not to break the lyrics with our laughter. *"But he's got high hopes! He's got high hopes! He's got high apple pie in the sky hopes!"*

After a couple rounds of the chorus, we laid back on the bed, hands intertwined. "Well, I think we just taught him what terrible singers his parents are."

Suddenly, as if in response, my stomach rumbled. "That's not the baby." I laughed. "Just my own stomach being mad at me."

"What do you want?"

"I'm actually really craving some Kimbap." I turned on my phone. It was already 10:00 pm. Even though it pained him, Ian had sold his beautiful car to make up for our lack of income. "But, really, it's okay. I'll just have a bowl of cereal or something. It's late."

"No. I'll go to that place you like on 6th Avenue."

"Ian—"

He was already sitting up. "It's fine, I'll take the subway."

"Do you know how many stories Halmuni told me about subway assaults? Or about being spit on?"

Ian looked at me. "You used to complain she did that."

"Well ... now ... I'm starting to think there was a point. Please, *please* don't go on the subway."

He looked me in the eyes. I could tell he was deciding how seriously to take my plea. He sighed, grabbing his black fleece jacket. "Okay, fine. I'll take your bike."

The Mantis. I had already accepted I would never get rid of that thing because that "thing" is how I met Ian. I turned the blanket in my hands, extracting a few pieces of fuzz.

"Kelly, don't worry."

I looked up. He pocketed his wallet and then put one knee on the bed. "It'll be fine."

"Okay, but I don't even know if it still works right. Why don't you just Uber it or take a taxi?"

"They'll charge an arm and a leg at this hour. Don't worry. I have good balance." He kissed me on the top of my head.

"You really don't have to go."

"It's not just you I'm feeding. I'll be back soon." He smiled, and then walked out, closing the door gently behind him. I laid back on the bed, still feeling that tug of worry in my stomach. Maybe it was just the hormones.

* * *

At midnight, I paced back and forth through the living room, occasionally glancing at my reflection in the black TV screen, seeing my worried face become more and more grave. I should've known not to label women's intuition as hormones. I called the restaurant again.

"Hi, sorry, I just wanted to really double-check that order of Kimbap for Ian was picked—"

"Miss. I already told you. Picked up," said a male voice with a Korean accent.

I hung up, putting the phone by my side, continuing to stalk the small space between his desk chair and the door. I was making myself dizzy.

My phone beeped. I immediately went for it, my nerves on edge.

Kevin: "Haven't seen him since yesterday when I was in the apartment!"

Nash: "Yeah, sorry, I'm at my gf's right now. Haven't seen him. Everything ok?"

No. It was not okay.

* * *

Ring. Ring.

My eyes flickered open. I barely took in the living room before hurling myself toward my phone. I must've fallen asleep out here. I wondered how long

I had paced before collapsing from exhaustion and worry.

"Ian? Ian?"

"Is this Kelly Hopkins?" The male's voice was not Ian's.

My heart stopped. I clung to the phone, knees buckling. "Yes."

"My name's Steve Korman. I'm an RN at Mount Sinai Hospital. You're listed as an emergency contact in the phone of Ian Anderson?"

This couldn't be happening. "Where is he? Is he okay?"

"He was in a hit-and-run accident."

I imagined Ian's face right before the impact, his nervous determination trying to control that stupid bike. I saw the splayed food from the takeout boxes, his body meeting the pavement, the blood. Why had I ever let him go?

"Now, I want to warn you ... he's—"

Somewhere in the time it took me to fling the door open I managed to hang up the phone, punch in for an Uber, grab my keys, and run. I would commit any crime if it meant I could ride in a police car to get there faster.

* * *

I only saw two colors in the emergency room. White walls, white sheets, white gowns, white curtains, and blue scrubs. They blurred past as a female nurse led me through the lobby doors, past the panic-stricken victims on gurneys waiting for rooms.

In the distance, I made out a man's guttural yell, followed by a woman's shriek in what I think was Spanish. Desks occupied by nurses clustered in the middle, surrounded by signs labeled X-RAYS, EXIT, and LABORATORY. I was in a maze I didn't want to find the end of, the hallways only leading to more suffering.

An elderly man in a wheelchair dashed past us, muttering incomprehensible things to the male nurse by his side. I turned away, looking at the nurse as we stopped in front of a closed curtain. Her face was steady, unmoving. I realized I was merely part of another scene in her nightly horror show. What would devastate me was routine to her.

I grimaced as the curtain's slider scratched against the metal pole. My inability to recognize the person in front of me made me freeze.

A shell of Ian laid in the bed. His arms, ribs and legs were mummified in a thick, white cast. His arms hung in the air, lifted by an apparatus above the bed, his legs elevated on pillows. His face was the only thing left unwrapped. His expression was blank, like a slate wiped clean, his lips set in a thin line. The monitors were poised on his right, scattered with neon numbers. On the other side stood an I.V. bag, its liquid contents slowly dripping through a tube leading into a needle planted in the middle of his hand.

I think the nurse offered me a chair, but I stood there staring, hoping if I looked long enough, I would realize my eyes were just playing tricks on me. I think this was what doctors meant by shock. I couldn't move. I kept thinking any minute his eyes would blink open and match mine. I would go over and kiss him, feeling his lips, again and again.

"Excuse me, miss?"

I snapped my head to the right, the nurse finally coming into focus.

She scrolled through the computer. "He broke both arms, legs, and a few ribs. He's in a coma, so we're keeping him stable."

I took two steps to collapse in a worn, purple chair by the bed, reaching out to grasp his fingers.

"Do you know who his insurance carrier is?" She looked at me expectantly, her fingers on the keyboard. I started calculating in my head what all of this would cost: the E.R. visit, the casts, the indefinite treatment. Ian's words rang in my head. *I'm not the one pregnant. I'll be fine.*

"I don't think he has any, or if he does, it's probably just the basic plan... " I said quietly. I couldn't believe I didn't force him to get insurance. Or that I let him get me food. Me. My stupid cravings. I should've kept my mouth shut. I shuddered, sinking deeper into the chair, realizing the full weight of this nightmare. *This is my fault.*

The nurse breathed in. "Okay, so, we will still treat him to the best of our ability here. But for as long as he's in the coma … um, these costs…"

I didn't want to hear the estimate. "It's okay. I know who to call."

* * *

It was the first time I had ever seen Beverly unkempt. And it would probably be the last. She wore black yoga pants and a hastily thrown on zip-up jacket, one side hanging off her shoulder, exposing the strap of a tank top. Her blonde hair was thrown back up in a bun, and her eyes were slightly swollen, remnants from foundation still hanging on to the creases of her eyelids.

She lunged toward the hospital bed, narrowly missing the cast on Ian's leg. She sobbed, her knees crumbling beneath her.

I had no idea what to do. I had already spent an hour staring at Ian's new form, imagining the fragments left below the skin. I had already done what she did: cried and sobbed, not caring if anyone could hear me. But I didn't know if any of this made me qualified to comfort her. I stood up, uneasily, instinctively putting a hand on my stomach, then stopped. *She can't know.*

She must've seen me move out of the corner of her eye. She caught her breath. "Why doesn't he have his own room?"

"Well, this is a room—"

"No. *A room.* Walls. Not curtain separators."

I stood, unmoving.

"You don't know what to do," she snapped.

The monitor reading Ian's heartbeat beeped. That was the one thing I clung onto: a steady beep. As long as I could hear that, my own heart could keep thumping.

"You should go," she insisted. "I'll take care of him," she said. "I'll let you know when he wakes."

No. With Ian literally between us, I could not let her pull him away. "I'm not leaving him," I said sternly.

She shook her head, disgusted, then leaned into me, her blue eyes dangerously close. "Unless you do what I say, I'm not going to pay a dollar."

Monster. She knew. She knew he didn't have insurance. What if she had been spying on us? What if she already knew about the baby? What if she could find a way to blame this accident on me? Most important, how could I let Ian end up here, in a full-body cast, unconscious, with his mother lording over him? The kind of woman who would threaten to cut off his care just to spite me?

I gasped, realizing the full impact of her words. "You'd do that?"

I'd called her bluff. *She couldn't really hate me this much, right?* I stared back into her eyes and shivered. Maybe it wasn't a bluff. Maybe my instincts had been right all along: she really *was* evil, a black widow of a woman biding her time to strike.

Beverly looked away at last. "Just do what I say and get the hell out of here, or I promise I will make life *very* hard for you."

Ian, where are you when I need you? He could tell me how to play this hand with his mom: which cards to show, what bets to make.

"I've already lost my husband," she told me between gritted teeth. "I won't lose my son. You've done enough. You've destroyed what's left of my family."

"Beverly, please," I pleaded. "Please let me stay. I know you are upset, but so am I. I ... I don't know what I would do without him. Please have some sympathy for me and Ian. I know he would want me to be here with him." Tears welled in my eyes.

Beverly didn't seem at all fazed. "You've done enough. I've never liked you. You're probably the reason he's in this coma. Why the hell would he be riding a bicycle at this time of night? Just leave. I promise I will get the best medical care for him. Once he's better, I'll make sure he contacts you. Right now, I don't want to be distracted by you."

Every atom in my body told me to stay, but I was trying to think of the long-run—convincing myself there would be a long-run—and how Ian would've wanted me to react. Just let her have this round. *There will be others.*

I cleared my throat, grabbing my phone. "I'll be back tomorrow."

"No, you will not be back tomorrow. Like I said, give him a few days. I'll make sure he contacts you when he is out of his coma."

I stole one more glance at Ian, then pulled back the curtain and walked out, tears sliding down my face, the hospital once again becoming a blob of white, an occasional blue uniform scurrying past.

I would be back. And Ian would be, too.

CHAPTER TWENTY-SEVEN

I waited four whole days until I couldn't take it anymore. I just kept staring at my phone, but still not a word from Beverly or Ian. When I tried their numbers, the calls would go straight to voicemail. When I called the hospital, they would tell me Ian was still in a coma or, worse, Beverly would answer and tell me to leave him alone so he could get better.

My worry became an all-consuming obsession. I barely ate. I missed all my classes. I explained my situation to Melissa, Roy, Kevin, and B.B., and they all agreed I needed to let Beverly have her way. For now. Ian needed the best medical treatment available, and Beverly—and Beverly alone—could make that happen. But after four days, my impatience overwhelmed my better judgement, and I decided to go to the hospital.

When I arrived, I discovered Ian had been moved to the ICU three days earlier. After noticing my shock, the nurse explained this was standard protocol for coma patients. I tried to convince myself Ian's situation was "standard" as I stood in the glass elevator watching the lights blink up and up. 7... 8 ...9...

Turning around, I looked out the window, nervously cracking my knuckles as the ground dropped away. Below me lay the sprawling medical campus. Doctors with lanyards casually walked between buildings, some on cell phones, others holding a salad or water bottle. Just another normal day. I was suddenly relieved Halmuni pushed me to become a lawyer and not a doctor. There was no way I would ever be able to handle interactions with the patients' families: the look on their faces as I broke the terrible news, the tears, the grief. *No, don't go there.*

Recalling how Ian had looked four days earlier, wrapped up like a battered, bloodied mummy, made my stomach ache. I just wanted to get off this elevator and be with him again. I prayed his eyes would open, that everything would go back to normal. With each ascending floor, I wondered if he was passing further and further beyond the realm of medical help. *Stop that. Positive thoughts! Be strong. Ian needs you.*

Exiting the elevator, I followed the signs to the ICU lobby. In spite of the terror growing inside of me, I appreciated the hospital's attempt to make this a friendly place: the wooden paneling, a smiley face behind the hands of the clock, the numerous magazines fanned out on the table offering glimpses of happy families and better times.

However, the checkered linoleum floor told a different story. Dingy and scuffed, its many skidmarks told the real truth: it evoked mental images of nurses darting between dying patients, patient-laden gurneys hurriedly rolling their occupants to their ultimate fates, the heels of desperate spouses uselessly pacing, pacing, pacing. The walls may have tried to mask so much suffering, but the floors gave it away.

I approached the receptionist, a young woman in her late twenties with straight, brunette hair. A baseball player bobblehead wiggled on her desk.

"I'm here to see Ian Anderson, please."

She clicked away with her mouse, frowning with each new click. "Ian Anderson II?"

Why is she asking so formally? Is it because he's no longer with us? "Yes," I said, no saliva in my throat.

"Looks like he was already discharged. About two hours ago."

That made no sense. "But the person downstairs—"

"The system probably hasn't updated yet. Yeah, looks like they cleared him to go home."

"So, he must've been awake? He was in a coma," I added.

She looked at me like I was stupid. "We don't normally discharge patients if they're still unconscious."

It wasn't worth getting into with this person. Obviously, she hadn't been hired for her kind bedside manner. I pulled out my phone, dialed Ian's number, praying he'd pick up. I needed to hear his voice again. To confirm he was okay.

It rang once, then went straight to voicemail. I started to leave a message, then changed my mind. His phone was probably off, and he wouldn't know I had called. I had a better idea, anyway. I pulled up my Uber app, hoping there was still enough money left in my checking account to get me through the long ride.

* * *

Outside of agreeing to schlep me two hours to the Anderson compound in Connecticut, Sal, my driver, didn't have much to say. Usually I wouldn't have minded the silence; I might have even welcomed it. But today it oppressed me. It forced me to swim in my darkest fantasies. *What if Beverly won't let me in the house? What if she turns me away at the gate?* In my mind's eye, I kept seeing Ian in his full-body cast. *Would he ever be the same again? Would* we *ever be the same?*

My palm kept leaving little sweat stains on the windowpane of Sal's Toyota Corolla. What Sal lacked in the verbal communication department, he made up for in cleanliness. The black leather was freshly vacuumed, and the interior smelled faintly of Windex. I nervously tapped my foot against the passenger seat in front of me, playing with a paperclip left in a tray by the door handle.

Recognizing the exit, my already frazzled mind slipped to near-panic mode. To stop myself from falling to pieces, I visualized summoning a sorely-lacking inner strength. I ran through a scenario in which I suddenly acquired that "tough, gangster type attitude" B.B. assumed. He would always say, "Don't be a wimp; stand firm."

I wouldn't merely *request* Beverly let me inside, that heinous bitch—I'd *demand* to see Ian. If Beverly still refused me, I would slam my fists on the wrought iron, screaming to be let in. At least Franco would understand. *Right?*

"It's just at the end of this street," I said to the back of Sal's tanned neck.

It felt eerie being back in this neighborhood, taking in the sweepingly ostentatious show of wealth once more, noting the endless lawns immaculately manicured. The enormous houses with their private gates staffed by suited foot soldiers seemed to all but challenge me: *What are you doing here—again?* Noticing just how far the horizon went, knowing the acres of land belonged to individuals so monumentally out of my league, left me deflated. *What power do I really have here?*

"Here, here." I pointed to the gate. Sal eased up on the gas, slowly turning the wheel and rolling to a stop. I unbuckled as he shifted into park.

"Would you wait here for me? I need to go inside and get him."

It sounded so casual, I surprised myself.

Tucking my jacket closer, I steeled myself against the biting wind. I was just walking over the curb toward the intercom when I noticed a security guard posted on the other side of the gate. *Was he here before? Where was Franco?*

Middle-aged and bald, the guard's gut spilled over the top of his pants. He wore a white, long-sleeve button-up and black slacks. An iPhone and a heavy-duty flashlight were clipped to his belt like a gunslinger's six-shooters. I did a double-take when I noticed a taser. Talk about overkill.

Beady, humorless brown eyes stared back at me. He kept both hands poised beside his weapon as he barked, "Can't park here."

Stay unruffled. "That's my Uber. I'm just here to pick up Ian."

He shook his head extra slowly as if to demolish any possibility of conciliation. "You need to get off the property."

"If you'd just let me speak to Franco—"

"Miss, you need to leave now. You're trespassing."

Could I *call the cops on him?* I thought about case studies from class. What had Professor Mendez said about parental and spousal rights? Hadn't Beverly disowned Ian? Did she have any right to him at this point? *Shit. Why hadn't I just married the man already?!* I may have had a case that way.

I glanced back at Sal. The car was still running, but his head was down, fingers typing away on his phone. At least he was stranded out here along with me. Actually, that wasn't true. He could drive off any time he wanted.

Something moving beyond the gate caught my eye. I turned to see Beverly at the wheel of a golf cart. She had assumed her usual look: a superbly fashionable outfit, hair straightened, face done, hands adorned in white gloves. Seeing her formidableness, I tried to summon that stronger version of myself again: the one who would scale the gate, tip over the cart, and make a break for the house. I wished.

Instead, I did my best attempt to sound menacing as I rushed gate. "You had no right to just take him away from me! I'm his fiancé!" I yelled at the top of my voice.

The security guard stepped forward, reached through the gate and uncurled my fingers from the metal. Behind him, Beverly gazed on at me with wonder, like I was a tiny spider that managed to land in her lap. "Steve, it's okay. I saw her on the monitor," she said calmly.

I glared at the guard, who stepped backward to give me space.

"So how'd you get the hospital to release him?" I yelled to Beverly. "Pay someone off? You told me you would have Ian call me as soon as he was conscious again. You are a liar!"

Beverly killed her electric engine, then stood behind the gate, a picture of icy calm. Finger by finger, she tidily removed her gloves. "You don't wear anger well, dear."

I breathed heavily, blowing away a loose strand of hair stuck to my face. The guard didn't make any moves, but I noticed him grip the taser.

"Ian needs to rest," she said coldly. "He needs peace and quiet to get stronger."

"Let me see him."

"You can email him."

"*Email him?* Let me *see* him!" Rage tore through me. My whole body trembled. I grabbed hold of the gate again and shook it as hard as I could. "Let me IN!"

It happened so fast. I only caught a blur, then two large hands came at me through the spaces in the gate and pushed me back. "Miss, I told you to stand back from the gate," the guard named Steve growled. "Do not threaten Mrs. Anderson and do not, repeat, do not grab hold of the gate again."

Stumbling backwards, I reached for anything to stop me. I hit the ground at a funny angle, my legs and arms splayed out on the cold, hard concrete.

I never meant to say it. It must have been pure instinct. "The baby," I whispered, covering my stomach with my hand.

"What?" Beverly's eyes widened unnaturally.

My legs shook. Little bits of gravel clung to my jacket. My hands were red and scratched from the impact.

"The baby," I said, loudly. "*Our* baby." I glared at her. Challenging. *What can you do now?*

Her eyes traveled from my face to my stomach, and vainly to the guard. He stood still, unsure of his role, crossing his arms, frowning.

I remained staring at Beverly until she straightened her posture, clearing her throat. "I'm sorry," she said quietly.

You're sorry? Well, that just makes everything better, doesn't it? I propped myself against the car, not even daring to look at Sal. I hoped he wouldn't try to take off after all of this. I wished the baby were already kicking so I would know it was okay.

"I'll have Ian email you."

"No—"

"I would have him call you," she quickly followed. "But he can't right now. Trust me. You'll hear from him. That baby needs to be taken care of. After all, it is ... family."

Trust you? Family? I wanted to tear through the gate, commandeer the golf cart, and race to Ian's room. The adrenaline surge would give me such superhuman strength. I would carry him out myself, the three of us together again. The way we should be. *But I can't do that to the baby.*

I looked between Beverly and Steve. "When Ian finds out that you didn't let me in, he will never forgive you. And trust me, I'll be back," I promised, for the second time. No matter where she moved Ian, I would find him.

I turned, slowly walked back to the car, and opened the door. "Sal. It will just be me. Please take me back to Columbia." I grimaced, imagining the last two hundred dollars of my bank account dwindling to zero. I would figure something out. I had to.

He started the engine. "Are you—?"

"Just go."

I was confused. I didn't understand why Ian wouldn't call. Was he blaming me for what happened? I should have never let him take the stupid bike. *Ian, where are you? Please. I need you.* I put both my hands on my tummy. We *need you.*

As Sal backed the car out of the driveway. I stared at Beverly through the windshield. She looked at me for a few moments before leaning forward through the bars to say something to Steve with a hand in front of her mouth. I tried to control my breathing as we drove away, finally turning the corner out of her sight. No matter what she said, this would not be the last she'd see of me. I must speak to Ian.

CHAPTER TWENTY-EIGHT

To: Kelly Hopkins <kh2358@columbia.edu>
From: Ian Anderson <iananderson2@gmail.com>
Subject: **I'm Sorry**
February 20, 10:02am

Dear Kelly,

I'm sorry I didn't contact you until now. My mother told me to call you, but I needed time to think things through. I also prefer to email rather than talk because I want you to read what I have to say. I don't want to argue with you. I'm emailing you from my personal email account because I told Columbia I'm not returning to law school and they shut down my email.

Now that I am back home, I've had a chance to reflect on everything that has happened since I've met you. I've made many mistakes in my life and this accident has caused me to realize I need to make amends. In particular, it has reminded me how important family is to me. I cannot run away from my obligations of being an Anderson. As the only child, I have a duty to take care of my mother, as well as my father's business.

During these weeks of recovery, I have come to realize how unfair I have been to you. I used you. I wanted normalcy in my life, and you were the perfect stranger who was there, at the right time. I used you to run away from my problems. Only now do I realize the extent of my insensitivity. I am truly, truly sorry. My mother was right in saying we come from two completely different worlds. We don't belong together. We will end up fighting because of our differences. And because you can't get along with her, it has caused a rift between myself and her, which has made me miserable. If I have to choose, I must choose my mother. It was stupid of me to think otherwise. You belong with someone who is more like you. Someone who understands where you come from and can appreciate you more than I can.

Our child needs a more stable father, a role model. Not someone like me who has made a horrible mistake. I wish I could tell you things will get better, but they won't. I also think you should consider aborting the child or giving it up for adoption. It doesn't make sense for you to keep it when the baby won't have a stable family. I will wire you $50,000 from my account. Please do it for the sake of the baby. Don't bring a child into this world whom you can't take care of. I did love you, but for the wrong reasons. And love isn't enough anyway. I realize that now. I'm sorry, Kelly. Please forget about me and move on.

* * *

To: Ian Anderson <iananderson2@gmail.com>
From: Kelly Hopkins <kh2358@columbia.edu>
Subject: **Re: I'm Sorry**
February 20, 10:20am

Ian,

This is crazy! I've read your email three times, and I just don't get it. I don't understand how you can suddenly change like this. I think we just need to talk. Are you angry at me because you think the accident wouldn't have happened if I didn't have that stupid craving? I've been blaming myself every day since you were hurt. I know you say I act like a victim sometimes, but I think I have every right to be upset by what you just sent me.

I love you so much—that has not changed. Are you scared for me to see you? I don't care if you can't move a muscle in your body; I will always want to be there by your side. If you can just convince your mom to let me through the gate, then we can see each other. Then you can remember why we have always made this work. Can you please just call me? I've already called your mom, but she won't pick up. I'm going to keep emailing you until we see each other again.

You did not "use" me. I never felt used by you. Do you remember that pinky promise you made me after the Thanksgiving from Hell? You said that money and status weren't important to you. I don't believe you can suddenly say that you need to go back to your duties as an Anderson. You've never wanted to do that. There must be another reason. Please, please let me see you.

And I also don't believe you would want us to abort or give up the baby. I'm not going to do it because I know you are just saying this now out of anger or maybe your mom is making you say that—I know you don't truly mean it. I'm keeping this baby, Ian, because he/she is a part of me and a part of you.

Love you. Always.

* * *

To: Ian Anderson <iananderson2@gmail.com>
From: Kelly Hopkins <kh2358@columbia.edu>
Subject: **Are You Getting These??**
February 27, 8:02am

I've been writing to you every day and I'm not sure if you are getting my emails? I haven't heard from you in a week. Please send me something—anything—so I know you're okay. Please. Do you want me to go to your mom's place again? Can you walk out to the front of the gate? Please Ian.

I love you. Always.

* * *

To: Ian Anderson <iananderson2@gmail.com>
From: Kelly Hopkins <kh2358@columbia.edu>
Subject: **Ian?**
March 21, 11:35am

I hope you're still checking this email. This is now #30 of my daily emails and I'm really trying not to give up hope. Or lose it.

I re-read your email every day, but it still makes zero sense. If you were using me, why would you propose to me? We're engaged! You came to my grandmother's funeral because you said you can't live without me. Why have you changed your mind? Why can't you pick up the phone when I call you? Are you being brainwashed by your mom?

Ian, will you just *please* call me? I miss your voice so much, and I know the minute we talk you'll remember all the reasons we're together.

This month has been absolute torture. I don't get sick anymore, but my back and feet hurt, and I know you would've given me massages all the time. I miss your hand on my stomach. The way you look at me in the morning. The random, funny texts you used to send me all throughout the day. I can't imagine having this baby without you. He hasn't kicked yet, but I feel like you've already missed so much.

Also, Melissa came over yesterday. (Had to remind her again that Kevin and Roy were taken, LOL.) By the way, they say hi. I hoped they would be able to get through to your mom, but she's not answering their calls, either. I really hope you know we're all trying.

Anyway, Melissa came over, and I lost it in front of her. She was trying to cheer me up, making fun of the boyish stuff in your room, but it's all too hard. She stayed with me for a while, hugging me on the bed, but all I could think about was the comfort of your arms. You always knew exactly what to say.

And I love Melissa. She's a good friend. She even promised to be there at the hospital when Jack is born (I think I told you this in my last email—we are having a boy!!!). But right now, the baby and I need you.

Ugh. Here I go, crying again. This isn't right. You're supposed to be here. I know in my heart that we are meant to be together, and you are meant to be the father of this child. Please, please, *please,* just reply. Anything! My thoughts go back and forth from you being completely gone (I seriously check the news every day), to you trapped in your mom's basement somewhere, to you really meaning that you don't want to be together anymore. But I have a hard time believing any of those. We were happy. I don't understand. Please help me understand.

Love you. Always.

* * *

To: Ian Anderson <iananderson2@gmail.com>
From: Kelly Hopkins <kh2358@columbia.edu>
Subject: **I'm Leaving NY; Please Reply**
April 28, 1:37pm

I'm packing my bags. It's been two months since I've heard from you, two more months of Jack growing bigger and bigger. I can't concentrate in school. I owe Kevin and Roy $1,600 for rent. BTW, I refuse to use the 50K that you wired me because I am not getting rid of the baby. They've been nice to cover me, but I can't keep doing that to them. B.B. said he'd let me live with him, so I'm heading back to L.A. tonight. I'm not going to tell Melissa. I can't handle her reaction.

I walked around Columbia one last time today. Everywhere I went reminded me of you. I kept looking around like I might suddenly see you. How dumb is that?

These past few months I kept hoping you would come back and everything will return to normal, but now I realize that will never happen. You are not here. You will not be back. Everything in New York makes me think of you. Anything and everything. I can't stay in your room, can't stay with your friends, can't even see my own friends because they ask about you.

I can't afford tuition anymore, even with my scholarship. And there's no way I can still go to Columbia and try to be a lawyer while raising a kid alone. When you're ready to talk, I will be here. But otherwise I need to try to accept the fact that you are completely done with me. So, that means I need to move across the country and try to build a life on my own again.

You can send me back a blank email. Anything. Something so I know that you got this and that you know where your fiancé and son are.

* * *

To: Kelly Hopkins <kh2358@columbia.edu>
From: Ian Anderson <iananderson2@gmail.com>
Subject: **Please Stop Emailing Me**
May 1, 4:05pm

Please, do yourself a favor and stop contacting me. I just want to be alone. I think we rushed into the engagement without thinking things through. Please use the $50,000. I told you to abort the baby and now it is too late. At least consider putting him up for adoption. I won't be the father of this child. I want to start anew and I can't if you keep him. I hope you are not doing this in order for me to pay you child support. Then you will become exactly what my mother said you were, which is a gold digger. Perhaps she was right? If you have the child, it will be an embarrassment for both of us. It will tarnish my family's reputation and yours. So please do the right thing. Start your future without me. And for both of our sakes, please do not contact me ever again.

* * *

To: Ian Anderson <iananderson2@gmail.com>
From: Kelly Hopkins <kh2358@columbia.edu>
Subject: **Re: Please Stop Emailing Me**
May 1, 4:25pm

I have no idea what to say. For months, I have emailed you and tried to call you with no response and finally you reply with this ridiculous message. I can barely see the screen right now I'm crying so hard. Never in a million years would I get rid of our child. And I don't want your filthy money. So don't worry, I will not be asking you for child support. I will make sure that Jack doesn't even know who his father is.

All I wanted was to be a lawyer. To be independent. Have a beautiful child together, as a family. You took that away from me. I thought you were different. I loved you. But you disgust me even more than your mother. I should have ended it when I went back to L.A. for my grandmother's funeral, but you begged me to take you back. You swore you would always be there for me. How can you be such a liar?

How could I have been so wrong?

* * *

To: Ian Anderson <iananderson2@gmail.com>
From: Kelly Hopkins <kh2358@columbia.edu>
Subject: **Update**
June 8, 2:34pm

I don't know why I'm updating you. Why do I feel the need to? Why do I still miss you so badly? Why do I still think about you? Maybe it's more for me. A way to write things down, a way to pretend you're still listening. Even if you delete this account, I don't care, I just need to pretend for a minute that the Ian I knew still exists somewhere. Because he would care.

Sometimes, when B.B. is feeling bad for me, he takes me out to lunch at Halmuni's favorite place. Everyone can tell I'm pregnant now and you should hear what these people say in Korean about me. They think they're whispering. *Look at that girl. So heavy. So fat. I heard she's having a baby on her own. A disgrace. I'm surprised her friend even still associates with her.* I'm a freak show to them. Sometimes I am to myself, too.

I had another doctor's visit today. Jack is healthy. Kicking a lot. I started crying in front of a nurse while I was on the chair after the ultrasound. I was embarrassed even though I'm pretty sure every nurse at that hospital has seen me cry by now. It's not easy carrying a child by yourself—trying to grab things when you feel like you can barely move; when you're crying in pain and no one knows; when the doctors and staff ask you where your husband is. They've tried to walk me through the delivery process a few times, but I couldn't handle it. It seems too scary to deal with on my own.

"Do you know who's going to drive you home?" they ask. "Do you want to take this info home to your partner?"

Every time I have to say no. I have to explain it's just me.

Imagining these moments used to make me so happy: you smiling at the ultrasound pictures, nodding over the brochures, calming me down at the end of the day. You would've been the perfect coach, the perfect hand to squeeze.

Jack wakes me up in the middle of the night a lot with his kicking. Reminding me he's there and he's coming. Whether I'm ready or not. I watch Halmuni's favorite Korean dramas to try not to feel so alone. To try to think about her and not you. To try to forget what it ever felt like to touch your hand. Remembering is too painful.

* * *

To: Ian Anderson <iananderson2@gmail.com>
From: Kelly Hopkins <kh2358@columbia.edu>
Subject: **Update 2**
July 20, 8:09pm

I had my 22nd birthday on July 16, and you weren't there to celebrate it with me. How different things can be after only one year. Do you remember last year when you came back from work and you brought all my favorite Korean food and a bottle of wine to celebrate I'd reached the legal drinking age? We were so happy then. I still can't understand what's happened to us.

I also can't believe my due date is in a few weeks. I cry every day. I have no idea what to do. B.B. can only help me out so much financially. I'm going to use the 50K you wired me. I haven't yet because I've been hoping this is some sort of bad dream. But I need the money now. It's not for me, it's for Jack. That's what I keep telling myself. Don't worry, I'm not going to ask for child support. Your mom always thought I was after your money, so that is the last thing I want to do because then she will think she was always right. But you know that isn't the truth. Right, Ian? But I guess it doesn't matter anymore.

I was going to pawn the engagement ring, too. I was standing outside the pawn shop, ready to get rid of it forever. Get rid of you. But I couldn't. I guess a tiny part of me still hopes you'll show up at my door like you showed up at Halmuni's funeral and smile that mischievous little grin and tell me it's okay. Giving away the ring would be like finally giving up all hope for you. And I'm still not ready—don't know when I'll ever be ready—to do that.

Part of me still just doesn't know what happened. It's like falling off the swing set when you're a kid. One minute you're up in the air and the next you're eating wood chips. You don't remember the space in between. One minute you were kissing me on top of the head, determined to get me something to eat, then the next you disappeared forever.

I still love you, but I guess you don't.

I wish I didn't.

* * *

To: Ian Anderson <iananderson2@gmail.com>
From: Kelly Hopkins <kh2358@columbia.edu>
Subject: **Welcomed Jack Hopkins into The World Today**
August 4, 6:30am

Ian,

Our son was born today. I couldn't get a hold of B.B., so my Uber driver had to deal with my screaming. I know I told you I was going to try to have a natural birth, but they're right; you ask for all the drugs in the world once the contractions get closer together. The nurses and doctors were amazing, trying to make up for the heavy absence in the room. After about eight hours of pain I thought would never end, Jack made his way into the world. He was born at 5:05 am at 19 inches, 7lbs, 8oz. He is absolutely beautiful. I never thought I could love something this much. Looking at his eyes (blue!!) with black hair.

This is the last email that I will send you. Since you haven't replied, I will just assume you really didn't love me and I will let you go. But I still can't help going back to the night of the accident. Perhaps you do blame me for it. If you do, I'm sooooo sorry. I wish I could go back in time and tell you not to leave for that stupid Kimbap, or insist that you take an Uber.

B.B. has been telling me to be strong and let go. He said that you are a complete jerk and asshole and that he hopes you rot in hell. He also said that you don't deserve me and that I will have a much better life without you. I guess he is right that I need to let you go. I have to start a new life for Jack. I have to look forward, rather than backwards. I don't know what the future will bring and I'm scared. But like B.B. said, I have to stay positive, and he keeps reminding me about my dad telling me to have "high hopes." I don't even sing that song anymore. An ant can't move a rubber tree plant, so that song is just stupid and unrealistic. Life is hard and just having high hopes doesn't make it better. It's best to have lower expectations. But, I have Jack now, so I will try to remain positive for him.

I loved you, Ian Anderson, with all my heart. I'm sorry that I wasn't good enough for you and your family. I will miss you.

IAN

THREE YEARS LATER

CHAPTER TWENTY-NINE

"Ian. *So good to finally meet you in person.*"

Craig Harrington, a 40-something hotshot investor, shook my hand firmly. He had become a billionaire ten years earlier when his first investment, a startup tech company, went public with a big splash. I had only ever heard his voice over the phone, but it matched his large, muscular frame and sharp features.

"Likewise," I replied.

We stood beside a table in a fancy-enough restaurant in downtown Los Angeles. I was surprised Craig hadn't made a bigger effort to impress me. But then again, he did reserve the entire back room, so we were one of the only parties on this side of the restaurant. The empty space made the waiters in the corner more noticeable; in fact, they looked practically eager to pounce on us in hopes of getting a large tip. Julia, Craig's wife, shook my hand. Like Craig, she was all smiles for this meeting. She wore a conservative black dress, and her hair appeared to be modeled after my mother's. I had to hand it to Craig; he was doing his damnedest to ingratiate himself with us.

I was just turning to introduce my fiancé when she stuck out her arm. "I'm Camy," she practically shouted. She wore a skintight orange dress, completely inappropriate for this casual dinner. But I hadn't said anything earlier. Why bother? I knew by now not to challenge her wardrobe selections. *Why is she even here again?* Oh, right. My mother invited her.

"And I'm sorry again it's been so long." Craig sat down, motioning for us to do the same. He shook his head at himself, doing the whole self-deprecating act. "I'm the guy who calls you on Thanksgiving five years ago, interrupts family time, then disappears for a couple of years. Well, at least we're finally getting this done."

More disarming smiles from the Harringtons filled the pause between breaths.

"It's just that, with my CFO calling it quits back then," Craig continued, "we went into reorganization mode. That's why I didn't contact you for a while. But I can assure you, Ian, we are very much back on our feet, ready to make this deal happen. And I just want you to know..."

Craig blathered on some more, piling on platitudes and compliments about my mother, my late father, and, of course, the investment company he founded. The more he bloviated, the more I checked out.

The paper lamps bathed the private room in a warm light. We sat in the cozy glow, shadows dancing off Craig's bushy eyebrows. I remembered to nod my head, doing my best not to let my eyes glaze over. Craig seemed nice enough, but his eagerness—bordering on desperation —made me uncomfortable. To buy our company, he would probably shine my shoes right now if I asked him to.

I stretched my right leg out to the side so I could keep it straight—the only way the dull, throbbing ache below my kneecap would abate. Noticing Craig's lips had stopped moving, I threw in a "Sounds great."

Honestly, I used to care. I really did. I enjoyed working a room and was good at it. It was a joy to make mental calculations, to detect which personalities I might get along with best. The volleying give-and-take of conversation was an art form I excelled at. Not only could I resuscitate dying chitchat, I helped shy people feel comfortable. I liked the challenge, to see if I could get others to have a good time. My mother always called it my "natural charm," but I was genuinely interested in learning about others.

Plus, all those people are right about how near-death experiences force you to reevaluate your life. Ever since my accident, I had one plan of action: sell my dad's company, take the money, and start my own law firm. Despite the excruciating physical therapy sessions I had endured and all the missed coursework, I was finally close to earning my *juris doctorate*. Then I could move onto my goal of creating a firm giving a voice to the voiceless. Yes, this meeting was part of that plan, extricating me from the family business, but it was also a colossal bore. All my life, I've done the social dance with the Craigs of the world. Summoning the will to pretend like he wasn't a big fat phony, even to get what I wanted, well, it felt just too exhausting to attempt.

"So, how's the leg?" Craig topped off my wine glass with Pinot Noir.

"Still doing rehab. Guess *The Nutcracker* will have to go on without me."

Camy laughed, a little too hard.

"Ah, well, I'm sure with your work ethic, you'll be running a marathon in no time," Craig said. Julia nodded beside him.

"I'll be alright," I said with a grin.

Camy leaned into me, brushing her finger along my scar, which traveled from my temple to my jawline. "Too bad we can't rehab that out."

I smiled at Craig and Julia. *Isn't she hilarious!*

Julia chuckled politely. "It makes him look tough."

Camy squeezed my arm, her manicured fingers almost stabbing through my sports jacket. "He is my little muscle man."

I stared off at nothing, trying to suppress the scream building in back of my throat.

"So, Ian, where'd you meet this beautiful young woman?" Julia took a piece of molasses bread and dipped it in a plate swimming with oil and balsamic vinegar.

Camy cut in. "Oh, we've known each other since high school. And our mothers are friends. They were always trying to set us up." Cute as a button, Camy laid her head on my shoulder. I wanted to pick off the strands of that chemically straightened and colored blonde hair with a lint roller.

"Ah, Beverly the matchmaker." Craig turned to his wife, still chewing her bread. "Sounds like B.B.'s mom."

"You know someone named B.B.?" asked Camy. "Like the gun?"

"Yeah. Lawyer friend of mine. Real name's Brian. He likes to use 'B.B. Chu' because he thinks people will remember his name better—like BBQ."

"His mom's a hoot, too," Julia chimed in. "She's always trying to set him up with someone new."

"Never seems to stick, though." Craig nodded to Camy, using the piece of bread in his hand to point at her ring finger. "Ian, looks like she will stick with you, though!" He said with a knowing wink.

Camy held up her hand, scrunching her nose. She liked to make sure no one forgot to notice the rock on her finger. "We are so excited."

I hated when she said "we."

Julia's mouth went agape at the huge emerald-shaped Harry Winston monstrosity my mother had picked out.

"It was just meant to be." Camy took my arm again.

Removing it, I took a long gulp of wine and poured another. I didn't have to worry about saying anything; Camy would take over this part of the conversation. She always did.

"It's easier when you know the same people," Camy explained. "You just really understand each other."

I smiled at Craig and Julia, nodding along. *Perfectly.*

* * *

My hand instinctively reached for the bill, but Craig stopped me. "Don't even try." He grinned wide as the Cheshire Cat. It's like his smile just widened and widened as the night went on.

I capitulated. "All right. But next time, it's on me." I put my hand on Camy's bare shoulder. I already knew she was going to ask for my jacket later. Why didn't she just wear warmer clothing? "Ready to go?"

"Nonsense," Julia said, writing down a tip. "Come over to our place. We have this huge chocolate mousse pie in the fridge just waiting to be eaten. I insist."

"That's very tempting, but we should get going," I replied.

Camy tugged at my arm. "Oh, come on, darling. We never do anything fun."

I looked at her, at those imploring blue eyes that looked Photoshopped. *Empty and blank with no soul behind them.*

"Besides, we just live up the street," Craig added.

* * *

I lost the argument and the night dragged on. Leaving the restaurant on Bunker Hill, we accompanied Craig and Julia a couple blocks downtown. Buzzed, Julia staggered crookedly, one arm draped over Craig as we made our way toward the beckoning lights of the Staples Center.

"You guys spend a lot of time in D.T.L.A.?" asked Craig.

Before we could answer, Julia called back. "It's gotten so cool!"

"Like Manhattan," Craig noted. "But with better weather."

I could see Camy wasn't impressed. She preferred Rodeo Drive in Beverly Hills. She only wanted to stay where the über rich stayed—where all the high-end stores like Chanel, Louis Vuitton, Gucci were. I knew she didn't like this area because if you wandered even one block off the main drag, you were deep into Skid Row.

"Looks dirty to me," Camy whispered into my ear. "Trash on the streets. Graffiti everywhere." She pointed to the tarps beside a half-completed construction site as she wrapped my sports jacket closer.

Craig waited for us to catch up to them, then turned to me. "We got in early, you know. Before gentrification," he whispered.

"We've always been early adaptors," Julia smiled huge again.

I started to return her smile, but then Julia stumbled on a beer can and nearly took down Craig with her.

Once in their building's elevator—made of glass so you could see the two, unfairly split worlds below— Craig pushed the button for the 15th floor. The penthouse. We rocketed skyward. With each passing level, I felt we were rising above the everyday struggle of "ordinary" people's lives. Obviously, I was grateful for my family's wealth—and too often I had taken it for granted—but ever since the accident I found myself slowly despising it, especially after being forced to spend a year living with my mother. She had insisted I stay with her after to supervise my recovery. She wouldn't let me check my emails, watch TV, or call friends because she wanted me to "focus 100 percent on my rehabilitation." Lacking the strength to argue, I gave in to her.

I did manage to message my old roommates, Roy and Kevin, a few times. When I mentioned I was now engaged to Camy, they seemed genuinely shocked and disappointed, as if I had committed some heinous crime. I had been dating Camy right up until the day of the accident, so why did Roy and Kevin seem so surprised? After a year of physiotherapy, with armies of specialists coming and going through my mother's place in Connecticut, I was finally well enough that I could return to Manhattan, but whenever I called them to announce I was coming in, they would always make an excuse not to see me. What had I done that they wanted to avoid me, I wondered.

When I asked my mother why Roy and Kevin seemed so surprised that I was engaged to Camy, she explained that we had never announced it formally. Yes, we had intended to, but then the accident happened. I also asked her to explain why I had been riding a bicycle in the middle of the night. Both Camy and my mother said that I had been under a lot of stress at school and just wanted to get out and enjoy some fresh air. *Why can't I remember any of this?*

We walked into the Harringtons' vast and swanky duplex loft, decorated in the minimalist style you saw marketed on trendy, redecorating reality shows. Spotless, cold, and clinical, it resembled a modern nightclub before the clubbers arrived. The duplex must have been at least 6,000 square feet. The kitchen and living room blended together in a splash of white, images from a 60-inch flat-screen TV the only spot of color in the high-ceilinged room. Doorways branched off to bedrooms in a narrow hallway. To my right, a floor-to-ceiling window showcased the neon rainbow of lights from skyscrapers buttressing the building on every side.

Camy made some comment about interior design that sparked Craig's interest. He bobbed his head as she continued talking, his mouth parted, just dying to say something interesting as soon as she paused in her monologue. Meanwhile, Julia excused herself to the kitchen. I collapsed onto the startling white leather couch, straightening out an already-straight pillow.

As Camy and Craig chatted, I didn't even try to keep that stupid smile on my face. Something was gnawing at me, like a bad dream you didn't quite understand. That name, B.B. Chu, sounded familiar. Each day I remembered something new, but it was usually trivial. It was frustrating; I felt like my brain was wasting all its memory power on the mundane while missing the bigger picture. After the accident, the doctors told me I was suffering from retrograde amnesia, that the blow to my head had erased whole sections of my memory. They said the condition could be temporary, but it could also be permanent loss. Only time would tell. Well, it has been three years already. Did this mean I would never remember the missing years before the accident?

"Honey?"

Shit.

Craig and Camy looked at me expectantly. Julia did, too. She held out the chocolate mousse cake on a large plate. *What did she want from me? Is she waiting for me to cut the cake and hand out fucking slices?*

Camy looked embarrassed. *Great.* She was definitely going to bring this up later. "Darling, why don't you try the cake? It is amazing."

They were all waiting for an answer. "I'm not hungry right now. I'm still full from dinner. Can you please direct me to the bathroom?"

They blinked back at me for a second before Julia put the plate down. "Let me show you. It's complicated. I got lost the first time myself."

* * *

I walked out of the bathroom, wondering if I could pretend to get lost for an hour. Then I heard it.

"Just what makes that little old ant ... think he'll move that rubber tree plant ..." A woman's voice filtered through a half-open door on my right. The sound made me stand still. I couldn't breathe. I knew that song. That voice. Where had I heard it before? There was something there. Something ... I couldn't put my finger on it.

I loitered in that hallway, ears perked, trying to make my mind work. The voice ebbed, replaced by the shrill sounds of children giggling. Something rose up in me, some unknown feeling. I had to lean against the wall; otherwise, I thought I would split in two. Though I didn't remember it being warm when I entered the Harringtons', beads of sweat formed on my brow. I wiped them away and pulled myself to my feet.

"What's the matter with you?" was the first thing Camy said to me when I rejoined the others.

"Huh?" I just wanted to lie down and sleep for a month.

Craig and Julia were digging into their cake. I could see my piece was still sitting there, but I didn't want it.

When I said nothing more, Camy went right on with her conversation. They were discussing the differences between the islands of Greece. I listened absently for a few moments while I watched a line of cars snake onto the 110 onramp.

"Excuse me. I need to use your bathroom again."

"Again?"

I didn't wait for them to interrogate me further. I just got up and went back down the hall. In the distance, I could hear Camy apologizing for me being weird.

The melodic singing picked up again along with children giggling as I passed down the long corridor. I leaned my ear against a door so I could hear clearer "... *He had high hopes! He had high hopes! He had high apple pie in the sky hopes! So any time you're feelin' low, stead of lettin' go, just remember that that ant. Oops, there goes another rubber tree ... Oops, there goes another rubber tree ... Oops, there goes another rubber tree plant ...*" The tiny hairs on my arms stood up, and I had to hug the wall for support. My throat felt dry, and I couldn't swallow. Nothing made sense.

Pushing the door open the slightest crack, I stopped and peeked in. Faint illumination from a child's night light reminded me of my own childhood, a feeling I hadn't recalled in years. Safety and longing intermixed. It felt like I was outside of time looking in at my own self years earlier. The singing woman stood with her back to me. Opening the door a bit more revealed three little boys in two different twin beds. Two of them were white and appeared to be twins. Another seemed faintly Asian, but I wasn't sure because he had blue eyes, and he sat off to the side, staring up at the woman. He must have seen a flicker of movement and turned his eyes up to me.

"Look." He pointed at me.

The woman whipped around, and I was instantly pulled into her dark brown eyes. They, too, looked remotely Asian. They swallowed mine in their pain. It was like she drowning and had to grip onto something—anything or she would sink. But quick as a blink, they let go and a hardness papered over her whole face. Bitterness tore down the corners of her mouth. She tightened her jaw and backed away from me.

She stood there, staring at me, rocking back on her heels as if she was either going to fall over or bolt from the room.

It was so soft I wasn't sure I heard her say something at first.

Then she repeated it. "Get out," she hissed.

Her brown eyes now glared, hatred pouring out. She looked like she wanted to hit me, or worse.

I stepped back. "Okay, sorry, sorry. Didn't mean to intrude."

I quickly shut the door, startled. Maybe she was mad I had been listening. But I didn't think she would've been *that* mad. The door had been open. Whatever the source of her rage, it seemed ... *personal.*

I returned to the living room, shaken, while everyone scooped chocolate mousse into their mouths.

"So, you up for talking final details, or do you want to wait for another time?" Craig asked, finishing a bite.

I looked past his head. *Do I know that face? And why did that song pull me in like that?*

I felt Camy's hand on my arm. She turned to Craig. "Sorry. He's a bit of a space case sometimes."

I removed her hand. "I'm fine."

Craig looked annoyed for a second, then changed his demeanor, turning his expression into a smile and nod. Just like me. Practiced.

"You know ... we should probably call it a night," Camy said.

"Yes, plus, we'll see you both tomorrow, with Beverly. We can talk more then."

Julia took away plates as we stood up.

"Sounds lovely. Looking forward to it," Camy said, filling the silence. She waited for me to do something, so I smiled.

* * *

Camy and I stepped outside to a cold gust of wind. She took my jacket from me again. "You're always so distracted."

"Yeah."

She placed her fingers in mine, whispering seductively. "You know what could make you feel better ..."

"I actually think I want to take a walk."

"Alone? It's midnight."

"I'll take you back first."

She looked at me, her eyes flickering with rage. Two angry women in one night. At least I understood her reasons. "This is exactly the kind of thing I was talking about on the plane," she said. "You need to try harder. I have certain expectations you know ..."

I let her continue her tirade all the way back to our hotel. She ranted about the usual stuff: the inattention, the aloofness, all the times she felt disconnected. I apologized for it all. I made no excuses for myself. I told her everything she wanted to hear, until we hit the lobby of the Beverly Wilshire.

"I'll be back soon. I just need some fresh air."

"What?"

I could hear her screaming after me as I pushed past the doormen into the night. Jacketless, I shivered as I headed toward main streets, witnessing more high-rise hotels, expensive couture shops, and over-priced restaurants.

I could not get the strange woman out of my head. She was so angry. Even more than Camy. You didn't get that angry at someone unless you knew them. But I didn't know her. Or did I?

Why can't I remember?

CHAPTER THIRTY

I had hoped the massage and sauna would do me some good. With my mother arriving in just a few hours, the walls felt like they were caving in. Just like they always did when she showed up. Soon, she, too, would be staying at the Beverly Wilshire Hotel. In a different suite than Camy and me, yes, but her mere presence would suck all the available air out of the hotel. Before that happened, I had to get away. Had to regroup. This trip to the pool and spa would have to be my reprieve. Otherwise, I would crack. I could feel it.

I purposely set my alarm for 5:00 a.m. and stabbed it off before Camy awoke, before she could ask me a zillion questions. Always a deep sleeper, she was bound to be out until noon after washing down her nightly Ambien with the room's complimentary bottled water.

The less Camy asked me, the better. Not only did I not feel like talking, I had no answers for her. After circling much of Rodeo Drive for hours on end last night, I was still no closer to understanding any of what had occurred in Craig's apartment. I went to bed with the sinking feeling I would never unravel this mystery.

For years, my physical therapists recommended I make swimming my workout to rebuild the plasticity of my joints. Though I always promised I would, I seldom made the effort. It used to drive Camy crazy.

"Take care of yourself," she said. She also let me know in no uncertain terms I had let myself go. And she was right. Whenever I looked through old photo albums, I could barely recognize the skinny kid in the even skinnier jeans. It wasn't just that I didn't have the scars back then; I looked lighter, happier.

Whatever. That's just what being young is. Being too stupid to realize you're, well ... stupid.

But today I did heed the meddling well-wishers. The first one downstairs, I swam lap after lap until my sides ached and my eyes went blurry from the chlorine. Even then, I kept slapping and kicking the water until I could barely hold myself up to tread water.

Stepping out of the pool, I wobbled over to the metal bar where I left my towel. My calves burned, and I was dying for water, but I felt good. My mind was a beautiful blank. No thoughts. No worries.

"Okay there?" a middle-aged woman in an eggshell swim cap asked me from one of the lanes.

"Good, thanks."

I could feel her eyes on me as I ripped open the sauna door. The blast of dry heat calmed me even more as I landed on the wooden slats. A miniature clock provided the only noise, ticking away the minutes below a smudgy red lamp.

I put my elbows on the towel draped over my knees, clasping my head with my hands, glad to be the only occupant. Within seconds, the water evaporated from my skin. I felt a tightening in my chest as I tried to take in deep breaths. Sweat ran down my cheeks, pooling between my feet. As usual, all of the weighing concerns overtook my peace of mind, and I was back in worry-mode, my usual state of being. Crises and potential crises swirled around, each one begging for my attention: our impending wedding, our impending company sale, our impending ... life. I put my head in my hands, dreaming of blackness, the absence of thought. Just to make it all wash away.

I closed my eyes as the minutes passed, feeling the heat do its work, breaking down the layers of tension, the anxiety. The longer I sat, the more I relaxed. I gave up trying to make sense of things, returning to that calmness from a few minutes ago. When the concerns slipped away and I could lay back against my towel in peace, she returned.

The singing woman with the children. That song. That face. *Who was she?*

I still couldn't shake that image. The woman's anger was... abnormal. She really hated me. But why?

I hummed the song to myself, over and over, the sound bouncing off each wooden wall. The tune remained right in front of me, teasing, suspended in the growing heat. It had to be a key to something.

* * *

I opened the limo door for Camy. We were parked outside the Beverly Wilshire, minutes away from grabbing lunch with Craig and Julia to finalize the acquisition. This time, she wore an outfit my mother would approve: knee-length pencil skirt, a pink button-up T-shirt, and dangly earrings that nearly touched her shoulders. Her blonde hair had been slicked back into a high, tight ponytail.

"Hey." I said as I took her arm as she stepped in. "Do you want to skip this? I don't think my mother needs me."

She narrowed her eyes like I had just said the most asinine thing imaginable. "What? Last time I checked, this was *your* company."

I waved my hand. "It was my father's."

She found the farthest possible seat away from me and removed a Perrier from the mini-fridge. "And now it's yours. We'll be fabulously rich once you sell it."

I sighed as our driver pulled away from the curb. Sometimes I saw flashes of who I imagined Camy was before her parents forced her to attend debutante balls at age 13. That Camy would have skipped lunch and gone on an adventure. I knew that Camy existed because sometimes late at night, as her Ambien kicked in, vestiges of her former self appeared.

In those moments, she would surprise me by telling some story about a mischievous prank she pulled in junior high or at summer camp. Unfortunately, if I laughed too hard, she got the wrong impression and would shrink, embarrassed, reverting back to the "public Camy" others expected. After the accident, my mother repeatedly reminded me how much I loved Camy and how ecstatic I had been when Camy accepted my proposal. But then why didn't I feel "in love" with her? Why does everything she do and say irk me, instead? Did I lose all my feelings for her because of the accident?

I kept my eyes on Camy as we took the short drive down Santa Monica Boulevard toward West Hollywood, hoping to extract the real version of her. She had to be there, somewhere, deep down—the woman I was supposed to love.

"Tuck in your shirt," she said as she sipped from her Perrier. "Looks sloppy."

* * *

My mother sat at the table at the Fig and Olive in Melrose Place, waiting for us, surrounded by a mountain of papers, a glass of Sauvignon Blanc within easy reach. She removed her sunglasses and stood up when she saw us, wrapping her arms around Camy and kissing me on the cheek. The image of them together made me shudder. Camy looked like my mother's Mini-Me: similar wardrobe, faces caked with makeup. Forget daughter-in-law, Camy would've made the perfect *daughter* to Beverly Anderson. Camy even ordered the same drink just as soon as she slid into the plush booth.

Sunlight poured in through the open windows, reflecting brilliantly off our water glasses. I reluctantly sat down, neatly folding my napkin in my lap. Camy and my mother made small talk about the scene in New York versus Los Angeles. Though I only half-listened, they both made the case with equal intensity that the former far-outweighed the latter.

"It just comes down to *culture*, don't you think?" Camy said, to which my mother readily agreed.

Julia and Craig walked in, smiley eagerness plastered on their faces again. They behaved as if nothing at all was weird about last night, but I sensed they would strike any imaginable pose as long as they could walk away with my company. *Fine. They could have it. Just get me out of here.*

After shaking hands, I sat back down, letting my eyes travel up to the ornate mural on the ceiling many feet above our heads. There, a group of angels wafted heavenward with upturned cherubic faces. They looked so happy and carefree. If it were at all socially acceptable, I would keep my neck craned to stare at them until this whole deal was inked.

However, that was not to be. No one ever lets you off so easily. They actually want your attention. My mother and Craig reviewed details like the warranties and dividend shares, every now and then searching my face for assent. Whenever this happened, I kept my expression determined and serious as I hummed that haunting song in my head.

At some point, my mother began handing over paper after paper to Craig. He was ready with his pen each time, smiling away. Julia looked on like she was watching a NASCAR race. Halfway through the thick packet, Craig excused himself to go to the bathroom.

I used the break to lean into my mother, who was dog earing the next few pages. "Hey, I think I'm gonna go."

"What?"

Camy rolled her eyes at me from the edge of the table.

I ignored her, as well as Julia's frozen smile. "You have my Power of Attorney, anyway. Sign for me."

She looked at me as if I had slapped her across the mouth.

Camy took me by the hand.

"Don't," I said with a stern look.

I dropped her hand and stood up. I opened my mouth to say something else, to give Camy a reasonable excuse, or to go the other route—to say I didn't give a shit anymore, but then I closed it. I had no words. Instead, I turned and walked out, not daring to look back at their stunned faces.

* * *

I could have gone back to the hotel. I could have gone anywhere really—to a bar to watch sports, to a bookstore to browse, to a part of town I hadn't yet visited. Instead, I asked my driver to take me downtown.

An African-American security guard sat at the front desk of the Harrington's high-rise in a high-backed leather chair. Behind him, a split-screen monitor displayed various sections of the premises. An older man in his 50s, with a grey, bristly mustache and deep-set crevices, he kept his hands crossed in his lap as he leaned back to stare at me.

Okay. Fine. Time to use that "natural charm."

"Hello there, I'm here to visit Craig Harrington."

He studied me for a second. "You were here last night."

"Yes, sir. He's buying my father's company." *Literally. Right now. Somewhere else. But you don't need to know that.*

He mumbled something I didn't catch.

"So, can I go up?"

For a second, I thought he would say no, but then he waved me through.

"Appreciate it."

I took the elevator up to the penthouse floor. Trembling, my stomach felt like it was bouncing. *Why am I so nervous?*

The elevator doors opened. I readjusted my sports jacket, trying to take a deep breath but failing. *What is wrong with me?*

I stepped past two doors, then knocked on Craig's. Moments later, it swung open. In front of me stood the woman from the night before. This time, I noticed her enchanting face showed complexity. She had seen much joy. And much sadness. Tall and slender, she looked to be in her 20s. Dressed in a plain black T-shirt and yoga pants, she stood with one hand on the knob, the other holding a stuffed dog toy.

She wore the same expression, like she was vacillating between punching me in the nose or running away. Behind her, I could see the three children, also playing with stuffed animals. The loft actually looked like a real home today, with toys sprawled around the living room, plates with half-eaten PB&Js strewn across the table.

"What are you doing here?" Her nostrils flared. Heat behind her eyes.

I tried to straighten up. *You're charming. You are.* "Look, I know this is crazy. But I feel like I've met you before..."

Her eyes widened. If I thought she looked angry before, I had no idea what extremes she was capable of. This wasn't just anger. This was *rage.* I had to say something. "Um, that song. I know that song. I just don't understand—"

"*You* don't understand?" She gripped the door harder, eyes on full-alert.

"No. But I really want to."

"Is this some kind of sick joke?" She raised her arm up, the toy dog coming with it. She grit her teeth like she was preparing to throw a hand grenade. "Are you pretending not to know me because it may jeopardize the deal with the Harringtons? Are you scared that I will tell them that I know what a complete asshole you are? If so, don't worry I won't tell them what an insensitive jerk you are, because I don't care. I don't want to waste my time talking about you. You've ruined my life, but it doesn't mean that I have to be vindictive and ruin yours. I'm not like you. But look at what you've done to me ..."

She started something else but her voice broke. She couldn't continue. She was shaking now, her eyes filled with tears. I wanted to reach out to her, but didn't dare try. The nervous feeling in my stomach spread to my chest. I couldn't breathe. I felt dizzy. *What have I done to her? How did I ruin her life?*

"*Ian?*"

I turned around. Craig and Julia stood at the door behind me. "What are you doing here?"

I turned to look at the mysterious woman once more. She had managed to wipe her eyes in the meantime.

"Is there a problem?" Julia stole a glance at Craig.

"Beverly said you weren't feeling well," Craig said, frowning. "We didn't expect you to come … here."

I cleared my throat, catching a glimpse of the little handsome boy who looked a bit Asian, who was now standing behind the woman, arms wrapped around her legs, one eye peeking out, watching me.

"I thought I left my sunglasses here last night." *You weren't even wearing sunglasses, idiot.* "I asked your nanny to help me find them."

"Oh." Craig looked at the woman. "Did you see anything, Kelly?"

Kelly? Kelly. Kelly. Kelly.

"No," she said, still glaring at me.

Craig frowned again. "Sorry, Ian. We'll keep an eye out. Do you need a ride back to your hotel?"

"No, I'm okay."

I was just about to go when the little boy weaved through Kelly and Craig's legs. He ran up to me, holding out a pair of cheap, toy sunglasses. "Here," he said quietly.

I stared back at him, amazed at how he held my gaze. He had jet black hair and beautiful blue eyes.

Craig looked down at him and chuckled. "I'm not sure those will fit Mr. Anderson."

Julia smiled, patted the kid on the head, then disappeared down the hall. The woman they called Kelly quickly grabbed the child's hand and led him away. It was now just Craig and me in the foyer.

"Talk to you soon, Ian," Craig said, still a little on edge.

Kelly didn't look back once. A moment later, I heard the door close.

CHAPTER THIRTY-ONE

I pushed through the Beverly Wilshire's entrance doors, ignoring the obsequious greeter at the front desk, searching for any bright Hermes bags or shiny Valentino high heels indicating the presence of my mother. A wedding reception was in progress, and the dizzying crush of tuxedoed men and women in formal gowns—combined with people queuing for The Blvd Lounge—made it difficult.

I squinted as I maneuvered through the crowd, smartphone flashes popping all around me. I raced around young couples, slipping through plush couches and wooden chairs. More employees took up the greater lobby, smiling, eager to assist me with anything I wanted. I broke off eye contact. There was only one person who could help me now.

I found her seated with Camy at a table of the lounge tucked away in a private corner.

"Mother!" I shouted.

She and Camy turned, each with a hand caressing a glass of champagne. Camy avoided looking at me directly and took a distracted sip from her champagne flute.

My mother settled on her signature look of disappointment. "Don't shout." She waved her hand, annoyed.

I sat at the empty seat between them. My mother searched in her purse for something. "You couldn't stick around for a few more minutes?" she asked, clearly annoyed. "Your dad would have been furious you weren't there to actually sign the documents yourself."

I didn't care about the deal. "Did I—was there someone I used to know named Kelly?"

I thought my mother was having a heart attack. Her breathing seized. She dropped her purse, spilling credit cards, keys, and lipstick. All the color in her face drained. Then, just as quickly, she regained her composure.

A waiter saw the spillage and came over to pick the items off the floor. "Let me help you with that, Ms. Anderson," he said as if he had been responsible for the accident.

"Thank you."

She and Camy watched the waiter recover each item as if it was the most interesting thing they had ever witnessed. It was obviously a tactic they were using to avoid answering my question.

After what seemed like an eternity, the waiter finally left, and I asked again, "Mother, did I know someone named Kelly?"

She assumed a nonchalant pose, stood up from her chair and said, "She isn't worth talking about. Please be a dear and sign the bill. I'm very tired."

"Who was she?"

"Oh, just some girl from Columbia. To be honest, I had completely forgotten about her."

There was obviously more she wasn't telling me. I glanced at Camy. She looked bored. She handed my mother her bag and stood up, as well.

"She was just some gold digger," my mother said casually, adjusting her strap. "Used to follow you around like an eager puppy. Honestly, it was pathetic."

I looked between the two of them, trying to see who would crack first. Camy kept her expression blank, except for a tinge of annoyance. She rubbed the space between her eyebrows and sighed. "Ian, can you just get the bill so we can go? We all know you had many admirers at Columbia. Do we need to make a big deal about each one?"

My mother stared past me. "See? Now you're making Camy upset. I'm going up to my room."

I didn't budge. When my mother took me home from the hospital, she not only become my primary caretaker, but my memory-supplier, as well. With retrograde amnesia, I remembered who I was, as well as most of the major events in my early life, but the two or three years before the accident were a black hole. When I needed more info, she supplied it. Supporting her was Dr. Root, an A-List psychotherapist, whom I saw regularly for therapy sessions to "enhance cognitive function," as my mother would say, but also to make me "talk about my feelings."

During all this time, there had been no mention of a "Kelly."

"He's not moving," Camy said quietly as if I weren't there.

I looked over at her, at those startling bright blue eyes. So beautiful. So empty.

After one year of physiotherapy and psychotherapy sessions, I could have returned to Columbia to finish law school, but my mother insisted I go back to work at my father's hedge fund. During this past year, my mother and I constantly fought. Rage would erupt in me without warning. It didn't matter the context. Once I kicked a wicker chair so hard I shattered its legs. Another time, I put my fist through a mirror. I spent the next hour picking shards of slivered glass from my palm and wrist.

Dr. Root called these moments "my episodes." My bouts of explosive anger seemed to matter little to my mother. Even if we were in public, she hid away these inconvenient outbursts with calm just as efficiently as this hotel tucked away its Prohibition-era lounge behind an innocuous front.

Looking up at the uncanniness of her wrinkle-free face, I suddenly found myself marveling at the ways she always managed to avoid inconveniences. Whatever unpleasantness threatened to topple Beverly's cool pose—the death of my father, money complications, mortality itself—she faced it with cold, uncompromising resolve. Nothing ruffled her. She just clicked right past it in her high heels, smashing through any barrier, leaving the Camy's of the world to pick up the pieces.

This epiphany opened the floodgates in my damaged brain. It revealed something so basic, so incredibly simple, yet monumental. I didn't belong to Beverly Anderson. I didn't belong to Camy, either. Or to anyone else in this make-believe world. None of it had anything to do with me.

My mother couldn't force me to accept unwanted obligations. Especially not marriage. She couldn't even lord wealth over me. Per the contract I had helped draft, I owned a large chunk of the proceeds our company sale delivered. I was now independently wealthy. Set for life. She couldn't do a thing to me. Not anymore.

Turning around was easy. Slipping into the elevator was easier. I heard them call after me, but I was gone.

The number of revelers in the lobby had grown in my absence. I slipped between them, skirting past the celebrants in their dressy finest. I even saved an apologetic grin for the greeter I had earlier ignored.

* * *

"I need to remember," I said impatiently to Dr. Root.

I was beyond frustrated by what had happened in Los Angeles. Here I was, sitting in a chair in Dr. Root's Upper East Side office, trying to understand why I felt the way I had when I met Kelly and, more important, why was she so angry with me. Had I been a complete A-hole before the accident? Is that why I'm no longer friends with Roy and Kevin? Had I become like my father, a selfish prick who just wanted to make as much money as possible, friendships be damned? Was that possible?

I didn't want to believe that about myself. I could imagine spiraling into depression at the thought of this, so I focused on where I was, hoping perhaps Dr. Root could help me. As was his habit, Dr. Root, bald, with a ridged forehead and a grey beard, leaned forward like he was a swimmer at the blocks, ready to launch himself into the water, his fingers steepled at the base of his long thin nose.

"Ian," he said slowly in his characteristic monotone, drawing out both syllables. This was his game. Deaden your life force with slow-motion drudgery.

But I hadn't taken the red-eye here to get entangled in his human quicksand. "Look, I just need help remembering. Are you gonna help me or not?"

The more I seethed, the more he stalled. He kept his fingers close to his face, almost as if he was playing some invisible trumpet as he leaned back. It took him so long to hit the straight back chair, it felt like a full minute had passed.

"We've *talked* about this before," he said, elongating the pronunciation of each word. If I were a stenographer transcribing this moment, I would put an ellipsis between each one—that's how slowly he talked. "When you suffer from a traumatic injury like you did, sometimes the mind can do things. Strange things. Like make you forget."

Great, thanks for the help.

"We could try hypnotherapy."

"Isn't that for like, people who are into Tarot cards and Ouija boards?"

Even the way he shook his head looked smug. "Not necessarily. We can try a hypnotic regression session. It could serve to release past memories, items locked away in your subconscious."

I sighed. *I'm ready to try anything at this point.*

After placing a warm blanket over my shoulders, he instructed me to remove my shoes and get comfortable. I dropped my hands into my lap and closed my eyes just like he instructed, taking slow, deep breaths.

"Now ..." He began. At least he had a soothing, quiet voice. I could imagine him giving tax advice on some AM radio station. Granted, it would be a station I would turn off for fear of falling asleep at the wheel. "I want you to imagine an empty room ..."

I had tried guided meditation apps before and had some familiarity with what we were doing. As he proceeded to offer suggestions, I relaxed my limbs, allowing them to grow heavy like they were weighed down by bricks. The more he continued, his calming, lullaby voice pulled me in deeper. A few minutes in, I felt like I was in the room he was describing, floating on air, all my muscles slack.

"Ian?" I felt a hand on my shoulder.

I blinked my eyes open.

"It's okay. You just fell asleep during our session."

"Shit. Wait. Is that a good thing?"

Dr. Root sat back down, noting something on his yellow legal pad. "It means you were very relaxed, so that's always a good thing."

"No. I mean for my memories. Will I remember stuff now? Ask me something."

Dr. Root cleared his throat. "Ian, I'm afraid it doesn't work that way. Hypnotherapy only decreases your anxiety. It relaxes your mind and body, allowing you to open up for greater recollection. If I asked you what kind of things you were doing one year ago, even after a few hypnotherapy sessions, you still may not be able to tell me. It may not happen immediately."

Then what the hell was the point of what we just did? I could feel the frustration rising in me again. "Are you just trying to scam me?"

Someone else might take offense. Not calm Dr. Root. He even chuckled. "Certainly not. I only suggested this alternative because you are understandably keen on accessing your memories—"

"Well, Jesus Christ. Who wouldn't be?"

"… I'm doing all that I can to help you. Patients with amnesia may be able to uncover some memories eventually, but the more likely outcome is that those years in your life will remain opaque."

"Then, what was the point of your hypnotherapy session?"

"As I just told you, it is part of a coordinated treatment course to mitigate your tendency toward anger and anxiety."

I stared back at him, unmoving, unspeaking.

He finally broke the silence. "I'd like to recommend we reconvene in two weeks. You can tell me what progress you have made in the interim."

"I have to go," I said, knowing I would never return.

* * *

I walked out of Dr. Root's building and toward the blue Porsche I had bought that morning. I didn't want anything associated with my mother, including her limo, so I had made a stop at the dealership and made the purchase in what must have been record time. No haggling. I paid the full MSRP, leaving behind a very happy salesman. I hopped into the car, inhaling the delicious new car aroma, feeling the smoothness of the leather seats. I made sure I had a few minutes left at the meter and checked my phone. I started typing in google.com/flights, but a text from Camy popped up first.

"I'm going out with friends dancing tonight. Come if u want."

I started to type a response, then changed my mind.

I swiped out of the screen and went back to the flight info. I clicked on the first flight to Los Angeles I could find. One-way ticket. Sold.

CHAPTER THIRTY-TWO

Is it possible to fall in love with people without really knowing them? Kelly and her son, Jack, were strangers to me. Strangers who wanted nothing to do with Ian Anderson II. Yet, after returning to LA, I was compelled to rent a two-bedroom apartment in a high-rise across the street from Craig's. Undoubtedly less glamorous than his, the apartment was also sparser. *Spartan* was a better word. *Minimalist*, better still. Zero furniture except for the futon wedged in the corner. It didn't even have chairs. When I wanted to sit down, I perched on the windowsill with the view toward Kelly and Jack.

Days went on and on. I felt like a shivering man in the fallen snow, forever locked out of a cottage with a warm hearth, heat blazing inside. I remembered well what Craig's apartment looked like the day I barged in: the pajamas, the toys. Life. The happy mess. That's what I wanted.

I was hoping that by watching Kelly, I could begin to remember what really happened during those missing years. I stared out the window, affording me a kaleidoscopic view of the bustling city below. Teeming with diversity—honking cars, rich and poor, planted trees in the concrete urban jungle—I thought perhaps its alien vastness would trigger something inside me. Something demanding to be set free.

Unfortunately, it did no such thing. Unless you can count the hunger it unleashed in me. Not for food, though. For Kelly. For Jack. For any sense of belonging. And while my hunger for connection grew, I shriveled. Pounds melted off as the summer swelter baked me in my concrete cocoon. I never ran the AC. I let the heat punish me with its stifling fieriness. It cooked me alive in that hollow unit all through July.

As drops of sweat pooled and dripped from my forehead to my bloodshot eyes, it blurred everything, including the smeary city with its never-ending hullabaloo of noise and sights. But whenever Kelly came into view, my whole being sharpened. More than a hundred feet below, she came into view, a dreamy vision in this maddening island of steel and glass.

I learned her schedule through repetition. Every morning, she left the building with the kids hand in hand. The twins usually looked distracted, their blonde hair matted, lips chattering, but the little boy, Jack, he always looked happy just to be holding her hand, just to be there. I longed to grip hers, too. To feel her fingers intertwine mine.

She would take them to some playdate or preschool, then return to the apartment alone, looking exhausted. I watched it all, holed up in my 16th floor airless prison. For the first time ever, I had all the time I could ever want. I could do anything with all my payoff money. Yet I desired nothing else but to sit, to watch.

It went on like this into August. By this time, I was nearly unrecognizable as the man who inked the massive hedge fund sale. My hair had grown out, and I had lost more than 20 pounds. To keep my sanity, I began a new health regimen: 20 push-ups every 30 minutes, 30 sit-ups on the hour. I did this all day, every day, until my abs poked through my shrunken stomach and the veins in my biceps bulged just from stretching.

One morning, I decided to shave my thick beard that had grown in the last few weeks. Looking at my reflection in the bathroom mirror, my eyes haunted me with their starved look. I was a man alone, apart. Was I punishing myself for not remembering? For what I had done to Kelly? I didn't know. And I felt ashamed for not knowing.

Ever since the accident, I would wonder why I felt so empty. Why things didn't seem right. Why I despised my fiancé, Camy. Why something inside doubted the stories my mother told about those missing years. It wasn't until I saw Kelly that I knew something was truly wrong. All those doubts and questions suddenly seemed justified, and I had to know the truth. But looking at my reflection, I realized self-punishment wouldn't help me discover anything. I couldn't go on this way. I had to get out of this apartment. I had to see Kelly again face to face.

After clapping the pockets of my now-baggy jeans to make sure I had wallets and keys, I ventured out. Pushing open the glass lobby doors, I stepped onto the rough concrete, feeling the sun sear the top of my head. I had to shield my eyes from its glare. A couple of security guards outside the building nodded. They knew me as the weirdo who popped out at odd hours to buy peanuts from the store across the street.

A motorbike whizzed past, forcing me back onto the cracked sidewalk. When I looked up again, I froze. *It's her.*

My feet moved before my brain did. I started walking in the same direction, slowly, so she wouldn't see me. As usual, she dragged the three kids with her. The twins wore backpacks designed to look like characters from *Cars*. Jack held Kelly's hand. On his back hung a green backpack with a picture of a Minion from *Despicable Me*. She wore a black T-shirt and jeans with flip-flops. She didn't have any makeup on, and her long, black hair flowed past her shoulders. Her natural, carefree look was refreshing compared to Camy's artifice. I felt drawn to her. My heart raced just looking at her.

She made the kids wait at the crosswalk to turn on Frank Court. I had just weaved around some parked cars when my phone rang. The tone was some high-pitched chirping sound Camy had installed. *Shit.* I immediately fished for it in my pocket, trying to turn it off. A picture of Camy's face—another thing she had installed—popped up. I turned it off and slid it back into my pocket, trying to keep up with the trio as the walk sign appeared. The chirping started up again.

I answered, keeping my head down. "Camy, what is it?" I asked, clearly annoyed.

She didn't waste any time. "I'm seeing someone."

I turned the corner, lifting up on my tiptoes, trying to catch Kelly above the crowd of people. "Great. I'm happy for you."

She snorted. "You really are a narcissistic asshole, just like everyone says. You know, I waited for you for you to call—"

I hung up.

Kelly kept walking straight ahead, heading toward a group of white tents set out in the middle of the street for the Farmer's Market. She stopped beside a vendor selling fresh organic produce.

"Miss Kelly, how are you?" I heard the man ask.

Another voice chimed in. "Ah, our favorite girl is back!"

Kelly flushed under the attention. One of the guys reached down to give Jack a high-five. Kelly pretended to put a head of lettuce on his head as a hat. He looked up at her with adoring eyes, giggling.

For some reason, this small interaction—the hat, the laugh, those eyes—took my breath away. The twins were busy at another stall, but Jack stayed close to Kelly. He clung to her leg, pretending to be a monkey. I had to laugh, then turned, realizing tears were coming.

A moment later, a tall, thin Asian man with square glasses and slicked back hair came up to her and gave her a hug. The kids flocked to him, and he gave them squeezes in return.

They shared a kiss that ripped me apart. Holy crap, she *isn't* single! I scooted closer. I needed to hear their conversation.

"I thought you were at church," I heard her say. I edged toward a pyramid of avocados, keeping my head down.

"Got out early," the man said.

She bent down to pick up some strawberries and scooted the children out of the tent. I followed.

"I was hoping to use today to study," Kelly said. Even her speaking voice was melodic. I just wanted to go up and talk to her, all day, every day.

"You want me to take 'em for a few hours?"

"You can take the twins. Jack wants to go with me there, but every time they come along, he freaks."

"Yeah, I can do that. Hey, boys, want to play some Wii?"

"Yeah!" they shouted in unison.

Pangs of jealousy tore through me as I watched him kiss her again. Then he took off with the twins, leaving Kelly and Jack alone.

"Ready?" she asked him.

He took a flower from the vendor, who gave him a high five, and followed after her.

"Oh, Jack," I heard her say.

* * *

I stood near the market entrance, watching customers weave through stands selling everything from fresh fish heads to costume jewelry. Anger rose inside me. Seeing that man kiss Kelly made me crazy. I had to put the pieces of the puzzle together *now*. Who could help me? Dr. Root was useless. My mother would never tell me the truth. Then it came to me. I put my phone in between my ear and shoulder and waited for him to pick up.

"Ian. What's up?"

"Hey, Craig. Sorry to bother you, man, but, you know, I feel like I know your nanny from somewhere."

There was a long pause. I could tell Craig was debating whether to hang up on me, or worse, call the cops.

"Oh, gosh. I don't know." I could tell from his voice that he was feeling uncomfortable.

"That's why I was there that day. Just making sure I didn't know her from somewhere."

"Yeah."

"Can you tell me anything about her?"

"Tell you anything about my nanny?"

"I know this sounds weird ..."

"It sounds really weird, dude. I come back here and you're fricking stalking her like some—"

"Look, Craig. Just tell me something about her. Anything and I promise you'll never have to talk to me again."

He didn't say anything for so long I checked my screen to see if he ended the call. "Camy called Julia. What happened between you two?"

"Nothing. We broke up. But seriously, Craig ..."

"Look, I'm gonna go now. Please don't take this wrong. I appreciate everything you and your mom did. It's just ... it's creepy, you know?"

I wanted to scream at him, to tell him I knew it was nuts—*absurd*—insane. I understood all the reasons he must think I was a mad man. "Craig, please." My voice broke as I said it. I was at the end of my rope.

"All I know is her parents died when she was young. When B.B. Chu told me she was looking for work and that she had a kid, too, I decided to give her a try. Now my twins love her."

"B.B. Chu. Like BBQ. That's the lawyer you mentioned—"

"Look, I gotta go. You take care, okay?"

* * *

I pushed through the doors of B.B. Chu Law Offices, nodding to the secretary before noticing a familiar-looking man in an office surrounded by glass. Built with the kind of chest that comes from doing repeated bench presses, he sat hunched over his computer. After confirming with his secretary I was the person who called looking for a new IP attorney, she let me pass.

When he saw me enter, his mouth gaped open.

I put out my hand. "I'm Ian Anderson."

B.B. shoved my hand away like I just insulted his mother. "I know who you are. Why the fuck are you here?"

Not exactly the greeting I expected. "Wh—"

He didn't let me finish before rising to his full height. He had a good three inches on me and was intimidating. Especially with his neck heating up to an ugly crimson. "You'd better walk out that same door you just came in."

I could hear the secretary shuffling outside and sensed a crowd might be forming. I dared not check. This guy looked spitting mad, like he might put my head through the glass if I made the wrong move.

"Kelly—"

He didn't let me get the word out. "How could you do that to her?"

"Tell me what I did."

I snuck a look back. Sure enough, half the office had gathered.

B.B. shook his head, appalled. "Jesus, man. Get out of here."

"Please, I—"

He reached over. I thought he was going to hit me, but instead he opened his door wider. "I can't be in the same room with you for another minute. And if you don't drop this, I'll knock your damn teeth out."

"Kelly—"

"Kelly has her life on track now. Finally started dating someone. Let her be."

"Just tell me, what did I do?"

Murmurs from behind me.

"Don't test me, man. You're starting to piss me off. If it weren't for Jack, I'd punch your fucking pretty-boy face into ground chuck."

He shoved me toward the office door. Feeling punch-drunk and stupid, I staggered past my audience. Just like B.B., they glared at me, too, like I had done something unforgivable to them. *But what?*

Outside on the street, I paused beneath an overhang. To my left was an automated parking garage. Why did he say, 'If it weren't for Jack?' *What did Jack have to do with anything?* I started toward Wilshire Boulevard as I tried to piece together clues. My mother said Kelly went to Columbia, too.

I took out my phone and tried accessing my old Columbia email account. Inactive, it must have been shut down. Next, I tried the archive of my work email account, *@andersonfunds.com,* and searched "Kelly." Nothing came up.

I took a deep breath. I had no choice but to speak to the one person who must know the truth. I dialed her number, steeling myself. "Mother, I need to talk to you—"

"You haven't called in weeks. Camy is a wreck. You know that, right? I don't blame her if she never speaks to you again. It's unforgivable—"

"I need to talk to you about Kelly."

"Oh, God, this again?"

"There's something you're not telling me."

She sighed. "I didn't want to have to tell you this, but she blackmailed you."

"Blackmailed me?"

"For 50 thousand dollars."

"That makes no sense."

"She said she was pregnant and that you were the father. Completely ludicrous."

I thought of Jack. "*Was* it mine?"

"I doubt it. She disappeared after I paid her the money."

"*You* paid her? When?"

"Ian, she's not a good person. I have a copy of the wire transfer receipt in my personal email account. Do you want to see it?"

"I have to go."

I paced back and forth on the sidewalk, trying to make sense of everything. After watching Kelly, I knew that she was not a gold digger. I've met plenty in the past, and Kelly was nothing like them. Blackmail? Fifty thousand dollars? It can't be true. Suddenly, it occurred to me. *Why was I checking my work emails?* I needed to check my personal account. My iPhone remembered the login, but the cursor in the password bar blinked back at me. *What was my password?* I hadn't used it in so long I couldn't remember.

Anderson9089

Wrong.

Boomer2002

Childhood dog's name. Wrong.

I stopped. Looking up at the cloudless sky, it hit me. *Ilovekelly*

It worked. My heart sped up as the email loaded.

You have no messages.

I stopped breathing. The inbox had been cleared. The sent boxes were also cleared. Someone had deleted all the emails.

Wait. *What about the trash folder?* I clicked on it. There were hundreds of emails. Hundreds of emails from Kelly. I felt sick. What had I done?

CHAPTER THIRTY-THREE

I walked away from the business plaza, weaving through the throes of oncoming foot traffic, phone clenched in my hand. *Think, think, think.* Kelly's boyfriend took the twins. Kelly had Jack. She said they were going to visit his grandparents. She couldn't be talking about my parents, and Craig said both her parents were dead. *Jack wanted to bring flowers ... dead parents ... a cemetery.* They were going to visit her parents' graves.

Turning to my phone, I found emails about a cemetery and someone named Halmuni's death. Vague memories swirled in me— an heirloom ring, seeing her relatives packed at a vigil. The more emails I read, the more I started to remember, little by little like a dream ... how confident I was back then. *Brazen* would probably be a better word. I felt sick thinking of what Kelly must have been through in the last three years. I had to find her.

I guessed that wherever this Halmuni was buried, Kelly's parents would be nearby. Somewhere within the emails was the information I wanted. Evergreen Cemetery. That's where we went to bury Halmuni that day. I didn't remember it, but I had to try.

I called for an Uber and hopped in the black SUV, barely saying hi to the driver. I sat in the back passenger seat, bouncing my knees like a restless five year old.

Usually, I felt prepared for any kind of social situation. But for this, I was flying blind. What do you say to the person you wronged—unknowingly—for years?

Fifteen minutes later, the driver turned down the hum from the radio and pulled up to the curb. I scanned the cemetery from behind the fingerprint-stained window, but didn't see anybody.

"Here's good. Thank you." I threw another $20 bill in his direction.

The morning's furnace blast had begun to wane as the sun climbed higher in the sky, but the heat still made me dizzy, like I was feverish. I had to stop to catch my breath. Ascending the hill just beyond the gated cemetery entrance, I looked around. Patches of brown crabgrass thirsty for water bled into a healthier green carpet the closer I ventured toward tombstones. It had been years since I visited my own father's grave, and regret filled me as I glanced at so many bouquets wilting on stone markers.

Far from the roar of the city, this place offered comforting silence. I could see no one in any direction, reminding me there were still places even in LA where you could still slip away from it all—even if you had to hide away among the dead. I walked as fast as I could, careful to avoid trespassing on any of the plots. I couldn't help doing what I always did when it came to cemeteries: study each of the dates listed on the graves. Somehow, these always surprised me, either because of how long the person had been around or how little.

"Beloved mother ... Adored father ... Once met, never forgotten ... More times..." Reading the epitaphs, I tried to imagine how Kelly felt as a teen losing her parents. Did she get any say when it came to the inscriptions? I pictured her coming here, placing her own yellow roses on their graves, filling the silence with her own thoughts, her own fears and worries. I had to choke back my tears.

At last, I saw two specks in the distance. Without another thought, I took off running. Blurred at first, they came into view, and I had to stop. I thought my heart would burst. Kelly held Jack's little hand as he bent down over a grave to say something.

Then she slowly led him away. They continued in the opposite direction toward a gate on the other side of the sprawling park. Several hundred feet beyond was the street, scattered with meters, parked cars, traffic lights, glowing storefronts. Everything normal and alive.

Ignoring the pain in my legs, I plunged after them. I hadn't run like this since my accident, and my body just wouldn't respond like I wanted. If only I could run faster.

"Wait!" I shouted.

My throat burned and my sides ached. I yelled again, but they couldn't hear me. They were about to leave through the gate.

Wheezing, I threw everything I had into catching up to them. I could hear myself gasping, and every breath felt like I was inhaling fire, but still I kept on.

"Kelly! Kelly!"

I was panting so hard now I could barely get the words out. And still they were so far away. I wasn't going to make it. They were at the gate now, her hand on the door. They were slipping away.

Then Jack turned and pointed. When Kelly saw me, she brought him closer and went for the gate.

"No. Wait!"

One more surge of energy blasted through me, and I raced ahead. I caught them just outside the barrier where the cemetery met the road. Kelly backed away, her eyes wild with fear.

"Don't come any closer."

I had nothing left. I dropped to my knees, scraping them as I hit the hot pavement.

"You … can't go." I panted.

I wanted to say something more, something meaningful but I could barely breathe. Tentative, Jack studied me like I was an alien. He looked unsure, like if I made any wrong move he might bolt.

"I will …. stay right here," I said, summoning the air to continue. "Begging … on my knees until you let me explain."

"Explain? Explain what? That you pretend that you don't know me? That you left me when I was pregnant and that you said we weren't right for each other?" Kelly pulled Jack tighter to her chest.

"Kelly, you have no idea how sorry I am for all the pain that I have caused you. But, if you leave, I'll go wherever you go. I'll follow you to the ends of the earth until you hear what I have to say. I swear it."

Jack squirmed in her arms. "Mommy, what's wrong?"

"It's okay, honey," she said, leaning down to him, speaking softly.

I tried to match her soothing tone so I wouldn't frighten him. "Please, please let me talk."

In spite of everything, it felt so natural to be with her. *Didn't she feel that, too?* She took a deep breath but didn't make a move to leave.

"I ..." I stopped. How do you begin the most important thing you'll ever say? "The accident ... I had brain damage. Retrograde amnesia. I lost years of memories. Memories my mother filled in for me. But they never added up—"

"Amnesia?" She frowned. "How is that possible? You wrote those emails."

Jack looked between us, unsure.

"Please, believe me." I held up both hands in prayer position.

She squinted. I could tell she thought this was ridiculous.

"Today I went to see B.B.," I said hurriedly, not wanting to lose her. "He wouldn't tell me much, but that's when I realized my mother lied to me all those years. Then I found the emails. The ones I never wrote. It wasn't me, Kelly. It wasn't me." I was shaking my head now, barely able to hold the tears back. *Please, I'll do anything to prove it to you.*

I heard her inhale sharply.

I took that as a sign I was getting through. It was certainly better than her turning and walking away. "I'm so angry at myself for not remembering. And what she did. It's just … evil."

Her face was a mask. I couldn't tell what she was thinking.

"Look." I dropped my hands and stood up, the pain in my legs excruciating. "I know you're dating someone …"

She cocked her head to the side, uncertain how to react.

"I, um … I've seen you together."

She straightened up. "Who I'm dating is none of your business. *I'm* none of your business." She pulled Jack closer. "He's none of your business. How am I supposed to believe you? Do you know what you did to me? You broke my heart, Ian. You completely, utterly shattered my heart."

"I cannot tell you how sorry I am, Kelly," I said as the tears I was trying desperately to hold back started to cascade down my cheeks. "I never meant to hurt you. The moment I saw you at Craig's home an emptiness that I felt for the last three years was lifted. I knew there was something between us … but my amnesia was preventing me from knowing. Once I started reading the emails, my memories slowly started coming back, and then when I realized what I have done, I felt sick to my stomach. You have every right to—"

She cut me off. "I still can't believe anything you're saying. Your mom has done some mean things, but she wouldn't be that evil."

"I know it sounds crazy ... but please believe me. I'm telling you the truth."

I looked at her: the way her chin quivered, her beautiful dark eyes. In spite of their hardness, there was still vulnerability. She was still the girl I fell in love with another lifetime ago.

I looked down at Jack, as the tears continued to stream down my face. I wanted to scoop him in my arms. I wanted to take him to the park and play tag and make him sandwiches and ask him how preschool was. I wanted to share everything with them, and be there, forever, for both of them. I needed to convince them why I disappeared, why it would never happen again.

"I've missed so much," I said, my voice breaking. I was no longer strong and sturdy. I let myself be an absolute mess as words came tumbling out. "Three years of his life. And he doesn't even know who I am."

The rest of the world no longer existed. It could all stop. Buildings could fall, the ground could split beneath our feet, I wouldn't care. I bent down again, this time not out of pleading, but because I couldn't support myself with how violently I was sobbing. This wasn't how it was supposed to be. I didn't know what I would do after this. There were no next steps.

Suddenly, I felt a warm hand on my arm. "Deep breaths," she said in a calm, soothing voice.

I looked up. Tears formed in her own eyes. Her face softened. She gave me a small smile. Jack stood behind her, looking at me with those beautiful blue eyes.

"I would never have hurt you. You know that. It wasn't me. I had no idea. I want so desperately to make things right," I said. "If that's even possible. I understand you can't forgive me now, but all I ask is for a chance. Just one chance to start over."

Kelly brought Jack closer to us. Her shoulders drooped, and it was as if something broke in her, too. Suddenly she threw her arms around me, sobbing.

"Ian, Ian, I've missed you so much," said Kelly with her head against my head crying uncontrollably. I embraced her back, falling into her.

I squeezed her harder, never wanting to let go.

As she wiped her tears away, she looked up at me and asked coyly, "But what makes you think I would say yes?"

The sun hid behind a large oak tree, casting a shadow on her face. I cleared my throat. A memory came to me. "You told me once your dad sang a song to your mom when she said no." I knelt down. "*Just what makes that little old ant/Think he'll move that rubber tree plant…*"

My voice was ragged and off key, but when I was done, Jack clapped. Kelly couldn't help but giggle and put a hand over her mouth.

"You know, you knelt like that the first time you begged me to go out with you."

I tried to suppress a smile, singing louder. *"High apple pie in the sky hopes..."*

When I was done, she said nothing for a long moment. Then she reached beneath her shirt, revealing a necklace. In the middle, was a familiar-looking ring.

"You kept it?"

She nodded shyly.

"He's got high hopes!"

I turned. Jack was singing the rest of the song in his own high-pitched voice. I crouched down to him. He stretched his little arms out to me. I glanced up at Kelly.

"It's okay," she whispered.

I wrapped him in a hug, letting the tears run down my face.

"Why're you crying?" he asked.

I couldn't talk. Kelly joined us, throwing her arms around me. Taking a wild chance, I kissed her. It was soft and beautiful, and when I was done, I found myself kissing every part of her face. Jack was laughing, but I couldn't stop kissing her.

We squeezed into another group hug as the tears kept falling. A lifetime later, we walked away together, holding on to each other, supporting each other as a family. Together at last.

Made in the USA
Middletown, DE
29 November 2018